"*Vita Nostra* is ⌐
read."

#1 *NEW YORK TIMES* BESTSELLING AUTHOR OF *BABEL*

"*Vita Nostra*—a cross between Lev Grossman's *The Magicians* and Elizabeth Kostova's *The Historian* . . . is the anti–Harry Potter you didn't know you wanted." —*WASHINGTON POST*

"I was stunned by [*Vita Nostra*]—not just by the story, which was a revelation to me in itself, but also by the vividness and fluency and power of Hersey's translation. *Vita Nostra* has become a powerful influence on my own writing. It's a book that has the potential to become a modern classic of its genre, and I couldn't be more excited to see it get the global audience in English it so richly deserves." —LEV GROSSMAN,
NEW YORK TIMES BESTSELLING AUTHOR OF *THE MAGICIANS*

"*Vita Nostra* takes the trope of young people selected for a school for magic and transforms it into an unnerving, deeply philosophical coming-of-age tale. . . . Hersey's translation is plain and straightforward, a wise choice that enhances the deep strangeness of this trippy, vivid novel." —*PUBLISHERS WEEKLY* (STARRED REVIEW)

"This dark, ambitious, and intellectually strenuous novel will feel like a fresh revelation to fantasy readers glutted with Western wish-fulfillment narratives." —*KIRKUS REVIEWS* (STARRED REVIEW)

"Amazing book. Dark Harry Potter on steroids with a hefty dose of metaphysics." —ALIETTE DE BODARD, AWARD-WINNING
AUTHOR OF *THE TEA MASTER AND THE DETECTIVE*

"*Vita Nostra* is utterly fascinating. Readers will crave to learn what's next, and they will be wrong every time. This story is bold

and refreshing and demands a higher plane of thought from both characters and from readers alike. It's like a drug; the more you read, the more you have to read. A unique premise, mind-blowing magic system, and spellbinding conclusion make this one of the best reads of the year." —CHARLIE HOLMBERG,
BESTSELLING AUTHOR OF *THE PAPER MAGICIAN*

"*Vita Nostra* reminds us that language and knowledge are the greatest powers, and it's through the word that we've shaped everything around us." —*PASTE MAGAZINE*
(BEST BOOKS OF NOVEMBER 2018)

"Imagine that Hogwarts has opened a satellite campus inside Harry Haller's Magic Theater from *Steppenwolf* by Hermann Hesse, and assigned Kafka, Dostoevsky, and Rod Serling to oversee the curriculum." —*BOOKPAGE*

"*Vita Nostra* is a dark, enthralling fantasy quite unlike any other. . . . One part coming-of-age tale, one part contemporary magic school, and a sizable part dark reality, *Vita Nostra* is a beautiful, aching, nearly debilitating fantasy that bruises, and thrills, the heart." —NEW YORK JOURNAL OF BOOKS

"The Dyachenkos have produced a remarkable novel and one that will linger long afterward in the reader's thoughts."—POPMATTERS

"*Vita Nostra* is the purest version of the magical academy fantasy setting." —MANHATTAN BOOK REVIEW

"This goes magnificently into an adult direction that will blow the reader's mind. It twists and turns between wonders and horrors, taking a reader on a magical, psychological trip that won't be forgotten." —SCIFI PULSE

"It is a thought-provoking, twisting tale that has highs and lows, unlike anything that most U.S. readers will have experienced. It is brilliant and well worth the time." —SFREVU

SCHOOL OF SHARDS

SCHOOL
OF
SHARDS

A NOVEL

MARINA AND SERGEY DYACHENKO

Translated by Julia Meitov Hersey

HARPER Voyager
An Imprint of HarperCollins Publishers

SCHOOL OF SHARDS. Copyright © 2025 by Sergey Dyachenko and Marina Shyrshova-Dyachenko. English translation copyright © 2025 by Julia Meitov Hersey. All rights reserved. Printed in the United States of America. No part of this book may be used or reproduced in any manner whatsoever without written permission except in the case of brief quotations embodied in critical articles and reviews. For information, address HarperCollins Publishers, 195 Broadway, New York, NY 10007.

HarperCollins books may be purchased for educational, business, or sales promotional use. For information, please email the Special Markets Department at SPsales@harpercollins.com.

Harper Voyager and design are trademarks of HarperCollins Publishers LLC.

FIRST EDITION

Library of Congress Cataloging-in-Publication Data has been applied for.

ISBN 978-0-06-322548-0

25 26 27 28 29 LBC 5 4 3 2 1

To my husband, Sergey Dyachenko,
and our beloved daughter, Anastasia

PROLOGUE

No one enrolls in this institute of their own volition. And yet, every year on September 1, students gather for the first day of classes. At the institute, the price for a failed class is the death of a loved one, the price of a failed final exam is a fate far worse than death, and fear is the lead teacher, stern and merciless. Students are asked to complete mental exercises that push the human brain far beyond its limits. As they perform these exercises, students cease to be human beings, transforming into Words of the Great Speech.

The Great Speech is the only true reality. All objects and actions submit to Its grammar. The Great Speech demands more and more new Words, and so every September, first years gather in the assembly hall and sing the old academic hymn, "Gaudeamus Igitur."

This is how things worked until a new student, Sasha Samokhina, stepped over the threshold of Torpa Institute of Special Technologies. She is a special Word; she is Password. She can manufacture new realities and destroy old ones. Sasha wanted to create a new world according to her own design—a world without fear.

But something went wrong.

PART I

CHAPTER ONE

f you press the red button, the hamster in the cage will die."

"Got it," the first year said, nodding. He was freckly, plump, and very diligent.

"Press the button."

The boy looked at her in confusion. He blinked, his eyelashes very light and very long, and pressed the red button. The small brown hamster twitched, fell on its back, and stopped moving.

"Why did you press the button?" Sasha asked, holding it together.

"You *told* me to," the first year said in surprise. "You're the professor, I am doing what you told me to do."

Sasha demonstratively looked at the clock.

"Session is over. For next time, exercises four, five, and six on page eight."

"But Alexandra Igorevna . . . I can't do these exercises. No one can. No one understands any of this. Not exercise one, not two, not—"

"I am your professor," Sasha reminded him. "And as you noted, you *will* do what I tell you. I don't want to hear 'I can't.'"

He wanted to argue but took one glance at Sasha and gave up immediately. Sad and disappointed, but not scared, he wrote down the assignment and left with a quick good-bye. Sasha didn't think he'd learn anything for their next session. He'd look just as blank.

Sighing, Sasha opened the cage, pulled out the dead hamster, and placed it on her desk.

She leaned over, pressing her palms against the edge. She *claimed* the desk, then the tiny cooling body. The hamster began to tremble. Sasha completed the metamorphosis, separated the animal matter from herself, and walked away from the desk to look out the window. Outside, young, recently planted linden trees glowed in yellow.

Someone panted heavily behind her back. Sasha turned to see a second year perched on the desk. The girl looked miserable, her face as pale as watered-down milk.

"Your thoughts?" Sasha asked.

"I don't like it," the second year said, sniffling.

"I didn't ask if you liked it. What are your thoughts?"

"Alexandra Igorevna, I don't understand. What do you want me to do?" the girl said. She was on the verge of tears. "I don't like being a hamster, and I don't like dying."

"Do you remember being given the same assignment last year?"

"Yes . . ."

"And do you remember pressing the button?"

"Because you told me to press it!"

"Session is over. Your homework has been sent to you electronically. See you on Thursday."

Avoiding Sasha's eyes, the second year said good-bye and left, but not without difficulties. She had trouble passing through the door and took half a minute to position the frame so she could squeeze through. Once the door clicked shut, Sasha leaned over the recently painted windowsill, opened the window, and lit a cigarette.

Sasha knew she was now that annoying person lighting up anywhere and making everyone breathe in secondhand smoke. Yet no one dared to reprimand her. She smoked during lectures, during department meetings, and anywhere else the mood struck her. If only they knew the danger wasn't cancer. No, the danger was that whenever she was lost in thought, the cigarette smoke would fold itself into a nebula, a new galaxy system; it would glimmer dangerously, and Sasha would have to pull herself together to avoid destroying gravity on campus. And yet, without smoking, there was no way she could ever teach a single class.

Aside from the admissions process, she kept a few individual student sessions, but only when it was necessary. The hamster test was one of her inventions.

There were many things the school handled differently now, including the application process. Now prospective students received acceptance letters; some arrived via email, some landed in tin mailboxes. Once accepted, they all matriculated—as before, no one had the option of refusing. But not because of fear for someone's life. Rather, acceptance letters automatically took away their will; there was no fear, no evil, and no choice. She remembered Farit talking about the ramifications of this setup, but Farit was not to be trusted—especially since Farit no longer existed.

Once again, out of habit, she approached the whiteboard and picked up a green marker. She drew a line: the horizon. She blinked, remembering something long gone, something that was unpleasant at the time, but—she knew now—was uniquely precious.

Here was the initial impulse: Password reverberates; the new world opens up. Galaxies form, the sun lights up on the periphery, the first cell divides on the third planet . . .

Sasha dropped the marker, leaving the line unfinished.

"As you know, Alexandra Igorevna, yet another incoming class is a disaster," Adele said. "All first years are going to fail their winter finals. The second years are a bit stronger, but half of them are having trouble recovering from deconstruction. How will any of them pass their third-year final?"

Adele had a deep, velvety contralto; she spoke with authority and conviction. The more trouble the department was in, the more elegant were her choices of perfume and makeup. Sasha had no idea where Adele found her bespoke jackets, suits, designer bags, and shoes, but she also didn't care enough to find out.

"They are incapable of making an effort," Adele continued. "They are wet noodles, not real students. Zero motivation, no matter what song and dance we're performing in front of them, no matter how hard we're trying to engage them."

"They are showing quite a bit of potential in Phys Ed," Dima Dimych said. He was perched on the desk, one leg crossed over the other. "Incidentally, I'd like to bring up the pool question again."

Sasha looked at him without saying a word, and Dima immediately backpedaled.

"I mean, I know it's not the most convenient time, but we talked about it at the end of last semester . . ."

Still silent, Sasha lit another cigarette. Dima wrinkled his nose and stopped speaking; a devoted athlete, he despised smoking.

Adele, unfazed, spoke again.

"The issue isn't just a matter of passing, but *who* is passing. The grammatical composition is unbalanced. There is a dramatic shortage of verbs. And most of the verbs we do have are in the conditional mood. Very few are in an indicative mood. And we do not have a single imperative one."

"To put it bluntly, the Great Speech is degenerating, and the grammatical structure is declining," Portnov said quietly. Unlike the others, he'd remained unchanged, and even his jeans, sweater, and glasses were the same as Sasha remembered from her own first year at Torpa. It made it all the more painful to see how much Portnov was changing from the inside. He held it together—he resisted the simplification of the Great Speech—but now and then he would get stuck like a second year during a routine exercise. Watching him, Sasha knew: every time he struggled, yet another block of meanings would break off, disintegrating into incoherent lowing, and eventually ceasing to exist. And so would Portnov himself.

"We will have to sift and eliminate," Adele said, knocking on the desk as if calling to order. "Let us keep one group, even if it's only ten people, but the ten capable of mastering the curriculum."

"They won't make it," Sasha said softly. A smoke ring glimmered dangerously, folding into a flat spiral with a dark cloud in its center. Sasha flapped her hand, forcing the emerging projection to disperse.

The room fell silent. The basement had no windows, so no noise came from Sacco and Vanzetti Street—no birds singing, no passing cars. The only sound heard was the humming of an old air-conditioning unit.

"This world that I created has a built-in defect," Sasha said. She winced at the inexact and false nature of human words, so inefficient in describing the processes of true Speech. "Yes, this world exists, and it's not that bad—some people enjoy it. It even has some ability to develop. But Speech cannot be fooled." She looked at Portnov. "Oleg Borisovich is right: all of us can see what's happening with the grammatical structure."

"Shocking," Dima said, batting his eyelashes.

"We will recruit a new class," Sasha said, putting out her cigarette. "Dmitry Dmitrievich, you will have to give up your current champions, because the recruiting efforts will take place last summer, three months ago."

"We're just running in circles," Portnov said, wiping his glasses with the hem of his sweater. "Our students are the product of their reality; you simply don't have anyone to choose from. Another round of recruiting won't solve anything."

"It will if I execute a grammatical reform," Sasha said.

Adele stared at Sasha like at a shiny shop window. Dima Dimych rocked back and nearly fell. Portnov narrowed his eyes.

"Are you planning to bring back prerevolutionary orthography?"

I am so lucky to have Portnov at my side, Sasha thought. *Even as tired, wounded, and disintegrating from the inside as he is right now.*

Dima swung his feet in their white sneakers, seemingly hypnotized by the bright yellow shoelaces.

"Dmitry Dmitrievich, please sit up properly," Sasha said. "You're attending a department meeting, not hanging out at a street corner."

"The local athletic society has a nice pool," he said, reluctantly moving to a chair. "We can get hours for the students, and we won't even need to pay—it's just paperwork."

"And what sort of a reform are you proposing?" Portnov cut in, returning his glasses to the bridge of his nose.

"I am not *proposing* anything," Sasha said. "This is my will."

At half past midnight, she ran out of cigarettes. Portnov showed up at twenty to one with a new pack.

"You smoke too much," he said disapprovingly, as he lit up his own cigarette with Sasha's lighter.

"At least that's something I excel at," Sasha said.

Her basement office had no windows either. Sasha could have easily opened a new window onto Sacco and Vanzetti, or Montmartre, or into space, but she didn't bother. What she needed was nowhere to be found.

"This new reform of yours is quite an interesting way of getting things done," Portnov said, straddling a chair. "You are an assassin of reality. Everything is happening the way you wanted."

"No," Sasha said. "The world, as you see it, is not real. And the way you imagine—it doesn't even come close."

He nodded appreciatively, smirking at the memory of the very first Specialty lecture for Group A and the first year named Alexandra Samokhina standing by the blackboard and staring into the darkness behind her blindfold. Today, she paid him back.

"The world exists the way you created it, Samokhina. Once a book reaches its audience, it's too late to rewrite it."

"Thank you for the cigarettes," Sasha said by way of dismissal. "I'll get you another pack, I promise."

She went up to the entrance between the two stone lions. Their faces had been worn out by frequent touching, but the right one still looked sad, and the left one—teasing, full of mirth. The lions gazed up into the sky, as if waiting for Orion's Belt to appear in the winter. Sasha held on to the tiny building as her place of strength, even though she could have lived—or rather, existed and functioned—anywhere.

She went up to her room. It reeked of cold cigarette smoke. A vintage table was littered with pencil drawings; dozens of them were pinned and glued to the walls, like in an investigation room at a police station. All of them were Sasha's self-portraits, and all were different. Some looked exactly like photographs, others like children's doodles, yet others resembled caricatures or butcher charts. A jumble of pictures had very little to do with a depiction of an actual human; some were perfectly symmetrical, some shapeless, some had nothing but a squiggle in the middle of the page or a single dot where the sharp point of a pencil punctured the paper.

But all were *her*.

The autumn morning was approaching. Sasha opened the door of the tiny balcony bound in yellow grapevines and looked up at the sky, at the same point in the distance as the stone lions. The constellations shifted; Orion ascended. Snow covered roofs and pavement: February had arrived. Sasha inhaled the frosty air: the world became brighter, and the grapevines turned a lush green. It was now late June.

The old clock struck seven. Sasha recalled another clock, a different house, different circumstances, and she locked up the memory until another day. She took a hot shower, warmed up a sandwich in the microwave, and made a pot of coffee. She smoked two cigarettes in a row and thought of buying a new pack for Portnov.

Dressed in a white linen suit and a pair of flat sandals, Sasha left her apartment and walked to work. Sparrows shrieked in the bushes. Two charter buses were parked by the entrance to the institute.

Sasha nodded to the guard and walked toward the courtyard located between the main building and the dorms. The courtyard was crowded: the new second years, equipped with colorful backpacks, duffels, and an occasional guitar, were leaving for their summer internships.

Some of them kept shifting from foot to foot, others stood still. They smiled or frowned. They kept touching their ears, cheeks, and noses making sure all their body parts were still intact. Now and then they touched each other, not to encourage or ask for attention but only to make sure that the world and the objects within it remained material.

All this made sense to Sasha, as she saw them from the *inside*: with noses on the backs of their heads, eyes on their bellies, broken attachments, cause-and-effect relationships, and twisted logic. This was just the regular destruction stage in the process, something every student had to go through during the first years of their education. If they worked hard, they would put themselves back together, and the Word would once again peek through the human shell.

She didn't like thinking of the alternative.

Sasha walked along the line of students, watching their faces. Some looked right through her, some smiled hesitantly. But she didn't care about their expressions. Rather, Sasha gritted her teeth, knowing most of them were frozen inside, lacking dynamics. And *all* of them looked like embryos inside their golden eggs, perfectly still and perhaps already dead. Were these the students Adele called "a bit stronger"? Because, if so, then the first of September this year was going to be a disaster. If they didn't truly apply themselves—to their full potential, not like last year!—they would remain crippled, lose their minds, fail their exams, and die.

Sasha barely resisted the urge to cancel the summer internships and send the students back to the auditoriums. Everything had to go on as usual, and today was June 26. They had plenty of time. Adele finished the roll call, waved her hand, and the students, one by one, trudged toward the street, to the charter buses. Clad in a leisure suit, a bag of volleyballs on his shoulder, Dima Dimych led the way, chatting with the girls. The girls giggled.

Adele looked at her questioningly.

"I am leaving," Sasha said. "By September 1, we'll have a new class and a new motivation."

Adele nodded to show that, while she did not quite believe in Sasha's mission, she still wished her luck.

Sasha had very few memories of Torpa in the summer. She'd always spent the best months of the year someplace else. The only thing she remembered of Torpa in the summer was a bag of dried linden leaves and flowers that made such good tea for the colder months.

The old linden trees had dried up not so long ago, and new, slender ones appeared in their place. This year most trees had lost their blooms early, and only a few bees still buzzed around.

Sasha walked to the oldest part of the town, which looked more like a village than a town. She slowed down in front of a house that boasted a huge fir tree behind the fence. A single silver thread hung off its top, too high to reach or simply forgotten when the decorations were put away after New Year's Eve. Inside, a ball bounced off the fence and children shouted: grandkids were visiting their grandparents. The youngest girl was four, and the eldest, twins, just turned eighteen.

Sasha stopped to peek through the fence. The twins were

going through the phase of trying to look as different from each other as possible. One was half naked, dressed only in worn-out swimming trunks, the other donned a pair of ironed jeans and a polo shirt. One was explaining to his little cousin that she was not allowed to step over the line as she threw the ball, while the other sat in the gazebo with a tablet balanced on his lap, his dour expression demonstrating how sick and tired he was of his younger relatives, including his brother.

The boys looked exactly like Yaroslav Grigoriev: two perfect projections. A clear case of paternity with no need for a test. Their mother, father, grandparents, aunt and uncle, cousins—everyone was alive, and this noisy family was perhaps the best thing Sasha had managed to create in the new world, where Password had reverberated.

Both boys were smart and talented, and both were slightly immature. Recent high school graduates, one was already accepted to the Polytechnic Institute, and the other had chosen biology. Both longed for separate summer vacations, with their own friends, instead of spending time in Torpa. Here, everything was sweet and familiar, but they were so sick of it now that they were practically adults.

They had something else in common, though, and that always made Sasha pause: inside of them both, she saw a glimmer of something more. A scent of hot resin. A sound that tasted of a drop of alcohol on one's tongue. All signs that both were potential Words, the instruments of the Great Speech.

They could have been left alone, allowed to remain human, to live their lives, and never learn the truth about the institute. Sasha had considered it exactly a year ago, standing by the same fence and looking at the boys, and she told herself it was too early, they had another year.

But now it was almost too late.

The Great Speech did not tolerate simplification. Should the Torpa Institute of Special Technologies fail to produce a new generation of strong, well-prepared graduates, the world would go mute and cease to exist—it was that stark. And Sasha, the creator of this sweet, kind, dying world, would be forever suspended in emptiness and loneliness. It would be a punishment fit for an assassin of reality.

A punishment she still wasn't sure she deserved . . . or craved.

She walked away just as the cheerful voice of Anton Pavlovich, the twins' grandfather, called from the porch:

"Lunch! Borsh, meatballs! And cherries! Go wash your hands!"

Unnerved by the sound of Yaroslav's father's voice, Sasha walked a couple of blocks, sat down on a bench, white with poplar fluff, and lit a cigarette. In one uninterrupted move, she drew a self-portrait: the spiral arms of a new galaxy and a shadow of an aircraft passing over a nucleus. A winged silhouette that had nothing to do with aerodynamics or physical matter in general. Thinking about it, she didn't notice someone approaching until they sat down by her side.

"Hello," she said without turning her head.

"Did you summon me?" he asked softly.

Sasha glanced at him; the summer sun glinted in his mirrored dark lenses. He was the same as before. Maybe a bit older.

"I did . . ." Sasha said, hesitating. "Are you mad at me?"

"No," he said, throwing his head back, poplar branches and floating fluff reflected in his glasses. "You won fair and square. And now you don't know what to do with your victory."

"I am a functional Password," Sasha said dryly. "I'll figure it out. Perhaps not right away, but I will."

"You'll figure it out," he said, taking off his glasses. When he looked at her, his eyes were perfectly human, tired, and so familiar that Sasha flinched.

"Where is he?" the man sitting next to her asked softly.

"He's happily married, he has two sons . . ."

"That's not what I asked."

Slowly, Sasha handed him her drawing. He put his glasses back on and moved the paper away, like someone farsighted. After a minute, he looked back at Sasha.

"This is the original projection," Sasha said, clearing her throat. "A starting point where I had *reverberated*. The world is built on the concept of planes never crashing. But—"

"But to live is to be vulnerable," her interlocutor recited, quoting something that was said a long time ago.

"And now this harmony is compromised," Sasha said. "I did it. I kicked the name of fear from the load-bearing structure, but I did not replace it. I thought that love as an idea would hold up the entire structure, but—it turned out in the world without fear, love is not enough."

Her companion looked back at the drawing: a shadow of an aircraft passing over a galactic nucleus.

"Are you trying to reach him?"

"There is a part of me left in him," Sasha said. "A tiny shard. I have to get it back."

A very long minute had passed.

"I will help you," the man sitting next to her said finally. "You can count on me."

"Thank you," she said, finally exhaling. She coughed, and the cigarette smoke merged with the billowy poplar fluff and tried to fold into yet another galaxy, but Sasha waved her hand, chasing it away. She put out her cigarette.

"Thank you, Kostya."

While Sasha was making coffee, he washed the ashtrays and took out the trash without being asked. He never commented on the state of her room, but when Sasha viewed it through his eyes, she realized how long it had been since the last time she'd cleaned it. However, just yesterday it was October, and now it was June: time moving backward ruined things, piled on trash, and left a felt-like layer of dust on tables and floorboards. He didn't judge, though: there had been times in Kostya's own life when old trash accumulated in piles both inside and outside.

And then she looked around through his eyes again, this time paying close attention. She realized Kostya remembered this room from a January day in the past, when there was a decorated tree, and a fire was lit in the small fireplace, when Sasha and Kostya were happy. It was just one night, a few hours before the exam in which failure would result in a fate worse than death.

"I've always thought the world was structured in a very dumb way," she said, forcing herself to abandon these unnecessary thoughts. "Until I took it upon myself to build one. I expected an ethical molecular hydrogen production, a benign formation of galaxies, lovely volcanoes, cheerful amoebas, a sincere Mesozoic era, an affectionate Middle Ages, and so forth and so on. I thought the Great Speech would sound different, yet just as perfect. I thought . . ." She paused, knitting her eyebrows. "You see, Kostya—all these billions of years are but one syllable. One squeak of an infant. A hole made by a pencil point. The real time, the history and development—they are all here in Torpa. And the real meaning is here as well."

Kostya said nothing, waiting for her to continue.

"I captivated them with the joy of creativity," Sasha said. "I awakened their curiosity. Transformed their learning process into a game. They loved each other, loved the whole world, but they kept breaking, Kostya. Only a few of them made it to the third year, and all of them failed the final exam."

"Are you saying you know where you've made an error?" Kostya asked delicately.

"I didn't make an error, though—I did exactly what I wanted to. But Password is just as much of a part of the Great Speech as a noun, conjunction, or preposition. I am the source of the universe, but I'm also just a cog in the universal mechanism."

Sasha lit another cigarette; when she exhaled, a faint spiral of a new universe floated around the room.

"I can *manifest* matter in any form," Sasha said. "But I cannot *manifest* Speech. I can only build it from scratch.

"Sit down, the coffee is getting cold."

"There is a bit of a draft," Kostya said, nervously watching the smoke spiral.

"Don't worry about it, it's just a picture," Sasha said, waving away the ghost of a galaxy. "Sit down."

Kostya sat down but left his cup untouched. Sasha glanced at the grapevine outside the window. Kostya waited.

"The Great Speech needs new Words," Sasha said; her voice suddenly seemed hollow, dull, and no longer young. "But human beings, even gifted ones, cannot become Words for the sake of kindness, beauty, love, thirst for knowledge, or a box of chocolate. I loved my students; I offered them all sorts of carrots. And now I want to *manifest* a stick."

"And abandon your main goal, the world without Farit and everything he symbolized?"

"Not abandon, no," Sasha said, picking up her cup of cold coffee. Her hand shook. "Farit is gone forever. But I must preserve the Great Speech and build a new balance for it. That means finding balance within myself."

She fell silent. Kostya reached across the table and placed his hands over hers.

"Do you want to save the Speech or bring back your pilot?"

"It's the same thing," Sasha said, gently freeing her hands.

CHAPTER TWO

Little Valya hated his name. This resistance was stupid, and what's worse, it upset his father because Valya was named after him.

"It's a girl's name," Valya would say in his defense.

"Do I look like a girl to you?"

"But you're big," Valya said bitterly. "No one would laugh at you."

"Tell me who's laughing at you, and I will take care of them."

"No one," Valya said, hiding his face. He cried easily back then, for any reason whatsoever.

"You can tell everyone your full name is Valentin; it's an Ancient Roman name and it means 'strong,' 'healthy,' and 'vigorous,'" his mom said when they were alone.

He nodded, not wanting to offend her. He'd been sick his entire childhood; he wore glasses—his vision dipped to minus five. He'd never had anything above a C in physical education, and even this was a pity grade. He didn't mind when his mom called him Valya, he even grew to like it, but then he found out it sounded like medication that treated anxiety. He couldn't bring it up to Mom again because he didn't want to upset her.

His father thought Valya was spoiled by his mother. Valya's poor health and their never-ending arguments over parenting principles almost caused a divorce, but Valya's dad was a decent person. He did leave his first wife and kids, but in that case, "things were different," he explained when Valya got a little older. And Valya believed him.

A long time ago Valya had a sister, Mom's daughter from her first marriage. Valya didn't remember her. Her name was Sasha. She had enrolled at some provincial institute, and one day she simply disappeared. Valya used to see a poster with her picture captioned *Please find me* everywhere for years. It kept popping up, as if of its own volition, on bulletin boards, in computer ads, on light poles.

"She was very jealous of your mother and me getting married," Valya's father said to him in confidence, a hint of bile in his voice. "At first, she ran away to that institute, and then she simply stopped communicating with us. Ungrateful bitch," he added under his breath.

"What if something happened to her?" Valya asked uncertainly.

"I highly doubt something happened to that girl other than her own selfishness. She might still pop up someday. Although if I were your mother, I'd never forgive her."

When Valya was thirteen or fourteen, he thought of his missing sister often. He even kept one of the posters, hiding it in his desk from his mother. Sometimes, when Valya stared at the face of his estranged sister, he felt dizzy, goose bumps would crawl over the skin, his pulse would race, and he'd struggle to breathe.

In high school, he all but forgot about his sister and threw away the tattered poster. All his classmates had started dating; Valya pretended he was seeing someone as well. He went to an optometrist and replaced his glasses with contacts. He got a gym membership and drank protein shakes, but every time he looked in the mirror, instead of a buff teenager he saw himself—a mama's boy, Little Valya.

He attended his high school prom but danced alone. Every few minutes he pretended to get important messages on his phone that required his immediate attention. He left as early as he could.

It was June 26. His home was only fifteen minutes away, ten if Valya was in a hurry. But today there was no reason to rush. He walked along a wide street, still full of people despite the late hour: summer brought out packs of teenagers, lovers holding hands, and dogs of different sizes walking their patient owners. It seemed that only Valya had no one by his side, but tonight, he didn't mind being alone. His grown-up life was ahead of him, and even though he wasn't crazy about the medical technology major his father had insisted on, Valya was proud of being accepted by and excited about starting college. He was looking forward to meeting someone special. Someone who didn't know him as Little Valya.

The girl stood by the store entrance, looking at the window display. She was dressed in a jacket and a pair of light trousers; her hair was slicked back. Valya glanced at her ramrod-straight back and instinctively squared his shoulders. Would he go over and introduce himself? Valya had never done anything like this before, but a nice suit and contact lenses gave him a boost of confidence. Plus, she was also alone. Was she waiting for someone at this late hour?

Sensing his gaze, the girl turned. Valya stumbled; she was nowhere near his age. She could have been twenty or forty, but the most terrifying thing was that she reminded him of someone so much chills ran down his spine and his pulse raced.

The girl turned away and took a few steps in the other direction. The entrance to the store was empty again, as if Valya had simply imagined everything.

He unlocked the door, trying not to wake up his parents. They had an early flight the next morning: they were going on vacation alone for the first time. Valya had worked very hard to convince them. It was mostly his mom who needed convincing—his father knew Valya was an adult and could be left alone for two weeks.

Tomorrow afternoon they would step into the warm sea. Valya promised to call and write every day and submit full reports on what he ate, where he went, and how he felt.

He left his bag with his diploma on a hallway shelf. The clock showed half past twelve. He didn't think prom was all that after all. People had been so excited about it, collecting money as early as September, and booking restaurants and boats for their parties, and now graduates couldn't wait to leave and forget each other as soon as possible. Or was he the only one feeling this way? Was he just naturally a loner?

He couldn't wait to start his university life. He knew he'd make real friends there. He was happy the university was close, and he could still live at home: "dorm" was a four-letter word for his mother. He could make the transition easy for her and still have a fresh start for himself.

The kitchen lights were on. His mother stood by the window looking at pictures on her tablet. Glancing over her shoulder, he saw sunshine, the sea, his much younger mother in a swimsuit, and a girl by her side, sixteen or seventeen years old, the same age as Valya now. Mom sighed deeply. Valya stepped back out quietly, then walked into the kitchen to ensure she saw his reflection in the window.

Mom turned to him, switching off her tablet.

"You are back so early."

"I did everything on the list," Valya said, smiling. "I got my diploma, I gave a thank-you speech, I ate, danced, and said no to the contraband vodka hidden in the bathroom. I wanted to get up early and help you with your luggage tomorrow."

Mom hugged him, tighter than usual.

"Promise me you'll be careful. Promise you'll cross the street only when the light is green."

A while ago she had been diagnosed with anxiety. She saw danger where healthy people would never even think of it. Judging by her mood, she must have been too busy packing and forgot to take her pills.

"I promise," Valya said sincerely. "Nothing bad can happen to me."

He thought of the girl in the picture. She was probably living her life somewhere, while their mother worried about her. Was it his sister's revenge for her mom's new husband, new son, and new life?

His thoughts jumped to another girl, the one he'd seen by the store entrance just a short time ago. The two girls merged in his mind, gazing at him in solemn expectation.

He shivered.

It was unbearably hot in Torpa that day.

After lunch, the eight-year-old Antoshka begged to go to the beach.

"Is it summer vacation or prison?" he asked dramatically.

Little Lora cheerfully echoed her brother: "Is it a prisoney prison?"

Grandpa began collecting his stuff—gathering towels from the laundry line and pulling fishing rods out of the shed—but Grandma gave him an ultimatum: no one was going anywhere until his blood pressure was measured.

That went awry. Grandma said that with this kind of blood pressure, she would never allow him to go anywhere in this heat. She herself had recently twisted her ankle and couldn't walk all the way across town, so she offered to hose Antoshka and Lora down and set them up with an inflatable kiddie pool.

Lora was about to start bawling, and that's when Pashka suddenly decided to step up.

"I'll take them," he said. "I wouldn't mind cooling off myself."

Grandma was visibly taken aback. To her, Pashka and Arthur, albeit recent high school graduates, were not that much older than Antoshka and Lora.

"I don't . . ." Grandma said vaguely. Lora smelled weakness and sobbed louder.

"Why not?" Grandpa said. "Pashka knows how to get there."

"Fine, but only if Arthur goes along," Grandma said immediately. "It's fine if both of you take the little ones."

In the garden, Arthur sat in the rocking chair listening to his podcasts. When Pashka pulled off his headphones and informed his brother of the plan, Arthur's face wrinkled like an old plum.

"Why would we go anywhere in this heat?"

"We're going swimming!" Antoshka was hopping around, a rubber ball and a snorkeling mask gathered in his arms. "We're going to the river! To the beach! Don't you want to go swimming? You're dumb!"

"Arthur, buddy," Grandpa said gently. "Please go with them."

It was only for him that Arthur relented (God knew he would never do this for his sibling). A few minutes later they were walking along the empty-at-this-hour street, up and down the gentle hills, over dry clay, asphalt, and gravel, while Antoshka and Lora ran around in circles, picking dandelions from the side of the road. The snorkeling mask dangled around Antoshka's neck.

Later, Pashka would often think of this day, of how differently the flow of the warm air over the ground felt at that moment, how reality appeared transparent, see-through, with another reality peeking from underneath. At some point, he had even worried that Grandma was right, and that he had been suffering from heatstroke.

In the moment, though, he just tried to get a grasp of where and when he was.

"What a strange place, this Torpa," he said out loud, needing to break the silence. "Where we live it's a real village. And here, in the center, there are all these buildings. But have you ever considered where their city-forming enterprise might be?"

Pashka had always had a systematic approach to life, or at least he tried. He was a STEM guy, unlike Arthur. But here in Torpa, in the summer heat, full of Grandma's food, Pashka felt dumber than ever.

"Not 'this Torpa,' our Torpa," Arthur said didactically. "Our predecessors have lived here for centuries."

They passed an empty bus stop and continued onto a cobbled stretch of Sacco and Vanzetti Street.

"If we had bikes, we'd be there in twenty minutes," Pashka said, shifting the backpack and fishing rods on his shoulder.

"If we had bikes, you'd pop a tire on this rock, and I would pop mine on that one," Arthur said. "Also, this was *your* idea."

Arthur was extremely practical. He chose the best rates for his phone plan, read and listened only to the most useful books, and calculated and predicted the consequences of any and all actions. Pashka firmly believed that Arthur would become a renowned biologist and someday would design a cure for all diseases; humanity would never again be bothered by coughs or sniffles. Right now, though, he was just his usual antagonistic self.

All kinds of linden trees lined Sacco and Vanzetti Street: old, massive ones that threw shade onto the cobbled path, and young, supple, barely rooted ones. Some new trees had dried up and stood like skeletons in the middle of the summer day, tied to wooden stakes. Those that had survived were still blooming.

"Lora, wait up!" Pashka yelled. "Don't go too far!"

For this trip, he took on the role of supervisor. Arthur did not want any responsibility; he simply agreed to go to avoid upsetting their grandfather. Their little cousins were behaving very nicely, better than at home, and Pashka wondered why they'd never gone alone to the beach before. Why did they make their grandparents walk all the way across town? Tomorrow they would go first thing in the morning, before the midday heat.

The little group caught up to the facade of what must have been the strangest building in Torpa: the Institute of Special Technologies. The tall doors were shut. It looked like the building was deserted, and no one had been inside for quite a while.

"Here is your city-forming enterprise," Arthur said.

"Is it still open?" Pashka said, catching and tossing the ball back to Lora. His backpack had slid down again, and he hitched it up on his shoulder.

"That's what they say," Arthur said, finally taking the fishing rods out of his brother's hand. "Right now everyone is on vacation, though. The neighbors say it's where the drug dealers are, and no one knows what they are teaching there. But every year they get a bunch of new students."

"What kind of people want to study here, I wonder?" Pashka said.

"Who knows? Those who failed to get into any other schools?"

From Sacco and Vanzetti Street, they turned onto the very short Peace Street. Just ahead they saw reeds swaying in the wind, and the air smelled of the river. Pashka took Lora's hand to make sure she stayed close. The tiny reed-lined beach was empty, traces of an old rain barely visible in the sand. *Torpa is such a weird little place, but that's part of its charm,* Pashka thought.

"Stay in the shallow water," their grandma had said. But in the summer heat, the river had dried up so much, they would be hard-pressed to find any deep places. Lora pulled off her dress and promptly plopped into the water, showing off her bright pink swimsuit. Antoshka followed, and Pashka recalled splashing around with his brother when they were younger.

The old boat pier had been dry and boatless for a while. Down the stream, a lonely figure stood on the wooden foot-bridge: a fisherman, dressed in a hooded canvas jacket, despite the heat. The fisherman turned his head and glanced at Pashka, the sun reflecting in his dark glasses. He was probably annoyed by all the noise from the little ones scaring off the fish, even though the footbridge was at least a hundred paces away.

"We should try fishing," Arthur suggested. "What was the point of dragging all this stupid gear with us?"

"Go ahead, I will watch the kids," Pashka said firmly.

Arthur untangled the rods; a few minutes later Pashka saw his silhouette on the humpbacked bridge. He suspected that Arthur wasn't going to catch any fish—he simply liked watching the float . . . and having his own space. Pashka had learned this a while ago.

Lora and Antoshka tossed the ball back and forth, arguing about something. Ignoring their chatter, Pashka took off his T-shirt, the smell of sunscreen filling the air—Grandma had been generous with the sunscreen, smearing it all over the four of them like mayo on a sandwich.

"I can do it!" Lora shouted. "Look! I can swim!"

Water sprayed into the air above the reed thicket. Lora wasn't exactly swimming, more like floating in the water, occasionally pushing off the shallow bottom with both hands. But Pashka nodded encouragement anyway.

He looked back at the bridge, but the fisherman was gone. He must have decided to try his luck someplace else. A gray wooden fence in great need of paint threw its shade onto the grass. Across the fence, graffiti proclaimed: *The world is not what you think.*

Amused by the local Banksy's confidence, he picked up a shard of a brick—who knew what it was doing there—and wrote underneath: *What is it then?*

Screeching, Lora jumped out of the water and ran over to Pashka.

"He's tickling me! I can swim, but he is drowning me!"

"No monkey business in the water!" Pashka said. "You might swallow river water, eat some bacteria, and end up with diarrhea. Let's get you toweled off."

The fence no longer displayed the graffiti. Pashka's question was also missing. Instead, a single line in green marker said:

You'll know soon enough.

Valya's parents always arrived at the airport well in advance because of Mom's anxiety—she was terrified of missing the flight. Today, they got up early, double-checked their luggage, and called a cab. They sat down for a minute to ward off evil spirits as per an old pagan custom and then headed out, Valya wheeling the heaviest suitcase.

The familiar road seemed somber and important as if they were on their way to a space center rather than an airport.

Perhaps it had something to do with the fact that his parents were leaving, and Valya was staying behind on his own. It was akin to a primitive initiation; thinking about it, Valya struggled to stifle his laughter. His parents would not understand the reason for his mirth. Plus, traveling already put Mom on edge.

Once they checked their luggage and got their boarding passes, Valya's mood changed. Suddenly, he longed to be little again, to go to the sea and jump in the waves, clutching his mom's arm. But his parents waved to him from behind the barrier and walked off, holding hands. Other passengers' backs hid them from view. Their vacation—and their second honeymoon—had begun. Valya shuffled off toward the exit.

Clusters of young people, couples, and families with children moved toward the check-in counters, carrying colorful suitcases and backpacks, all anticipating fun and enjoyment, not a single sad or indifferent face in the entire huge terminal. For a second Valya felt like an outsider. All of them were going on vacation, and he was left behind—but so what? He was now his own boss. He could bike to the park, go to the movies or aquapark, he could sleep until noon, or watch TV . . .

He stopped across from an enormous arrivals and departures board that took up the entire wall. It displayed a million different routes, to Singapore and Amsterdam, Tivat and Rome, Odesa, San Francisco, and Simferopol. *Our world is so big,* Valya thought. When he was little, he wanted to be a pilot, flying across seas and oceans, but those dreams ended with his acceptance as a medical technology major. Valya had plenty of time, though. Perhaps someday he'd get a second degree.

The Tivat flight board blinked and changed the status of his parents' flight from *On Time* to *Departed*. Valya frowned: Why had it departed so early? His parents had planned on waiting for an hour and a half at least.

The board blinked again. *Departed* changed to *Undefined*. The word "undefined" was not part of the flight schedule glossary.

Around him, people moved in different directions. Suitcases kept rolling. Children ran around with their tiny backpacks. The board blinked again, changing to *The world is not what you think*. Valya sighed with relief, realizing someone had hacked the board. Any second now everyone would start laughing and taking pictures with their phones, everyone but the airport staff, who would not be amused.

The board changed again. Red letters ran across it, for every line of every flight: *Crashed. No survivors.*

Pashka dipped his hat in the water and put it back on. Ghost graffiti was the last thing he needed.

Lora and Antoshka were still in the river, busy showing off their newly acquired skills. Wearing a snorkeling mask, Antoshka dived in and out of the shallow water, stirring up mud and picking tiny shells from the bottom. Lora used her ball as a flotation device and was attempting to swim, kicking the water up with her heels. Still wearing his wet hat, Pashka walked into the water up to his knees. He suddenly felt chilly, despite the oppressive heat. Dragonflies hung suspended in the air above water lilies; the sun was just starting to lean toward the west.

"Come out before you freeze to death," he called to the children.

"We're not cold!"

"Come out, now!"

They ignored him.

"I will tell Grandma, and she won't let you go swimming ever again!"

"Then we'll run away!" Antoshka said. He was clearly feeling cheeky; as Grandma said, he "had a burr under his saddle."

Pashka didn't feel like dealing with them. He reached for a dry towel and wrapped himself up, wondering why he was so cold—was he getting sick?

The fisherman in dark glasses came back and was now standing very close on the ramshackle dock. Pashka never even saw him approach.

A sharp twist of the rod, and a large fish flew up into the air and flopped on the sand. The fisherman effortlessly removed it from the hook and tossed it into a tin bucket. He glanced at Pashka—the dark glasses reflected the shifting sun—and smiled, proud of his catch. He wrapped a piece of raw dough around the hook and threw it back into the water in a dramatic, showing-off gesture; another twist of the rod, and another silvery body flew up in the air as if an entire school of fish had lined up underwater, waiting for the bait.

Carrying his fishing rod and net, Arthur walked up from the bridge. There was only so much meditation he could do by watching a motionless float, and having a skillful fisherman nearby probably did not help him maintain his composure. Arthur clearly meant to break the unwritten rules and take a spot right next to his lucky colleague; he even stopped to remove his shoes and roll his jeans up to his knees. He was strictly against shorts, even in this heat.

"They are not listening to me," Pashka said.

"Just let them be, they are fine," Arthur said philosophically.

He placed his sneakers next to his backpack in the shade of the wooden fence. *The world as you see it does not exist* was written on the fence in such bright paint that Arthur suddenly became very nervous.

"These idiots from the institute must have had a wild party here," he said. "All these empty bottles. What if they left needles or broken glass in the sand?"

He glanced at his bare feet with concern.

Pashka wiped his forehead, drenched in cold sweat. Dejectedly, he thought he must have caught the flu in the middle of the summer and now Grandma would medicate him to death with her linden blossom brew.

"There is no glass," he mumbled, trying to control his shivers. "We come here all the time."

The fisherman pulled out another fish, such a hefty one this time that Arthur forgot his fear of broken glass and walked over to the dock with his fishing gear.

"Do you mind if I fish here?" Arthur said. He had excellent manners.

The fisherman nodded, still wearing his glasses.

"You can take my spot. I am about to leave."

He picked up his tin bucket with visible effort and poured the contents back into the river. A dozen fish of different sizes flashed their scales, fleeing in different directions. Pashka thought that there was nothing dumber than ecological fishing: the fish would still die from their wounds or be eaten by another fish.

"The world as you imagine it does not exist," the fisherman said softly, and Arthur laughed with relief.

"Oh, so it's you who's painting all these murals?"

Pashka glanced at the fence. The brightly colored sentence was gone; instead, a black round symbol appeared, written in some sort of machine oil. Pashka thought it looked familiar. Then he thought it was shifting as if reflected in the water.

"I think I just spiked a fever," he said weakly. "Arthur . . ."

He saw his brother's face. Arthur stood frozen in his spot, his tackle in one hand and an empty metal net in the other, staring at the same thing as Pashka.

"What the hell?" Arthur said. His voice sounded hoarse and somehow foreign.

"Boys," the fisherman said, packing up his gear. "Where is your little cousin?"

Antoshka was treading water with the snorkeling mask still on, his head underwater and his butt—in floral trunks—and pale feet bobbing on the surface. When Pashka and Arthur jumped at him from both sides, he swallowed a bit of water and coughed, his face red with the effort.

"What? She's right there, I mean, she was just a minute ago . . ."

The shallow river flowed by. The reeds rustled softly. Lora's sundress and sandals lay crumpled on the sand, and her red rubber ball swayed gently by the opposite riverbank, carried away by the current. Pashka felt as if he were reading a book, trying—and failing—to close his eyes or turn the page.

"We need to talk," the fisherman in dark glasses said. He was now standing very close.

"Lora!" Arthur shouted. Ignoring the fisherman, Arthur grabbed Antoshka by his bare shoulders and shook him so violently that the snorkeling mask flew off. "Where is she?"

Antoshka couldn't speak through a bout of coughing.

"Lora! Lora-a-a-a-a!"

Still fully dressed, still wearing his watch, Arthur threw himself into the water and swam across toward the rubber ball, diving and pushing himself back to the surface, blindly searching the bottom of the river. On the shore now, Antoshka stood frozen, hugging himself with thin tanned arms.

"Fascinating," the man in dark glasses said pensively. "That's how this works. He knows nothing of drowned children, there is no such concept in his world. And yet, he has this very natural reaction. Truly fascinating."

Pashka felt like he was stuck in concrete. He couldn't take a single step, say a single word; he couldn't tell this psycho to go where no one had ever come back from.

"And you?" the man in dark glasses turned to Pashka. "Do you want to bring the girl back?"

A long second passed. Arthur dove and emerged, Antoshka trembled by the riverside; eddies swirled by the other shore— it was quite deep there, across the river.

"Do you want money? How much?" Pashka said softly. A terrible, aching hope sprung up inside him. He'd never been blackmailed before, but blackmail was a real thing, not a part of a nightmare.

"Nothing," the man in dark glasses said, smiling. Under different circumstances, Pashka would have called his expression "full of sympathy." Holding out his hand, the man said, "Take this."

He handed Pashka a small gold coin. Pashka recognized the round symbol on its reverse side.

"The world is not how you imagine it," the fisherman said softly. "Aircrafts crash. Children drown. Do you understand?"

But Pashka didn't. "It's not true," he said.

"Take the coin and swallow it, like a pill. There is nothing to be afraid of."

"I won't."

"I don't want to hurt you," the fake fisherman said. "Neither you nor your brother. But we're almost out of time."

Pashka watched the sun reflected in the dark glasses.

"Come on. Swallow it, like a pill. Otherwise, your brother is going to find her, but it'll be too late—she'll have spent too much time underwater."

Pashka put out his hand and felt the weight of the coin, too substantial for a small piece of metal. He brought his palm to his lips and swallowed the coin; it scratched his throat on its way down, but otherwise, he felt nothing.

I wish it was a dream, I wish I could wake up, he thought. His eyes shot open at the sound of a voice.

"I'm smarter than Pashka! I'm smarter than Antoshka!" Lora said happily.

Pashka blinked. Still in her pink swimming suit, hair wet and tousled, Lora stood by the old unpainted fence, banging on its smooth gray planks.

"You couldn't find me! I was playing hide-and-seek, and you didn't see me!"

Pashka screamed, hurting his throat, and rushed to her. He grabbed her by the shoulders, lifting her above the ground.

"Hey!" Lora said indignantly. "You're it, I won! Let me go!"

Pashka placed her back on her feet and, for the first time ever, smacked her swimsuit-clad bottom.

Valya bought a soda from a vending machine and drank it in one swallow, tasting nothing. It was only when the empty tin hit the bottom of the dumpster that he knew what he'd drunk: it was an energy drink with caffeine, which was a very bad choice. Mint tea with valerian root would have suited Valya's nerves a lot better, but not a lot of machines sold that.

How did he manage to see something on the board that was not there? Everything was just fine; his parents' flight had left on time and later tonight they would dip their feet into the warm sea. There would be just the two of them, and pines, and sand, and tiny pebbles, and they would be alone for the first time in many years. Mom would be cured of her anxiety, and they would come back tanned, joyful, and happy.

Yet . . . if this was done by hackers, why had no one at the terminal seen the terrible display? Why had no one reacted at all? A hundred people had been watching the display, but only Valya saw the morbid message. What was wrong with him?

Was it his wild imagination? But if so, where had it come from? He was sad to see his parents go, sure, but not scared. What prompted this awful, terrifying vision? He felt as if the world he was born and grew up in, this kind, safe world, had suddenly lifted its benevolent mask and showed such a ghastly face that it almost made Valya, nearly an adult, wet his pants.

Valya decided not to think about it anymore. He would go home, clean up after the early breakfast, and stretch out on the sofa with his tablet.

With that in mind, he headed back to town. And as soon as he turned the key in the lock, as the aroma of his home enveloped him, a mere half a step from his calm, comfortable world, he sensed a foreign presence in the empty apartment.

Somebody was waiting for him.

"You had no right to hit a child!"

Quiet on the way home, Lora cried harder now.

"Grandma, we nearly lost our minds," Arthur said softly. He hadn't stood up for his brother in years, but now he was all in. Still, he was pale, his cheek muscles twitching nervously and his hair standing on end. "If I hadn't been in the water at that moment, I'd probably have killed her myself."

"Don't say this," Grandpa said anxiously, hugging Lora and patting her head.

"You were supposed to watch her," Grandma said. Her lips barely parted as she spoke and pulled into a thin thread during each pause. "You were supposed to keep your eyes on her at all times. You promised me!"

"She ran off and hid," Arthur said. "How is this *our* fault?"

But Grandma just pulled Lora out of her grandfather's arms and led her back into the house, speaking softly into the girl's hair. At the threshold, Grandma turned back and motioned to the unusually quiet, subdued Antoshka to follow them. Pashka, Arthur, and Grandpa stayed in the yard, under the shade of the old fir tree.

Pashka pressed his hand to his belly. He thought that the gold coin he swallowed of his own volition had begun its independent, dangerous existence inside him. He chased away all those ridiculous thoughts: it was obvious that he'd never swallowed any coin; he was simply experiencing a temporary lapse of perception as a result of heatstroke. He didn't want to explain it to his grandmother—it would look as if he were lying to make excuses for himself.

"He only smacked her a couple of times," Arthur said softly. "She really scared us."

"She's a child," Grandpa said, and his voice sounded hollow and tired. "She thought it was a game. And why were you so scared, anyway?"

Arthur and Pashka exchanged glances, mentally questioning each other. The day had cooled off, and they felt like idiots who'd spent too much time in the sun to think and act intelligently.

"Sure, she could have swallowed some water and choked, or stepped on a sharp rock," Grandpa continued. "You would have helped her immediately. But she wanted to play hide-and-seek.

You could have gone along with her game, you could have looked for her in the reeds, and you would have found her right away."

"But she didn't *tell* us she was playing a game. She just disappeared. How would you feel?" Arthur asked.

Yet, once more, his grandfather didn't respond to this logic. And with that nonresponse, Pashka and Arthur simultaneously concluded that it was time for them to go back home. Summer Torpa was nice and all, but only up to a certain limit.

His head down, Pashka went into the house. In the kitchen, Lora had been changed into dry clothes and Grandma was feeding her some wild strawberry preserves, the ones that were supposed to be savored on New Year's Eve.

"Lora, I'm sorry," Pashka said, trying to make it an official apology. "I'm sorry, Grandma. I think Arthur and I are going to head home tomorrow."

Grandma looked up, her face full of regret that, in just another second, would be replaced by sympathy. She shook her head and sighed. It was then that the gold coin in Pashka's stomach turned into a red-hot dagger.

He winced and rushed to the bathroom, but it was occupied by sniffling Antoshka. Pashka ran out of the house and went around the corner, to the thicket of nettle that should have been mowed a while ago.

Overcome by nausea, Pashka fell on all fours; the coin flew out of him, gleaming like a goldfish. Before he had a chance to enjoy his miraculous release, he bent over again, and four more coins flew into the grass.

Valya's first impulse was to step back, close the door, and immediately call the police, but he didn't want to become a laughingstock. It was likely that the person inside his apartment was their next-door neighbor, stopping by to water the plants—his parents always left her the spare key when they traveled. There was no reason to call the police. It would be embarrassing, and he could even get in trouble for making unnecessary calls.

"Olya! Is that you?" he said in the friendliest way he could muster.

"It's me," a female voice said softly, definitely *not* Olya's. It was the voice of a stranger, and yet Valya knew it, knew it so well that the sound of it sent shivers down his spine. "Come in, Valya, and close the door."

Like a marionette, Valya followed the voice to the kitchen. A young woman sat at the table, where they had left all the breakfast dishes. Now the table was clean and empty, and the uninvited guest was sipping tea from Mom's favorite cup.

"You . . ." Valya began, then stopped. He recognized her. Of course it was her. Now everything made sense, except for how she got hold of the keys. Did she get them from their neighbor?

"You decided to come back after all," he said, using as few words as possible to demonstrate his independence and remind her of their blood ties.

"Yes, that's me. I am your sister, but you can address me formally, by my name and patronymic," she said, pulling out a cigarette. "It's Alexandra Igorevna."

"You can't smoke in here!" Valya said firmly.

His guest looked at him, almost amused, as she flicked the lighter on and inhaled elegantly, like a character in an old movie.

"I assume you don't remember me," she said. "How I used to take you for walks in your stroller. Or how you lay here, on this table, a baby, and how I nearly killed you thanks to my ignorance."

As impossible as it was, Valya did remember. He remembered the cold, the white ceiling above his head, and this face, her face, just younger and with a totally different expression: that of curiosity and greedy power like a girl cutting apart her doll to look at its insides. He remembered the awful sensation of his life, his mind, his identity being sucked out of him. Although, what identity could a tiny baby possibly have?

"Forgive me, I didn't mean to do it," she said, smoking and watching him. "It was a miracle that I managed to fix you. I had help. I couldn't have done it on my own."

Valya inhaled cigarette smoke and coughed.

"Are you following their flight?" she asked casually, glancing at her smartphone. "How long do our mother and your father have until they reach their destination? Lucky ducks, going to the warm sea, aren't they?"

"Please go," Valya said softly.

"Do you remember what you saw on the display board at the airport?" she said, smiling. "*The world is not what you think*. Millions of people will never know this. But you already do, Valya. You know."

"I am going to call Mom and tell her everything," he said, clenching his fists. "And I will call Dad as soon as they land . . ."

"*If* they land," she said simply.

The world went dark for a moment, but almost immediately the helpless haze was replaced by anger. Not even anger; fury.

"Get the hell out," he said, straightening his shoulders and trying to look taller. "Leave before I kick you out."

"Lovely," she said, looking at him with renewed interest. "Such an appropriate, healthy reaction. I am very pleased by this, Valya. I would have been gentler with you, but unfortunately, we're out of time. You'll just have to deal with it."

She left, leaving behind her crumpled, still-smoldering cigarette.

Grandma pleaded and cajoled, telling Pashka she was no longer angry with him, that things happen, and it was time to move on. Lora came as well, not as benevolent but coached by Grandpa, with an offering of vegetable ragu and mint tea. Pashka refused the food and drink. He was still sitting cross-legged by the nettle thicket, like a sick bird in its nest.

In his fist, he held five gold coins. He didn't need to look at them to recall the round symbol on the reverse sides. The nominal value of the coins was zero. Worse, the informational value was even less, because it was impossible to explain what had happened earlier at the beach, not even as by hallucination or hypnosis.

Grandpa came over with a blanket. Pashka thanked him but left the blanket on the ground.

Arthur showed up. He hugged Pashka (it had been ages since Arthur had allowed himself to show affection) and offered him a thermometer, an old one, the kind with mercury. Pashka held it under his arm for ten minutes, but the result was normal: 98.6. Sounding a bit unsure, Arthur brought up some sort of mushrooms; if one stepped on them, they blew up in millions of spores, causing hallucinations and visions. He'd seen something about it on some TV show. Pashka was about to show him the coins but held back; instead, he asked to be left alone for a few minutes and promised he'd return to them shortly. He swore he was going to eat supper, get a good night's sleep, and be perfectly fine by morning.

Arthur left but came back almost immediately. Pashka was about to say something when he realized that it wasn't Arthur. Tiny lights reflected in the black lenses—a jarring effect in near-darkness. The man sat next to Pashka, where Arthur had been sitting just a few minutes ago.

"All of us have been through it. All this, and much worse. How many coins?"

As if in a bad dream, Pashka opened his fist. He had clenched it so tightly that the five gold circles left imprints on his skin.

"Wonderful," the man said happily. "Very good, keep these. Put them aside somewhere, in a sock or something, and don't lose them! Tomorrow I will be working with your brother, and you will need to support him. Things will be easier if you stick together."

"Tomorrow, we're taking the first train out of Torpa," Pashka said, barely moving his lips.

"No," the man in dark glasses said, moving slightly away from Pashka and shaking his head with regret. "You will stay here. Both of you are on the hook, and if you try to move, you will be hurt."

"Who are you? Why are you telling me this?"

"My name is Konstantin Faritovich. You can call me Kostya."

CHAPTER THREE

Closer to midnight, Sasha knocked on Portnov's office door and placed an unopened pack of expensive cigarettes on his desk.

"Thanks," he said after a brief pause. "Not sure how I can pay back your kindness."

"Keep lending me some when I run out," she said, and he laughed.

"The reform has begun," Sasha continued. "By September 1, we'll have two groups of first years. We will give the lost tools back to the Great Speech. Among them, we'll have a verb in the imperative mood."

Portnov looked at her inquisitively. He carefully cut the plastic film off the cigarettes.

"Genetic ties don't guarantee success," he said. He knew exactly what she meant. "If they did, half of our students would be related."

"It's not about genetics. When my brother was a baby . . . when he lay on that table, gutted like a chicken," Sasha said, shuddering. "When I got hold of Farit, and Farit called Nikolay Valerievich . . . When back in that kitchen, I tried to restore the human in Little Valya, while his parents were trying to break down the door . . . Back then I left an informational fragment of myself inside Little Valya. I left a projection of myself inside his structure. I left a tiny beacon."

Portnov stared at her.

When he opened his eyes in the morning, Valya knew exactly what he was going to do that day. He'd skip breakfast and go to the shopping mall to buy a few things. Then he'd search the Internet for locksmith services, door installation, or something like that. By that evening, he'd have new locks. Let her try to come back in.

Luckily, the front door had a deadbolt, so Valya could lock it from the inside and sleep well. But he wanted to make sure that every time he left the house, no unwanted guest would break in and make herself at home.

He decided not to say anything to his parents. He knew they would immediately come back—his mother wouldn't be able to enjoy her vacation if she knew her precious Sasha had returned. Valya wondered what Mom would think of this Sasha now.

He heard voices in the kitchen. As if bitten by a snake, he jumped up from his bed, chills running down his spine. For a second, he thought he hadn't locked the door before going to bed. But he did! He'd locked it and checked it. This wasn't possible. He wondered if he was still asleep.

"Valya, sweetie," Mom said cheerfully from the kitchen. "Are you coming to the airport with us?"

Wearing only a T-shirt and underpants, he ran into the kitchen, stumbling over stacked suitcases on his way. Mom and Dad were finishing their hurried breakfast. One plate was covered, keeping his own breakfast warm.

"What's wrong?" Mom asked when she saw his face.

"A nightmare," Valya said hoarsely. "A bad dream."

"What was it about?" Dad asked, giving him a sympathetic glance.

"I don't remember," Valya said, squeezing the words out with an effort. "What day is it today?"

"Really?" Mom asked, lifting her eyebrow quizzically. "It's the twenty-seventh, obviously. Did you forget our vacation dates?"

This time, the familiar road seemed long and difficult to Valya. He put a lot of effort into making sure his parents did not suspect anything. Luckily, they were too busy with their own issues: Mom was trying to think of the crucially important things they'd left at home, and his father was cracking jokes, attempting to assuage her worries—in other words, adding fuel to the fire.

Eventually, they once again checked their luggage and got their boarding passes. At the last moment, Valya had to stop himself from grabbing Mom's hand and begging her to stay. This childish impulse terrified him. Giving in would have been deeply embarrassing.

His parents waved to him from behind the barrier and walked off, holding hands. Their vacation—and their second honeymoon—had begun . . . for a second time. Valya remained standing as if glued to the shiny floor.

Clusters of young people, couples, and families with children moved toward the check-in counters, carrying colorful suitcases and backpacks, all anticipating fun and enjoyment, not a single sad or indifferent face in the entire huge terminal. For the first time in his life, Valya realized that all of them were vulnerable, that, as they reached for happiness, all of them were risking their lives by going up into the clouds in a tight aluminum cylinder full of complicated devices, and someday one of those devices would stop working . . .

I am suffering from anxiety, he thought, gritting his teeth. *Like Mom, but worse. Mom knows that she's unwell, and she takes medication for it. She knows that her fears are made up, they are nothing but reflections of the chemical reactions in her brain. They must be regulated, hence doctors and medication. Psychotherapy and all that.*

He remained frozen, afraid of moving, afraid of walking by the display board, and terrified of going home. He still hoped *it was a dream.* He'd come home, and it would be empty, no strangers inside. To make sure it was true, he needed to—

"Valya," someone said behind his back.

He shuddered but did not turn his head.

"Let's talk," his sister said. "I swear I am not your enemy."

"Obviously, we're leaving," Arthur whispered in the darkness. "But it would be better if we left in a couple of days. We can call Mom. We can prepare Grandpa and Grandma. Don't worry, he won't get to you, this maniac. I will be by your side."

"But we can't wait, don't you get it?"

Arthur sighed. He did get it. He and Pashka had shared a long life, almost eighteen years of various experiences. They had been assigned to different classes, then brought back together, and the doctors used to say they were like conjoined twins, but conjoined mentally, not physically. Some suggested separating the boys and sending them to different cities to ensure proper formative conditions for their personalities, but their parents resisted. And when they finally outgrew the difficult times, accepted each other's limits, and consciously abandoned their painful connection—that's when that hot day on the beach had happened and when everything had returned.

Arthur fought back. He stuck to his belief that Pashka was sick and had even brought him the thermometer. But once Pashka told him the whole story in the dark, there was no room left for doubt: something otherworldly and incomprehensible had crawled into their lives. They had to get out first, then figure out what it was later.

Pashka tossed and turned on the sofa, Arthur on a cot by his side. The house was asleep or at least pretended to be. Grandma took her medication with a sip of water, Grandpa patted her shoulder, and Lora sniffled in her sleep knowing she had caused all this trouble. Antoshka slept soundly, despite the traces of river sand on his pillow and sheets.

"It's Torpa," Pashka began again in a whisper. "Do you remember when we were little, we used to say it was a special city, with a black tower and a building guarded by lions, and all this other stuff? We thought someone, or something, that didn't exist anywhere else lived here, in Torpa. Well, I think we've found that someone and something, and we are going to leave Torpa, and that'll be the end. We'll never return."

"What about Grandma and Grandpa?" Arthur said after a pause.

"*It* won't touch them. They are locals."

"What about Lora and Antoshka?"

Pashka had considered it. He had considered it long and hard.

"If we are not here, *it* won't touch them either." He wasn't sure how he knew this, yet nothing could shake him from this now apparent fact. "But if we stay, they will be used to blackmail us. And we can't take them with us, Aunt Irina and Uncle Roman would kill us."

Another pause.

"Have you packed?" Arthur said, and his voice broke. The plan was becoming a reality.

"Yeah, whatever I could. If we forget anything, not a big deal, Grandpa and Grandma can bring it or send it later. The first train is at six. Then we change trains at the district center."

"One ticket?" Arthur said, smiling in the dark.

They had done it many times before: taking exams for each other; taking the train with one twin showing the ticket, the other jumping on board right before departure as if he had forgotten something at the last minute. "I was just grabbing some food! You remember me, don't you?" one of them would say, the twins always taking turns sleeping on the berth and the luggage shelf, and never once getting caught.

"We'll see," Pashka said hesitantly. He suddenly realized that they had switched roles. Arthur used to do all the planning and all the brainstorming. "It's a long trip." And he had no desire for this escape—for that's what it was, he realized—to be brought up short by youthful chicanery.

They listened to the sounds of the sleeping house. Grandma and Grandpa had stopped talking and were hopefully asleep. Their little cousins, Lora and Antoshka, had settled down after their big adventures and were hopefully experiencing nice, calm dreams.

"Let's not wait until morning," Pashka said softly.

```
Grandpa, Grandma, sorry we left
without saying good-bye. Please
don't worry, we're adults and
can handle things. Please don't
call Mom yet, we'll tell her
everything when we get back.
```

```
Thank you for a wonderful
vacation. Hope you come
for a visit soon.

        Arthur and Pashka
```

Arthur wrote the "wonderful vacation" piece. Pashka wanted to add, "Your pancakes are the best pancakes in the world," but the look on Arthur's face stopped him in his tracks. This wasn't the right time for jokes.

They made the distance from the house to the town center in half an hour. For some reason, they thought that it would be easy to get a cab from there to the train station, but the app informed them that there were no drivers available in the area. The first bus was scheduled for half past five. Pashka and Arthur were alone at the bus stop; all the windows in the nearby buildings were dark. The streetlights burned at half power.

Half past three. Quarter to four.

"Let's just walk," Pashka said. "We'll get there by six. Or hitchhike on the way. Look at the stars! Might be a nice walk."

Arthur nodded and picked up his backpack. Pashka felt strange joy as if the two of them were going back to school, the same one, the same class, to the displeasure of their parents and their psychologists.

They both had good flashlights but decided to use only one to save batteries. After the first half hour they had reached the town limits, but saw only two cars, both going in the wrong direction. Neither of the cars had stopped for them.

"We should figure out what to tell Mom," Arthur said, breaking the silence. Along the quiet road under the stars, the sense of the idea of running away from Torpa no longer seemed all that sound.

"And what we're going to tell Gran when we call," Pashka said, aiming the flashlight far ahead. In front of them was a vast rippling field.

"We will tell her . . . Like I said, we should figure it out," Arthur said.

They continued walking for another hour until they heard a strange sound coming from afar. At first, it was so soft that they didn't even understand what it was—just some low humming, chirping, rustling, and creaking. A few minutes later a chain of lights popped out from behind the hills. Strange-looking machines with rotating jaws and closely set bright headlights moved across the fields in a diagonal.

"Combine harvesters!" Pashka said in surprise. "In the middle of the night?"

At least they no longer needed the flashlight. Pashka and Arthur saw the road awash in lights and their long black shadows ahead; a moment later they realized the beams were coming straight behind them, and another half a moment later they jumped to the side of the road, letting the column of empty grain-carrying trucks pass by.

"And that's how we found ourselves murdered by agricultural indifference," Arthur said with disdain.

"Driving like blind bats," Pashka said, coughing up the dust. "Can't they see live people in their path?"

As if in answer, the chain of lights in the field drew closer as if the combines saw no difference between people and grain.

"They are not going to drive down the road," Pashka said vaguely. "I mean, theoretically they shouldn't."

"Theoretically, people don't walk along this road in the middle of the night," Arthur said. "And harvesting grain overnight is a widespread practice in certain regions."

Not that that information was useful now. And as the lights

grew brighter, the sensation of being caught in a sticky net washed over Pashka.

"*He* said we'd never get out of Torpa. Even if we wanted to."

"*He* is not the head of the agricultural co-op," Arthur said sternly. "He doesn't control the combines. It's just a coincidence."

"Arthur, please, let's walk faster," Pashka said, feeling sweat trickle down his back. "You said it yourself: they are just drivers—they are harvesting wheat."

"It's rye, actually."

"Fine, it's rye! We have to go."

"We're already halfway there," Arthur pointed out.

"Then let's get all the way there!"

The chain of combines was very close. The one on the right kept grabbing the side of the road with its spinning maw. The headlights turned night into day. Arthur pulled Pashka out of the way, and the enormous, smoke-wrapped mechanical monster drove clanging by. A silhouette of the driver flashed in its window. The driver held up his third finger.

"They can see everything perfectly fine," Pashka muttered. "Come on, let's go."

They waited until the grain cart that followed the combines passed by, wiped their eyes of dust and tiny fragments of straw, and ran, covering their faces and trying not to breathe too deeply. The sound of the engines had died down and it became dark again. Arthur and Pashka slowed down to a walk. To the right, the field had been mown and now looked forlorn. To the left, the field continued undulating, as if mocking them with its heavy crops.

"Arthur," Pashka said hoarsely, simply to avoid the silence. "Do you think the new crops know what happened with the old ones? Does grain have genetic memory?"

"Mmm-hmm," Arthur said. "They pass their experience from generation to generation. They write books and compose songs."

He always got As in biology. Pashka laughed. Ahead of them, at the edge of the field, a forest belt came into view.

"Imagine them simply growing," Pashka said. "Thinking that nothing bad would ever happen. And what could happen to them? A drought, maybe, but not humanity. There are all these modern tools, watering mechanisms . . ."

Arthur stopped.

"Speaking of which," he said. "I need to pee."

"Want me to light the way?" Pashka said, offering his flashlight.

"No, you moron! Go ahead, I'll catch up."

"Please hurry."

"Can't rush these things," Arthur said with dignity.

Pashka walked on, pointing his flashlight at the dusty uneven road, adjusting the strap of his backpack, and trying to think of simple, pleasant things such as what kind of girls he was going to see at the university next year. Traditionally, his major was chosen mostly by boys, but he heard that more girls had been applying in the last few years, and all of them were awesome. Pashka used to be too shy to meet girls. A couple of times Arthur even made the initial contact, and Pashka showed up later. But nothing ever came of those dates.

This time, though . . .

"Hey, Arthur? Where are you?"

He pointed the flashlight to the road behind him. He could see about two hundred meters back. The tall wheat swayed in the wind. Or was it rye?

"Idiot," Pashka said. "Are you playing hide-and-seek, like Lora? Right now?"

He heard the familiar rumble, then saw the lights: a group of combines was returning from the other side of the field.

"Arthur!" Pashka screamed. "Where are you? Come back!"

He ran back to where he left his brother. He threw himself into the sea of crops, piercing the stalks with his flashlight, hoping to see his brother sitting (or lying?) on the ground. There was no sign of Arthur or his backpack. The headlights made the dark disappear. The mechanical jaws cut through the crops, twisting the stalks and shaking out the grain, and it looked like the entire field was alive, roaring, waving, and blazing away. The rye, with its short uneventful life, was as terrified as Pashka. *The world is not what you think, poor little grain.*

The combines moved with the speed of a train. Pashka barely made it from the side of the road to the harvested part of the field, where the sharp stubble poked Pashka's feet through his sneakers. The closest monster moved over the spot where Pashka had been standing just a moment ago and tossed a dark object up in the air, along with straw and dust.

It was Arthur's backpack.

The grain truck drove over the backpack with its heavy tires. Pashka sat down, deaf and nearly blind. The headlights had moved on, and he seemed to have lost his flashlight.

Both sides of the field, separated by the road, now looked naked, shaved, with only a few remaining stalks still standing here and there, in the same state of shock as Pashka. The combines had disappeared as if they were never there, and the rumble had gone with them. The sky began to grow paler. It was very clear, not a single cloud in sight. The stars appeared washed out. Still, Pashka got up. He wasn't leaving until he found his brother. Whatever was left of him.

• • •

Sasha's biggest challenge was to ignore her sympathy toward Little Valya. Sympathy was poison; to pity the boy now was to prolong his torture.

"Let's go sit on that bench and chat."

The bench was directly across from the large display board. Valya sat down gingerly, as if the metal was red hot, and lowered his head.

Sasha saw right through him: a jellied layer of humdrum on the outside and claylike mediocrity underneath, followed by softness, plasticity, and infantile conformism—and the golden light coming from his depths, where the unsaid Word slept soundly under the blanket of his ordinariness. Treasure inside, useless trash on the outside. Sasha wanted to dissect the boy on the spot, right there and then, to bring harmony back into the Great Speech. Valya sensed her desire and shrunk, turned inward, removing himself, hiding from reality.

"You thought the world was safe and kind. And it's true. Or rather, that's how it was. But someone must pay for the world's kindness."

Sasha paused. The boy kept his eyes down; he may not have heard her.

"Eventually, you'll know I am right, and everything I do, I do to save reality, the reality most people are aware of. You will know how the world is configured and you'll know your place in this world. And everything will be fine. But right now, Valya, you will simply have to do what I am telling you to do."

"You are nobody to me, Alexandra Igorevna," he said, raising his pale, focused face to her, his cheek muscles twitching tensely. "I will tell my mother everything."

He's resisting, Sasha thought, and found herself both frustrated and impressed. Even now, when she'd broken his impression of the world and scared him out of his wits, he was still resisting her. There was some hope.

"Shanin, Valentin Valentinovich," she said in an official tone. "Taking into account your previous achievements, you are accepted into the Institute of Special Technologies. We'll skip the entrance exams as an exception. On September first, you are expected at Torpa, 12 Sacco and Vanzetti Street."

At the sound of the familiar name, he looked up.

"Did you say Torpa?"

"It's a lovely little town."

"Mom's not going to let me go to Torpa," he said with a nervous giggle. "It's totally out of the question."

"The thing is, she's my mom, too," Sasha said with a sigh. "And I won't let anything truly terrible happen to her."

"Like what?" he said, shuddering.

"Like things you actually wouldn't be able to believe in this reality. Just know that, years ago, she let me go to Torpa. She didn't want to. It was just how it worked out in the end. Do you understand?"

"Why me? Why do you want me?" he asked softly. In his question, Sasha heard her own pleading voice from many years ago. Many billions of years ago. Facing Farit Kozhennikov.

She wondered if she should try explaining it to him. But no, it wasn't possible. He wasn't ready. It would be as effective as making coins out of clay.

So instead she simply said, "You have almost an entire free summer ahead of you. Enjoy it—swim, take walks. Don't tell your parents, don't say anything to anyone. I will make sure Mom lets you go to Torpa."

"She won't!" he said with conviction. "She won't let me go, and neither will Dad!"

Sasha smiled wistfully, letting this naïve dream germinate a little longer.

Pashka picked up Arthur's backpack with both hands. Inside something clinked like shards of glass. His phone? Tablet? Sunglasses? The sunrise made everything look gray, and the air was filled with straw dust, but no matter how hard he tried, Pashka could not see any blood.

"This is not real," he said into space. "This is a dream! Tell me it's a dream!"

"It's not a dream," someone said behind his back. Pashka dropped the backpack and turned, ready to fight, ready to rip apart with his bare hands that ghoul, that monster borne of the terrible town of Torpa.

He saw himself, as if in a mirror: a gray, terrible face, with huge eyes, and black lips as thin as a single thread. A second later he realized it wasn't his reflection; it was his brother's.

"Let's go," Arthur said, his voice strange and dull, either hoarse or simply sick. "Hurry up."

"Where were you?"

"Never mind. Let's go back."

"Go back? You mean to the train?"

"Back. Now."

Arthur picked up his squashed backpack and ran down the straw-covered road. Suddenly he stumbled and fell on his knees, coughing.

Small gold coins rolled in the dust.

That morning their grandparents, along with Lora and Antoshka, woke up late; they must have been exhausted by the adventures of the day before. Pashka and Arthur managed to return to the house, destroy their note, hide all the evidence of their trip, and climb into their beds before their escape was discovered.

The sun rose high and was beating mercilessly into the windows.

"Listen," Pashka said when he could no longer stay quiet. He heard voices and the clinking of spoons coming from the kitchen.

"Don't ask me," Arthur said.

"I thought—"

"I won't talk about it. We can't leave this place, and I am not crazy. And *he* is not a maniac."

Arthur turned on his stomach and pulled the blanket over his head.

"What if we ask *him* what he wants from us?" Pashka asked.

Arthur took so long to respond that Pashka didn't even expect an answer.

"He wants us to . . . Today he wants us to go to the Start supermarket," Arthur said from beneath the blanket. "He wants us to steal a box of chocolates. Just one."

Pashka laughed. It was hysterical, nervous, stupid laughter, but Arthur jumped up and tossed the blanket aside.

"Do you think this is funny?"

Pashka shut up immediately, as if someone had put a hand over his mouth. Red spots burned on Arthur's cheeks. His eyes were full of tears; he looked ill.

"Valya, sweetie, it's Mom! We are here, we made it, it's so beautiful here! Have you eaten? Both lunch and dinner? How are you doing?"

From the sound of her voice, Valya knew immediately that

she was tired from traveling and missed him already, but also that her anxiety had eased up. He had been waiting for her call and yet, he found he wasn't ready for it.

"Everything is great," he said, hoarsely but cheerfully.

"What's wrong, why do you sound like this? Are you sick?"

"No, everything is fine," Valya said, clearing his throat. "Send me some pictures, I want to see where you are."

A stream of photos followed: pines by the shore, tiny pebbles, yachts in the distance, selfies of Mom and Dad hugging in front of a hotel, the sea, and the beach.

He was going to tell them everything. They would cancel their vacation, change the tickets, and come home. Mom would be radiant with hope, Dad would be bewildered. Mom would ask: "Where is she? Where is my Sasha?" And what would Valya say, how would he present Alexandra Igorevna, who stayed behind at the terminal? When he returned home, the apartment was empty.

So he said nothing. "Awesome pictures," he said, paying close attention to his voice. "Have a great time."

That night he deadbolted the door and turned on the TV, knowing he couldn't sleep. However, he did doze off by half past one. At six-thirty he woke with a start, jumped up, and ran into the kitchen.

There were no suitcases in the hallway. The kitchen table was empty of yesterday's dishes. Valya's phone showed today's date, June 28.

"Everything is fine," Valya said softly. "Everything is perfectly fine. I am suffering from anxiety. Everything is peachy keen."

He laughed and kept on laughing until he had to stick his head under the cold water. He forgot to take off his glasses and the glasses almost broke.

CHAPTER FOUR

Sasha came home in the early evening, before dusk. She put a bunch of daisies into a vase and lit the fireplace—in the middle of the summer—opened the window, and lit a cigarette.

Kostya showed up almost immediately, with a gentle knock on the door.

"Come in," Sasha said. "Door's unlocked."

He showed her a paper bag with an unfamiliar logo.

"It's Chinese food, from a new place. I haven't tried it but heard good things."

"Thanks," Sasha said, blowing smoke out the window.

"You are right, both have potential," Kostya said. He filled the kettle with water, switched it on, and found a tin of loose tea and cups. Sasha watched him indifferently. He had a right to feel at home in her tiny place. Billions of years ago she'd given him permission to do so.

"Let's eat," he said, arranging plastic and cardboard containers of complicated food and sauces on the table. "We are made of flesh, after all. We can indulge now and then."

"Should I send them the letter of acceptance?" Sasha said, wishing he'd simply nod.

"Not yet," Kostya said, busy with the tea leaves. "They have this one peculiar feature: They reflect each other. Like a pair of mirrors. Or planets connected by gravity. They revolve around each other, unable to break the connection, but incapable of merging. It's quite interesting."

"What's the point of torturing them if they are ready?" Sasha asked, putting out her cigarette.

"You asked me for help," Kostya said, sitting down and opening one of the containers. "I'm a very responsible person. By the way, Sasha: Who are these boys to you in the grammatical sense?"

"It's too early to discuss their grammatical affiliation," Sasha said. "But it's quite an interesting case, you're right."

"Who am I to question Password," Kostya muttered. Sasha knew that meant, *You don't have to answer, but I will file it away.*

To at least give him a morsel, Sasha said, "They are my sons—in the grammatical sense, obviously." She felt a wave of anxiety and lit up another cigarette. "Biologically they are not related to me; they have a mother and a father. And you know all this perfectly well, and still, you're asking me about it."

"Do you always smoke this much?" Kostya asked grimly.

Not bothering to answer, she said, "In each of these boys, there is a fragment, a reflection, a projection that is very dear to me, and that I need very much."

"If you need them this much, we cannot afford to pity them," Kostya said, removing his glasses in such a familiar gesture that Sasha flinched. "On September first they will enter the assembly hall along with everyone else. Your responsibility is to teach them.

"Mine is to make sure they work hard."

Pashka and Arthur pretended to be sick. It was easy: they simply slept through the morning, only occasionally opening their eyes. Grandma was worried and even wanted to call a doctor, but the boys talked her out of it by claiming they were feeling better. They finally got up and got dressed, and even had Grandma's truly excellent pancakes.

Lora and Antoshka wandered around the yard, picking pointless fights with each other. As soon as Arthur and Pashka made an appearance, the little ones ran into the kitchen, claiming they were starving. Each had something to say: Lora presented a beetle she'd caught and kept in a cardboard box, planning to liberate it later. Antoshka, who never liked to read, took a Jules Verne book from Grandpa's library and attempted to pull Arthur into a literary debate. Both little ones felt that something strange was going on, that something was trying to take their older cousins out of their lives and that something had almost succeeded, but if Lora and Antoshka worked hard at providing a distraction—like Lora's beetle—Arthur and Pashka would forget all the bad stuff, come back to the routine, and stay.

The little ones didn't realize that, by their cousins staying, they were even more likely to lose them.

Start supermarket in the center of Torpa was open until 10 P.M. Arthur, who had witnessed something Pashka still had no knowledge of, began preparing when the sun was still high in the sky:

"Gran, do you need anything from the store? We were going to take a walk, so we can swing by the supermarket."

This was a first for Arthur: he'd never offered to run any errands before. While Grandma pondered the question, Grandpa got very excited.

"Of course, we need all sorts of stuff! I went there two days ago and completely forgot to buy lemons, and there are none in our local grocery store. Let me give you some money, get lemons and something for the little ones—cookies or chocolates."

At the mention of chocolates, Arthur's cheek muscle twitched, but the only one who noticed was Pashka. Arthur lowered his head just in time.

"We wanna come, too!" Antoshka shouted, but Arthur looked at him, and Antoshka shut up immediately.

"We won't be long," Pashka said, grabbing Arthur's elbow and pulling him out of the kitchen. He felt as if both he and his brother were branded with an invisible stamp, covered with an elusive layer of unreality. It was contagious, and Pashka worried that it could touch and hurt those who were near them, those who were innocent of any wrongdoing.

Then again, what wrongdoing were Arthur and he guilty of?

It was a perfectly ordinary, peaceful summer evening. Arthur picked the right time: the supermarket was very crowded. Toddlers sat in the grocery carts, swinging their legs, while their mothers checked expiration dates on packaged foods. Young couples filled their carts with beer, chips, cold cuts, paper towels, and other party supplies.

Pashka entered first. Holding an empty basket, he strolled along the shelves, trying not to look toward the cameras. The supermarket had an impressive surveillance system. In addition to the video cameras, a stocky guard at the entrance watched as the customers walked in and out the door.

Pashka had never stolen anything in his entire life. He'd never even considered the possibility. But Arthur . . . In those few months when the brothers were forced to separate and attend different classes, Arthur had joined a new group of slightly older friends. Stealing from supermarkets was their favorite pastime.

They stole candy and chips, T-shirts and earbuds, and once they emptied the cash register of a small kiosk. Eventually, Arthur got caught; his more experienced pals managed to escape.

Pashka was the only person who understood what Arthur felt when somebody else's fingers closed on his wrist. Pashka knew the price of being called a thief and the weight of the conversation at the police quarters. But the worst thing was the expression on their father's face when he returned from his flight. It wasn't an accusation or anger; it was of childlike surprise—his son, a thief?

Once again, a team of psychologists was called to the rescue. In those few days, Arthur had lost himself, with Pashka as his only lifeline, and Arthur needed Pashka to share his identity with him like a diver running out of air and looking to share another diver's oxygen tank.

Eventually, the case was hushed up, and the brothers were allowed to attend the same classes; it was the only good outcome. Six years later they had graduated from high school and by then Arthur had learned to laugh at the old story. And yet, the man in the dark glasses knew his pain points.

The question was: *How* did he know them?

Stop, Pashka said to himself. *This is Arthur's trauma, not mine. I am different, I will deal with it, this is easy for me. It's just chocolates.*

Facing the camera, he picked up three lemons, a bag of oatmeal cookies, and a box of chocolates from another shelf. He placed everything into his basket, paid at the register, and took the receipt.

He walked toward the exit, and, just as he reached the door, he slapped himself on the forehead and, smiling apologetically at the guard, doubled back.

Cocooned in a hoodie up to his nostrils, Arthur was waiting for him in the corner. Pashka waited for a young couple with a full cart to block them from the cameras and dropped the box of chocolates into Arthur's bag. His hand twitched and the chocolates fell on the floor. Customers nearby turned their heads.

"Shit," Arthur said.

"Want to leave?" Pashka asked quickly.

Arthur shook his head. He was ready to continue the mission at any cost. Shuddering, Pashka wondered once again what the man in the dark glasses had shown Arthur back in the field.

"Just go, you're not doing anything wrong," Pashka said. "The chocolates have been paid for. Go."

Arthur lowered his head even farther, pushed down his hood, and shuffled toward the exit. Pashka wanted to shout: *Stand up! You look straight out of a Wanted poster!*

Arthur reached the guard and pressed his bag against his hip, perhaps on purpose, perhaps out of fear. The guard turned his head, about to say something.

Arthur walked through the doors without activating the sensors. He walked faster, expecting to be arrested at any moment.

The guard lost interest and went back to watching the entrance.

Smiling nervously, Pashka approached the shelves, picked up the same box of chocolates, and put it in his basket. He stepped through the doors, and the sensors screamed, making everyone at the store stop and look at him. Blue and red lights flashed as if Pashka had just taken millions of dollars from a bank.

"Open your bag," the guard said.

"I don't have a bag," Pashka said, showing him the plastic basket. "Here is my receipt: lemons, cookies, chocolates."

"Mila, you missed something again," the guard yelled at the cashier.

"The receipt has everything," she yelled back. "The barcode is not working, that's a tech support thing."

"Can I go?" Pashka asked softly. Trying to avoid a traffic jam, the guard waved him through.

Arthur was waiting for him in the park across the street. A drop of blood had dried in the corner of his mouth. He held something in his right fist. Pashka smiled and clapped him on the shoulder.

"That's all. I hope he leaves us alone now, and—"

A bout of coughing made him bend over, his throat turned inside out, and a handful of gold coins rolled down the brick path.

"How many?"

The man in the dark glasses stopped them on their way back home. The evening sun reflected in the windows, the red promise of tomorrow's wind. The man stepped into their path even though the road was empty just a second ago.

"Six for both of us," Pashka said haughtily. "Three for me, three for Arthur."

He pulled his hand out of his pocket. The golden circles felt very heavy in his palm. The man in dark glasses glanced at them.

"You have four, Arthur has two. It's not enough. Not good, guys," he said. He wasn't blaming or scolding them; he was simply disappointed like a coach whose team had just lost the game.

"We did everything you asked," Pashka said, handing over the box of chocolates.

"Keep them, I don't need any chocolate," the man in dark glasses said with a vague smile.

"Then what do you need?" Pashka asked. Despair made him brave. "What else do you need?"

"Do you remember my name?" the man said, smiling wider. "I did introduce myself."

Pashka grew silent. He remembered some name being mentioned, a perfectly human name, but at that moment, Pashka had lost his ability to hear or remember anything important.

"My name is Konstantin Faritovich," the man said, his tone more serious now. "And I can see that there is no reason to give the assignments to both of you together. It's not effective enough. You'll have to work separately."

Throngs of psychologists who had worked with Pashka and Arthur echoed in his voice: *Separately . . . on their own . . . independently of each other . . .*

Before Pashka figured out what he could say in response, Konstantin Faritovich motioned for Arthur to come closer. As if hypnotized, Arthur complied.

The man in dark glasses leaned over to Arthur and whispered something in his ear, something not long but not too short.

"Just do it," the man said placatingly. "And then everything will be well. Go home, everyone is waiting for you."

Konstantin Faritovich disappeared around the corner of the nearby fence as if he never even existed. Arthur remained rooted to the spot. His long shadow lay on the sidewalk, melting into the shadows of young chestnut trees.

"What did he tell you?" Pashka asked. Awkwardly holding the shopping bag, he came closer.

And saw Arthur's face.

At the drugstore, Valya bought a jar of valerian root capsules—an herbal treatment for anxiety. He would have preferred his mother's medication, but that required a prescription, and Mom had packed hers for the trip.

It was hard to wake up in the mornings. Every time Valya opened his eyes, he listened to the silence in the empty apartment, trying to figure out: These steps, were they coming from outside or from the next room? This squeak—was it the neighbors' door or his parents' bedroom door?

He called Mom every day, making sure he sounded calm. Despite his efforts, Mom was beginning to suspect something, but she blamed the tension in his voice on his new experience of being alone and not the existential crisis he'd somehow been forced into.

"Do you make oatmeal in the morning? Eating cold cereal every day is not good for you! Are you getting enough fruit? Why don't you call one of your classmates and go to the movies?"

Her fussing, routine and slightly annoying, calmed Valya down faster than the valerian root. *Just let them come back safely,* Valya said to himself, *and I will tell them everything. And when Mom sees her precious Sasha—and she will see her—she'll have someone else to bother about eating more fruits and vegetables . . .*

Valya's imagination stopped at that point; he would start laughing and immediately feel better. Just let them come back. Less than a week remained until their return. He cleaned the apartment, rode his bike to the park, and on Friday he went to the beach. He sat under a faded tent, watching some girls dive into the water from a tin pontoon. Their microscopic bikinis looked nearly transparent in the water, and Valya decided to come back to the beach on Saturday.

In the morning he called Mom as usual, but she didn't answer. It was a little strange but not yet alarming. She could have lost her phone in the sea. She could be in the water, and the phone on her towel. There were so many reasons to not answer, and yet . . .

He called Dad. His father answered, and the sound of his voice made Valya freeze.

"I can't talk right now," Dad said. "I'll call back later."

"Is Mom okay?" Valya shouted.

"She's okay. Everyone is okay," Dad said, his voice heavy as a rock, making it clear nothing was okay. "We'll talk later." And he hung up.

Valya circled the room like a fly caught in a glass jar. Alexandra Igorevna had said: "This is my mom, too, and I won't let anything truly terrible happen to her." But what about something only marginally terrible?

He didn't go to the beach. He spent the entire day at home, missing a gorgeous July day. He kept checking his phone: Was it fully charged, was the connection stable, did he miss any calls? He even brought his phone to the bathroom. Finally, three hours later, Mom called.

"Valya, darling, your father and I are coming back tomorrow," she said, her voice very soft, very fragile. "We managed to exchange the tickets for an earlier flight."

"What happened?" Valya said. The way she said "your father and I" made him imagine something implausible, like a hole in the sky.

"Later," she said, as if slicing off a string. "You don't need to meet us at the airport."

Of course Valya found the only flight from Tivat arriving tomorrow. Of course he went to the airport.

The flight was three hours late. Gritting his teeth, Valya watched the scheduling board. It was his own long personal battle against Alexandra Igorevna. His eyes had begun to water, but Valya kept staring at the lines. He expected the board to break or for Alexandra to show up in person. Instead, he got a call from his mom.

They were already home. They'd flown back from Dubrovnik, not Tivat, and got home early. Mom was upset that Valya went to the airport, when she had explicitly asked him to wait at home.

Valya got a cab; it was a dumb waste of money, but he couldn't wait for a bus or a train. The cab got stuck in traffic. By the time Valya got home, the apartment smelled medicinal. Swimsuits and other summer things lay on the living room sofa; in the bedroom, Dad was packing his other clothes: button-downs, slacks, suits, dress shoes.

"Finally," Mom said.

She stood by the window, facing away from everyone, and didn't even turn around when Valya came in.

"Mom, what happened?"

"Valentin, you can tell him," Mom said and went into the bathroom.

Watching the door close behind her, Valya's father got up slowly, glanced at Valya, and immediately looked down.

"Your mother is kicking me out."

His words sounded nonsensical to Valya. The noise the water made in the pipes was much more logical and significantly more intelligent.

"I assumed she'd give me a chance to explain, tell her why it wasn't what she had assumed," Dad said in a monotone, hiding behind the simple action of packing dress shoes into a plastic bag. "I made a mistake, I admit it, but we're grown people, adults! It was an isolated case, a temporary lack of judgment, the only thing that's ever happened, and we've been together for so long! We have a life together, we have you . . . but she won't even listen."

"Dad, are you both insane?" Valya said, struggling to move his dry lips.

It felt as if the sun rose inside his head. It wasn't joy, not at all, but sudden clarity of what was happening here.

"Wait," he said, putting out both palms as if trying to hold his father back from fiddling with his shoes. "I will explain everything. Just wait."

He rushed to the bathroom and pounded on the smooth wooden door.

"Mom! Sasha was here! Alexandra Igorevna! Your daughter! It's all her fault!"

The door opened. Mom stepped out, and only then Valya realized how old she really was.

Dad left in a cab, with a single suitcase.

"Don't worry," Mom said, smiling vaguely. "He'll be fine. When he left his first family, with the two sons, he was just fine."

"Mom, she manipulates time. She can make the same day repeat. Everything that's happening is a lie. Dad loves you. Even if he had a summer fling . . ."

This sounded so vulgar that Valya blushed.

"Valya, I get it," Mom said, shaking a pill out of a small bottle. "It's your defense mechanism at work. At seventeen, you are letting your imagination run as if you were eight."

"Mom!"

"This, too, shall pass. All these emotions will die down. You are an adult, so you and your father can meet whenever you want, on neutral territory. He may even introduce you to his new family."

"He doesn't have a new family! And he never will!"

"She's young and beautiful," Mom said pensively. "I used to be like her. When he appeared in front of me, at the seashore, at sunset. I fell in love so deeply I ignored the fact that he was married, I let him leave his family. I stopped taking care of my daughter. It's karma, honey."

"Mom, are you listening to me? Alexandra is back! She—"

"If Sasha had come back, she would have called," Mom said. The only thing she heard was the voices in her own head. "She would have called me immediately."

She pointed at the ancient phone in their hallway. When Valya was born, this landline was already old, but it was still functional. A few numbers were jotted down on a piece of clear plastic. Mom always kept one of them fresh, tracing the fading digits with a black marker.

"She would have seen this number here and she would have called me. But you're making things up right now to distract both you and me. And while I appreciate it, I'm tired and need you to accept this."

Mom swallowed her pill with a sip of water and hugged Valya; he stiffened in her arms.

"I am very sad, too. I also didn't want to believe it at first. But it's just life, life can be like this. There is still time left until the end of our vacation. Let's go away—you and me. One of my coworkers has a nice dacha, and it's empty right now. It's in this beautiful place in the woods, and there is a lake . . ."

Valya should have told her about Torpa. The very name of the town would have pushed Mom out of the deep denial she'd buried herself in. And yet Valya knew that at this moment, the very mention of Torpa would have finished her off, and no pill would have been enough.

He just had to accept it, as she said. Until, that is, he wouldn't be allowed to anymore.

Sasha sat on a bench in the familiar courtyard overgrown with old poplar trees. She watched Valentin put his suitcase in the cab. Valentin was a gift from fate to Sasha's mom. Valentin was Mom's second life, her true and last love.

The generous fate was named Farit Kozhennikov.

"Thank you, Farit," Sasha said, addressing the man who could no longer hear her. "It was a great idea. Watch how I'm going to recycle it."

CHAPTER FIVE

A rthur handed the grocery bag to Pashka. He didn't explain anything, just said he was going for a walk and needed to be alone.

"What did he order you to do? You can tell me."

"No," Arthur said firmly. "I can't."

"What would happen if you don't do it?"

The immense pain in Arthur's eyes made Pashka shut up.

They went their different ways: Pashka shuffled back home, and Arthur went down one of the side streets, disappearing from view. Pashka stopped a few times, looking back and wondering if he was doing the right thing. Should he have followed his brother, and stayed with him, by his side, no matter what happened? What would be better for Arthur: for Pashka to follow his instructions? Or ignore them and try to protect his brother? Pashka thought of his attempts to "protect" his brother back on the field, with the combines, and shuddered.

He threw the stolen chocolates into a trash bin. The rest of the groceries he brought home. Lora and Antoshka attacked the sweets, while Grandma pleaded with them to save half of them for the next day. Both grandparents wanted to know where Arthur was.

"He ran into a friend of his," Pashka said, then continued

lying. "They went for a walk. They haven't seen each other for a while."

"A friend?" Grandpa said skeptically. "Perhaps a female friend?"

Pashka marveled at reality building itself like a salt crystal or a simple snowflake. Their grandparents knew that neither Pashka nor Arthur had friends in Torpa. There were few young people in Torpa in the summer, and it was hard for vacationers to befriend the locals. And yet, a lovely picture had formed in Grandpa's mind: Arthur had met a girl and offered to walk her home, the weather was beautiful, and the evening turned out to be warm and romantic, so let the kids enjoy themselves.

Pashka watched his grandparents create a microcosm of confidence and tranquility, an indestructible calmness and joyful predestination. Pashka wanted to hide in this microcosm with them, but he was afraid of puncturing a hole in its fabric. His new knowledge of the world was a threat to this cozy old house.

And so he left and went into the front yard. It smelled of wilting grass; Grandpa had mowed the nettles behind the house, and the piles of stinging shoots lay scattered on the ground, clearing the way to the old chin-up bar by the far side of the fence. The chin-up bar was so old that Pashka remembered trying to reach it and failing, no matter how high he jumped. Now all he had to do was stand on his tiptoes.

He pulled up once, twice, three, five times, hopped down, and stretched, stepping over the cut nettles. He went back to the chin-up bar and began to pull up again without counting, simply because physical effort took the edge off his anxiety.

Pashka's T-shirt had stuck to his back and the sky turned dark when he finally heard Arthur approach. Pashka recognized his brother's steps even though they sounded unsteady and weird.

Arthur opened the gate and stepped into the yard, swaying. Pashka had never seen his brother drunk before. He'd never imagined him *being* drunk, if he was being honest. Yet here he was. Arthur could barely stand; his T-shirt was covered in vomit and some other stuff. It looked as if he had rolled in the gutter before returning home. And that smell—even outside, even at a distance—made Pashka's nostrils turn inside out.

"Wait, go behind the house," Pashka said quickly. "I'll bring you a towel and some clean clothes."

Arthur shook his head, losing his balance and nearly falling. Determined, measuring every step, he proceeded toward the entrance, and at that moment Grandma opened the door.

The light from the windows fell onto the veranda. A ray of streetlight reached as far as the front door. On the top stair, Grandma wrung her hands. Standing on the bottom stair, Arthur was almost the same height as her.

"My poor boy," Grandma said gently. "Did you have an argument? Did she upset you? Girls can be so mean; I remember feeling like an evil mother-in-law when your dad was only two years old. Let's get you washed up; I'll get you some aspirin."

Standing in the shadows, Pashka watched Arthur swaying, shifting his weight from foot to foot, as if preparing to jump from a springboard. Preparing for something. His eyes looked glassy, but not from alcohol. It seemed as if Arthur was regretting not being sufficiently drunk.

"Arthur!" Pashka shouted, but he was too late. His brother uttered a short choking sound, and slapped his grandmother on the cheek, making her head snap back.

Arthur ran out the gate and immediately disappeared. Pashka wasted another second to fight his paralysis. Then he ran over to his grandmother.

Holding on to the railing with her left hand, she touched

her right hand to her face: to her lips and her bloody nose, the blood still gushing, faster and faster.

"Grandpa! Help!" Pashka yelled in despair.

Grandpa ran out and held his wife in his arms.

"What happened?"

Pashka could not explain. Neither could his grandmother—she was in shock. Grandpa carried her into the house, and immediately Lora and Antoshka started to scream.

At least Pashka could count on his grandfather to provide first aid. He couldn't bear being there, answering questions, explaining stuff—it was too much. He still saw Arthur's face, the expression his brother had when he received his next assignment from the man in dark glasses. Whatever Arthur had seen in the rye field, whatever the man had told him, meant he could no longer ignore the assignments. He had just completed the next one, bewildering and horrifying as it was. What would happen now?

What would Arthur be asked to do next?

The house phone rang after Mom had already taken her pills, falling asleep in her empty bedroom. The hospital staff had tried to call her, but Mom's phone was turned off.

"Yes, I am his son," Valya said. He felt his hair stand on end. "Why?"

Mom woke up a minute later. Five minutes later she was pulling on her clothes, getting tangled in her sleeves and pant legs. It was as if she hadn't taken any pills at all; perhaps in the few hours she'd been asleep, the time had stretched to several days in her dreams.

Half an hour later they were in a cab, another half an hour and they had reached the hospital reception, still unsure what exactly was going on. Valya was shocked by how strong and willful his mother could be when all hope seemed lost.

Somehow, he found himself alone in a corridor where trolleys transported patients back and forth—most of them looked ancient, wrinkly, but still alive. *It's natural,* Valya said to himself. *Once you get close to a hundred years, you might as well give yourself up to the medical personnel who will drive you back and forth along the hospital corridors. It might be kind of fun, but it won't matter that much.*

But wasn't his father too young for this sort of entertainment?

Mom came out of the intensive care unit looking like a very different person. Valya could not understand why he thought she looked old before; now she appeared younger than she did in Valya's baby pictures.

"He is better. He has excellent doctors, and tomorrow he'll be transferred to a regular room. Go home, I'll stay here with him."

She caught his eyes and brushed her hair away from her forehead. He was about to say something—he wasn't quite sure what—but whatever his mom saw in his face made her think he was upset at her change of heart.

"Valya, I . . . It's important to learn to forgive. Especially if you truly love someone."

Was he supposed to forgive Sasha for this?

Pashka found his brother exactly where he expected to find him. As if Arthur were the North Pole, and Pashka a compass arrow.

A riverbank. A crumpled figure on the sand under the bridge. A compulsively clenched fist. Glassy eyes.

"How many?" Pashka asked softly. Arthur flinched, but

Pashka was not wearing dark glasses, and Arthur recognized him at a second look. Arthur glanced at his fist but could not unbend his fingers.

"The world is not what we thought it was," Pashka said, sitting down next to his brother. "But you have me, and I know what's going on. And I have you. There are two of us, and he's all alone."

Arthur tried to speak, but his lips remained stuck. He shook his head and finally began to speak.

"I heard you calling me. The combines were making all this noise. I heard it. I was pulled in, but *he* came and stopped time. He rewound it a little so that I could go from mincemeat to myself again. But I feel like I'm still mincemeat, hamburger, ground up, broken. I can't forget the steel chewing me up, and I have a feeling I'll never forget. I wish I'd just stayed there."

He got up, swaying, staggered out from under the bridge, and tossed something into the water. Gold circles splashed in the glow of a distant streetlight on the corner of Peace Street. Concentric circles spread on the water.

Kostya came at dawn when Sasha stood on the bridge over the shallow river, watching pond skaters scurrying along the riverbank, a school of minnows just under the surface, and concentric circles dispersed by the larger fish frolicking around. Frogs croaked loudly; it was the coolest hour of the hot July day, and it was still balmy. Sasha's linen jacket hung off the dried-up railing.

"Fish are biting," Kostya said, staring at the river. "Wish I had a rod with me."

"Yum, up to your elbows in fish slime, and worms writhing on a hook," Sasha said, smirking. "So romantic."

"I never use worms for bait," Kostya said sternly. "I think it's sadistic. I use raw dough, and I always let the fish go."

Sasha looked into the water. Small gold coins with a round sign on the reverse sides lay on the sandy bottom, surprisingly free of silt. There were eleven coins in total.

"You broke the boy," Sasha said. "You broke Arthur. Why did you do that?"

"Because you summoned me," Kostya said dryly. "You want something from these twins, don't you?"

His sudden fury made the wind blow through the cattails and the water ripple.

"I know what you see when you look at them," Kostya said. "I know *whom* you see. But they are no one until you teach them and they *reverberate*. And they will not learn on their own. There is no more Farit, and so I must do his work. It would be easier without your attitude."

The fish disappeared. They didn't like what was happening on the bridge. A small wave broke on the sandy bank.

"I know how important the twins are to you," Kostya said, squeezing the railing with his slim fingers. "I tried—for you!—to maintain dynamic equilibrium. I didn't break Arthur, I fractured him. I left Pashka untouched. That means they would have different potentials, don't you see? One is a straight-A student, the other one is a lazy bum. One is a fatalist; the other is a rebel. Sasha, I tried so hard—even Farit couldn't have managed better!"

"I don't want to hear his name," Sasha said through gritted teeth.

"You're right," Kostya said. Suddenly, he seemed tired and sad. "A pronoun does not call the one they replaced by their proper name. It simply refers to them. Like I do."

Sasha sighed and put her arm around his shoulders, her

eyes still on the river. Surprised, Kostya froze on the spot like a mouse facing a basilisk.

"I am so grateful to you," Sasha said softly. "I understand everything. I just can't get used to it."

"Over millions of years?"

"Even over billions."

The minnows came back to the shallow water. Two light brown ducks swam out of the cattails and began plucking the grass by the riverbank.

Grandma could no longer tell Arthur and Pashka apart.

She'd always been great at this, even when their father was still struggling, when the twins wore identical overalls and spoke to each other in a special language only the two of them understood. Grandma never made a mistake, as if the twins had identifying marks on their foreheads.

After what had happened on the porch, she seemed to have lost her ability; she was now looking at them the same way, avoiding calling them by their names, convinced she wouldn't get it right. No excuses or explanations helped. It no longer mattered why Arthur was drunk, what he must have seen, why he did what he did—none of it mattered. Everything had changed. The very air in the house was different.

Grandpa had made it very clear that it was time for the brothers to leave Torpa. Grandpa didn't know who Konstantin Faritovich was, and the twins could not explain it to him. Not that it mattered. An assault on their grandmother—on his *wife*—was the last straw.

"It will end soon," Pashka said every night when, after wandering around the town all day, they would finally creep up to their room past midnight, without dinner. "It can't go on like this forever. It's almost September. We will have to start school."

The omnipotence of the academic calendar seemed sacrosanct to him; perhaps that's how ancient farmers felt about the change of seasons.

"When we were little, we used to say Torpa was a special town," Arthur said, wrapping himself in a blanket. "And that if you want to be free of it, you must run away."

"That's right."

"But we were wrong, Pashka. That's the problem. It doesn't work like that. Torpa is simply his lair. He's everywhere. There's no 'getting away.'"

Out of the eleven coins Arthur threw into the river in desperation, they only found nine. Arthur went to the beach every day and kept looking around the seaweed-covered sand. He hoped he would find the missing gold and avoid punishment for . . . whatever malfeasance losing thrown-up coins was in the eyes of the man with the dark glasses. Pashka realized that Arthur was not only afraid, but was also—conversely—hoping Konstantin Faritovich would come soon.

Eventually, he did come.

It was raining; fall was around the corner. Pashka and Arthur took shelter under the bus stop awning, eating pies they bought from a street vendor. It was the same stop where the bus departed for the train station. At this hour it was empty: the morning bus had left a while ago, and the evening one wouldn't leave for a few more hours.

"Hello, boys."

Arthur choked on his pie and coughed. Konstantin Faritovich slapped him lightly on the back. Arthur twitched but stopped coughing.

"Congratulations." Konstantin Faritovich smiled benevolently. "Both of you have been enrolled as first years at an established educational institution. You will be in the same group, just like you wanted to."

Pashka swallowed the rest of his pie and wiped his hands on his pants. Konstantin Faritovich knew that they had already been accepted, back in the spring, Pashka to the polytechnical university, Arthur as a bio major. "'The same group'?"

"Arthur, you lost two coins," Konstantin Faritovich continued just as calmly. "But there is no reason to panic, because between the two of you, you have the passing score. You know where the Institute of Special Technologies is located, don't you?"

"No," Pashka said quickly.

"What do you mean, no? You've walked by it a hundred times, along Sacco and Vanzetti!"

"No as in we're not going there! We've never applied to this place—Arthur, tell him!"

Arthur was smiling beatifically as if the fact that he'd been forgiven for losing two coins outweighed all the other news.

"Arthur gets it, don't you, Arthur?" Konstantin Faritovich said gently. "And you do, too, Pashka. You no longer have to live with your grandparents, the institute has wonderful accommodations, a cafeteria, a library—everything at your fingertips. You can move in whenever you want starting tomorrow, but on September first you must be present at the lecture hall. All the coins must be turned in at the administration office when you register, all right?"

Pashka may have imagined Arthur sighing with relief.

One day in mid-August, Sasha stood by the fence she knew so well—down to the tiniest detail in the wood pattern, down to the last nail. The lilac bushes concealed her from view, even though she wasn't trying to hide. Behind the fence, in the gazebo, father and son were talking.

Yaroslav Grigoriev had returned from a long business trip. The news that awaited him at home had caused quite a shock, and now he was consulting his father, a witness to the recent events.

Sasha watched them through the cracks in the fence, through the lilac branches, through the rips in reality. The man whose face she knew to the tiniest line was Yaroslav Grigoriev—and yet it wasn't him. This man was but a faint shadow: in the world Sasha had created aircrafts did not crash, and that meant there was no need for people capable of preventing a catastrophe.

Equally a shadow was his father: Anton Pavlovich had lost a lot of his vigor in the last few weeks. He blamed himself for what happened to the twins. They had been difficult children and complicated teenagers, but in the last couple of years they seemed to have grown and matured, and their grandparents very much enjoyed their company. And then suddenly, this summer, at first Pashka had lost all his common sense, followed by Arthur. It was still incomprehensible, what Arthur had done.

"Something happened to them," Anton Pavlovich said, and Sasha's heart ached at the concern in his voice. "I can't figure it out. Something bad. At first, I was angry, I pushed them away, I couldn't understand. If there was a way to reason with them . . ."

He was sensitive and kind, and he loved the twins. But what they did . . . was it unforgivable?

"I will take them both back home," Yaroslav said heavily. "To reason with them?" Then he shook his head, clearly disagreeing with himself. "We've been 'reasoning with them' way too much! All these psychologists, nannies . . . it's too much. They are going to college, wherever they got accepted, or enlist—and that's it!"

"We're staying in Torpa," someone said. Sasha heard the voice but did not immediately understand who it belonged to. Then she saw Arthur; he came quietly and now stood next to the gazebo. A dry fir needle fell from above and got tangled in his hair.

"No," Yaroslav said. "I am your father, and I get to decide. Go pack your things, we're leaving."

Sasha blinked, yet again reminded that while the man in the gazebo looked exactly like Yaroslav, this projection was distorted by the world without fear. The real pilot Yaroslav Grigoriev would have understood. The real one would have felt, just like Anton Pavlovich, that something was going on with his sons, that it wasn't just them acting like spoiled brats or playing games.

Kostya is making the boys do all the heavy lifting, Sasha thought, struggling to keep down her anger. The idea that Kostya was abusing the Grigoriev twins out of jealousy was stupid and not just human—it was infantile. But the fact was that now Arthur had to prove to their father that he and Pashka had better be left alone.

What she didn't know was *how* he would prove that.

Silently, Arthur entered the gazebo. He picked up a glass of water from the table and threw it in Yaroslav's face.

In early August, they got a place at a rehabilitation clinic in India, at one of the super-advanced medical centers. Dad's illness turned out to be quite rare, and the doctors were hoping to learn something from it while curing the patient. "He is too young to have heart problems, medically speaking," Mom said,

86

smiling coyly. She had forgiven her husband once she realized how much he'd regretted his mistake. Mom rejoiced in her own goodness like a child. Dad practically dissolved into a puddle in her presence. This was their third honeymoon, the happiest one despite everything.

Valya never mentioned Alexandra's name again. He did not speak of her return. On several occasions, he thought he saw her on the street, but it turned out to be a stranger every time. Valya felt like a frog being boiled very slowly; by the time Mom and Dad had made definite plans to go to India, where Dad would undergo treatment, and Mom would work remotely, and the whole treatment and rehabilitation would take at least six months—by then Valya had lost his ability to protest.

The events had been stacked up like stones in a pyramid. If it wasn't for the sudden "summer fling," the fury and jealousy, the immediate breakup, the cardiac arrest, the rehabilitation, the guilt, and, finally, the amazing medical center in India that Dad's colleagues had suggested; if all these factors hadn't come together in time and on the emotional level—would Mom even consider leaving Valya alone for six months? She had struggled with leaving him alone for two weeks, and now there was barely a second thought.

Of course, Mom had arranged for her relative, Nina, to move in with Valya, cook his meals, and watch over the boy. Valya was not in the least surprised when, a few days before her move, Nina broke her leg in three places. The unfortunate woman had become an innocent victim who happened to stand between Valya and the town of Torpa.

Mom was terribly upset, but postponing the visit to the clinic was impossible. Trying to diminish her suffering, Valya gathered all his strength and said:

"Mom, please don't worry. I will have lunch at the university cafeteria, I can make hot cereal in the morning. Plus, I'll be in class all day and only come home to sleep. And Olya, our neighbor, would tell you right away if I had a big party or something!"

"You've grown up so quickly," Mom said, turning away to hide her tears. But she didn't disagree with his plan.

Dad was taken to the airport in a wheelchair. Mom promised that when they got back from the clinic, he'd be running and dancing. Whatever devotion she had, Mom now poured into her husband, as if he were her child. And what about Valya?

As she'd said, Valya was all grown up.

"I will make sure Mom lets you go to Torpa," Alexandra Igorevna had said. Valya was almost sure that when he returned from the airport, his sister would be sitting in the kitchen. But the apartment was empty.

Valya sat down at the table and started to cry. He realized how easy it was to make his parents betray their beloved son.

PART II

CHAPTER ONE

September 1 was hot, even this early in the morning, and only the color of the sky made one think of fall. The surviving young linden trees looked lush and green, not a single yellow leaf in sight. The dried-up dead trees were gone; the day before, the town services had dug them up and utilized them for kindling.

Sasha entered the main entrance of the institute, greeted by an old-fashioned bow from the guard in the glass booth. The second years stood in front of the scheduling board, the whole mass of them limping, hunched over, twitching: disassembled. Sasha wasn't bothered by it; all students looked like that at the beginning of their second year. However, these projections of Words locked in human bodies had not developed. They'd frozen and hardened; the summer internships did not work. And that would have bothered her if she hadn't set this new first class into motion.

At the wide staircase leading to the second floor, the English professor who'd worked at the institute long enough to teach Sasha herself waved without interrupting her phone conversation. No one ever remembered this woman's name, even though she was called something quite ordinary; she also did not age, no matter how many years or decades had passed outside Torpa's town limits. The English professor spoke with a heavy accent, but this was not considered one of her quirks.

Sasha nodded back to her.

Third years had gathered farther down the corridor, by the staircase leading down. Nineteen out of the original twenty-five, enrolled two years ago.

"Good morning, everyone. Congratulations on the start of the new academic year."

They muttered some sort of greeting. Nouns, adjectives, prepositions. One verb in the subjunctive mood—a tall blond guy, who reminded Sasha of Yegor.

"We have a lot of work to do this semester," Sasha said. "And that means everyone will be well prepared for the winter exams."

They continued to stare, stone-faced, except for the blond guy, who smiled sadly at her words. Six of their classmates—people who had sat next to them in the auditoriums, shared their dorm rooms, occasionally smoked a single cigarette together, who had kissed them and slept with them—six people had disappeared within two years, and all because of seemingly natural causes. What could be more natural than disappearing without a trace in the town of Torpa? What could be more natural than being expelled for bad grades and going back home, leaving all their belongings in their dorm rooms, and forever dropping off the radar, with no address, no telephone number, and no way to find them ever again?

But it wasn't easy to just ignore that a quarter of your cohort no longer seemed to exist.

Still, they don't feel any fear, Sasha thought. *Only dumb obedience. They are no longer people, and they may never become Words, and I will never be able to teach them—none of us could. Me, Portnov, Adele. I don't think even Sterkh could do it because the very settings of Speech are broken. The Institute of Special Technologies has stopped producing specialists—as if a factory that used to manufacture precious vases was now mass-producing broken bottles.*

And it was all up to her to figure out a way to once again give the world useful vessels.

Somewhere, behind the temporal wall of fifteen years, fourth and fifth years were beginning their studies. Weak, operational, ordinary parts of Speech; some would get their second-rate diplomas with their C's, some would fail, and Sasha would not be able to help any of them. All her hope lay with these new students, the ones sitting in the assembly hall.

As soon as this thought crossed her mind, the sounds of "Gaudeamus Igitur" filled the air. The first lines of the student anthem could be barely heard this far into the vestibule, but the third years shivered. They must have remembered standing in the same assembly hall two years ago, unaware of what was ahead, but full of foreboding.

Somewhere in the assembly hall, the Grigoriev brothers were listening to the anthem. Sasha tried not to think of them, but it was like trying not to think of a white bear. The last few seconds flew by; the thing she was waiting for, here in front of the equestrian statue, was about to happen.

Behind her, the front door opened.

"Where are you headed, young man?" the guard said sternly.

"To the institute," Valya said, his voice hoarse and full of challenge, as if the boy wanted to know where the line for the chopping block was supposed to form.

Sasha turned around. Valya recognized her and stumbled back instinctively.

"Have a seat."

He seemed unsettled by the lack of windows in her office. And yet, he was ready for anything, even a dungeon with chains. A wheeled suitcase by his feet was too small to fit three seasons of clothes. He wasn't thinking of his future when he packed.

"You're late," Sasha said once he perched on the edge of an old leather chair. "You missed the new student orientation. What happened?"

"I took the wrong bus from the airport," he said, removing his glasses and wiping them on the hem of his denim shirt. Sasha was suddenly reminded of Farit.

"No one is going to cut you any slack just because you're my brother."

He shrugged, demonstrating his indifference. He had already taken his step into the abyss, right after he discovered that the College of Medical Technology had no one with his name in their records, neither a student nor even an applicant. He made a frantic call and finally got hold of his mom, only to realize that she wasn't all that happy about his call: it was right at the time of their visit to a very important doctor. After, Mom texted him and asked him to stick to communicating in writing because the connection was terrible at the medical center, but otherwise everything was simply great. The doctors said Dad would soon run, dance, and swim again.

That's when Valya rebelled for the first time in his life. He packed a suitcase and got on the plane. Sasha had bought him a ticket. Rather, she had been buying him a ticket for every day starting on August 20, but Valya waited as long as possible. He flew in around midnight on the thirty-first, spent the night on an airport bench, and in the morning, he took the wrong bus and was late for the new students' welcome.

"May I ask a question?" Valya said, putting his glasses back on.

"Yes," Sasha said, tensing up in surprise.

"My mom . . . All my life I thought she cared about me, almost too much. I felt like she was always by my side. And now that she has turned away from me, is this magic? Or does she simply no longer care?"

"Let's leave 'magic' to Hans Christian Andersen and the Brothers Grimm," Sasha said. "People act differently under different circumstances."

"That's not an answer," he said.

It certainly wasn't. "Mom hasn't turned away from you, and she hasn't stopped loving you. Mom knows that you are currently attending the College of Medical Technology, that you like it there, and that you are living at home. Mom lives in an informational bubble in which you are doing well and everything is going according to plan. It's a solid, comfortable reality.

"Trust me, it would have been much worse if she continued to be a helicopter parent," Sasha said, thinking of the Grigoriev brothers.

"So she hasn't forgotten me?"

"She hasn't given you much thought," Sasha said frankly. Valya looked aghast, so she forged ahead. "We need to go to the administration office, where you will turn in your documents and get a room key and your cafeteria pass. And then you're going straight to class, the first session. You can move in after today's classes are over. It's your own fault for being late."

"What is Torpa?" he asked, without moving.

"Torpa is where you're going to get answers to all your questions," Sasha said gently. "As long as you work hard and do your best."

...

Hearing Portnov's calm voice behind the doors of auditorium 1, Sasha felt shy for a moment, as if she were the student coming in late. She forced herself to knock.

"Yes?" Portnov said.

He was sitting behind his professor's desk: gray sweater, glasses in thin frames, light hair gathered in a ponytail. He watched Sasha the same way he'd look at any latecomer, with cruel fascination. His gaze lasted a fraction of a second.

"Get up, everyone," Portnov said, rising from behind his desk.

Following him, the first years got up, reluctantly, as if surprised by the seemingly militaristic order, but knowing by now that any sign of disobedience would be costly.

"Alexandra Igorevna Samokhina is the provost of Torpa's Institute of Special Technologies," Portnov said softly. "She's also a lady. I ask you to rise whenever she needs to interrupt our class for some reason."

Portnov was on top of his old-fashioned manners, as usual. Sasha appreciated his sarcasm, but laughing at it would be unseemly for someone in her position. Instead, she simply motioned for Valya to come in.

"Oleg Borisovich," Sasha said. "This is Valentin—Valya—Shanin, a first year. He is a late arrival."

She waited for Portnov to nod, and only then looked at the class. Twelve people, Group A, stood with their backs to the well-lit window. The auditorium, big enough to fit twenty, seemed spacious. The Grigoriev brothers had taken the last double desk on the left, the same one Sasha herself had liked best.

Twelve silhouettes lit up by the sun. Twelve barely distinguishable, deeply embedded sparks. Each one of them could potentially grow into a Word and *reverberate,* become a part of the Speech, and resurrect it. Then again, perhaps they couldn't.

If only I could use a can opener and pull your Word out of all of you, Sasha thought wistfully. *I would gut you more brutally than I did baby Valya, feeding on his information like a larva on nectar. But Words cannot be cut out of human beings, the Words would die in the process. Word can only be nurtured, step by step, breath by breath. And we will nurture and cultivate it, and you will fight and scream, and that would be the best outcome. It would be much worse if you broke immediately, and the Word that chose you as its projection would never reverberate.*

"Sit, please," Sasha said. "Have a great class. Congratulations on the beginning of a new school year."

As she left the auditorium, she heard Portnov say to Valya:

"Take that seat in the first row, please. And consider yourself lucky we haven't gotten to *S* yet."

CHAPTER TWO

O n their birthday, August 28, Pashka bought two bottles of beer in addition to their daily meat pies. The salesperson asked for his ID; blushing, she wished him a happy eighteenth birthday.

She was very young and had dimples in her cheeks. Perhaps a crazy thought had crossed her mind—would the birthday boy invite her to a birthday party? There were so few options to meet anyone in Torpa.

But that wasn't a possibility. Instead Pashka thanked her, put his purchases into a bag, and went back to the dorm. They popped the caps off the bottles on the edge of the desk, leaving unsightly scratches. They weren't the first ones to do so; the entire desk looked as if it had been gnawed on by beavers.

Half a bottle in, Pashka asked:

"We're family—they know us as well as we know ourselves. Why was it so easy for them to believe that we're absolute trash?"

"Because we behaved like absolute trash," Arthur said evenly. "I mean, I was the shittiest of the two, but you were no angel, either. That's fine, it's better this way. Unless you want to . . ."

He stopped and took another sip. Pashka thought about Arthur carrying this constant hell inside him. While Pashka occasionally managed to distract himself and even found some positive aspects of their new status, Arthur existed in a world where any sort of trouble could happen at any moment. Arthur even made up and multiplied potential troubles inside his head.

"Let's cross that bridge when we get to it," Pashka said, stealing their mother's favorite expression. Arthur smiled wryly. He also read some of Pashka's thoughts and knew that Pashka had just diagnosed him with anxiety.

"Do you remember my saying that *it* won't touch Grandma and Grandpa because they are local?" Arthur said. "*It* had explained to me that, as long as we're nearby, our grandparents aren't in danger. And our parents, too. I'd rather get beat up by Dad and would much rather be a total shit than . . . than for something to happen to them. I . . ."

He fell silent, hiding his head in his shoulders. Pashka knew Arthur was thinking of Grandma.

Pashka put his hand on Arthur's shoulder.

"Let's pretend it was me. If *it* had ordered me, I'd have done the same thing. It could be me, right?"

Arthur smiled faintly, not quite relieved, but Pashka knew his brother felt better.

"Let's turn on our phones," Pashka said with a sigh. "See if we got any birthday wishes."

They turned on their phones exactly once a day to text their mother: "Alive and healthy." In two weeks, Mom had answered only once: "Ready to apologize yet?"

This time, when they turned on the phones, two identical messages arrived simultaneously: "Happy birthday. Anything you want to discuss?"

"They are waiting for us to return soon," Pashka said. The beer made him a little nauseated. At least, he blamed the beer.

"And if we don't come back, what are they going to do?"

"Mom will come here," Pashka said, choking on cabbage pie.

"And then it'll be your turn," Arthur said pleadingly. Pashka had never heard his brother sound like this. "I won't have to do anything like that again, will I?"

Pashka felt cold sweat streaming down his back under his T-shirt. No, he would never hit Mom, and he wouldn't let Arthur do it, either. Konstantin Faritovich terrified Pashka, but for Arthur, his very name had a paralyzing effect. If it came to that, Pashka's mission was to stand between the two of them and protect his brother.

Pashka recalled a child's beach ball washed up by the current. A simple reminder that death existed, that it was very close, and could show up at any moment, without asking for an ID.

At some point, the dorm suddenly stopped being empty. At first, the second years returned. Stumbling upon them in the corridor, Pashka felt as if he'd swallowed a porcupine. It wasn't only that they limped, twitched, stuttered, and had lazy eyes; people could be different, and so could Torpa's students. It was their facial expressions that terrified him, something in their eyes. They said, "Hey," and "Oh, look, a first year," and "Wow, are you twins?" And yet Pashka felt that second years weren't quite human, as if aliens had put on humanoid masks and repeated all sorts of clichés hoping no one would crack their disguise.

"Arthur, we shouldn't eat at the cafeteria anymore," Pashka said. "Looks like they are all addicts here, and who knows what the institute puts into their soup."

"No, addiction is just a cover story," Arthur said after a pause. "It's to make sure Torpa residents don't ask any questions."

"Then what's wrong with them?"

"Want to ask them?" Arthur offered.

Pashka laughed nervously but had no desire to do any such thing.

Then the third years showed up. Pashka waited for their arrival, peeking from a latticed first-floor window. He was the first one to see a group of people with suitcases; somehow, they all arrived together. Some of them limped, some twitched, but they all had perfectly human eyes, at least as far as Pashka could tell.

On the day of their arrival, the third years gathered in the second-floor kitchen. Feeling brave, Pashka approached the group. Nine males, ten females. None wanted to talk to him.

"You'll find out eventually," they kept repeating.

"The second years, is that a special class? Are they special ed students?"

"You'll find out."

"Why are there so few of you? Was it a limited enrollment?"

"You'll find out."

Pashka gathered all his courage and asked his most pressing question:

"Who is Konstantin Faritovich?"

They shrugged.

"No idea. Who is he?"

Agitated, Pashka reported back to Arthur.

"We'll find out eventually," his brother said, and in his voice, Pashka heard an echo of the dull voices of the third years.

First years showed up last, on August 31. Three girls moved into room 8, next to theirs. One of them caught Pashka's eyes with her striking looks—cropped black hair and very blue eyes. Considering it a good omen, Pashka asked casually:

"Girls, do you know Konstantin Faritovich?"

It turned out to be the worst possible way to start a conversation. The blue-eyed girl looked at him with horror and revulsion, her roommates pretended not to have heard him, and all three retreated into their room. Pashka heard the deadbolt click.

Strangely enough, he felt calmer. It wasn't exactly logic he saw, but more like a pattern. He saw an ocean in a drop of water: all first years knew Konstantin Faritovich. All second years had physical disabilities. All third years kept things close to their chests, but none knew Konstantin Faritovich. He had answers that led to more questions.

Those would have to wait until September 1.

Then September 1 arrived.

Valya didn't sleep all night; he felt groggy, and this made it easier to accept reality. He had his picture taken at the administrative office and was given his student ID. From that moment on, Valya willed himself to think that everything was going according to plan.

The massive building of the institute, the academic office with its eternal bureaucracy, and the scheduling board put him into a trance. He knew he would have experienced the same things as a medical technology major. However, the equestrian statue in the vestibule was slightly unusual. It wasn't simply gigantic; it was bizarre and irrelevant. Who was its rider? A founder of Torpa? An old trustee of the institute? Why was his face hidden from the public?

Pretty quickly, Valya gave up trying to solve the mystery. He was more concerned with the fact that Alexandra Igorevna was the provost of this institute. How could Mom not know this? Luckily, the sleepless night helped him put off complicated questions. From his first-row seat, Valya didn't get a chance to take a good look at his classmates. Behind him, they conversed softly: everyone already knew each other, chatting and cracking jokes to gain popularity. One of the girls kept dissolving into high-pitched giggles. *What if I don't make any friends here?* Valya thought wanly. *I was dumb enough to be late. I didn't wear my contacts and chose the wrong glasses, the ones with an old ugly frame. Is that why she's laughing? Is she laughing at me?*

The professor calmly finished the roll call. Valya felt something akin to trust toward him: the professor also wore glasses, and looked serene, phlegmatic, clearly experienced. Just as calmly, he instructed them to write down his name, Oleg Borisovich Portnov. Then he looked up from the attendance journal and glanced at the students from above his glasses. The small auditorium grew colder. The girl with a high voice giggled again.

"Zhuravleva," the professor said softly, squashing the giggle and all the other voices for the next half hour. The first years fell mute; no one wanted to hear their name pronounced in that tone of voice. *Poor girl,* Valya thought. *She hadn't done anything wrong, and he slapped her down like a fly. Who is this hapless Zhuravleva?*

The minute hand twitched on the round clock above the door. Portnov spoke about honest hard work, of necessary daily efforts, of the winter exams, which were closer than they appeared. In the dead silence of the auditorium, his measured speech made Valya very sleepy.

"Shanin!"

Valya felt as if someone had poked him with a red-hot iron. He jumped up, not quite aware of who he was and where he was. He fixed his glasses with both hands.

"No sleeping in class," Portnov said dryly. "Take these books. Everyone gets a copy."

Valya began to move before he understood what was required of him. He picked up a stack of new textbooks, sharply smelling of printing ink, without even looking at the title. He thought he was still sleeping; in his sleep, he placed each copy on each desk made of pale wood.

"Open your books. Page three, paragraph one. Pay attention and don't miss a single line."

Valya began to read. He was definitely asleep. As it sometimes happens in dreams, the lines folded themselves into a nonsensical mass that gave him an instant headache and made his ears itch. He concentrated on waking himself up when he heard some whispering and chattering behind his back. Finally, one voice asked loudly, bravely, and even with a hint of irony:

"Did you know your books are damaged?"

"Perhaps it's you who's damaged, Grigoriev, P.," Portnov said, glancing over his glasses. Fleetingly, Valya was happy Portnov wasn't looking at him. "Read on. Try hard. And remember, Group A: I will be reporting any and all academic issues to your advisor."

Silence reigned in the auditorium once again.

Anton Pavlovich was alone in the gazebo. A broom leaned against the wooden balustrade: Anton Pavlovich had come out to sweep the yard, but suddenly found himself tired or simply lost in thought.

A pink children's bike stood forgotten on the porch. Everything was quiet, the only noise coming from a squirrel trying to peel the leftover holiday tinsel off the top of an enormous fir tree.

Sasha remembered this yard to the last fir needle and the house to its last scratch and its last nail. The house remembered her, too. In both past reality and this current one, this house reflected a singular idea: the place one returns to. The place one could, and had to, defend. The place one pulled out of a fire.

"Good afternoon!" Sasha said loudly and opened the gate, not waiting for an invitation. "Delivery for Grigoriev, Anton Pavlovich!"

The house looked the same, but an invisible wormhole ran along the facade. Where before there was an imprint of unconditional love, now doubt and disappointment clouded the view and belief in evil swirled around.

"Delivery," Sasha said. "Sign, please."

She wore a uniform: a dark red vest, a cap with a vague logo, and a large delivery backpack.

"Hello!" Anton Pavlovich said. Jerked out of his thoughts, he tried to be friendly. "Does Torpa even have delivery services?"

He rubbed his eyes to ensure that Sasha wasn't a dream.

"I am here, aren't I?" she said, smiling. "Where would I come from, if there were no delivery services in Torpa?"

"But I didn't order anything."

"Someone else did," she said, unloading two bags and a long cardboard box. "People order deliveries as gifts all the time."

"But who was it?" Anton Pavlovich asked. He stopped in front of her, observing the packages—and Sasha—with a great deal of suspicion. He took another look at her and squinted; his vision must have gotten worse. Or perhaps he thought Sasha looked familiar but couldn't recall how he knew her.

"It was anonymous," Sasha said solemnly. "But it's someone who wishes you well. Have a good day!"

Leaving, she worried that Yaroslav's father wouldn't even touch the packages, that he wasn't a fan of mysterious gifts. But curiosity took hold; from behind the gate, Sasha watched Anton Pavlovich open the cardboard box.

"Anton, who was it?" someone said from the porch.

Sasha walked faster. The scent would reach his nostrils by now. And in another second, he'd feel a burst of happiness. Fresh flowers, autumn asters, were carefully arranged in a cardboard box. And fruit and ice cream packed tightly in refrigerated bags. The Grigorievs always celebrated the first day of school: Grandma used to be a teacher.

Kostya appeared by her side as if he'd accompanied her the entire way from the supermarket.

"Samokhina, why must you complicate my life?" he asked reproachfully. "If the old couple believe that the gifts were sent by Arthur and Pashka, if they want to see them, if they decide to snatch the children out of our evil cult paws . . ."

"I calculated all the risks, don't worry. Let's cut the old people some slack. We're not here to teach *them*, are we?"

"I wonder what it's like, to live in Torpa all your life and know nothing about the institute," Kostya said after a moment. "Not know the truth, I mean."

"They can feel it," Sasha said with a sigh. "It's like a shadow in your peripheral vision, something you can't look at directly, yet it is always there. It must be quite unpleasant. But people get used to everything."

"Do you remember coming here for the first time?" Kostya asked wistfully.

"Of course I do," Sasha said, laughing. "I remember you carrying my suitcase."

A few passersby stared at Sasha's dark red vest and the cap with a vague logo.

"I saw your brother," Kostya said.

"And?"

"He doesn't look like you at all. It's quite strange."

...

"Shanin!"

Valya jumped in his seat. Had he fallen asleep during class? The room smelled of dust, rubber, and leather: the odor of a gym. Valya found his glasses and put them on: there was no desk or books in front of him. There was a gym mat and next to it a stack of other mats, protecting Valya from prying eyes.

Previously protecting him from prying eyes. His hiding place was no longer a secret. A man stood in front of him: a tracksuit, a whistle on a cord around his neck. The jacket hugged the sculpted shoulder muscles. Valya had always dreamed of such a physique.

Physical Education, Valya recalled. The second class was Phys Ed. And this guy, who just called out his last name, was the gym teacher. He was so young, nearly Valya's own age. Valya had forgotten his name. San Sanych?

"I am sorry, I fell asleep," Valya said sincerely. "I was up all night."

"That's not good," the gym teacher said, and Valya froze, suddenly realizing that everything was, in fact, not good. He was in Torpa. He'd forgotten about being there, relaxed, and fallen asleep.

The sun was setting. How long was he asleep? A few hours or a week? If he looked in the mirror right now, would he see himself as an old man? Torpa was the kind of town that made people disappear.

"You were late on the first day of classes," the gym teacher said somberly. "You played hooky during English and Philosophy. That's a bad start to your year. One hundred squats. One hundred push-ups. And fifty loops around the yard. For starters. Let's go."

• • •

Pashka didn't think he'd see the end of that day. But eventually, evening did come.

The institute looked very different from a bench they were sitting on than from its front facade. The first floor resembled the foundation of a medieval castle, the second, a redbrick manufacturing plant, the third looked like a gingerbread house, and the fourth like an old wooden shed.

Loud music was shaking the dorm windows; someone laughed hysterically, someone swore, and it sounded as if heavy furniture kept falling over.

"They're boozing it up," Arthur said with a hint of disgust. "Good thing we have a private room."

"Who is that?" Pashka asked, looking across the yard toward the institute. "Is that the guy from our year? The nerd who was late on the first day?"

The nerd in question shuffled out into the yard, looking as if he was about to keel over, his knees buckling, followed by Dima Dimych, or Coach—the gym teacher, the instant crush of all the first-year girls. Every single one of them had signed up for table tennis.

Dima Dimych was not wasting any of his charm on the nerd. He said something and gestured around the yard as if drawing a large O in the air. The nerd began to run; at first, he simply hobbled, then walked quickly, breathing through his mouth and stumbling. Instead of sneakers, he wore dress shoes; instead of gym clothes, jeans and a T-shirt.

"He arrived late, and then missed English and Philosophy," Pashka said. "Looks like they have the same disciplinary methods as in some dumb-ass penal battalion."

The nerd ran by the twins without looking in their direction. Still running, he took off his fogged-up glasses and put them into his pocket, then began the second loop. The gym teacher stood leaning against an old linden tree, pensively watching the nerd run.

"What if we punch him in the face?" Pashka asked suddenly.

"Who, the nerd? Don't you think he's had enough?"

"Coach," Pashka said, scowling. He got up. "He's just a pawn around here, same as the English teacher. I hope Konstantin Faritovich won't object."

"Konstantin Faritovich would object," someone said behind his back. Pashka turned. The man in dark glasses stood by the fence, in a space empty just a second ago.

"Guys, don't mess around with this thing," Konstantin Faritovich said gently. "Even I wouldn't mess with him. With Coach. The world is not how you see it, isn't that obvious? Or not yet?"

The running nerd fell. Coach approached him and said something softly. The nerd got up and continued running, drops of moisture falling off his chin.

The twins just sat there, watching.

What would happen if Valya said no? If he refused to do push-ups or run? What would happen—would they reprimand him? Would they kick him out of the institute? Why did this stupid gym teacher hold such power over him?

Valya felt like a sheep on a leash. A piece of warm Play-Doh flattened with a rolling pin. Nasty memories flooded his brain: Why didn't he protest when his fifth-grade teacher blamed him for something someone else had done? Why did he agree so meekly to apply for a medical technology major? Why did he agree to go to Torpa just as easily?

"Valya is so easy-going," Mom used to say, making it sound like a compliment. He never argued with his parents. He couldn't convince Mom that Alexandra Igorevna was real. He didn't try to stop his parents from leaving for six months. He didn't even attempt to tell them he was terrified. He was nothing but a piece of Play-Doh being pushed through a narrow mold.

He came to in a washroom with tiled walls. He was drinking from the faucet, cold water streaming down his face.

It could be worse. It was Torpa, after all.

"He violated disciplinary rules on my time, during my class."

Shirtless, Dima Dimych was performing a series of pull-ups. His muscles in motion were hypnotizing, like a windy sunset or a firepit in the snow. Sasha stood a few steps away, the air by her feet swirling into tiny dangerous tornadoes. Coach managed to wound her, on September 1, the very first day of classes.

"He's a verb in the imperative mood," Sasha said, barely containing her fury. "He should be dragged out of submission, not beaten into it!"

"He's not a verb yet," Coach said, jumping off the bars and grabbing a towel. "At this point, he's simply your brother. Whom you've brought here of your own volition. Without any entrance exams. Without motivation. To be afraid for those you love—oh my goodness gracious, what a terrible, cruel world. But when those he trusted from birth suddenly no longer love him—oh yes, then he will study. He'll study so hard. He'll totally punch above his weight for you. You're hilarious."

Sasha didn't want to look into his eyes, didn't want to see a structure that had never been human. A structure whose only function was to cut worthless, defective morphemes out of the

Great Speech. This structure was sturdier and simpler than Portnov, but even Coach was beginning to deteriorate from the inside. It was just a question of time.

"I've spent millions of years looking for students capable of making an extreme effort without being motivated by fear," Sasha said through gritted teeth.

"You could have looked for a chlorine molecule that is actually hydrogen."

"Why don't you want to help me? At least out of self-preservation?"

"Because I am an instrument, a tool," he said with a hint of rather insincere regret. "But not yours. I am an instrument of the Great Speech. Which you're killing, by the way. I can't help you, but unfortunately, I can't stop you, either."

"You can't stop me," Sasha agreed. "And you never could, by the way. My brother will be exempt from Phys Ed. Officially. If you want to exist, stay away from him."

Coach wrapped a towel over his shoulders, rubbing his palm over his forehead. He looked extremely human.

"Yes, I want to exist. I wish to exist. But you made a different decision, and it's your choice as the assassin of reality. I thought everything would happen very fast, but you don't look for easy ways. Your time is Cosmos, you long for extended agony. Let it happen your way, Password."

From experience, Sasha knew not to trust him. If she allowed herself to believe him, even for a split second, she'd lose hope and give up. No one was going to help her, no one was going to reach out and bring an important piece of news that would change everything at the last possible moment.

"I will arrange for pool time for the students," Sasha said. "Two-hour sessions twice a week; would that be all right with you, Dmitry Dmitrievich?"

"I've always valued you very highly, Samokhina," he said after a pause. "But it doesn't change anything."

By half past ten, the dorm had more or less settled down. Exhausted from all the new experiences and too much alcohol, first years collapsed into their beds and fell asleep, and second years—

"We didn't ask why second years all seem damaged," Pashka said. "And we meant to ask."

Arthur did not reply. He was reading his textbook. He'd been reading it for three hours; beads of sweat shone on his forehead. Now and then, Arthur would step out to wash his face, pace around the room, and rub his temples; over and over again he'd come back to page three.

Pashka opened the book three times. Every time he'd start feeling nauseated by page four and take a time-out.

"They must have had a dedicated enrollment last year," Pashka said. "For students with special needs."

He mused at how deftly the routine had constructed itself. Like a salt crystal, or a snowflake. How easily ordinary rationalizations draped themselves over insane facts.

"You should study," Arthur said, drawing a deep breath with each word. "Did you hear what he said? About all the academic issues being handled by the advisor?"

"There is no academic issue." Pashka fell onto his bed and tossed his feet still in their sneakers over the footboard. "What's the problem? That I didn't memorize six lines of bullshit? Worst-case scenario, I will make a cheat sheet the likes of which none of these professors—"

Someone knocked at the door. Arthur and Pashka flinched, immediately checking whether the other noticed their fear.

The door opened. A boy stood at the threshold: nerdy glasses,

113

a dark green wheeled suitcase, and a rolled-up mattress under his arm.

"The custodian sent me," the boy said in a barely audible whisper. "She said I will be living in room 6."

"This is a two-person room only," Arthur said grimly. "Go back to the custodian and ask her for another room."

"She's already left," the nerd said softly. "It's too late."

"Look around here," Arthur said, pointing at the room. "Where do you see the third bed?"

The nerd obediently looked. Arthur and Pashka had disassembled the third bed a while ago. It was now stashed behind the dresser.

"All right," the nerd said after a pause. "Good night."

He left, shutting the door behind him. Pashka stared at Arthur. Arthur pressed his finger to his lips.

"This is not our problem," he said, then continued. "Pashka, don't lie to yourself. What cheat sheet, what are you talking about? Do you know who our advisor is?"

"Calm down," Pashka said gently. "It's already happened. Are we students? We are. At Torpa? Yes, at Torpa. But we've been here before, if not *here* here. I'll think of something before the test."

He went out into the hallway. The lights were on in the kitchen; some people were still there, drinking and singing softly accompanied by an out-of-tune guitar. The nerd sat on the floor next to his suitcase, leaning against the rolled-up mattress. He seemed to have fallen asleep.

"What's your name?" Pashka asked.

Valya learned to tell them apart immediately. One had old bruises on his face as if someone had slugged him a few days ago. This twin now speaking to him looked older and was quite rational: The room was too small. Why would they want a third roommate? Surely, Valya had other options.

This other twin was nicer, perhaps because no one had hit him.

"We're classmates," he said, dragging the disassembled bed from behind the dresser. "We should stick together. Give me a hand, Valya."

The first twin sat on a squeaky chair behind a tiny desk, turned on the lamp, and opened his textbook—all without saying a single word.

"My name is Pashka," the second twin said, putting the bed frame together while Valya held on to the mattress.

"I have a favor to ask of you," Valya said. "Please call me by my full name. Nothing short or affectionate. Just Valentin."

"Got it," Pashka said, nodding. "Do you know Konstantin Faritovich?"

"No," Valya said. He thought for a second and shook his head, very sure of his answer. "I don't."

The first twin tore his eyes away from the textbook. Pashka narrowed his eyes and stared at Valya with curiosity.

"How did you end up here?"

"Long story," Valya said sincerely. "I can't tell you, not right now."

The brothers exchanged glances. Valya had a weird feeling that they were exchanging information without words, without gestures. Like two devices with remote access.

"I am Arthur," the twin who wouldn't let Valya in said. "No girls in the room, and don't be a slob."

He went back to his textbook, his hands pressed against his ears.

···

Sasha stood on the balcony, gazing at the night sky. It kept changing colors: orange, crimson, milky opalescent, pearly white, emerald, violet, and dark blue. Sasha inhaled the spectrum, became the colors; she tasted them on the root of her tongue, and this game—the universal data read by human nerve endings—helped her to get into the proper mood.

The countdown had begun. The True Speech would either get new Words or disintegrate.

Sasha blinked. The silhouettes of the gothic rooftops became visible against the once-again-dark sky. For a second, she imagined a man with folded wings and ash-blond hair falling to his shoulders waiting for her.

"I truly miss you, Nikolay Valerievich," Sasha said.

Sterkh hadn't had any need for a human shell in a long time; it had been left in the past, in the previous version of the universe. Surprisingly, Sasha still missed him. She felt sad that Sterkh would never again sit across the desk, sharp chin resting on his steepled fingers, and say: "What is it, Sasha, my dear?"

The informational fragment that used to bear his name had dissolved in a multitude of meanings. She could have resurrected his physical shell, one that he wore as a sports jacket or a raincoat. She could have reconstructed Sterkh in the flesh, in the next room or on the roof of the next building. But it wouldn't have been *him*.

She respected him far too much for that.

The September evening was soft and warm. The stone lions stared up at the sky, but in September Orion rose later, in the early morning hours.

CHAPTER THREE

G rigoriev, A."

"Here."

"Grigoriev, P."

"Yeah."

"Danilova, Eva."

"Here."

"Zhuravleva, Stephania."

"Here."

Valya's muscles hurt. He'd barely made it to auditorium 1. It hurt to sit down and it hurt to get up. He'd experienced muscle soreness before, usually after skiing trips or beach volleyball at Dad's office picnics. But the pain was never as bad as what he was feeling after September 1.

"Klimchenko, Irwing."

"Here."

"Makarova, Antonina."

"Here."

"Mikoyan, Samvel."

"Here."

He recalled parts of the previous day: talking to Alexandra, the administration office, and his student ID. And almost immediately—the gym, and his muscles disobeying, and Coach standing by his side, holding Valya by an invisible leash: "Sixty-eight, sixty-nine, seventy. This one does not count; you didn't bend your elbows."

"Shanin, Valentin."

A long pause followed. Valya wondered if the roll call was already over or if someone else was supposed to answer.

"Here," he mumbled eventually.

"Individual sessions start today at one P.M., auditorium 38. Arthur Grigoriev will create a schedule."

No one answered. Valya cast a careful look over his shoulder. Arthur was sitting behind the last desk, closer to the aisle, and his bruises looked worse than last night.

"Grigoriev, A., did you hear me?" Portnov said again. "You are now the prefect."

"Fine," Arthur said without expression. Portnov glanced at him over his glasses, made a small, vague sound, and went back to addressing the class.

"Open your textbooks. Page three, paragraph one. This is your last chance to prepare for the individual sessions, and I strongly suggest you use it."

During a break between classes, Alexandra Igorevna blocked his path.

"Come with me."

"I have gym," Valya said dejectedly. "And if I am late—"

"You're released from Phys Ed," Alexandra said, starting to walk away. "You don't need to attend gym classes anymore; your teacher has been informed."

"Really?" Valya said, letting his joy show. Alexandra gave him a sideways glance but said nothing.

They went to the basement floor, where her office was situated among other bizarre spaces. With every step, Valya felt his aches and pain subside and his mood lifted because he no longer faced the prospect of lining up in front of Coach, of running races, doing push-ups, of remembering Coach's name, whatever it was. It definitely wasn't San Sanych. But it no longer mattered, and Valya felt light and happy. He even skipped down the steps.

Once in her office, he felt chilly and uncomfortable again. Alexandra Igorevna sat behind her desk, pulled out a pack of cigarettes, and lit one. It was terrifying to watch her smoke, even though Valya no longer minded the fumes.

"Have you read the paragraph?" she asked briskly.

She looked at Valya; he felt held to the light, like a delicate tree leaf.

"You didn't read it all," Alexandra Igorevna continued without a pause. "You didn't learn the last part."

She opened a desk drawer and took out an envelope.

"Here's some cash. Go to a pet store, it's not too far from the downtown area, 7 Labor Street. Buy a hamster."

"A hamster?" Valya said. He thought he'd lost his ability to be surprised. "What kind of hamster?"

"Any hamster. Choose the one you like," she said. She exhaled powerfully, like a steam engine, and for a split second Valya imagined the smoke folding into a flat spiral with red and blue sparks. Alexandra waved her hand, and the illusion dissipated.

"It's a twenty-minute walk to the store," she said, business-like. "Twenty minutes back, plus ten minutes to purchase a hamster. I'll be waiting for you in auditorium 38 in fifty minutes. Starting now."

Auditorium 38 was Portnov's place. It was located at the semi–ground level, impossible to find just by following numbers, and all first years had been late to their individual sessions at least once. Every one of them had been severely reprimanded.

Valya was on time. He must have asked someone for directions. In both hands, he held a glass jar with no lid. Inside, on the straw-covered bottom, was a plump, fluffy, caramel-colored hamster.

"Good job," Sasha said, pointing at the side table mostly used by Portnov as an ashtray holder during his lectures. Currently, the ashtray was replaced by a cage, made of steel bars, plexiglass, a bare metal floor, and a large red button on a side panel.

"Give it to me," Sasha said.

It didn't look as if Valya had any experience with hamsters. Afraid of picking up the animal with his bare hand, he also wasn't in a rush to just shake it out of the jar. Finally, he wrapped his hand with his light jacket and—very carefully—transferred the hamster along with a couple of tiny drops of excrement into the prepared cage.

"Did you choose it yourself?" Sasha asked.

Valya nodded. He watched her cautiously, probably wondering if he would be taught animal husbandry among other things.

"If you press this button, the hamster will die," Sasha said.

Valya's pupils widened. He had certainly been aware that he was in Torpa, that strange and disturbing things were par for the course, but so far, his imagination had not gone past penalty pull-ups and push-ups.

"Press the button," Sasha said. She looked *through* him.

She'd seen him before: treasure inside, garbage outside. The worst part was the layer of weakness, which had grown thicker in the last few weeks. It wasn't fear, it was helplessness, stupor in the face of the inevitable. And now, once she'd issued her order, the obedience membrane had squeezed him tight, as if the boy were buried alive in a giant condom.

This is not the end, Sasha thought, fighting a lump in her throat. *He'll study, and I'll strip him of this trash, I will peel it off like rotten skin. With every murdered hamster, it will get harder and harder for me, I will feel sick just looking at this boy, but at some point, I will finally turn him inside out and harvest the verb I so desperately need.*

He was delaying the inevitable. Demonstrating the same feeble indecisiveness.

"The button," Sasha said.

Again, Valya sensed he was being held against the light, but now he wasn't a leaf—he was a boulder of ice under the burning sun. He felt himself melt, become soft and pliable. His hand reached for the button of its own accord: nothing would happen to the hamster, she was bluffing. And if the hamster did die, so what? It was just one hamster. A small, fluffy, terrified hamster.

The ice boulder rose up, blocking his throat.

"The button." The outside pressure had become unbearable.

He couldn't say a single word. His mouth filled with saliva that tasted like poison. Impulsively, Valya spat at Alexandra Igorevna. She was sitting across the auditorium, so of course he missed, the glob of saliva landing on the floor.

The puddle of mucus made him sick. Valya retched, and small yellow coins burst out of his mouth, bouncing on the thick linoleum. *I am losing my mind,* Valya thought. His knees buckled.

He saw his own hands pushing against the floor. He heard a dull, rustling sound: the coins rolled around, reflecting the dim overhead lights.

"Stop," Alexandra Igorevna said. The coins spun on their edges and fell over as if commanded to freeze.

In her bag, Sasha found a small thermos. That morning, she wasn't sure why she'd brought it with her; now she knew.

"Drink it."

He needed a few seconds to tell the difference between a friendly offer and an order. And he obeyed, holding the plastic cup with both hands and drinking the warm sweet tea, with each swallow realizing how thirsty he really was.

She poured him another cup.

It's crazy how dangerous I was during my second year, she thought distractedly. *If only they knew. But they did know, didn't they? Portnov did, and so did Sterkh. And Dima knew everything, of course, and . . .* Now Sasha understood Coach so much better than ever before.

And that's considering that this boy is no more than a shadow of me, Sasha thought. *Nothing but an embryo. He hasn't even finished the first paragraph of* Module. *I did the right thing when I sent him to buy a real hamster. This is a pure experiment. The purest. He refused, he dared to refuse.*

For the first time in millions of years, she felt the weight lifted off her shoulders. Sasha fought the urge to grin like a total idiot. Valya wouldn't have noticed anyway; he was still in shock.

He finished the second cup. There was a little tea left in the bottom of the thermos. The coins still lay all over the room. Sasha didn't bother counting them; there was no need. There must have been over fifty coins—even though he had a human throat, a human mouth, and a human tongue.

From the cage, the hamster stared at them with shiny black eyes, as if comprehending the importance of the moment.

"What's happening to me?" Valya asked in a barely audible whisper.

"Nothing terrible. We're past the worst."

She rubbed his shoulder, thinking: *Later, you will learn that I lied to you, and later yet you will forgive my lies. Because we will both survive; we have something worth fighting for.*

"Here at the institute, we work with ideas, projections, informational structures," she continued. Her tone was friendly, as if she were explaining to her preschool-age brother where clouds come from. "Coins are the projection of internal processes. They are symbols, tokens, chips. Unsaid words. Valya!"

He flinched and refocused his blurred gaze. Sasha took the hamster out of its cage—the animal felt weightless on her palm—and put it back into the glass jar. She handed it to the boy.

"Here is your hamster. It depends on you now. Go back to the store, get a cage with a wheel, a water bowl, food, whatever it needs. Ask them how to take care of hamsters. You have a little bit of time, but do not be late for Oleg Borisovich's individual session. He does not tolerate tardiness."

"What's all this for?" he asked, watching the hamster burrowing into the straw.

"What do you mean, what's it for?" she said, pretending not to understand his question. "Did you buy this hamster? You did. No one is going to feed it if you don't. Hurry up, Valya."

Without a warning knock, the door opened, and Portnov walked in. He seemed unfazed by seeing Sasha, Valya, or the hamster. Only the gold coins scattered on the floor made him raise his eyebrow.

"My apologies, Oleg Borisovich," Sasha said quickly. "We are done. The auditorium is all yours."

...

Arthur chose the path of least resistance: he picked up the class list at the dean's office and created a schedule for individual sessions in alphabetical order. He put himself first, Pashka second, and their nerdy roommate last. All Pashka had to do was wait in the hallway for fifteen minutes. He couldn't hear anything at all: once Arthur entered auditorium 38, it was as if he had disappeared deep into a pile of cotton wool.

On the other hand, what was Pashka expecting to hear? Portnov leading vocal exercises?

"Is that auditorium 38?" someone asked behind his back. The voice was loud, sharp, and surprisingly aggressive.

Pashka turned his head. The girl stood a few steps away from him, clutching *Textual Module* to her chest and staring at him with icy blue eyes.

Her name was Eva Danilova—Pashka had learned it earlier. Her cropped dark hair stood on end like a hedgehog's needles. The girl was hard, and sharp, and a little strange, as if hastily carved out of a piece of wood.

"It's here," Pashka said, nodding at the faux-leather-upholstered door. "You have a little time, you're third on the list—after me."

The corridor was empty; the two of them stood side by side, looking in different directions, and the silence was growing more tense with each second.

"Is he expecting us to memorize this?" the girl asked nervously. "I didn't learn anything. Practically nothing."

"No one has memorized anything," Pashka said. "I didn't even try to learn it."

"Aren't you scared?" Eva asked softly, and the hair on top of her head drooped a little.

"There is nothing to be scared of," Pashka said firmly. "Look at me. I'm not afraid."

For a moment they were silent. Eventually, Eva's face relaxed, and her white cheeks turned a faint pink.

"Are you Pashka or Arthur?"

"Pashka," Pashka said, taken by surprise. "Why?"

Eva smiled.

Pashka had read enough classical literature to know that a smile could transform someone's face, showing their true nature, and all that. But he never thought he'd see a wooden face become alive, watch a pair of icy blue eyes turn warm and deep, like the sea.

The door opened, and Arthur came out, looking surprised and confused, but also somewhat content, for the first time in many weeks.

Riding a wave of relief, Pashka winked at Eva.

"See? Arthur made it, and we will, too! We have nothing to be afraid of!"

Sasha hated going to auditorium 14—too many memories connected to that room—and Adele was fully aware of this. Whenever she didn't want to run into Sasha, she simply stayed on the fourth floor. She did this today while the second years attended their classes. The door kept opening and closing; Adele continued working without breaks.

Sasha stood on the landing in front of the stained-glass window. The sun streamed through, and the floor and all the walls were awash in turquoise, pearly white, and emerald. Second years wandered around the creaky hallways like ghosts: some wearing headphones, some blindfolded, some crawling on all fours trying to read the patterns of the cracked floorboards with the tips of their fingers.

Human shells fit them crookedly, like poorly tailored suits, heavy, tattered, and badly stained. The new structures inside them—the future Words—were suffocating because the channels carrying the life-affirming information had been blocked or had never formed in the first place. Sasha felt physical pain just looking at them.

The students scattered out of her path.

The window of the auditorium faced Sacco and Vanzetti Street, letting in the fragrance of the fall; as intense as it was, it could not overpower the lovely scent of Adele's subtle, elegant perfume.

I should ask her for a sample, Sasha thought. Every time she entered this room, she thought of Adele's perfume to stop herself from thinking about Sterkh.

A student in front of Adele looked distraught. Tears fell from the girl's glassy eyes, rolling down her face and dripping from her chin. The book of exercises, volume 2, was opened on page twenty, the paper warped slightly from the moisture, past and present. Inside the student, a tiny, just-born projection was trying to form into a Word, but the girl didn't have enough willpower to complete the necessary work. It was a fruitless effort. A guaranteed failure of the winter exams.

Adele looked at Sasha, exhausted and unhappy to see any uninvited guests in her auditorium, especially Sasha, especially at this time. Sasha stared at the girl; it was a reproach—Adele was failing as a pedagogue.

"You want to try?" Adele said grimly. "They are lazy and inept. This world you created makes it impossible to teach anyone."

. . .

Auditorium 38 stunk of cigarette smoke.

"It's been a while since I've seen decent students," Portnov said pensively, studying Pashka. "I was pleasantly surprised by your brother. I hope you have studied hard as well, just like him. You are identical twins, aren't you?"

"We are not identical," Pashka said dryly. "And I didn't study at all. Studying this stuff makes me sick."

The corners of Portnov's mouth turned down as if Pashka were a bride who'd just changed her mind at the altar. Pashka shrugged, as in *Do whatever you want, but you can't make a hedgehog out of a mouse, or a good student out of me.* Inside this cramped, smoky room, Pashka felt constraint but not fear. "I'm not afraid," he'd told Eva, and at that moment he realized he hadn't been lying to her.

Portnov got up, put out his cigarette, and stretched lazily. Something had shifted in the auditorium; Pashka felt a chill.

For the two weeks before the classes began, Pashka had served as a counterweight to Arthur, who was living in his own nightmare-induced hell. For two weeks, Pashka had created a model of their former world, where his brother could feel calm, cozy, and safe. And now, watching Portnov's catlike stretch, Pashka understood that the world as he knew it was gone for good.

They'd warned me, and yet I hadn't listened.

And now, he felt like what he'd told Eva was a lie.

"Look right here," Portnov said, raising his hand with a ring on his index finger. The ring wasn't there before. It clashed terribly with Portnov's sweater and jeans, and with his mannerisms. The ring had a pink stone in its center, possibly onyx. *Little Lora loves bling,* Pashka thought weakly.

The pink stone turned violet, slicing across his eyeballs, and Pashka lost his ability to move or breathe.

An hour passed, then a day. A year had gone by. Pashka was imprisoned within a stone. A tiny fragment of the Earth's crust, once burned in a primordial lava stream, would exist for the next several millennia, with Pashka inside it, alive and conscious of every passing second.

His ears were ringing as if a hundred windows had shattered at once. Pashka gasped for air. He found himself in the middle of the auditorium; the minute hand on the wall clock moved two markers of the dial, but the clock did not tell him what year or which century it was.

"For the first and last time, I will not write a report to your advisor," Portnov said. "If you come unprepared again, you will have to deal with Konstantin Faritovich."

At the sound of this name, Pashka felt nothing. He was still a yearslong prisoner of the stone.

"And then you will really feel 'sick,'" Portnov said. "For our next session, paragraphs one and two, and work hard, like your brother. You may go."

As he left, Pashka nearly collided with Eva. She saw his face, and he saw her eyes widen in terror, pushing out the irises, leaving nothing but narrow blue rings around the pupils.

Like an eclipse, Pashka thought.

The second year in Sasha's office was named Alyssa.

Watching her, Sasha felt as if she were watching a child dying of thirst next to a pitcher full of fresh water. She couldn't get the child to drink, but only show her the pitcher and convince her to pour the water. *The effort would be worth it. Here is the pitcher. Figure out how to pick it up.*

"Again, Alyssa."

"Alexandra Igorevna, I can't do these exercises, I just can't!"

What made me decide I was a great pedagogue? Sasha thought bitterly. *Even Sterkh made mistakes, even him.*

"You have a whole year of studies under your belt. You passed the exams twice, so you have certain skills. These exercises are simply a tad more complex. Concentrate."

The girl used to think of Portnov as the most terrible executioner. Eventually, that role was transferred to Adele Victorovna. And now it was Sasha who'd become the main merciless, implacable evil.

"Alexandra Igorevna, I will try tomorrow."

"Take a deep breath, Alyssa. Close your eyes. *Imagine two spheres of the same diameter. Combine their centers so that the spheres do not touch at any point.*"

Alyssa stared into nothing. Her eyes went glassy, and Sasha realized she was about to fail. The girl wasn't trying; her will was paralyzed. The new Word inside her was dying, like a thirsty child sitting next to a pitcher full of water. *Do it, come on, do it, you passed your exams before, you got your passing score somehow, didn't you?*

The girl's eyes twitched under her eyelids. Something had begun to develop, something chaotic, but increasingly more confident. The child Sasha saw inside her mind had figured out what the pitcher was for and reached for it with her small hand. *Here you go,* Sasha pleaded silently, *you're doing it, just finish!*

The girl flinched and stepped back, losing the logical thread of the exercise. The imaginary pitcher in the middle of the desert cracked and split into shards.

CHAPTER FOUR

t only took half an hour for the fluffy hamster that Valya refused to kill to become his best friend. The hamster was the only normal thing amid the madness of Torpa and, just like Valya himself, the animal was terrified. It also fully depended on its new owner, as Alexandra Igorevna had rightfully pointed out.

There were no small cages to be found, so Valya bought a huge one, in addition to a drinking bowl, a running wheel, and a bag of litter. And a mineral chew, as instructed by the store staff.

"You'll be happy with me, little dude," Valya murmured. He couldn't recall whether the hamster was male or female; he thought it was male.

Busy with making a comfortable home for his pet, Valya forgot about Torpa. Only the heavy steps in the hallway and a key turning in the lock brought him back to reality.

Valya thought the twins were about to kick him and his hamster out of their room. He even had a chance to plan his response to their reaction to their new roommate. He even opened his mouth.

The twins didn't notice Valya or his hamster. They saw absolutely nothing.

Usually so calm and friendly, and now as gray and wrung out as a dishrag, Pashka was holding on to the wall, trying not to fall. Arthur sat him down on his bed, ran out to the kitchen, and brought back a glass of water. Pashka drank, spilling most of it on his T-shirt. Arthur was saying something to him, so softly that Valya couldn't hear anything. He thought that the twins were communicating in their own language, completely obscure to everyone else.

"What happened?" Valya asked delicately.

"Don't miss your slot," Arthur said through gritted teeth. "Your individual session is coming up."

Only now Valya realized that Arthur had spent multiple hours studying, that Pashka had opened the textbook exactly three times for exactly five minutes, and that he, Valya, had read only two lines during Portnov's morning class. He realized that if Portnov had a system of penalties for idleness, Valya would be in more trouble than Pashka.

He was almost on time, only thirty seconds late. Portnov was busy making a pattern out of golden circles. Valya recognized the coins and stopped in his tracks, barely managing a weak "hello."

"Sit down," Portnov said, pointing to a chair. He didn't look up. "Did you bring *Module*?"

It took Valya a second to recognize that Portnov meant *Textual Module*. Yes, he had brought *Module*: on his way, Valya had tried to read at least something, running into people and walls, and falling at least once.

"Open to page three, paragraph one. Read slowly, thinking it through. Silently."

The book was very new. The traitorous edition clearly demonstrated where and how many times it had been opened.

"I can't see very well," Valya said, trying to postpone the inevitable.

"Want to borrow my glasses? To put over yours?"

The sarcasm was evident; Portnov didn't even bother shaking his head. Valya envied his hamster. The hamster was sitting in its cage, chewing on its food, and no one was watching it from above a pair of narrow glasses. Portnov's gaze implied a whip in his hand.

Paragraph one. Valya read these words five times before lowering his eyes and allowing them to crawl along the line as if along a chicken wire.

As his eyes fought through the nonsensical lines, a roaring noise grew in his ears, and his head began to hurt; something changed inside the room, and inside Valya himself. On the page in front of him, he saw the pattern Portnov had made on the desk out of gold coins.

Valya turned the page. The pattern moved over. Valya read, trying not to move his lips. The pattern grew very bright, then began to dim, and Valya lost his ability to blink. He couldn't stop reading. His eyes burned as if full of sand, but he kept on reading.

He turned another page, and everything in his line of vision turned red. He got to the last paragraph, the one he was supposed to memorize.

"Stop," Portnov said, just like Alexandra Igorevna had said earlier. Valya knew he could now close his eyes and did just that. He wished he could remain like this, his eyes shut forever. "That's how you should be studying."

In the dark, Valya heard the sound of a lighter and smelled

cigarettes. The smell was not unpleasant, it was actually kind of nice.

"You must work like this every day. Got it?"

Valya dared to open his eyes. In front of Portnov was a tall pile of coins; he looked like a medieval money changer.

Portnov looked at him.

"My advice: ask Alexandra Igorevna to cancel your gym exemption."

"I have health issues," Valya said, quietly but firmly.

"Exactly. So you need to support your health with physical education and sports. Alexandra Igorevna wants to monopolize you, which is understandable. But Dmitry Dmitrievich's class is necessary for your overall well-being."

Dima Dimych, that was the gym teacher's nickname. So stupid.

"It's up to Alexandra Igorevna to decide," Valya said, surprised by his resourcefulness. Portnov squinted, gazing at Valya through cigarette smoke, and for a second Valya felt as if he was being studied and seen right through.

"Oleg Borisovich, about this hamster thing," Valya said. This was the first time he'd ever used Portnov's name. "The cage with the button. Does it really kill them, or is it an illusion?"

"It kills them," Portnov said, taking a drag of his cigarette.

"Does she like dead hamsters?"

"She doesn't like submissive students. She seeks balance between weakness and fear, readiness to carry out any order and the ability to go above and beyond. But you won't understand it even if I decide to explain it to you."

We shall see, Valya thought. Out loud, he only said:

"What did you do to Grigoriev, P.?"

Portnov put out his cigarette.

"Have you met Konstantin Faritovich?"

"No," Valya said. He recalled Pashka asking him the same question.

"I gave Grigoriev, P., a jolt of motivation," Portnov said. "And I did not report him to his advisor. I felt sorry for him."

"You felt sorry for him? Are you serious?"

"Obviously not," Portnov said, suppressing a yawn. "When one speaks to first years, one must adjust to their ideas of the world. I don't feel sorry for anyone, there is no relevant function. But Grigoriev, P. is a reasonable young man, and he understood me."

Valya bit his tongue. He was so very close to asking why Portnov wasn't treating him the same way he'd treated Pashka.

"Because you're two different people, and you have different destinations," Portnov said softly. Valya choked.

"But you understood exactly what I said, too, Shanin," Portnov said, and his tone made Valya pull his head into his shoulders. "Go and work hard."

All Valya had to do was walk to the end of the hallway, cross the vestibule, and break out through the back door into the open world under the dark sky. If he managed to sneak back into the dorm, there would be no Alexandra Igorevna tonight, and no conversation about going back to the gym.

When fifty paces remained between Valya and his temporary freedom, he saw Alexandra. She was speaking to a dark-haired woman in business attire. The woman was flawless; she was ideal. Yesterday, when Valya had found out she was teaching second years, he regretted bitterly that Portnov couldn't be substituted for this symbol of perfection.

He changed his trajectory to hide behind the equestrian statue and wait it out. He hoped the two women would finish up their conversation and leave; no way they would stick around in the lobby for long. The bronze stallion loomed over him with all its anatomical details, and Valya wondered yet again, what was the point of this statue? What was it doing here? Old universities had all sorts of bizarre approaches to décor, but this statue was not an ornament. There was something heavy and oppressive about it.

"We should move this discussion to auditorium 14," Alexandra said. "No reason to make this sort of decision on our feet. Shanin, come out!"

She must have noticed Valya even while facing the other way. Valya stepped from behind the statue, looking as innocent as his hamster.

The beautiful professor was walking up the stairs, her narrow heels clicking on the marble floor, pencil skirt hugging her hips. Valya couldn't help but watch. His nostrils twitched, detecting a wave of delicate, elegant perfume.

"You're looking in the wrong direction," Alexandra said, smirking. Valya blushed and that made him even more embarrassed. Ignoring his feelings, Alexandra came closer and looked *through* him again, and Valya forgot all about perfume and swaying hips.

"Great," Alexandra said gently. "What were you going to tell me?"

"Me?"

Alexandra offered no assistance whatsoever. She simply waited.

"Oleg Borisovich disagrees with your decision," Valya finally said. "But your decision is still final, right? You have the last word?"

"You're quite the manipulator," Alexandra said, smiling. "What exactly does Oleg Borisovich disagree with?"

"With my Phys Ed exemption," Valya said, trying to look as naïve as his hamster. "But I trust your opinion."

"Things have changed," Alexandra said. "Oleg Borisovich is right. You are going back to the gym."

Valya's muscles immediately began to ache. Alexandra nodded and walked up the stairs. Her low-heeled shoes made no sound. To Valya, she looked like a bloodhound following the subtle scent of someone else's perfume.

CHAPTER FIVE

We've never done anything like this before!"

Adele felt obligated to contradict Sasha in everything, even when they were fully in agreement. This conversation should have only taken a minute; instead, it had been going on for half an hour, and Sasha was starting to get annoyed.

"You know nothing about 'before,'" Sasha said evenly. She glanced at the door. "And you know absolutely nothing about 'never.' Please choose your words carefully; you and I are no longer first years."

Under her gaze, the door opened, and Kostya walked in. The lamps reflected in his dark glasses.

"Good evening," he said.

Adele immediately pointed to the chair next to hers, ensuring that the two of them would be facing Sasha. She wanted Kostya to be on her team.

Sasha studied them: two pronouns, replacing others so smoothly that the fabric of Speech showed no wrinkles. As a falling guillotine knife becomes a projection of the universal law of gravitation, Kostya served as a functional shadow of Farit Kozhennikov. Adele was destined to compete with Sterkh ad infinitum. For Sasha, Sterkh was still real, even though he had long ago merged with the informational mass of the universe.

"Samokhina, will you stop smoking for five minutes?" Kostya said.

His concern lay not with himself and not with Adele, whose elegant perfume lost its battle with the cigarette smoke. Kostya just wanted to force Sasha back into the world where she was human and had to worry about her physical health. Somehow his efforts never bothered her. Almost never, to be exact.

Sasha put out her cigarette and calmly informed Kostya of everything she'd just said to Adele. *Repetition is the mother of learning,* she thought.

"Implementation will not be trivial," Kostya said. "But if that is your wish, Password, I will comply."

"Fine," Adele said, nodding as if she had any decisive voice in the matter. "I have only one request: Alexandra Igorevna, please stay out of the academic process. Let me do my job without you interfering."

"Perfectly fine with me," Sasha said. "Kostya—thank you. What's the weather forecast for tomorrow? Right, we're expecting a downpour. That's going to help them get in the right state of mind. By the way—Adele Victorovna, the assessment will be based on the weakest students. Everyone will remain in the loop until the last student completes the assignment."

Adele's skillfully lined eye twitched ever so slightly—or perhaps Sasha only imagined it.

"Thank you for your time," Sasha said casually. "Kostya, will you stop by for a moment?"

The two of them stepped into the creaky hallway, and Sasha felt inexplicably drawn to the stained-glass window. The sun had gone down a while ago, the streetlights were on, and the yellowing leaves twirled in the wind, as always.

A man stood on Sacco and Vanzetti Street facing the institute. For a second, Sasha thought it was she, Sasha, caught in the loop, that events were repeating for her, and that, like millions of years ago, once again she saw Yaroslav anxiously watching the windows.

"Hold on a minute," she said to Kostya.

"Good evening, Yaroslav Antonovich."

In the glow of streetlights, he seemed older than his age; his face bore an unfamiliar expression, and that made Sasha happy. This wasn't her pilot. This was a shadow, a projection of a very courageous man on the world where fear did not exist—and hadn't existed until now.

"My name is Alexandra Igorevna Samokhina, I am the provost of the Institute of Special Technologies. Are you looking for your sons?"

"You're the provost," Grigoriev repeated, studying her face in surprise. The streetlight on Sacco and Vanzetti popped out from behind a linden branch and hid again as if flirting. "I need to speak with someone from the administration."

"You need to speak to me," Sasha said. "Our institute is a renowned academic organization with established traditions, an excellent jump start for successful careers. Do you have any questions for me?"

"I filed a report with the Prosecutor's Office," Grigoriev said. "I believe your institute is a drug den and I will insist on forcing my sons to test for narcotics. Further, I will insist on treatment, should the diagnosis be confirmed."

"You have an interesting approach to pedagogy," Sasha said, smiling. "Is it true that Arthur hit his grandmother?"

Grigoriev staggered back. Sasha looked away, unwilling

to see his face. He did resemble the real Yaroslav. Not a lot, but there was some similarity. She didn't want to see him on his knees.

"Do you really think that narcotics, even if that were the issue, could force your sons to renounce their family? Or did you miss something? What were you thinking when you struck your son on his face, while he chose not to defend himself? He never even tried to avoid your fists. Did you think he was going to run straight back into your arms?"

"It's none of your—"

His voice cracked. Sasha continued.

"How much time did you spend with your sons in their entire lives? Considering all your business trips? Admit it, you picked up a lot of overtime, more than was allowed. The airline management closed their eyes to that. I realize it was much easier to take off at sunset and descend on a glide slope at sunrise than waste your time with two snotty ankle-biters who couldn't even talk until they were three years old."

I am behaving worse than Farit right now, Sasha thought, looking at Grigoriev's shadow on the old street cobblestones rather than at Grigoriev himself. *My world is a curious place: There is seemingly no fear. Death is so old that it no longer frightens anyone. But the sense of guilt that he's experiencing right now—the one I am making him experience—is it similar to death? Or is it just a placebo?*

"It's none of your business; you don't know anything," he said, still trying to fight back.

"It *is* my business. Your sons are my students. So, Yaroslav Antonovich," Sasha said gently, "if you want to see the twins again, listen to my advice:

"Get out of Torpa."

Tangled in the linden branches, the streetlight went off.

...

At seven in the evening, doors slammed all over the dorm. In the kitchen, students were cooking and drinking, and the building reeked of burned food. The sound of clanging bottles filled every floor.

Room 6 was overly bright with all three desk lamps switched on. Pashka hunched over the textbook, covering his face with his hands. When he looked back at the page filled with nonsensical words, the lines would start crawling to the left, like tiny departing trains or a family of snakelets. Pashka sighed so deeply that a stone would shed a tear. A stone would, but not Portnov.

I failed Eva, Pashka thought. *I told her there was nothing to fear. I wanted to comfort her. If only there was a way to tell how her individual session turned out. If only I could go over there, ask around, and learn something useful.*

"Keep reading," Arthur said, tearing his eyes away from his book. "Pashka, listen to me. I know better."

"For sure," the bespectacled nerd said, clearly excited about joining in the conversation.

"No one is talking to you," Arthur said sharply, and the nerd wilted.

"I know better," Arthur continued, ignoring the nerd and his feelings. "Think of Grandma and Grandpa."

The nerd looked wary. He wanted to ask something, but his pride got in the way. His hamster was hiding in its tiny house; the creature had had enough adventures for one day.

Pashka sighed again. The memory of today's unpleasant experience, a gift from Portnov, had already faded in his mind in the last few hours, and Pashka was beginning to bargain with himself, despite agreeing with Arthur: But maybe this was plenty? He'd read for a while, wasn't that good enough?

No one in his entire class could memorize these red lines; even Arthur had managed to memorize only the very beginning, he'd said so himself.

Someone knocked softly on the door. The nerd jumped up: he finally had a reason to stop reading the paragraph and talk to another human being. Arthur turned to the door. Pashka sighed and hunched over the text.

"Excuse me, may I speak to Pashka?"

Pashka twitched and almost fell off his chair. Eva stood by the door, her blue eyes bright even in the semidarkness. Her coarse hair bristled gleefully on the crown of her head. She didn't look frightened or broken; on the contrary, she looked as if she were challenging everyone—*yes, I visit strangers' rooms all the time, got a problem with that?*

"You want to speak to Pashka?" the nerd confirmed, a hint of disappointment in his voice. He glanced at Pashka over his shoulder.

"Hey, Eva," Arthur said, getting up. "I have some pies in the fridge, assuming no one has stolen them. Want to check with me?"

He went out to the hallway, and through the open door they could hear Eva's tone, lighthearted and teasing, nothing like earlier that afternoon.

"How are you feeling? You really helped me today. But you looked so awful when you came out. Are you sure you're okay? He said I did well, can you imagine? I didn't think he was physically capable of praising anyone."

Arthur responded sweetly; their voices grew distant. Pashka's roommate stared at him, the light of three desk lamps reflected in his glasses.

"Doesn't she know which one is which? You two are so different!"

She doesn't know, Pashka thought. He laughed, surprising his roommate.

Taking on a girl was a very Arthur thing to do. Just like in good old times when Arthur would go on a first date and then pass the girl on to Pashka, and the girl would treat him like an old friend. Things were easier for Pashka this way. Usually, those dates led nowhere anyway, but Arthur insisted he needed to socialize.

Fine, Pashka would read the damn textbook at least for show. He'd read and memorize that stupid paragraph and pass Portnov's test. And tomorrow—tomorrow he'd see Eva again and he'd make her smile. He wondered if he would need to brush up on some jokes.

Pashka hunched over the page. Revoltingly meaningless symbols attacked his eyes, pain radiating in his ears. Pashka kept on reading.

. . . removed his glasses. He wiped his tears and called softly, "Darling." As if waiting in the wings, Grandma stepped outside, saw Pashka and Arthur, and took a step back.

"Grandma," Arthur said hoarsely. "We . . . I love you very much. Please . . ."

Grandma took a step off the porch, stumbled, and nearly fell. Arthur threw himself forward and caught her, and she held on to his shoulders.

"Oh, Arthur, honey."

She could always tell them apart.

The letters disappeared. The picture behind the lines faded into nothing. Pashka jumped up, scaring the nerd and his hamster.

He meant to run to the kitchen to tell Arthur, but reaching just outside the door, he froze. What would he say? That he'd had a vision?

"What just happened?" the nerd asked softly.

Pashka shook his head to say that he couldn't explain anything. He came back to his desk, opened the book to paragraph one on page three, and felt his mood shift.

Was it a vision? What if it wasn't? What else was this stupid book capable of?

As he waited for Sasha, Kostya passed the time by trimming the grapevines on her balcony. Sasha never bothered with landscaping, and so the grapevines had grown long, climbing into her room and blocking the window. A few dried-up stalks hung off the live vines like old crimes on the perpetrator's conscience, dramatically spoiling the view.

Kostya pruned the dry parts, freed up the living ones, and propped them securely on the intricate balustrade. Sasha watched him with admiration; he was exceptionally good at this. Her meeting with Yaroslav's shadow had left a lump in her throat, so she welcomed a chance to breathe and not talk.

Kostya finished pruning and picked up his dark glasses.

"Those grapes are edible, by the way, not just decorative. You should be able to pick a few."

"We don't get any sun on this side of the street," Sasha said. "They never get ripe enough."

"It's too early to discuss it," Kostya said irrelevantly. "The classes have only just begun."

"I wasn't going to discuss anything," she said.

She held him in her arms. It was in her power to trim off any information outside of this touch, the scent of his skin, and grape leaves; to toss out and forget everything, forget both Yaroslav Grigoriev and Farit Kozhennikov. To *manifest* love and to fill the world with love. He wanted it, too; for one long second, he was full of hope, just like he was back then, during their first year.

She let go. Kostya took a step back immediately. He knew the moment had passed, and nothing would ever happen again.

Valya had a fitful night of sleep. At first, his hamster decided to test out its new wheel, and it rumbled like a medieval cart driving a condemned man to the execution site. Arthur moaned in his sleep and put a pillow over his head. Pashka sat hunched over his textbook as if it was an absolute page-turner and he couldn't tear himself away even for a moment. The hamster kept running.

Valya circled the cage, trying to recall everything he'd been told by the pet store staff. Nothing useful came to mind. Finally, he saw a wooden clothespin left behind by the previous tenants, waited for the right moment, and blocked the wheel. The rumbling stopped. The hamster looked disappointed. Such a silly animal, it could have enjoyed lifetime no-gym privileges; it could have been sitting inside its house, doing absolutely nothing. Valya had had this privilege for one fleeting moment and lost it almost immediately, and now he would have to drag himself to the gym along with everybody else.

He fell asleep instantly, jerking awake a few hours later, drenched in cold sweat. He dreamed that his mother was making frantic calls: to their home, their neighbors, the institute's administration, his father's colleagues, and all their family friends, trying to figure out what had happened to her son. Valya picked up his phone after ignoring it for the last two days. The last message from his mother was sent four hours ago.

It was a long, detailed message. Mom described their everyday routine (so well organized), and his father's treatment and rehabilitation plans (so effective). She sent pictures. Dad looked a lot better; the pictures showed him smiling in a garden, surrounded by parrots. In her message, Mom thanked Valya for telling her about his first days at the College of Medical Technology; she truly enjoyed his descriptions of his faculty and his new friends, and even girls. Mom was very pleased with their neighbor Olya for offering to cook Valya's meals. Of course Valya was an independent adult and could cook for himself, but he was so very busy. Before, students never had a workload this heavy. These were his best years; he should spend more time relaxing and having fun. How about going to the movies on Sunday, or perhaps Valya could invite a few of his friends over?

Valya scrolled through the entire thread and found the messages sent to his mother from his phone. He experienced a momentary confusion: Had he written these messages himself? It was his style, his sense of humor. He felt as if reality had split, as if there were, in fact, another Valya, a freshman at a university close to his house, who was studying chemistry, physics, and public health, and eating dinners prepared by his neighbor.

He didn't think he could fall back asleep. And yet, the second his head hit the pillow, Valya fell into a distant spring day, when he was eight years old, and his dad taught him to make paper sailboats and send them off in puddles, and the rain was washing away the remains of the snow.

The rain pounded the window, which was slightly ajar, and Valya woke up just in time to prevent a flood. Pashka slept, his face planted in the pages of his open textbook, undisturbed by the rumbling rain. Arthur's bed was empty. Valya shut the window and wiped up the puddle forming on the linoleum floor.

He glanced through the wet glass. Outside, on the lawn near the dorm, a group of people stood in the pouring rain. It was a bunch of girls, and they weren't simply standing there. They were kicking someone lying on the ground.

"Hey!"

As soon as Valya ran out into the rain, his glasses fogged up. What was happening, what were all these girls doing? It didn't matter who was having tea with whom, and what happened later; the important thing was that Arthur was being beaten up again, and what could he possibly have done?

"What the hell are you doing?"

They finally heard him, turning his way. At first, he didn't recognize anyone, but a second later he realized that he was staring at a group of second years. Only yesterday, they appeared crippled and strangely distorted, but today every single one of them looked fit enough to play for a women's handball team. Their wet T-shirts and leggings hid nothing from the imagination. Big, strong, young women stared back at Valya, and their eyes were clear and sharp with anger.

It wasn't Arthur by their feet on the flattened grass. It was another girl; she lay on the ground, curled in a fetal position, covering her head, and her knees looked battered and skinned through the holes in her jeans.

"What are you doing?" he asked again.

Valya hadn't even considered the danger to himself. The world was certainly not what it seemed, but girls running amok and ganging up on a classmate was still wrong.

Strangely enough, his shock worked as a cold shower, better than the pouring rain. The girls' eyes had refocused. They glanced at each other, but Valya couldn't read their expressions.

"Get the hell out of here, nerd," one of them said hesitantly. She was olive-skinned, with hair gathered into a ponytail. Rain streamed down the girls' faces, and it looked like all of them were crying.

"Forget it," another girl, with auburn strands plastered against her forehead, said sharply, nodding at the figure prone on the ground. "It's not going to help. Let's go."

She walked toward the dorm, and the others followed her, ignoring Valya and the girl lying in the wet grass. Valya's T-shirt was soaked; he would have looked good if only he had ever lifted weights.

"Are you all right?" he asked, bending over the girl. "They are gone. Let's get you up, or you'll catch a cold."

She remained curled up on the wet grass, covering her face with her hands.

Pashka woke up when the stupid hamster dropped something in its cage. Or perhaps it was a gust of wind banging on the tin roof? Pashka struggled to straighten up and rubbed at a mark left on his cheek by the book spine. Then he remembered everything.

There was something significant in this book, something Pashka was chasing throughout the night. A fragment of normal life in which Arthur and Pashka's grandparents had forgiven them and all the bad stuff got erased like pencil marks. Was it just a fantasy? A dream? But Pashka remembered the text, the part of the book that read itself. He didn't know who he could talk to about this. Portnov?

The door opened. Arthur walked in, a towel wrapped around his neck, grim confusion written on his face. A girl followed; she looked vaguely familiar to Pashka. Her hair was dripping on the floor, and her clothes were stained by grass and soil as if she'd fallen into a puddle. Valya entered last, also soaking wet, holding his glasses in his hand.

"Are you a second year?" Pashka asked. He wasn't surprised by her appearance and didn't bother to introduce himself. "What are you guys reading in your *Textual Module?* Yesterday, I saw some words in there, some meaning. As if I was inside the book, and it was happening in real life. You're a second year, you should know about this!"

"Pashka, she's been in a fight," Valya said softly. "With her own classmates."

Pashka took a closer look and immediately felt like the biggest jerk in the room. The girl had a black eye that was getting worse with each second. There was blood on her lips and under her nose, and a scratch on her cheekbone. Did Valya say her classmates did this?

"She might be concussed," Valya continued, his voice breaking slightly. "We should call the ambulance."

"I am not concussed," the girl said softly.

Valya threw his things off his chair and offered her a seat. She felt for the chair with her hands as if she were blind, then sat down gingerly, sideways. It became obvious that one of her shoulders was higher than the other, and her spine was crooked. The corner of her mouth was twitching. Her left eye squinted.

"What have they done to you?" the nerd said, trying to conceal his distress.

"It's not them," the girl said, her voice soft and hollow. "It's the *Modules.* From our first year. The same ones you're reading right now."

The room became very quiet; the only sounds were the rain knocking on the window and the hamster trying to engage the locked wheel. Not quite believing her, Pashka glanced at his textbook, then back at the girl.

"These books change people from the inside," she continued, her voice growing stronger and more confident. "If you study hard, you eventually become normal . . . on the outside. They said we didn't study hard enough."

"I saw your classmates in the showers," Arthur spoke up. "Only yesterday they looked crippled, but today—today they had changed."

"Because today—"

The girl suddenly burst into tears, making everyone uncomfortable. Valya rushed to get her a tissue.

"Alyssa, it's okay. Please stop crying."

"Today keeps repeating for all of us," the girl whose name was Alyssa said through her tears. "This day keeps repeating. I don't know how many times it has happened by now. My classmates all managed to complete their deconstruction phase. They've reassembled themselves. But no one can get out of the loop until everyone is done.

"And I am the last one."

Adele looked thin, pale, and exhausted. Careful makeup did nothing to hide the bags under her eyes.

"She must be expelled. It's unavoidable. If we don't expel her now, she will fail the winter exams anyway."

"First I need you to admit that it is possible to teach students in the world I have created," Sasha said.

"I will admit it after they pass their winter exams," Adele said sharply. "Better yet, after they graduate. Right now, please sign the request to expel Alyssa Ostapova and let me get back to my job."

"This signature will serve as the proof of your pedagogical failure," Sasha said.

"Alexandra Igorevna, you worked with her yourself," Adele said with a honeyed smile. "I don't remember any results."

"I watched her get very close—"

"Should I put 'very close' into her report card?" Adele asked. Interrupting Sasha was quite a move against authority. Realizing her mistake, Adele winced, then continued in a more reserved tone.

"The overall results of second years are indeed a success. As a team judged by its weakest member, they encouraged and helped each other. But now we're at a dead end. This girl had a chance, but she . . ."

Sasha left the constraints of her human body. She went outside the building, outside Torpa's town limits. She saw Earth from above, saw forests, rivers, towns as if from aboard an aircraft. She moved up, watching the planet in the orbit of a yellow dwarf, moved farther yet. She looked around.

Meanings had been worn out. Stars went out, disappearing simultaneously in the past, the future, and in all streams of probability, as if a wall of water had come in and extinguished all flames. Complex, multidimensional structures gave way first to plain sentences, then meaningless interjections, then . . .

Sasha opened her eyes.

". . . missed it," Adele said. She looked at Sasha warily. "Alexandra Igorevna, is everything all right?"

"Not everything," Sasha said slowly. "I believe you're right. All second years should be released from the loop so they can continue their studies. But we won't expel Alyssa.

"She will remain in this day indefinitely."

CHAPTER SIX

The first period was gym.

"I am exempt," Valya told the twins.

Arthur and Pashka had no idea that Alexandra Igorevna had canceled the exemption. They breathed a sigh of relief: just as he had taken custody of a hamster, now Valya took custody of this battered girl, essentially a stranger, who spoke of bizarre, disturbing things. They didn't owe her anything, but leaving her alone would make them feel like crap.

Valya would take care of her. He had a free period.

Relieved, the twins left for class. As soon as the door closed behind them, a wave of fear washed over Valya: How was he going to explain missing class to Alexandra Igorevna? How high would the price be of his disobedience?

He ran over to the kitchen to get ice for Alyssa's face, and on his way, he recalled Alexandra's verdict: "You are going back to the gym." She did not specify the date. And he would go back, just not today.

Alyssa was leaning over the cage, watching the hamster eat. Her ripped jeans dripped on the linoleum floor.

"Is this your hamster?"

"It is," Valya said, handing her a plastic bag full of ice. "Why?"

She wanted to ask a question, something unpleasant. Valya realized he didn't want her to, and she wasn't happy about it, either, and yet she was just about to . . .

"I bought it at a pet store," Valya said quickly.

Alyssa stopped herself from asking the question. He could tell that she felt better; she even attempted a smile.

"You need to ice your face," Valya babbled. "I once fell off my bike, and the nurse at urgent care kept asking who hit me. But I did fall off the bike and slammed my face into a bench." He wasn't sure why he felt compelled to tell that story, but he just needed to fill the silence. Eventually, he muttered, "An ice pack helped."

Obediently, Alyssa pressed the ice pack to her swollen eye.

"Tomorrow morning, I won't have a black eye. And later they will beat me up again. It's pointless, and they know it; it's just a way for them to let off some steam."

"Why wouldn't your classmates help you?" Valya asked gently. "Instead of taking their anger out on you? It would be so much better for everyone."

"They tried," Alyssa said, not meeting his eyes. "They tried a bunch of things. Do you think I was the first one to be beaten up? We have hurt each other in all kinds of ways. But the next day comes, and it all repeats itself. For everyone around us, it's a new day, but for us . . ."

She shuddered and shook her head wearily.

"They did try to help me. Especially those who managed to complete the exercises; they explained them, drew pictures, and showed me with gestures. But it's impossible."

"Let me try," Valya said eagerly. "What's so impossible about it?"

Alyssa sighed as if surprised by his stupidity.

"How about something simple?" she suggested. "The first

exercise from the very first *Module*. Imagine a sphere in which the exterior surface is red and the interior surface is white. Maintaining the continuity of the sphere, mentally distort the sphere so that the external surface is on the inside, and the internal is on the outside."

Valya contemplated the exercise. Alyssa stared out the window.

"I hate rain," she said softly. "It is always raining now."

"It was sunny yesterday."

"Yesterday was such a long time ago."

He had no response to that. "Is there any chance your classmates are lying?" Valya asked. "Nothing stops me from saying I have distorted the sphere inside my head. Who's going to check?"

"You're just a first year," Alyssa said, and by her tone Valya knew that deep inside, she was hoping for a miracle, hoping he could help her. "You don't know anything yet."

"I do know some things," Valya said, recalling the coins rolling on the floor of Portnov's auditorium. "By the way, what do your professors do, are they simply standing around watching you? Don't they have to teach us, explain things . . ."

He faltered. Alyssa pressed the ice pack to her face.

"We didn't study hard enough during the first year," she said. "And I was the worst one. It happened because we didn't work hard enough. That's a lesson to you: study hard."

It was the wrong moment to remember that he was missing gym. Goose bumps ran unpleasantly down Valya's spine.

Leaving for their annual Torpa vacation (when was this? A hundred years ago?), Arthur and Pashka did not pack exercise clothes, and now they had to attend gym classes wearing whatever they managed to buy at the local supermarket. Arthur picked out a red T-shirt, Pashka a black one, but they ended up with the same pants and sneakers—all no-name brands that might have embarrassed them at home. Now the idea of designer clothes seemed inconsequential.

"Her parents are dentists," Arthur said to him in a whisper, as they tied their shoelaces. "She wanted to be a pediatrician, or rather her parents wanted her to be one, and she didn't resist. But she didn't get into medical school. Don't ask her how she ended up here. Her favorite music is gothic rock."

"*What* kind of rock?" Pashka asked.

"Ask her, it's her favorite topic."

"Why are you telling me all this?"

"Because she thinks it's you who had tea with her in the kitchen last night. Have you forgotten?"

"Arthur," Pashka said after a pause. "I wanted to talk to you. I was reading *Textual Module* last night . . ."

As Arthur listened to him, Pashka watched his brother's face. Almost immediately, he deeply regretted bringing it up.

"You made it all up," Arthur said sadly. "I have similar dreams. Don't be mad, but it's just because you're tired."

"Alyssa said *Modules* change people from the inside."

"Why would some *Module* know anything about our grandparents?"

Pashka wilted. All his questions and quests just lost their meaning. Arthur was right, and Pashka was simply lying to himself.

Eva was waiting for them by the locker room door. She looked great: her blue eyes shone like a movie star's in the limelight, and even her makeup, rather pointless considering the rain, looked good. She took a step forward, smiling with a cheerful challenging expression on her face: *Yes, I have been waiting, so what?* Then suddenly, she looked confused. Pashka watched her eyes flicker from left to right. Two identical boys stood in front of her, one in a red T-shirt, the other one in black.

"Catch up, Pashka," Pashka said to Arthur. Arthur gave him a confused look. Pashka slapped his brother on the back and went to the gym, as Eva spoke behind his back in obvious relief.

"Hey, it's been raining so hard all day, we had to use table-cloths instead of umbrellas! Can you believe it—I used to hate gym class in high school, but it's shaping up to be my favorite subject! Isn't it funny?"

"Line up!" Dima Dimych said, in the same tone of voice he'd use to offer free ice cream at a children's party.

This time they were sorted by height, and Arthur and Pashka found themselves at the beginning of the line. Arthur kept glancing at Pashka sideways. *I know you like her,* his eyes said reproachfully. *I set everything up for you perfectly. I tried to make it work for you, and you have put us into this ridiculous situation.*

Arthur was right. Pashka was mad at himself. There was no need for this stupid game, it wasn't the time or the place. If Eva found out, she'd think they were making fun of her on purpose.

"Congratulations." Dima Dimych raised his arms to the sky like an ancient priest greeting the sun. "Starting next week, we'll have access to the pool. A great new pool. I'm almost envious of us! Please make sure everyone has swimming suits, towels, rubber flip-flops, swimming caps for long hair . . ."

Girls in line embraced each other as if they had been offered crowns rather than rubber bonnets.

"Today I wanted to exercise in the fresh air," Dima Dimych continued. "But because of the rain, we'll have to stay indoors.

Luckily, we have a small class, perfect for two volleyball teams. Where is Shanin?"

He inspected the line as if expecting the nerd to be hiding behind someone's back.

"He's exempt," Pashka said, surprised that Coach would forget something like this.

"His exemption was canceled yesterday," Dima Dimych said sadly. "Oh well. To your right! Ready, set, go! Grigoriev, you're the lead."

Pashka realized that Coach did not call Arthur by his first name. Did he see things, know things, did he choose not to upset Eva with her obvious crush? It was hard to imagine that Dima Dimych, so simple, kind, and sensitive, would push their nerdy roommate to his limits. Pashka wondered if there were two Coaches at the institute, twin gym teachers.

Running, Pashka thought about the nerd skipping gym on purpose to take care of the beaten-up girl. Did he know what price he'd have to pay?

Valya escorted Alyssa to her room on the second floor. Luckily, both her roommates were out.

"I wanted to move," Alyssa said as she changed her clothes, modestly hiding behind the closet door. Valya turned and faced the window, watching the rain. "There are vacant beds in this dorm. I'd move my stuff over, but the next morning I'd wake up here again. Before my roommates learned how to complete the exercises, we were so close, we'd hold each other and cry. And then they managed to complete them, and I still couldn't. I tried getting up in the middle of the night to catch the moment in time when the same morning would begin. But I'd always miss it, and every sunrise would bring the same day, over and over."

On her desk, Valya saw a textbook called *Exercises, Stage Two*. The book was thin and worn out. Valya picked it up and opened it without thinking. The first thing he noticed was the warped pages—as if someone had read the book in the rain and then tried to dry it out.

The second thing was that the text was not total abracadabra, like in *Textual Module*. The book contained exercises in tight, small print. Many, many exercises. "Imagine a sphere. Mentally place it into a four-dimensional space. Increase the number of dimensions to five, then decrease to two." *The pages are wet with tears,* Valya thought. *This book had many tears spilled over its pages.*

"You won't get any of it," Alyssa said behind his back.

Valya turned around. Alyssa stood in front of him, sporting a black eye and a scratched-up cheek, but wearing clean, dry jeans and a hoodie with a vaguely familiar cartoon character print.

"I have to go. I have an individual session at eleven. Always. Until I'm dead. I have my individual session at eleven forever."

One of Alyssa's roommates had swiped her umbrella. "They do this all the time," Alyssa said. "They keep stealing my stuff." Valya ran back to his room and found his own, practically new, umbrella.

"It's too bad we won't meet again," Alyssa said enigmatically.

"Why?"

"When today starts again, they will gather to beat me up someplace else. You probably won't see it. You won't know about it. You'll be too busy with your own life."

"Wait," Valya said. "I am not locked in *today*. I will have tomorrow!"

"You might be locked in but not realize it." Alyssa smiled sadly. "Perhaps you wake up every morning and think it's a new day."

Valya felt water in his shoes, water as cold as ice. Seeing his reaction, Alyssa dialed back.

"No, of course it's not like that for you. For you, everything will be different. Just study hard. They always told me, 'You can do it, just study hard.'"

"Let's go," Valya said hoarsely.

They ran all the way from the dorm to the institute's side door. Alyssa carried the umbrella, and Valya pulled his hood over his head. A thick rubber mat was placed by the entrance; it was soaked all the way through. A custodian rode a large floor buffing machine all around the lobby, trying to eliminate water stains. She couldn't care less about the students and their curriculum.

Alyssa handed Valya his umbrella and shuffled up the stairs like a condemned woman on her way to the scaffold, her head hanging low. Watching her, Valya wanted to find Alexandra Igorevna and say a few things face-to-face. Everything he thought of the institute and its methods. He didn't have to wait long: Alexandra appeared in the same place as the day before, by the equestrian statue, as if popping out directly from the horse's belly.

"Are you wearing contacts?" she asked.

Valya blinked. It was a weird question. Earlier that day he'd found his contacts and put them on for the first time since arriving at Torpa. His glasses got steamy on rainy days.

He thought contacts made his vision a little sharper, but he wasn't sure. Alexandra Igorevna looked a little different. Had she always had these lines at the bridge of her nose? Did they appear today, or did he simply not notice them before?

"You missed gym," Alexandra said coolly, not waiting for his answer.

His answer was rehearsed.

"You said I'd have to go back to the gym, and I will, but—"

"I didn't mention the exact date," she said, interrupting him. "You're a clever boy, but please don't ever manipulate me. You're not going to be happy, Valya."

His name on her lips worked like a trigger. A second ago he was chilly, and now a wave of heat washed over him.

"In Torpa, no one is ever happy," he said through gritted teeth. "You're not faculty. You're a group of sadists. You can't teach anyone anything."

Something in her shifted, ever so slightly.

"Maybe the world is not how I imagined it," Valya said. "But it's not what you think of it, either."

Somehow, he'd managed to surprise her.

"Mom never loved you," Valya blurted out. He felt the hot air quiver in front of his face. "No one has ever loved you!"

"Go see Dmitry Dmitrievich," Alexandra said after a very short pause. "Right now."

A minute ago, Sasha had been talking with Coach. Rain slammed into the large, barred windows. Dima Dimych walked around collecting stray volleyballs from under the benches, tossing them across the entire gym, and landing them in the large round basket every single time.

"You're not going to like what I have to say."

"I never like what you have to say," Sasha said.

"As far as I can tell, these twins . . ."

He paused, trying to trigger her emotions. Her emotions certainly got triggered, but Sasha's face remained neutral.

"These twins are built to consume each other. Only one of them can survive. During the course of study, the weaker twin will be disassembled; he will serve to strengthen the leader. Right now you can make your decision: Which one will be the instrument of Speech and which one will serve as fertilizer? By the time of the final exam, you will no longer be able to manage things. Chance will determine everything, or the Great Speech will."

"You have told me so much nonsense all this time," Sasha said. "I have no intention of taking this seriously."

"As you wish," he said, tossing the last ball into the basket. "Just look at this rain."

Streams of water washed the windows from the outside, as clear as a mountain waterfall. Torpa had long ago ceased to be an industrial town.

This is the first time he's let me know that my efforts are not in vain, Sasha thought. *Until now, Coach was convinced I was simply prolonging the agony and that all my efforts would amount to nothing. That I was still the assassin of reality. What has changed?*

"What has changed?" she asked out loud.

"By the way," Coach said, ignoring her. "Today, would you allow me to treat your brother as I see fit?"

Valya struggled to make his way up the stairs; he had to stop twice. He simply couldn't decide what would be considered a true rebellion at this point.

To go back to the dorm, feed the hamster, and go to bed? But he'd already missed one class. The stakes had to be higher.

To leave Torpa? This thought made Valya stumble on the stairs. That would be a true rebellion. But what if he would again wake up in the same dorm, on the same morning, waiting for Alyssa's roommates to beat her up?

He was such an idiot; when he spoke with Alexandra Igorevna, he didn't tell her the most important thing. He didn't phrase it properly, didn't throw it in her face. Those damn words: when he spoke to himself, he sounded sharp, biting, eloquent. But when he looked into Alexandra Igorevna's eyes, his words withered into feeble, unintelligible curses.

His wet boots squelching, Valya passed the locker rooms. The door to the women's locker room was open, letting out some chatter; the men's was mostly quiet.

The gym itself was empty and clean, not a soul in sight, and Valya considered leaving: What if he simply told Alexandra Igorevna that what's his face, Dmitry Dmitrievich, was nowhere to be found?

"You look different," someone said behind his back. "Are you wearing contacts?"

Coach stood by his office door, smiling, showing off his white teeth and adorable dimples.

"Did you bring sneakers? Any kind of athletic footwear?"

Valya shook his head.

"Then you're running barefoot," Coach said. "Take your shoes off."

"I am not going to do that," Valya said; he didn't like the way he sounded. His voice wasn't strong enough. It wasn't confident. Valya managed a grin, as wide as Coach's, and said calmly and with a hint of irony:

"I have my individual session in six minutes. I can't see Oleg Borisovich barefoot, can I?"

Coach murmured something. Valya felt an instant discomfort, as if his wet shoes weighed him down.

Coach picked a volleyball out of the basket. It was an excellent volleyball; it brought back memories of playing with Dad and his coworkers at a company picnic, and how his dad was so proud when Valya managed strong, precise passes.

Coach tossed the ball into the air and hit it lightly with his right hand. The ball flew across the gym and froze over a pile of mats. Valya blinked: the ball hung suspended in midair. Outside, the rain hung suspended in midair. A stream of water froze over the window.

"Two hundred squats," Coach said. "Two hundred push-ups. As soon as you're done, you can go see Oleg Borisovich. In six minutes."

Valya froze in his spot. Only Coach continued to move; he strolled back and forth, rubbing his shoulders, stretching, rising on his toes, and lowering back on his heels. His sneakers were as white as fresh snow on a mountain peak.

"I thought you were human," Valya said, with quiet reproach. "A real human, just hypocritical."

"I am a hypocritical nonhuman," Coach said lightly. "Please don't discuss what I am with any of your classmates. It's far too early for them."

"And is it too late for me?" Valya said. He felt slighted, like a small child. He'd put so much energy into his rebellion, but rebelling against *this* Torpa was pointless.

"If you are looking for compromise, how about this: don't take off your shoes," Coach said. "And you can choose whether you start with squats or push-ups."

Sasha could have washed her hands and let Adele deal with Alyssa Ostapova on her own. She should have done this. Sasha had enough to worry about: The Speech was disintegrating. The reality was shrinking like a piece of leather on fire. But since Sasha had made this savage decision, she felt that she needed to see it through.

Alyssa would remain in the time loop by herself. Her classmates would go on with their lives, turn the pages of their calendars, and check the weather report for the next day. Some time ago, Sasha had found herself dangling in a time loop, but there was a point to it, clear even from within the loop. It wasn't prison, it was training equipment. Her professors wanted results, and results they got. Sasha had hoped to break through, and she had.

Alyssa would live out her only day in the company of people who had no clue of the time loop, people who were sure of their tomorrows. Alyssa could get on a plane, buy a train ticket, or even jump off a roof, but in the morning, she would wake up in her dorm room, and her roommates would start the same conversation. There would be no point to this carousel, and no exit.

Sasha went up to the fourth floor.

In the hallway, Alyssa was waiting for her eleven o'clock session. She had been beaten up that morning, half her face puffy, one eye swollen shut. *At least they won't touch her again today,* Sasha thought. There would be no reason to. She'd get lost in the past. At first, she'd learn how to pretend, and eventually, she'd lose her mind.

On this rainy day, Adele's perfume seemed softer and warmer.

"Adele Victorovna, you're free for the next twenty minutes," Sasha said. "I'd like to work with this student myself."

For the first time in her life, Adele did not argue. She got up, picked up her bag, nodded, and left without making eye contact with Sasha.

"Thanks," Sasha said.

It occurred to Sasha that Adele was not devoid of sentimentality. With all her tough exterior, Adele knew Alyssa had to be expelled and preferred Sasha to do the dirty work.

Twenty-five. Twenty-six. Twenty-seven. Twenty-eight. Valya had started with the squats; the last time he had made it to one hundred, and his muscles just about broke in the process. This time he wouldn't make it to fifty.

"Change the vector of your will," Coach said, strolling along the gym. The volleyball still hung suspended in midair, and the rain was suspended in midair, and it was so very quiet. The only sounds were Coach's steps on the wooden floor of the gym, and his voice, calm and even friendly. "Redirect your will toward action, away from resistance."

Valya gritted his teeth. He straightened his knees; twenty-nine.

"Meaning is the projection of will onto the area of its application. Find the correct vector, and your actions will become meaningful."

I can't. These words filled his mouth, preventing him from breathing. These words gagged him, and somehow Valya knew he'd never say them out loud.

Thirty. Thirty-one. *Imagine a sphere whose external surface is red, and its internal surface is white.*

He saw the sphere. It hung suspended in midair like a volleyball, but it wasn't inside the gym. Valya saw it clearly; he saw through it. The inner surface was white. And on the outside, it was as red as the sunset.

Without jeopardizing its integrity, mentally modify the sphere so that its external surface would now be on the inside, and its internal surface would be on the outside . . .

Seventy-five . . . Eighty. Valya couldn't feel his legs. Where his knees, his hips, his calves used to be, now there was only pain, as if someone had dipped Valya into a vat of boiling oil. But the sphere still hung suspended in his line of vision, and it was perfect, like a pass into the ideal world, and Valya had power over it.

Mentally, he turned the sphere inside out, minding its thin, delicate shell. It felt like a sip of water after a long thirst, like the first spring day after a long, suffocating winter. The sphere turned into a moon, white on the outside, and inside it, the sun was shining.

Valya felt as if he had been paralyzed all his life, and now he'd got up and started to walk. This strange sphere shared his joy; pulsing, it changed its outline, split in two, challenging him, and Valya froze in sweet terror: Was this truly possible?

"Alyssa, I know it's hard for you. But trust me, it's not easy for me, either. If all your classmates managed to complete this set of exercises, then you should be able to do the same. What stops you from succeeding, in your opinion?"

"I didn't study hard enough during my first year," the girl said, as if repentance could save her.

"But now you have had time, a lot of time, and you tried very hard. Why can't you do it?"

"I am mediocre . . ."

Alyssa suddenly sat up and stared at Sasha, struck by an idea.

"I am nothing but mediocre! You should expel me!"

Sasha looked away; she didn't want to see hope on Alyssa's face.

"Let's try again," she said out loud; to herself, she added, *For the last time.*

The girl shrunk in her seat. Her hope dissipated, leaving behind helplessness, exhaustion, and pain in her battered body. Once again, Sasha saw a child dying of thirst next to a pitcher of fresh water.

One hundred eighteen. Valya had no idea how his muscles were still contracting. However, there was a clear, precise connection among his physical effort, this muscle pain, and the images that appeared in front of his eyes.

He saw two spheres. Without de-forming, they squeezed into a given point on a plane. The larger sphere fit into the smaller one, while their volumes remained the same. These spheres could not be drawn or modeled; they could only be seen by one's inner vision. One hundred sixty-one.

Why would Alyssa reject these exercises? These exercises were the key, the meaning, they were freedom and pleasure! All one needed to do was to feel the vector, to direct one's will to action rather than . . .

The memory of Alyssa pushed Valya out of the altered space. At one hundred ninety-eight, he fell and lost all feeling in his legs.

The girl shuddered as if electrocuted. Inside her, where just before the unsaid Word had dangled in the primordial broth, layers and strata had shifted abruptly, and the axes of coordinates had changed. Informational fragments reached toward each other and snapped into place, like parts of a reset joint.

The deaf, blind, dying-of-thirst child reached for the pitcher, touched her lips to the opening, and drank, one sip after another.

Alyssa's eyes were closed, her eyelids twitching slightly. The previously clogged, blocked informational channel had opened up, and the girl was now receiving chains of meanings stretching far beyond human experience.

Sasha leaned back in her chair and froze, afraid to move.

The volleyball landed on the pile of mats. The rain slammed into the awnings, water streaming down in currents. Groaning, Valya sat up. Coach's white sneakers seemed to glow in the dark.

Valya held his head. He felt as if he had almost jumped off a tall tower. Had he jumped? Or perhaps he'd lost something very valuable and couldn't remember what it was . . . or had he found something precious instead?

"One hundred ninety-eight," Coach said. "Two more. And then you can go see Oleg Borisovich."

Valya couldn't feel his legs, but he managed two more squats, lousy ones—more like jerking with his knees barely bent. Coach let him get away with it. Two and a half minutes remained until Valya met with Portnov.

"I saw—"

"I know what you saw," Coach said, nodding. "In a million years, I haven't seen a student who could simply do what they've been asked to do. You owe me two hundred push-ups, but we'll wait for another day. Don't worry, I never forget anything."

A strange noise pierced the building, coming from the lobby. Valya shuddered at the sound, like a multitude of wailing voices.

It was a howl of joy, and it made Valya's blood run cold in his veins.

"Group A, have a seat and open your books. Shanin, this includes you. Second years are going to get loud today, they have permission—it's a special occasion. And you—I'd like all of you to start thinking of your exams. And try to avoid what the second years had to go through."

On the way to her seat, Eva glanced in their direction. Silently, Pashka pleaded with her: *Please tell us apart! Who did you meet before class? Who did you drink tea with in the kitchen?* But Eva simply blinked her tinted eyelashes and turned back to the whiteboard.

Disappointment gave Pashka courage, and he raised his hand.

"Yes, Grigoriev?" Portnov said; his tone would make any reasonable student immediately respond with, "Nothing, sorry."

"Oleg Borisovich," Pashka said, glancing at his notebook to make sure he got his name and patronymic right. "Is it possible to read something . . ." He faltered. "Something like a fragment of . . ."

He stumbled again, realizing he couldn't verbalize his thoughts. Outside the auditorium, the noise went down, and the front door slammed over and over again. It sounded like the second years had been released early.

Group A twisted their necks to stare at Pashka, and only Eva still presented the prickly, stubborn back of her neck.

Portnov pushed his glasses to the tip of his nose. Pashka tensed. Portnov gazed at him with obvious curiosity, as if at a captured exotic butterfly.

"We can discuss it during your individual session," Portnov said finally. "Group A, paragraph two, let's begin."

●●●

That night, the second years celebrated their escape from a temporal loop and the arrival of the next day. They partied so hard the ceiling nearly collapsed. Alyssa sat at the head of the table, and the very same girls who'd kicked her that morning now brought her drinks and sandwiches. However, when Valya peeked into the kitchen twenty minutes later, Alyssa was no longer there.

He went up to her room on the second floor. The door was not locked. Alyssa was lying on her bed face down.

"It's me," Valya said softly, hesitating to walk in without an invitation but unwilling to leave. "Are you asleep?"

Outside it was raining and the streetlight made it look like drops of water were crawling all over the room. In the semi-darkness, Alyssa began to stir. She got up, went to the door, and pulled Valya inside. She kissed him on the lips and—their mouths still locked—began to remove her top and her bra.

She must have seen quite a few movies. Or maybe she'd slept with tons of guys before Valya. Or perhaps all her ordeals had made her lose her inhibition. Valya was way too inexperienced to guess what had prompted her aggressive actions. That day he'd had quite an experience himself, and he wanted to talk about the sphere that was red on the outside and white on the inside.

But it was impossible to talk with someone's tongue in his mouth.

Valya shook her off. He may have even pushed her away. He wasn't gentle.

"I want to be human," Alyssa said hoarsely. "I am terrified of what's happening, don't you see?"

Valya was afraid she was going to attack him again, but Alyssa turned away.

"It's fine. Just go."

"Shall we flip a coin?" Arthur asked, his voice sounding strangely guilty. He pulled a coin out of his pocket, a regular one, not a gold one.

The dorm floors shook, and windows rattled. Second years had clearly lost their minds. Some first years chose to hide, others joined the mad celebration.

"It's not a real date," Arthur said quickly, evaluating Pashka's reaction. "It's just a coffee, friends meeting casually at a café. Why are you looking at me like that? Fine, go yourself, I was just kidding. Go."

Arthur collapsed on his bed.

"No, you misunderstood me," Pashka muttered.

"I understood everything just fine. That evening, I thought I'd just chat with her while you were studying. But she . . ." Arthur shook his head. "I was wrong. She came to you, she called you. Go, she's waiting. It's not her fault that . . ."

"That there are two of us?"

Pashka bit his tongue. Why did he say that?

He thought of their kindergarten graduation. The designer responsible for their yearbook assumed one boy was photographed twice and deleted Pashka's photo, leaving only Arthur's. Pashka didn't mind, but their mom was very upset. She was heartbroken.

"Listen," Pashka said quickly, longing to move past the unpleasant situation. "Go see her and tell her your name. See what she says. Maybe she'll say, *Wow, that's what I thought, I'm so glad you're Arthur.*"

"But she fell for you!"

"Or you? When you had tea in the kitchen. Maybe she wants you, she just doesn't know it yet."

Arthur took a moment to consider his thoughts, torn between decision and doubt. Second years shouted discordantly along with the music outside their room.

"Are you sure?" Arthur asked finally.

"Go," Pashka said. "She's not going to lie to you. If she doesn't like something, she gets vocal about it. She might even get violent, so be prepared."

Arthur grinned. It had been a while since Pashka had seen his brother so happy and so free. Arthur shook his hand, put on his best sweater, grabbed his coat, and walked out into the partying and singing. Pashka was left alone in their room. *Textual Module* lay by the table lamp, and Valya's hamster rustled in its cage.

What would Eva say when Arthur admitted to pulling the prank? *Why would she care?* Pashka thought with sudden annoyance. *She can't tell us apart anyway, just like that yearbook designer.*

Pashka turned to paragraph two. He'd looked at it earlier but then cowardly put it aside. He felt it again: it was impossible to read; the clanging of unpronounceable lines merged with the music and squealing behind the wall, and it was clear that . . .

. . . removed his glasses, wiped his tears, and called softly: "Darling . . ." As if expecting it, Grandma stepped out onto the porch. She wore her blue house-dress and a kitchen apron.

She saw Pashka and Arthur and took a step back.

"Grandma," Arthur said hoarsely. "We love you. We love you and Grandpa, and Mom and Dad. Please forgive us."

Grandma took a step off the porch, stumbled, and almost fell. Arthur threw himself forward and caught her, and she held on to his shoulders.

"Oh, Arthur, honey."

She could always tell them apart, always, since the time they were born. Anyone could make a mistake, but not their grandmother.

Pashka opened his eyes.

Two hours had passed, according to the alarm clock. Music was still playing somewhere in the depths of the dorm, but now it was low and quiet. Paragraph two contained no legible words, only drivel.

At midnight, second years ran outside, raising their arms to the sky and screaming like shamans.

"The rain has stopped! There is no more rain!"

Arthur and Valya returned at the same time. Without his glasses, their nerdy roommate looked like a different person. Lost in thought, he busied himself with feeding his hamster. Valya's shoes were soaked through: he must have spent the evening walking in puddles.

"I didn't tell her," Arthur said. "We were just sitting there, talking, and it was so nice, and all these people were around. And then we kissed at a street corner."

The nerd glanced at Arthur as if wanting to ask a question but holding back.

"Pashka, what can I do?" Arthur said, his voice full of pain. "Now she's definitely all yours. I can't come clean. I just can't."

Pashka felt split in two. To kiss Eva after she'd kissed Arthur? Let's assume Eva thought it was Pashka. Let's assume Eva was in her room, next door, and he could knock on her door, and she would open it, and it was so dark and quiet in the dorm. But why would any of this matter when the book filled with unreadable texts contained a fragment that kept repeating over and over, and in this fragment their grandparents had forgiven them?

"What?" Arthur asked. He must have thought Pashka was jealous.

"Nothing," Pashka said, swallowing his justification like a handful of bitter pills. "It's late."

The rain stopped at midnight; the moon came out almost immediately. The fireplace was lit; conveniently, the autumn evening was raw and chilly—Sasha needed the fire. She'd spent many hours drawing her self-portraits. Voluminous and dynamic, they tried to escape the paper, and Sasha burned them in the fireplace.

The Great Speech kept changing, giving way to grammatical reform. Into the world without fear, Sasha sent fear, carefully chosen and titrated, just enough to give the students back their ability to grow into Words. But the carefully measured fear kept trying to escape, like boiled milk, its burned organic matter spoiling Sasha's plans.

She had made the decision to keep Alyssa in the time loop indefinitely. Such a decision could not be taken without consequences—and Sasha had changed. Her metamorphosis had left a trace.

Alyssa survived in the indicative mood, at least for now. Had Valya not established an emotional connection with her, kicking off the process and showing her how to complete the exercises—instinctively, unaware of his actions—

In the conditional tense, in the *if*, Alyssa remained in yesterday's loop forever.

Sasha's pencil produced a picture worthy of a preschool child, but four-dimensional, leaning toward the fifth. The balcony glass cracked. Sasha placed the unfinished work in the fireplace.

Farit was right about many things, yet he did make mistakes. Had he been right about everything: that there would be nothing left of Sasha, not a single memory, not a letter, not a molecule, and aircrafts would continue to crash, children would continue to drown, and people would murder each other by the millions?

Perhaps that was the only viable reality.

Someone knocked on the door lightly. Kostya always knocked before entering.

"Hi there," Sasha said. She didn't even try to conceal her joy; she needed to speak with someone, but not Coach, not Adele, and not even Portnov, who understood everything, but had never been human.

Kostya stepped over the threshold, carrying paper bags with a restaurant logo. Sasha didn't recognize the logo; Kostya must have gone outside Torpa.

"Halibut," Kostya said. "It's really good."

"Thank you," Sasha said. She wasn't thanking him for the fish.

She shuffled the ashes in the fireplace to make sure the last piece of paper burned all the way through.

"I am doing some debriefing here," she said.

She began to speak, and he listened. He must have known everything, or almost everything, but Sasha needed to talk. She needed to verbalize and relive certain crucial moments.

"That part of me, not much more than a shard, a projection I left in baby Valya—it's developing quicker than matter would allow. Valya is a chimera. A Word of immense power growing inside an ordinary boy. And now I don't know what to do first: to stabilize Valya or save the twins."

"Save the twins?"

"I don't want to sacrifice one for the sake of the other. That's not why I created this world."

"What did you create it for?" Kostya asked gently. He wasn't taunting her. He was helping her, and she was grateful.

"I am an assassin of reality," Sasha said. She washed her hands, sat down, and ripped the warm foil as if illustrating how violently she'd ripped apart the old world. "I am an assassin of that reality in which the twins could have devoured each other in their mother's womb. A multiple pregnancy meant limited resources and the survival of the fittest."

"What exactly do you need from the Grigoriev twins?" Kostya asked, taking a seat across the table. The night dragged on, the fireplace was burning out, and the sky was clearing up in the strong moonlight.

"I need them to send me in the right direction."

Sasha imagined a ray of light in the darkness and a shadow of an aircraft, outside of space, outside of time.

"In the right direction," Kostya repeated pensively. "Then you need a directional adverb, Samokhina. A very strong, powerful adverb."

Sasha got up and placed another log into the fire. The fire had stiffened for a moment as if surprised by her generous gift, then joyfully and loudly embraced the dry wood.

"Don't you think I know that?" she asked, looking at the fire.

Kostya winced.

"My apologies, Password."

Sasha smiled sadly.

"I am afraid to look in the mirror, Kostya," she said. "I know what I'm doing, and what I still need to do. Today, my brother told me my mom never loved me and that no one has ever loved me."

"He wanted to hurt you," Kostya said gently. "Because he is scared. Your mom still loves you."

"She doesn't," Sasha said, shaking her head. "It was a different narrative, a different time, a different girl. Have you ever loved me?"

"You know the answer," Kostya said, smiling. "Everything that used to be my life and my entire grammatical existence reflects you. It is filled and formed by you, and everything would have been different had we never met."

Sasha gazed inside herself. Kostya was right, and she had known it all along. She didn't reflect on it; she simply knew it.

"My next step should be apologizing to you," she said softly.

Kostya shook his head. He put a piece of flaky, steaming white fish into his mouth, closed his eyes with pleasure, and swallowed. Sasha watched him enjoy his meal; slowly, she began to eat herself, tasting absolutely nothing.

"May I ask you something?" Kostya said hesitantly.

Sasha tensed up but nodded.

"Your love for that pilot of yours—was it constructed?" Kostya asked, stumbling for a second. "And if it were, then by whom? By you, or the one we'd agreed not to mention?"

"What is the definition of 'verification,' Kostya?" Sasha asked after a long pause.

"It is an empirical confirmation of the theoretical provisions of science by 'returning' to the visual level of cognition when the ideal nature of abstractions is ignored and the abstractions in question are identified with observable objects," he answered, without a hint of surprise.

"It is possible that my love for Yaroslav had been constructed by someone at some point to solve some grammatical problems. But the verification of my love is an aircraft that lands safely in the thunderstorm, even though it should have crashed. This world that I've created still exists. And I intend to save it. Even if I must change."

PART III

CHAPTER ONE

On September 4, Eva knocked on their door, sporting her usual hooligan grin and a prickly haircut that resembled a terrified hedgehog. While Arthur kept his nose in the book, Pashka got up and went out into the hallway.

Unfortunately, there were a few witnesses to their conversation: Eva's roommates and a random second year who was transporting a towel-wrapped steaming pot from the kitchen into his room. Pashka didn't want witnesses, but Eva, as if supporting her "take charge" reputation, put her hands on his shoulders and smiled, as if they were alone. Pashka could have easily hugged her in return; instead, he said:

"We should be friends."

At first, Eva didn't understand him. She continued to smile, gazing into Pashka's eyes like a trusting puppy. Her roommates pretended to struggle with the lock, and the random second year nearly dropped his pot.

Gently but firmly, Pashka freed himself from Eva's arms.

"We should be just friends. There is too much work and not enough time for anything else."

He didn't waste any time looking at her or talking to her. He simply went back into his room and locked the door. Arthur was no longer leaning over his book; he stood by the window, pressing his fists into the windowsill.

"Why?" he asked softly, not looking at Pashka. "Why did you do this to her?"

"Because there are tons of girls, but I only have one brother," Pashka said, the words tasting bitter in his mouth.

Six weeks had passed since that day, and he and Eva said nothing to each other. Not a single word.

Fluorescent lights reflected on the surface of the pool. The reflections broke over small waves and refolded, like glass fragments inside a kaleidoscope. For some reason, Valya saw it in color.

With renewed curiosity, he refocused his gaze on his classmates. Whether due to the lights in the pool, the sprays of water, or the warm steam escaping from the ventilation vents, to Valya, it looked as if shadows, not people, were splashing in the pool. He didn't know who the shadows belonged to.

Valya felt he was about to fall into the pool, but not like he had before, yelling and splashing. He was about to become the pool, not dissolve in the water, but *be* the water, possess these reflections, and only then understand their nature; all he needed to do was to mentally reshape a four-dimensional object, and then—

A sharp whistle made his ears ring.

"Shanin, is everything okay?"

Coming to his senses, Valya saw a whistle on a chain, then a set of powerful pectoral muscles under a thin T-shirt, and only then realized that Coach was standing right in front of him. A second later, Valya saw that the splashing and all the movement in the pool had stopped, and everyone was looking at him, questioningly and with some concern. These were his classmates, not shadows. They were slim and stocky, wearing rubber caps or with their wet hair uncovered. Irwing was a redhead, Samvel had a thin youthful mustache, Stefa was covered with freckles, and Tonya Makarova's shoulders were worthy of a rowing team; there were twenty-four of them, Group A and Group B in their joint swimming session.

Valya glanced at the round clock on the wall. Twenty minutes had passed since he first contemplated the surface of the pool.

"Twenty minutes left, everyone, back to work!" Coach said cheerfully, his voice bouncing off the arched ceiling of the pool. The pool was enormous, as big as a train station. Swimmers took their places at the appropriate lanes, and an orange ball flew up in the air at the water polo station.

"Self-control," Coach said to Valya softly. "Have you heard of exercising it before?"

"Yeah," Valya said, trying not to stare at the mischievous, hypnotizing water surface.

"Can you just paddle, please?" Coach asked him, as if in confidence. "We're not interested in beating world records here. All we care about is a positive attitude and healthy lifestyle!"

He spoke to Valya the same way he'd speak with any other first year, like an older brother, a kind, understanding, caring one. There was a reason everyone loved him.

Except maybe Valya. And the Grigoriev twins, who were clearly wary of Coach.

The twins stood in the shallow end of the pool. They were talking, or rather it looked like they were arguing, which almost never happened. Pashka was trying to convince Arthur of something, Arthur was trying to interject, but Pashka would not let him, and Arthur was getting angrier by the minute. Eva

Danilova swam past in a clumsy crawl, splashing with each move, and the Grigoriev twins forgot their argument. They watched Eva, and she watched the bottom of the pool as she moved past. *Imagine a four-dimensional object whose projection is an impulse . . .*

"Stop," Coach said softly. "What did I just say, Shanin?"

"Positive attitude and healthy lifestyle," Valya mumbled, taking a step toward the stairs leading into the water. Coach placed a hand on his shoulder; it was an ordinary gesture of a coach, but it made Valya recoil.

"You must feel your body," Coach said quietly. "When it starts changing, you must control it, not allow your body to control you."

"I am controlling it."

"No. Right now you don't even understand what I'm saying to you. You are growing as a concept while remaining human."

Valya recalled Alyssa's words: *I want to be human. I am terrified of what's happening, don't you see?* The memory sent chills down his spine.

"As long as you remain material, your body must work and develop, as any young man's body. By the way, take a look around. You're quite popular with your classmates. Everyone is looking at you. You should take it as a compliment."

"Me?"

In the far corner of the cafeteria, Alyssa sat frozen, staring ahead with glassy eyes. Valya sat down at her table. The lunch shift was over, and the kitchen crew was waiting to close the place until dinnertime.

Alyssa blinked. She stared at the cooling bowl of broth in front of her, then at Valya, as if wondering whether she was dreaming, or whether he was an abstraction, straight out of her textbook.

"All's well," he said, smiling at her. "Are you doing the exercises?"

"Yeah," she said, dipping her spoon into her bowl. "It got cold. Have you eaten?"

"I had a few slices of meat pie."

"You should eat soup, soup's good for you," Alyssa said. She blushed and, avoiding his eyes, went back to her broth, by now topped with a film of cooling fat.

"All's well," Valya said again. "I just wanted to ask how you're doing. Are you . . ."

Valya faltered. He wanted to ask if Alyssa had managed to overcome her fear and whether she was feeling human again. He wanted to know if she was still mad at him. He wanted to apologize for his tactless behavior and convince Alyssa that he liked her and that he understood everything, but . . . He struggled to find the right words.

He didn't need to struggle. Alyssa grinned suddenly, as if he'd just said something extremely nice.

"Everything's great! I am the star of our year! Adele Victorovna keeps praising me in front of everyone! There is nothing scary about these exercises, and nothing scary about this institute, and when we graduate, everyone is going to be so envious."

She stopped smiling, sighed deeply, then continued:

"I've seen you almost every day. In the lobby, then in the dorm, on the street. You always look like someone who can see their goal. I used to say hello, but you never heard me."

"I was working," Valya said guiltily. "I am a kind of star, too. Portnov gave me the exercises for second years and told me that if I continue studying like this, he'll pass me automatically."

"Wow," Alyssa said, looking at him with renewed respect.

"I heard things about you. They say you're crazy smart. Not that I listen to gossip . . ."

She blushed even deeper. For some reason, Valya felt discombobulated, as if they weren't talking about exercises.

"Do you think they may let you skip a year?" Alyssa asked hopefully. "And move you up into our class?"

For a second, Valya believed it was possible.

CHAPTER TWO

The leaves began to fall when the darkness came, all at once, as if by request. The outskirts of Torpa were filled with darkness, the autumn ink, and above, the stars blazed as if scalded by boiling water.

Leaves swirled over the water, above the bridge, in the glow of the last remaining streetlight. The river overflowed after the recent rainstorms, and a narrow stripe was all that remained of the beach.

"Tomorrow," Pashka said.

Arthur gnawed on his lips.

"Tomorrow, the sun will shine bright," Pashka said. "And the leaves. Like in the text I've been reading."

Arthur was close to giving in. But he wasn't entirely there yet; something had to happen for him to agree. Arthur was very stubborn. Arthur was also very scared.

"We'll go in the morning," Pashka said. "We'll have tea and eat bagels."

They were walking from the river back to the town, along Peace Street, then along Sacco and Vanzetti. The streetlights were on, but the stars hadn't even considered giving up their positions.

"And then we'll go, Arthur. You'll see. Everything will happen organically."

Arthur winced as if he had a toothache. Silently, they entered an arch leading from the street to the courtyard, toward the dorm. They walked up the stairs and into the first-floor hallway.

"Whoa," Pashka said in surprise.

The hallway was filled with all the first years and a few second years. Scowling, Eva was dragging her suitcases and bags over the threshold, her blue eyes looking steely gray. Her classmates attempted to help her, Valya among them, but she hissed like a furious cat:

"I am fine! Leave me alone!"

Her roommates, Stefa and Tonya, were hiding in their room. Pashka stopped. The smartest thing to do at that point would be to go back to the courtyard and wait it out. But Eva was standing right there, with her ridiculous cropped hair. She was biting her lip so hard it was almost bleeding, and she had all that stuff, too much of it, as it always happens when people move.

Arthur and Pashka stepped up at the same time. The hallway suddenly seemed very crowded, like a bus at rush hour.

"What happened?" Pashka asked softly. "Where are you going?"

Eva ignored him.

From the stairs came a rumbling noise. Huffing and puffing, Alyssa was dragging a wheeled suitcase; she looked at the crowd and immediately located the bespectacled nerd, Pashka's roommate.

"Hey, Valya! We're going to be neighbors! Eva and I switched, so I'm moving in with the girls."

Stefa and Tonya, Eva's former roommates who didn't lift a finger to help her, now rushed over to pick up Alyssa's suitcase and backpack. Pashka watched Valya hesitate, then try to help, but Alyssa stopped him with a grin.

"Wait, our room's a mess! You can stop by when we clean up, neighbor!"

She gazed at Valya happily and was about to wink at him but felt too shy and changed her mind.

Avoiding everyone's eyes, Eva dragged her stuff up the stairs like an overworked ant. Her belongings kept slipping out of her grasp. Eva kept going back for each item, and taking another step, pushing herself up the stairs.

Valya caught up with her and tried to take her suitcase.

"Go away," Eva said through her teeth.

Valya could have said, *They like you, both of them, and they can't figure out how to share you.*

He almost said something like this, but at the last second, he shut his mouth.

When he returned to his room, something was happening between the twins. As always in moments like this, Valya thought they were talking without making a sound, like machines controlled remotely. Eventually, Arthur took a deep breath, lowered his head, and said, "Fine."

Fallen leaves covered the sidewalks and the benches, the lawns, the streets, and the roofs. The leaves floated in the few puddles like forgotten boats; some looked like wrinkled hands reaching for alms. An enormous fir tree was visible from a distance, through the yellow gardens, birches, and maples of Torpa's residential area.

"*Textual Module* is an intermediary between you and the archive of meanings that is available to you at this stage," Portnov said. "Anything can appear in it, including a fragment of the most likely future."

"Future?" Pashka asked greedily. "Possible future?"

"You're rushing," Portnov said. "And it's both good and bad. The good news is that you started applying yourself in September, and not in December right before the exams, like so many students here, which is never a good idea. The bad news is that, as a first year, you are not ready to fully understand *Module*. Don't expect *Module* to make predictions, it's not a fortune teller's parrot."

"But the future I read about, is that the most likely future?"

Portnov sighed and lit another cigarette. This happened six weeks ago. Since then—for six weeks in a row—Pashka had tried to get Arthur to agree to go.

"Why should we believe him?" Arthur said angrily. "I spend hours reading these paragraphs, and I see nothing!"

"But me—do you believe *me*?"

And, at least initially, he did.

They crossed the autumnal Torpa, passed the town center into the residential area, and turned onto the familiar street. Arthur began to drag his feet. Pashka was starting to feel uncomfortable himself, but he grabbed his brother's hand like a little boy's and led him toward the house.

In the yard, Grandpa was sweeping up leaves. He had headphones on and was humming along—Pashka could see his lips moving. Or perhaps he wasn't singing but rather talking to an imaginary interlocutor.

Pashka opened the gate as he had done thousands of times since he was a child. He walked into the yard and suddenly froze, unsure of his next steps. Behind him, Arthur breathed heavily.

Grandpa turned toward them and stood still. Slowly, wearily, he pulled off his headphones. Behind his glasses, his eyes seemed to be the same color as the sky.

"Grandpa, we love you very much, you and Grandma," Pashka said. "And Mom and Dad. Please, forgive us. Please."

Both the cafeteria and the library were open on Sunday. While the cafeteria was noisy with voices and the clinking of utensils, the library was empty, quiet, and dusty, just the way Sasha liked it.

The librarian had stepped out "for a moment"; she stepped out quite frequently—it wasn't worth sitting in one spot for the sake of a couple of stray students. Next to the box of old catalogs, a brass figurine of an owl hunting a mouse stood on the desk. A row of bookcases hadn't changed since Sasha's own college years. One glass-paneled bookcase was locked: that's where the library kept all the Specialty textbooks.

Portnov was already there. He sat by the switched-off desk lamp and watched the twirling leaves outside the window.

"Your reform is working," he said instead of a hello. "The first years are studying like crazy. Kostya is keeping a tight rein, and there is progress. I believe all of them will pass the winter exams, although perhaps not on the first try. As far as second years: you may want to discuss it with Adele, but they are doing fine in my class."

He took a long pause. Sasha waited. She was used to his mode of communication.

"But I wanted to talk about something other than their success," Portnov said, glancing at her above his glasses. "Your brother . . ."

Sasha was silent. The less she asked, the more he'd tell her.

"You're looking at him through a multitude of filters," Portnov said. "Human filters, from the past. Mom, family, a baby, taking him for a walk in a stroller, nearly killing him and then saving him. You see a big boy, remarkable only because he has a fragment of you inside him. Perhaps that's all he was when you enrolled him in the institute. But children grow up. And what's inside him is aggressive and unpredictable."

"Yes," Sasha said, thinking the library was very cold that morning. "It was my mistake—back then. Now, it's my hope."

"All right," Portnov said quietly. He waited for Sasha to ask the next question.

"And the twins?" she said, accepting the rules of the game.

"Grigoriev, A. is a hard worker, yet perfectly ordinary. He's like you: in the beginning, you succeeded thanks to working your ass off."

"Do you mean to say he might surprise us yet?" Sasha asked carefully.

"He'll pass the first exam, if . . . He's likely to pass it. As far as Grigoriev, P. . . ."

He paused. Sasha waited.

"Samokhina, these boys are not your sons grammatically," Portnov said, wincing as if he'd stepped on a sharp tack with a bare foot. "Don't lie to yourself. You simply see a reflection of your pilot in them. In them both."

"What about Grigoriev, P.?" Sasha asked through gritted teeth. "Is he not studying hard enough?"

"He's working hard," Portnov said. "He has learned to find meanings in *Textual Module* before anyone else. But since then, all he does is try to catch a single fragment, a version of the future. He refuses to see anything else. He's talented but quite unstable, and for him, any failure may be his last. Do you know who he reminds me of? Kostya Kozhennikov, during his first year."

"You failed Kostya back then," Sasha said, unable to hold back.

"Is it still important for you? You still remember, don't you?"

They fell silent. The old dark hardwood floors creaked of their own accord.

"If I could sculpt them like clay," Sasha said softly. "If only I could just tell them what I want. But they won't understand, they'll get confused, and it'll make things worse."

Suddenly, the library went dark: outside, the sun hid behind a storm cloud. Sasha tensed up: something important was happening. She sensed she was about to become a witness to some crucial event.

She looked around, grabbed the heavy owl figurine off the librarian's desk, ran over to the locked bookcase, and broke the glass in one blow. Triangular shards spilled on the floor.

"Well now," Portnov murmured.

Without thinking, Sasha reached out for *Textual Module,* volume 1. A multitude of meanings swarmed across the pages, layering on top of each other and intertwining, as if the text was mumbling in a million voices, and someone's life depended on each sentence. It was a simple textbook for beginners.

". . . dropped his broom dotted with sticky yellow leaves . . ." Sasha read.

Grandpa dropped his broom dotted with sticky yellow leaves and took off his glasses. Pashka froze. This was where the textual fragment from *Module* began, it was what he'd encountered in different paragraphs, with different details. It's when their grandfather would call their grandma . . .

"Arthur, Pashka," Grandpa said weakly, his voice as fragile as rustling leaves. "Did you send us flowers on September first?"

Pashka glanced at Arthur. Arthur stared back in confusion.

"Doesn't matter," Grandpa said, dropping his head. "Doesn't

matter at all. But your grandmother is not well, she's in bed. I'm afraid that . . . give her time. Give all of us time. Are you staying there, at that institute?"

His eyes brightened. He gazed at them with hope.

"We got acccpted," Pashka said quickly. "We need to study. That's what we're supposed to do. We got accepted, so we need to study. But we can come visit on Sundays . . ."

"I don't understand," Anton Pavlovich said helplessly. "Why do you hate your parents so much?"

"We love them!" Pashka said, raising his voice. "It's just that we're adults, Grandpa . . ."

Grandpa looked down.

"Do what you want. But please, I beg of you, don't bother your grandmother. She could get worse. Or . . ." He faltered. "Or perhaps you don't care how she is feeling?"

Pashka wanted to wake up leaning over an open book, but there was no book. There was reality, autumn, the sun was shining, and the leaves were twirling in the air. Everything had gone wrong; it was impossible, unfair, and against the rules.

The glass shards scattered on the hardwood floor. The librarian, alerted by the noise, ran back and now stood frozen at the entrance. The owl figurine lay on the floor, and it looked as if the brass mouse would have a chance to escape.

Portnov did not move. He sat still by the window, leaning his head as if listening to something. Sasha placed the textbook back on the shelf, instinctively trying not to move, not to step on the glass, not to make any noise. Portnov went deep inside himself. A multitude of processes were occurring inside his complicated nonhuman world.

"You could have asked for the key," the librarian said with reproach. "Now we have to replace the glass."

She caught Sasha's eyes and quickly corrected herself.

"I mean, it's your business, obviously. It's just that we can't get maintenance to come in on a Sunday. And this bookcase should be locked at all times, as per instructions."

"It's not an adverb," Portnov muttered.

"What?"

"It's not an adverb you're looking for, Samokhina. Perhaps someday we'll learn—if we make it—what it is, but it's already capable of changing the current reality. His brother had read a possible future, something very plausible. But he canceled it. He distorted the projection and brought the possibility to zero. Sasha, this is not an adverb, and it's filled with fear. Kostya did a good job."

"Kostya did what I asked him to do," Sasha said, barely moving her rubbery lips.

Portnov closed his eyes. With horror, Sasha knew that at this moment—this very moment—Portnov was rotting from the inside. Only a few semantic measures were left until the destruction of the Great Speech.

Arthur sat on the bench amid piles of yellow leaves, staring at his feet. Pashka stood over him in despair like a bird over a wrecked nest.

He had sworn to his brother that everything would go well. He'd promised. So many times, he'd explained that he saw the future: Grandpa would remove his glasses and wipe away tears of joy. Grandma would call Arthur "honey." Pashka's promises meant shit. His hopes meant shit.

"It doesn't mean anything," Pashka mumbled. "They need time. It's true, Arthur, we love them, they must know that. And I didn't lie to you, someday it will happen exactly as I described. If Grandma had come out, she would have forgiven us right away. It's just that she didn't come out, but next time—"

"Hello," said an unfamiliar voice.

Pashka turned around. The woman appeared out of nowhere: a light pantsuit, straight dark hair, and strange eyes that in turn cleared and dimmed, as if trying to focus properly. Pashka knew this woman; she'd accompanied Valya, lost and late, to Portnov's class, and Portnov had introduced her as the provost. Pashka had seen her around, but never like this, face-to-face.

"I was the one who sent them flowers on September first," the woman said slowly and clearly, as if giving a lecture.

A light wind rolled the leaves around Pashka's feet. Arthur looked up and blinked as if seeing a bright light after being in the dark.

"Oleg Borisovich is very pleased with your work," the woman continued calmly. "Our faculty is quite happy with the first-year students."

She sat down, carefully pulling up her pant legs.

"Why did you send them flowers?" Pashka asked hoarsely. He did not doubt her words.

"I wanted to please your grandparents," she said, and once again, Pashka knew she was telling the truth. "And they were pleased."

Arthur's eyes finally cleared; a frozen mask of pain had slid off his face. Pashka surprised himself by feeling jealous. He'd tried so hard to pull Arthur out of his stupor. He was Arthur's brother! This strange woman showed up out of nowhere, said a few words, and Arthur looked like he was about to smile.

Pashka immediately felt ashamed. Arthur felt better, and it didn't matter who'd helped him.

"You boys need to be patient for the sake of your love," the woman said. "Sometimes love is verified in this . . . I meant to say that sometimes love takes on such forms that it becomes hard to recognize. But we all operate in ideas, projections, and informational systems. We must see the point inside matter. We must see ideas. A source of meaning."

Pashka suddenly knew why Arthur believed her. It was the sound of a distant flute, a light in the window, familiar and homey. When the weight falls off one's shoulders, when the pressure stops, one can simply trust and listen.

"What is the point? That we treated our family like shit?" Pashka said, shaking off the illusion. "That instead of living our own lives, we are reading your *Textual Modules*? That every morning we wake up and make sure we are living in the next day and that we're not locked in a loop?"

"No," she said, smiling faintly and looking into his eyes. Once again, Pashka saw a shadow of that distant light. "The thing is, Pashka—I tried different things. I explained to the students what was going to happen. Long before their enrollment, I told them what they would be studying, what was their mission, and what was the goal. Those were the worst years of the worst failure. Because . . ."

She stopped. Her face changed as if speaking was difficult for her. A small tornado of fallen leaves twirled around the bench.

"Tomorrow, Monday, eight P.M.," the woman said, very businesslike. Her intonation made Pashka recall her name: Alexandra Igorevna. "Come for an individual session at my office. You don't need to prepare in advance."

●●●

Right away, Valya knew that the twins' plans had failed, and they had not reconciled with their relatives. Aware of how much this visit meant for Arthur and Pashka, Valya felt a jolt of fear on their behalf. However, aside from disappointment and unavoidable depression, the brothers had brought something else back. Strangely enough, it was hope. Even stranger, the source of that hope was Alexandra Igorevna.

Valya should have expressed some caution, asked some questions, and hinted that Alexandra Igorevna never gave out free gifts and that the twins should stay on guard. But that day Valya was preoccupied with something else. Upon finding out about their session at eight, he gathered enough courage to ask them to save his life.

Struggling to provide a cohesive explanation, he looked at them pleadingly.

"Just don't come back until nine. Please."

"What are you going to do, set a timer?" Pashka asked.

"First, he dragged in a hamster . . ." Arthur began wearily but then stopped. Perhaps, he recalled the morning when Valya brought Alyssa into their room to tend to her wounds. Their having felt some compassion for the girl, albeit short-lived and without strings attached, meant Alyssa was no longer a stranger to them.

"Alyssa and I are just going to sit here and talk," Valya said quickly. "I'm going to clean up around here. It's to your benefit, too. And when you come back at nine, we'll be in the kitchen, having a cup of tea."

Pashka and Arthur exchanged glances; to Valya, once more, it looked as if they exchanged inaudible signals.

But then Arthur nodded, and that was all Valya cared about.

CHAPTER THREE

A cage was placed on the desk. The hamster pressed itself to the metal floor and stared through the bars with its beady eyes.

"If you press this button, the hamster will die," Sasha said.

Arthur looked up in surprise. In the short time she'd gotten to know them personally, she'd managed to get Arthur to like her. At first, Arthur thought she was kidding, or offering a puzzle or a game.

"But I don't need to press the button," he said, smiling. "Why would I want to kill a hamster?"

"It's an exercise," Sasha said. "Let me explain the concept. And then, once you're fully informed, you will complete this exercise, okay?"

Arthur stopped smiling. He looked at the hamster; the hamster sat still as if hoping that not moving would make everyone forget its existence.

"I demand complete obedience from all first years," Sasha said. "You cannot study without it. But I also need a manifestation of your own will, because without it you won't be able to continue. A contradiction? No, dialectics, that's how progress happens. I am going to give you an order. If you don't follow it, I will immediately report you to Konstantin Faritovich."

Arthur grew very pale, and yet Sasha saw Yaroslav in him. The real Yaroslav, the one who landed planes in thunderstorms, who understood the unsaid, who commanded "Do not be afraid" when all the lights had gone.

"You get to decide whether to follow my order," she said, slowly, carefully, not quite believing her luck. "You have a choice, you are free, and you can disobey me."

Sasha forbade herself to look through him. *The observer influences the object;* she needed Arthur to make his decision on his own.

"But I will definitely report you, and that's the point of the exercise, do you understand?"

If he refused to kill, she wouldn't have to sacrifice anyone. The boy would become the direct projection of Yaroslav as a concept of courage and trust. He would open an informational channel for Sasha, allowing her to make corrections to the foundation of Speech and reinstate herself fully. Reality would be restored in all its complexity and many true Words would obtain new meanings.

"You have a choice," Sasha said softly. "Press the button."

In the center of the cage, Pashka crouched on four short legs. He heard their voices as if through broken headphones and saw their faces as if through the fog. The cage smelled unpleasantly of a terrified animal.

He thought he was Arthur, that it was he who stood by the desk, staring at the cage and feeling Alexandra Igorevna's gaze. As he pressed his soft fuzzy belly to the bottom of the cage, Pashka understood something important: Konstantin Faritovich, the embodied fear of death, was nothing but a device, a drill, a screwdriver. The big evil that had settled in Torpa, the center of the web that had entangled everything in its thread, was Alexandra Igorevna, the provost.

"The button," a voice said outside the cage, a black voice, viscous like molten lead. Inside the cage, Pashka closed his eyes and screamed inaudibly: "Don't press it! Look at me! It's me! Don't press it, Arthur!"

Sasha desperately wanted to roll the time back by one minute and give him a chance to think, but she willed herself to stay still. She stopped herself from pushing him toward the right decision. She held herself back from telling him who was crouching at the bottom of the cage.

Come on. Become a reflection of your real father. Show me Yaroslav as if in a mirror. Give me access. Come on, Arthur.

Arthur took a step forward and pressed the button as if calling the elevator. Through the bars, they saw the hamster convulse, fall on its back, and spread its twitching paws.

Arthur staggered back. His forehead glistened.

Sasha closed her eyes for a second. *I don't ask for the impossible,* Farit used to say. Sasha had asked for the impossible.

Arthur was broken. He'd already assaulted his grandmother and symbolically spat into his father's face. The fate of the hamster had been predetermined. Yaroslav Grigoriev—the true one, the one Sasha had seen in his son's face just a few seconds ago—was gone. The access was denied.

"Good," Sasha said slowly. "Oleg Borisovich will give you an additional book of exercises at your next individual session. You must work twice as hard, Arthur. You must meet the faculty's expectations."

He straightened up, trying not to look at the dead hamster, then said good-bye and walked out.

Her mind blank, Sasha opened the cage, pulled out the dead hamster, and placed the tiny body on her desk. She pressed her palms against the desk and *claimed* both the desk and the dead animal. She entered the metamorphosis, separated the alien matter from herself, and completed the transformation. She turned away and walked between the rows of desks toward the window.

The weather had turned for the worse. It was raining, and leaves that flew over Sacco and Vanzetti Street twisted into tornadoes without Sasha's assistance.

Someone breathed heavily behind her back. Sasha counted to twenty and turned around.

Pashka Grigoriev leaned over the desk, shaking, and staring at Sasha from beneath a wet lock of hair. Hatred swam in his eyes. Sasha recalled the scene in Sterkh's cabinet, when, having returned from the winter break, she'd learned that Zakhar had failed his exam. Back then, Sasha would have killed Sterkh if she could.

"We lost this battle," Sasha said. "But we haven't lost the war."

He said nothing, but his face was expressive enough without words.

"You're being overly dramatic," Sasha said. "Look at me—you have no idea what I have just lost. And all you've lost is the life of one little hamster. Your brother didn't know whom he was killing."

Silently, he stood up straight, swaying a little, and walked toward the door. A moment later, the door slammed behind him.

Sasha remained by the window, watching raindrops slide down the glass panels. Eventually, she went back to her desk and lit a cigarette.

The door was locked, a chair leg used as a deadbolt. It was Valya's idea. Valya had never been alone in a dorm room

with a girl before, but he did inherit his father's engineering skills.

Invisible to his female classmates, too shy to meet a girl at a birthday party, too awkward to pay attention to anything but his phone at school dances, Valya was terrified of appearing too weak, too spineless, too passive to Alyssa. He was afraid he'd lose his courage in her presence.

The room was clean, all the clothes stuffed in the closet, the twins' beds made up with blankets. A small orchid in a clear plastic cup stood on Valya's nightstand.

"It's for you," Valya said, offering the orchid to Alyssa. He suddenly decided it was a dumb gesture, but Alyssa smiled, and her eyes shone.

"It's pretty cool here, on the first floor. All these bars on the windows. We have them in our room, too."

Surprised, Valya glanced at the window. The curtains were tightly drawn.

"I love orchids," Alyssa said, taking the flower out of his hands. "Especially raspberry-colored, like this one."

"It's white," Valya said and immediately bit his tongue.

"My perception of the spectrum is skewed," Alyssa said casually, placing the orchid back on the nightstand. "What we see and what exists objectively are two different things. This orchid is raspberry-colored. You see it as white, but it may not even be an orchid at all."

The hamster began to fuss in its cage, trying to add to the conversation. Alyssa stared at the flower intently, as if completing a mental exercise. Valya wondered if her aggression toward him—that intense emotion that scared him so much—was nothing but a hysterical reaction to the shock she'd experienced.

"I don't like hamsters," Alyssa said ruefully.

Valya put his hands on her shoulders and sat her down

on his bed. Just yesterday, imagining this date had made him sweat profusely, blood rushing to different parts of his body, his ears ringing. And now his heart pounded in vain, the blood rushed nowhere at all, and Valya felt cold and empty, like a serpentarium freed of all the snakes. It looked as if he'd told the twins the truth: *Alyssa and I are just going to sit there and talk.*

However, Alyssa had no interest in talking. She simply stared somewhere off to the side. Valya counted to three, gathered all his courage, and kissed her on the mouth, as gently as he could manage. It was a very chaste kiss, their lips barely touching. The kiss produced a sound, delicate and a little funny, and Valya wanted to hear it again, so he kissed her again, and this time he tasted raspberries and salt. The raspberries came from her lip gloss, and the salt was Alyssa herself, her objective existence.

The orchid flew off the tilted nightstand. The bed creaked, accepting the weight of two bodies. The taste of salt led him on, like an ocean beckoning a newborn turtle or a ribbon of dried sweat along one's stomach.

And now Alyssa seemed to recognize it as well. Valya didn't rush; it wasn't his experience, it was pure instinct that told him to slow down, to allow them both to taste the honey of their secret places, and the salt on their lips, and the new, dizzying scent. Alyssa held him in her arms, responding gently, not aggressively like before, but bolder and more determined with each second. Valya felt their rhythms synchronize, and now everything was about to combine as if the two spheres connected at the center wished to restore the common surface area . . .

Remembering the exercise, Valya *claimed* Alyssa. He became Alyssa while retaining his own self. Caught in a hormonal flood, he had no idea of what was happening, but he wasn't scared. To him, sex he'd read about and seen in the movies was just like this: you feel your partner and you are your partner.

He learned everything about her: She was now scared of the rain. She had painful cramps. She dreamed of escaping the institute. She had one best friend in first grade, and then her family moved to another city, and she'd never been able to make other friends. She wanted to be with Valya because she didn't want to be alone.

A quarter of a breath later, Valya saw Alyssa, this girl with all her fears and fantasies, as a reflection of something bigger and something infinitely more important. Streams of meanings, layers, combinations of abstract images: concepts Valya could not understand but which he changed by his very presence.

That's when he got scared. He tried to push Alyssa away, to eject her from himself, but they were now a single entity, and the more Valya struggled, the deeper he fell into someone else's vague structures. Losing his mind in terror, he was about to turn inside out . . .

At that moment, he heard sounds coming through the door. Someone was kicking it in frustration. Under the force of the blows, the chair playing the role of a deadbolt toppled over, and the flimsy lock rattled, letting him know it wasn't going to hold out much longer.

Valya felt his body anew. He saw the room, the hamster's cage, and the orchid on the floor. He saw himself, his pants inexplicably pooled around his ankles, his shirt unbuttoned. Completely naked, Alyssa attempted to hide under the covers. Valya met her gaze, wondering if she knew what had transpired between them, but it didn't look like she had any idea. The knock on the door worked as an emergency brake, and all Alyssa remembered was that she was naked in someone else's bed and that an armed detachment of moral police was about to burst in. At least that was what all that noise indicated.

"Occupied!" Valya barked at the door, helpless with nervous laughter. He jumped up and pulled his underwear and jeans back on, then covered Alyssa up to the top of her head with a blanket. The door latch was living its last seconds on Earth.

"Who is it?" Valya asked, picking up the orchid and placing it back onto the nightstand.

"Do you know what time this is?" someone demanded behind the door, their voice full of quiet fury. Valya glanced at the clock.

"We still have one minute left," he said with dignity. "You're breaking our agreement."

"Open the door!"

"Arthur, one minute. That's all I ask."

"I'm timing you," Arthur said after a pause.

Valya leaned over the bed, lifted a corner of the blanket, and caressed Alyssa's warm head.

"Hey you . . . It was good, wasn't it?"

He was afraid of meeting her gaze. Not because he felt shy or ashamed. He was afraid of learning that she did know what he'd done to her.

Or what I'd almost done to her, Valya thought, shuddering. *I was ready to take her apart like a child with his toy. And I didn't know how it all worked.*

"Don't look," Alyssa whispered.

Just like before, Valya turned to face the window, waiting for her to get dressed. Outside, the rain had stopped knocking against the awnings. Oh, how scared she was of simple rain . . .

"I'm ready," Alyssa said.

Valya turned around. She stood in the middle of the room,

fully dressed, hair tousled, holding the orchid in both hands. The blanket covering the bed was slightly askew.

Valya stepped toward her and kissed her on the lips. The sound was delicate and a little funny. From the way she looked and smiled at him, Valya knew: She didn't remember, or she didn't understand, or perhaps she couldn't process the information. She even seemed happy, despite the banging on the door.

The door rumbled again, ready to fly off the hinges.

"Time's up!"

"It was really great," Alyssa said softly.

Passersby recoiled from his path. Staggering down the street, Pashka kept vomiting on the sidewalk. Gold coins rolled into the fallen leaves. At first, he picked them up, then he came to his senses and tossed out the whole handful. The coins jingled as they disappeared into the darkness.

It wasn't about those few minutes when he was a hamster and then he was dead. It was about Arthur's face, the human face leaning over the hamster's cage. The face Pashka saw every day in the mirror and could no longer recognize. Everything a team of psychologists tried to do when they were kids and then teenagers, everything was accomplished in one second. The thin threads connecting the brothers, the live nerves—cut, sliced, and ripped, but then restored every time—had been burned, and Pashka was afraid he wouldn't recognize his brother the next time he saw him.

After a walk along Torpa's streets, he felt marginally better. The decision came to him quickly and clearly. He didn't waver, not even for a second. He experienced something akin to joy as he stopped and inhaled the autumnal air. He realized he hadn't breathed since their grandfather went back into the house, leaving behind his broom.

From the hallway, he heard agitated voices. Peeking out from her room, his neighbor Stefa said:

"Grigoriev, your brother has gone crazy! He almost took the door off its hinges. We were about to call the super."

Stefa still couldn't tell the twins apart, but Pashka never had high expectations in that regard.

A single lamp was lit, and the room smelled of perfume and something else. The second Pashka realized that "something else" was the odor of a terrified hamster, he nearly lost all his courage.

"Get your goddamn rat out of here," Arthur said. He stood with his back to the door and spoke coldly, heavily. His stance and his tone made it very clear it was not an ordinary squabble between roommates. "Or leave with it."

"Or what?" Valya said, blocking the hamster's cage with his body. "It's my room, too. If you don't like it, feel free to leave yourself!"

"Arthur," Pashka said softly.

His brother turned. The lamp was right behind him, and so all Pashka saw was his silhouette.

"Pashka," Arthur said, his voice growing warmer. "Don't worry, I'll deal with it. This tail-less rat thing is not staying here in our room. Are you all right?"

Pashka reached for the light switch, but at the last moment, he changed his mind and left the overhead lights off.

"We need to talk," his brother said, reaching his hand to Pashka as he had done since they were babies. It was an offer to go off together, to leave everyone else behind, to talk without witnesses. "Come on."

"No," Pashka said, refusing to take Arthur's hand.

"I didn't think it was going to happen this way, and neither did you," Arthur said, his voice different now, low and tense. "I thought she was normal, adequate, that she was a smooth talker—but look at what she did! She made us do this . . . but hamsters only live two to three years anyway . . ."

Pashka recalled his struggle the night before to yank Arthur out of a stupor, trying—and failing—to find the right words. Last night Arthur did not believe Pashka; instead, he trusted Alexandra Igorevna, with her velvet gloves. And now, Pashka would have loved to believe Arthur, but he couldn't forget the face leaning over his cage.

He pulled his suitcase from underneath the bed, opened the closet, and began to throw stuff into the suitcase, trying to keep Arthur's clothes separate from his.

"What are you doing?" Arthur asked, his voice different yet again. "Where are you going?"

"I'm leaving Torpa," Pashka said.

Arthur stopped speaking. Pashka didn't look at his brother; he didn't want to see his face.

"They made you kill hamsters today," Valya said, not asking a question but rather thinking aloud.

Pashka stared into the nerd's face.

"They tried to make me do the same thing," Valya said, nodding. "She asked me to buy a hamster at a pet store. This hamster. I won't throw him away and I will never give him up."

Arthur took a second to process Valya's words. He sat down and held his head in his hands. Pashka couldn't see his face.

He lowered himself down on the floor, by Arthur's side. There was nothing left to say, as if the coins Pashka had thrown away on a cold autumnal night had been lost forever.

...

A table tennis lesson had ended long ago. Disassembled tables stood in the far corner of the gym; lost plastic balls hid under the benches like mice.

Coach strolled around the gym, picking up the balls and throwing them on the floor. If a ball bounced with a clear sound, Dima Dimych would stash it in his pocket. If a ball failed to produce a healthy bounce, Coach squashed it with his foot and tossed it into the trash bin.

One could watch it forever, Sasha thought, *like fire, running water, or the transformation of abstract concepts. That's how death walks around and harvests its victims. That's how Coach tests defective morphemes to remove them forever from the Great Speech.*

"Go ahead, speak," Coach said, picking up another plastic fragment off the floor.

"Why?"

"Why are you here?"

"I came to look at you," Sasha said tersely.

He transformed. Instead of a fit young man, Sasha saw an immense, multidimensional function, a trace of destruction, death, and decay within it.

"Have you had a good look?" he asked, restoring his human appearance.

"That's not what I meant, Dima."

"Then tell me. Lately, I've been struggling with understanding your hints, Password."

Sasha lit a cigarette and exhaled a puff of smoke. The gray cloud filled the entire gym up to its ceiling and formed a new system. Streams of meanings, ideas, and projections, fragments of the past and the future intertwined, changing, shifting, melting signs of decay into harmony, and destruction into development. Sasha admired her work: in its center, at the abstract point of the beginning of time, a spark rotated along the given orbit.

She would have liked to admire it a bit longer, but while she was sharing her plans with Coach, time stood still, and Torpa stood still, and soon the room felt suffocating and hot. Sasha exhaled. The window flew open, a gust of wind brought in a few yellow leaves, and the projection shattered.

"Have *you* had a good look?" Sasha asked.

"It's a gorgeous but faulty construction," Coach said. "You assume that your ideas would be implemented without a single bit of information lost in the process. And if your subjects, your molds, were complete Words, I'd be the first one to applaud your efforts. But they are people, Samokhina. That means there are an infinite number of unaccounted-for factors. Today you've split up the twins—"

"Because I don't want to lose either one of them."

"Because you expect the impossible from them. Did you really think that a first year and a hamster would open *the way in*? Just one first-year student? From a single access point?"

"He's a projection of an extremely powerful idea."

"He is a human being, first and foremost. He's inert and weak. Put away your cigarette. This is a temple of physical culture; you cannot smoke in here."

"Portnov has a different opinion," Sasha said, holding back her aggravation.

"Oleg Borisovich never enters the gym with the purpose of poisoning the atmosphere," Coach said, picking up a yellow leaf and tossing it out the window.

"Portnov thinks Grigoriev, A. is a powerful, valuable, possibly polysemic Word. And Pashka is a directional adverb, gifted, with a keen sense of vectors."

"They may have become these things if they had a chance to study. Time is against you, Samokhina."

Coach had an uncanny ability to confuse her, to stump her, to verbalize the most unpleasant versions of events. Defiantly, Sasha pulled another cigarette out of the pack.

"My brother is making amazing progress. He's developing faster than anyone else."

"Oh yes," Coach said, concentrating on the sound of a plastic ball hitting the floor. The ball jumped to the side, and Coach chased it down and squashed it with his foot like a tiny skull. "He's tearing himself out of matter just like you used to do. But back then, Farit Kozhennikov managed to hold you back, and there is no more Farit. Who's going to hold back your brother?"

"I will," Sasha said.

Coach shook his head.

"Good luck, assassin of reality."

Sasha flicked her lighter and realized that its source was spent. The lighter no longer worked, only a few sparks flew out. Gazing at the tiny fireworks, Sasha knew: something was happening to Valya right at that moment. Or perhaps it had already happened.

CHAPTER FOUR

Valya left the room carrying a backpack stuffed with textbooks and the hamster's cage. The hamster was gnawing on a piece of apple, unaware of being the center of all the passionate discourse. There was so much tension between the Grigoriev twins that Valya opted to leave them to their own devices, took his hamster, and got the hell out of their room.

There was no way Pashka would leave. Valya heard—Alyssa told him in absolute secrecy—that every first year packed their suitcase at least once.

Valya needed to see Alyssa as soon as possible.

In the next room, girls' voices lowered to a whisper, rose excitedly, then lowered again. Valya slowed down and stopped as if about to knock; instead, he pressed his ear to the door.

It was hard to make out individual words, but the tone of their voices was clear. Alyssa was saying something about different varieties of orchids, and how in the tropics they grew straight out of tree trunks. Her roommates did not ask any questions. Either they were the most tactful roommates in the world, or they understood what had happened and were jealous. He heard Alyssa laugh. If she only knew how close to the edge she'd got earlier that day. Valya himself wasn't quite sure.

"Are you eavesdropping? Trying to see if she liked it?"

His classmates, Samvel and Irwing, walked toward him carrying two bottles of soda. Considering their glee, the liquid inside the bottles was definitely not soda. This dorm was as transparent as an aquarium.

"Don't be jealous," Valya said, moving toward the exit. More than anything in the world he wanted to drink glass after glass of gin and tonic and laugh at dumb jokes.

In the lobby, a vaguely familiar second year was groping a girl with closely cropped hair. It looked like Eva had already recovered from heartbreak.

A second later Valya noticed her arms hanging listlessly by her sides. She didn't enjoy the touch of the second year's hands, she tolerated it because . . .

"Eva!" Valya said loudly. As if she'd been waiting for someone to call her name, she flinched and recoiled, and the second year lost his grip on her body. He was about to say something to Valya, something extremely rude, but one look at the cage with Valya's hamster made him change his mind. Valya realized this second year had been subjected to Alexandra Igorevna's hamster test before, and he most likely pressed that button.

In that moment, Valya wondered where Alexandra Igorevna got all her hamsters. Did they have that many at the store? Did hamsters procreate that quickly?

"I totally forgot," Eva said to the second year. "I need to . . . Tomorrow's class . . . I haven't . . ."

She smiled gratefully at Valya and ran; the second year gave Valya a dirty look and shuffled away without saying a word. Valya almost laughed at the absurdity of it, but just continued on.

He went out into the cold wet night. He sat on a bench near the dorm entrance and took out his phone. From his pocket, he pulled out a business card, the same one he'd wanted to throw away just like he'd thrown away a photo of a girl from the Missing Persons bulletin board.

He dialed the number, and a ringtone cried out only a couple of steps away. Valya flinched. Alexandra Igorevna stood by the entrance to the dorm, holding a ringing phone in her hand.

Her room in the attic was cozy and even nice, albeit very small. Valya would have thought a university provost could afford a private house, one of the many in Torpa. But this room was lovely, with a real fireplace, antique furniture, and a small balcony, and he could understand it's appeal, especially considering the commute.

Alexandra Igorevna opened the balcony door, unbothered by the cold autumnal night, and lit a cigarette. Valya moved closer to the fireplace. The cage stood by his feet.

The walls were covered with pages ripped out of notebooks, albums, and sketch pads. Most of them had been scribbled on, some displaying abstract patterns; amid them, black-and-white portraits of the occupant of this room stood out starkly. At a closer look, Valya realized these were not photographs but rather pencil drawings, more realistic than any photograph. From every portrait, Alexandra's eyes stared back at him, her gaze sometimes as piercing as a shard of ice, sometimes softened by shadows, as if turned inward.

"Are you scared?" Alexandra asked softly.

"Yes," Valya said. "I want to know what happened to me, and to Alyssa. I want to know who I am—what I am *now*."

. . .

Sasha watched him through the curtain of cigarette smoke. Perhaps that curtain in front of her eyes was of a different origin. Since that day in June when they first spoke face-to-face, Valya had grown up. He looked a little bit like his father, a little bit like their mom, but there was nothing of Sasha in him, nothing at all . . .

Aside from that tiny shard. That fragment that had become impossibly valuable. Aside from a shadow of a verb in the imperative mood.

"The thing is that you and I are doing great," she said. "We're doing exceptionally well. You located your free will when asked to kill a hamster. You showed immense talent by learning to work with mental transformations so quickly. You can ask me anything. I will always answer, and I will always explain."

"I don't understand," he said hesitantly.

"That's perfectly normal. You're still learning. Any kind of study starts with 'I don't understand.'"

"I didn't kill my hamster," Valya said. "But Arthur did. Even though he didn't want to. And now he feels as if he's murdered himself. Why?"

Sasha took a deep drag of her cigarette.

Arthur had killed Yaroslav's projection inside himself and murdered Pashka, so fluffy and so helpless at that moment in time. Pashka and Arthur used to think of themselves as one person, and in some ways, that's what they used to be.

Today, she'd separated them. Not surgically, with a scalpel, but with an ax, in one great blow. Perhaps she'd saved them. But maybe she hadn't.

But even though she had just said he could ask her anything, it didn't mean she'd have to tell him everything.

"Valya, when you refused to kill the hamster," Sasha said gently. "Can you describe how you felt at that moment?"

He thought about it, raising his hand to his throat as if fighting a bout of nausea. He shook his head.

"You can't describe it because you didn't understand it," Sasha said with a sigh. "It's too early."

"Why do we need to kill hamsters?" Valya asked, a hint of reproach in his voice.

"Because you *shouldn't* kill them," Sasha said. "I am very pleased with you, Valya. Even more, I am proud of you." She put out her cigarette and closed the balcony door.

"You ask what you are now. That's not so easy to say. What I can tell you is that you and I must solve a very important problem that will ultimately teach you how to answer that yourself. We must teach you internal discipline. That means that from now on all your work will be done either in an auditorium, at the library, or in my office—under supervision. That means that you will be attending gym classes, you will follow Dmitry Dmitrievich's instructions, you will eat at the cafeteria, you will take notes in your Philosophy class, you will read Shakespeare in your English class, but you will not attack any mental exercises on your own. If you do, these mental exercises will attack you back."

Valya said nothing. He was a quick thinker, much sharper than Sasha in the olden days. The times were a-changing indeed.

"If you try these exercises without supervision, you will lose direction," Sasha said. "You are going to feel omnipotent. You will see the world in a different projection."

"The way it really is?"

"No. You will see the most precise model of what you're capable of understanding. But it will be very different from what you're used to seeing since you were a child. It might terrify you."

He nodded and even managed a crooked smile.

"Anyway, when you begin to lose perspective, when you feel like you're falling into an irrational pocket, you must stop."

"*Can* it be stopped?" he asked hopelessly. "This curse?"

"Curse?" Sasha said, practically sputtering. "Valya, this is your future. It's your mission, your goal, and you will soon understand it. It will make you happy and it will make the world beautiful. All of this I promise you. But you're not ready—not yet. Because you can't control it. Let's take it step by step: first, control, then fulfillment. Do you understand me?"

He nodded again, still looking down. Sasha met the eyes of one of her self-portraits. As she watched, the image became three-dimensional, then four-, then multidimensional.

Sasha shut her eyes. She stepped toward Valya and stood very close, putting her arm around his shoulders. She remembered the scent of his head when he was a baby. The adult Valya smelled differently, but Sasha still felt their connection. She knew him so well, he was right there, and so was the Verb, the perfect instrument of the Speech, and all she needed to do was to reach over, and pull, and raise, and cultivate.

He's not an instrument, Sasha thought furiously. *He's still a person, he's my brother, and he deserves to be loved.*

"I need you, honey," Sasha said, holding him tight and listening to the quickened beating of his heart. "If only you knew how much I need you. I can't explain everything to you now, you simply won't understand. You might get scared. But you need to know that everything I am doing and will be doing is necessary. There is no other way."

Sasha let go of him and stepped away. Instinctively, Valya moved closer to the fireplace as if Sasha's embrace had made him frost over.

"Speaking of control and discipline," Sasha said in her normal voice. "I would like to introduce you to someone."

There was a light knock on the door, and Kostya entered. He never came empty-handed, and this time he brought a large cardboard box that smelled of baked goods, and a toolbox.

"Valya, meet Konstantin Faritovich," Sasha said.

Judging by Valya's expression, he'd heard that name before.

Valya imagined Konstantin Faritovich as an ancient, ugly creature. In front of him stood a man no older than thirty, with a pale, delicate face, half obscured by impenetrable dark glasses. He wore jeans and a short black coat. Had he met this man on the street, Valya wouldn't have noticed him—if it weren't for the glasses.

"Hello," Konstantin Faritovich said. "You can call me Kostya."

Valya glanced at Alexandra questioningly. A few seconds ago, this woman had managed to surprise him yet again. He more or less knew the difference between hypocrisy and true tenderness, both sisterly and familial. He wasn't ready to accept this tenderness from Alexandra Igorevna, but she gave it a good college try: having essentially lost his parents, Valya was pretty close to buying it.

But now, there was this man in dark glasses.

"Next time you see the world as a system of meanings and another person as a sum of informational streams, you must stop and return to what we're going to call a normal state— this terminology should be familiar to you," Alexandra said gently. "If you don't stop on your own, help will be provided. But then it will be considered a failure on your part, and you will have consequences."

Valya looked back at Konstantin Faritovich. The man smelled of baked goods. *Will I hate the smell of fresh bread for the rest of my life?* Valya wondered.

"Alyssa is very attached to you," Alexandra said. Valya flinched: What did Alyssa have to do with any of this?

Alexandra nodded, pleased with his quick reaction.

"Every time you fail, Alyssa will be placed into a temporal loop. At first for one day, then for two, then proportional to your mistake. It won't be tragic, but she won't like it."

"It's not fair," Valya said hoarsely. "Why her, not me?"

"Because that's how this works," Alexandra said, smiling sadly. "It all depends on you. If you act responsibly and concentrate on—"

She fell silent, as if someone had pulled or jerked her from within. She frowned, speaking inaudibly to someone invisible, then glanced at Konstantin Faritovich.

"Sex," Konstantin Faritovich said softly. "Can't ask for the impossible. Remember the hormones."

"Right, they are all so hypersexual at this age," Alexandra murmured, as if quoting someone, as if there was some hidden meaning in all this, as if it were funny.

Konstantin Faritovich smiled a crooked, very human smile. He placed the pastry box on the table and his toolbox on the desk, on top of papers and pencil sketches.

"Don't touch Alyssa," Valya said as firmly as he could. "Don't touch her, she's already been damaged by you! If necessary, I will never approach her again!" His voice cracked. "I will live my entire life without sex! It's not that big of a deal."

Konstantin Faritovich opened his toolbox and took out a strange metal contraption. Valya stared.

"You can look away," Konstantin Faritovich said softly.

"But it's not scary at all. What is scary is you being unprepared and falling into an irrational pocket—that is terrifying indeed. And this—this will just make you fashionable."

Konstantin Faritovich pressed on the top of Valya's head like a policeman stuffing a criminal into the cruiser, forcing him to sit down in front of the fireplace. Valya felt his hand on his skull. Konstantin Faritovich didn't have to hold him; Valya was paralyzed, like a caterpillar stuffed into a black wasp's nest. Something touched his left ear, and he felt a sharp pain that went away almost immediately.

"Don't touch it before you wash your hands," Konstantin Faritovich said, a worried look on his face. "It should heal properly very quickly, but if you have any issues, you can call me. Take a look in the mirror."

Konstantin Faritovich took a round mirror from one of the desk drawers—he clearly felt right at home in this apartment— and handed it to Valya. Valya saw his own pale face, dark circles under his eyes, and only then—a tiny earring in his earlobe. It was a plain hoop made of white metal, no stones or embellishments. There was no blood, and the earlobe was only slightly reddened.

"I'll make sure Mom knows you got your ear pierced," Alexandra said, looking at him as if judging his new jewelry. "She'll be mad, but I'll make sure she's happy you only pierced your ear, and not your belly button or something worse."

Konstantin Faritovich packed the piercing contraption into his toolbox. Seeing both himself and the room from the outside, Valya felt a jolt of surprise: it was simply a small piercing tool, and yet that toolbox looked like it contained a vast multitude of torture devices. Was it a version of an executioner's bag? Valya's classmates must have had reasons to be that terrified of the man because he wasn't that far off himself.

"That earring is going to protect Alyssa," Alexandra Igorevna said. "Sooner or later, you will find yourself in the throes of passion and will see the girl as a system of meanings. You'll want to analyze this complex projection and take over the resulting information. The earring will signal for you to stop, and you will not suffer consequences."

Konstantin Faritovich nodded in agreement and slapped a plaster over Valya's earlobe. Valya didn't even get a chance to flinch; all he saw was his own doubled reflection in the dark lenses.

"The earring works only on hormones," Alexandra continued. "In all other cases, please control your own urges. If you don't, you will get reported, and Konstantin Faritovich does not accept apologies."

"I wouldn't mind apologies," the man in the dark glasses said under his breath.

"Valya, go home," Alexandra said, smiling. "You can leave your hamster here for now, I'll take care of it. Right now, your hamster would not be welcomed in your room."

Arthur blocked the door, pushing his arms against the frame.

"I won't let you go! You don't know anything!"

"I know more than you," Pashka said, hitching up his backpack. "I am not staying here. Let them stop me."

"We've tried to run away before, remember?"

"I'm not afraid anymore," Pashka said, stepping toward the door. "If you don't want to come with me, let me go."

Arthur slowly shook his head.

"No. I can tell you what's going to happen. One, they will bring you back. Two, Grandpa and Grandma's house will burn down. Grandpa is going to go blind in the fire, Grandma will lose her will to live. Three—"

"None of this will happen!" Pashka screamed. "Enough of your bullshit. I'm going to tell Dad everything, and he's going to come and get you out of here!"

"Idiot," Arthur said, pushing his back against the locked door. "He's not coming. His plane will crash with all his passengers. And only wreckage and debris will be found."

He spoke as if he'd already seen all of this, down to the minute detail. He looked as if the burning debris reflected in his eyes. Pashka's inner gaze saw things that Arthur hadn't even mentioned: the harvested field, ambulances, trucks, confused and shocked medical personnel who didn't know what to do. An airline logo on the tail of the aircraft burned to a crisp.

"No," Pashka said, shaking his head to rid his mind of the nightmares Arthur had manifested. Almost immediately, he recalled a child's inflatable ball by the tall riverbank—a symbol of death that comes to everyone, always unannounced. A ball by the riverbank, gold coins in the grass, Arthur's face over the cage. The world was not the same, it was different again; the world turned another facet toward Pashka, then another, and every facet was more horrifying than the others.

Should he tell Arthur who that hamster really was? Or shouldn't he? What would Arthur do if he found out? What would Pashka do if he managed to stay silent?

"I wanted to—" Pashka began hoarsely, but at that moment the broken latch flew off, and the door opened. Arthur nearly fell backward into the hallway. Valya barely managed to jump off to the side.

Valya carried his backpack, but not the hamster's cage. His

left earlobe was covered with a piece of plaster. Pashka wondered if the hamster had bit him.

"Are you taking your clothes for a walk?" Valya asked, looking at Pashka's backpack.

Arthur blocked the door once more.

"I'm not letting you go," he said again.

"Leave me alone," Pashka said heavily. "I'm not leaving, I'm just moving. To another room. I can't look at you, and I can't listen to your bleating anymore."

He took advantage of the fact that Arthur had lost both his ability to speak and his steam and walked out.

"You were there, weren't you? What happened, do you know?"

Alyssa pulled Valya into her room, adorned by a single orchid. Stefa and Tonya seemed to have been waiting for him to arrive. Everyone complimented his new earring. Alyssa held his hand, and Valya felt a little better.

"What was the fight all about? They even hit each other; did you see that? Was it because of Eva?"

"No idea," Valya lied.

"Where's your hamster? They say you took it back to the store; did you actually?"

"I just gave it to a friend for a few days."

Valya's lies were clearly written on his face, but the girls were too preoccupied to notice.

"Don't worry," Valya said to Alyssa. "I'll deal with the twins."

She didn't know what he meant but still responded with a smile.

"I'm not afraid."

She lightly touched the earring in his aching ear; Valya didn't know if her gesture caused more joy or pain.

...

"Listen carefully, my young friends," Sasha said. She wanted to straddle the chair, as Farit liked to do, but she didn't think it would be appropriate. Instead, she sat up straighter, reached for a new sketchbook, and picked a freshly sharpened pencil out of a cup. Without looking, she began to trace perfect circles on a blank page, all different diameters, but with a common center.

The conversation was held in her basement office. She wanted to get up and move, but the Grigoriev brothers had excellent manners: remaining seated while she was up on her feet would make them feel awkward.

Pashka wanted to get up as well. As a matter of fact, he wanted to move and throw punches. Swaying back and forth in his chair and clenching his fists, he stared at Sasha with hatred as if longing to kill her right there, in her office, in the politest way possible.

"For starters, regarding your voluntary room assignments. We've had issues with random moving before, and the super has been too lenient. She's been reprimanded. Grigoriev, P., you are to return to your originally assigned room 6. Grigoriev, A., you are to move to room 28. You will have one roommate, a third year. You should not have any issues sharing a room with him."

Frozen in his spot, Arthur nodded without saying a word.

Sasha glanced at the sheet of paper in front of her. The primitive harmony of concentric circles had been disrupted. It drowned in chaotic lines and tangled threads. Sasha's hand moved independently, tracing a portrait from within, a portrait of a shifting, changing world.

"I'm going to do something," Sasha said, pointedly looking at the brothers. "You know that words are actions, right? I am going to say something, and it'll change both of you. Get ready."

She took her time choosing a new, sharpened pencil to replace her dull one. Both Grigoriev brothers stared at her, and only at her. Arthur sat up straighter, and Pashka stopped fidgeting.

"Arthur, Pashka didn't tell you all the truth about the day you killed that hamster."

"Don't!" Pashka said, rising from his chair. The reflection of Word inside him became brighter. Sasha squinted: the Speech needed these two, but oh, how difficult it was to work with them. It was truly unbearable.

Her pencil was about to tear through the paper.

"Arthur has a right to know—it's crucial for both of you. But it would be better if you told him yourself, Pashka."

Grigoriev, P. stepped toward the door. Sasha wondered how many times he'd left the room like that, holding his head proud and high. A rebel, as Kostya called him.

"Stop," Sasha said softly. Pashka froze by the door. As if not trusting himself, he turned and looked at her in surprise, unsure of the force that held him back.

"Sit down," Sasha said, pointing at his chair. "We are not done talking."

He went back and sat down, still looking very surprised. *It's such a pity I can't order you to study,* Sasha thought. *But I can't. An obedient idiot who doesn't mature and overcome obstacles will never become a Word.*

"Arthur," Sasha said, putting the blackened page into a plastic folder. "You did not kill that hamster. That hamster was your brother, whose material form I had changed temporarily. This action is not beneficial for matter in general because it violates the laws of physics, but it does not affect grammatical laws. You should think of it as the hamster being just as alive as your brother. Pashka didn't betray you—he simply needed time to recover from the trauma."

A reflection of a Word stirred inside Arthur. Sasha gripped the edge of the table: no, it was not an adverb. Portnov was right. What was it? The spectrum was so wide. It wasn't a verb, wasn't a noun. Perhaps clouding her ability to read it was that there was a hint of Yaroslav in him, the real, true Yaroslav.

"Starting today, additional individual sessions will be scheduled for you," Sasha said. "With me. We will study here, in this office, every Wednesday and Saturday. I will give you all the necessary study materials. I want to see both of you at each session, at eighteen hundred hours."

"Stupid old bitch," Pashka said.

Arthur flinched as if poked with a live wire.

"I know who you are," Pashka said, spitting out each word with cold fury. "You are Torpa itself. You're the spirit at the heart of this cursed place. I know, I saw it. How dare you send flowers to our grandparents? How dare you say the word 'love' with that filthy mouth of yours? Just die already!"

He took a step toward Sasha's desk. Silently, Arthur flung himself onto his brother's shoulders. At that moment in time, both were so powerful that Sasha felt genuine fear on their behalf.

"Stop," she said quietly.

Arthur let go of his brother and stepped back. Pashka kneeled in the middle of the office; his nose was bleeding. Sasha reached for a pack of tissues and tossed it to Pashka. The tissues landed right next to the first few drops of blood on the hardwood floor.

"Calm down," she said to Arthur. "No one is reporting this. Arthur, go ahead and move your stuff to room 28. It'll be good for both of you to live separately, meet new people, and diversify your experience. I will make sure Konstantin Faritovich leaves you alone—until your exams, obviously."

Pashka dripped blood all over the floor, ignoring the tissues. Sasha waited for the door to close behind Arthur.

"You'll understand everything in time," she said to Pashka. "I promise. And he will understand everything as well. Come to your individual session. I will try to explain as much as I can."

He looked up, his eyes dry, bright, and furious.

"I am not coming back here. Do whatever you want."

PART IV

CHAPTER ONE

was eighteen years old. I came home for my winter break. We lived in the same apartment. The baby's crib was in Mom and Valentin's bedroom, and the second bedroom was still mine. I grew up in that room. I was going back to Torpa the next day, and I had no idea what would happen to me next, whether I would ever return, and whether I would remain human. Look, it's snowing. It was snowing then, too, but it was February, not December."

The fire was burning in the fireplace; the draft pulled the smoke out of the chimney, and a hint of it came back through the window. *Everything is a circle,* she thought. *Or a spiral.*

Very recently, Valya learned that birch made the best firewood. Outside the balcony door, snow fell in large clumps, a real, fluffy, New Year's Eve type of snow. A plate of orange biscuits stood in front of Valya. He held a cup of tea with both hands, warming them on the white and blue porcelain.

Now he knew why she never came home. She wasn't jealous, she just didn't know how to admit to Mom that she was no longer human. There was no way to bring things back to where they were. She couldn't explain; there was no way to explain anything.

"What am I going to tell my parents when they come back?"

Valya asked, holding his hand over the steaming cup. "They planned on being away for six months, so they are coming back in February."

"They'll stay in India a little longer and come back in July," Alexandra said. "Don't worry. They won't think anything's wrong, just don't mention Torpa in their presence."

"Talking to them will be weird," Valya said, looking at the hamster in its cage. It looked like the hamster was well taken care of; its fur was very shiny.

"You'll only be home for a week in the summer, and then you'll leave for your summer internship."

"Alyssa told me," Valya said, nodding his head. "To harvest cherries, plums . . . apples. Essential skills for academic studies."

"The internships are usually held during the deconstruction period," Alexandra said, acknowledging his irony. "It's a simple, calm, monotonous life with plenty of fresh air. Adequate physical efforts, beautiful views, nature . . ."

Valya tensed up. Alexandra wasn't exactly lying, but she was hiding something important, perhaps the most important thing.

"Yes," she said, answering his silent question. "Our plans may change. It depends on the readiness levels."

"Whose readiness?"

"Many people's," she said vaguely. She pointed to the plate of biscuits. "Try one."

"I don't really like sweets, thanks."

"Perhaps you'll like this one. Just try it."

Valya sniffed a biscuit. The smell had nothing in common with Konstantin Faritovich's box of baked goods. There was a hint of orange peel, cinnamon, and something familiar. He struggled to remember.

"Mom keeps our phone number the same," he said, surprising himself. "And she never changes the lock on the door. In case someone comes back and can call or enter right away."

"It's a ritual," Alexandra said wistfully. "She stopped waiting a long time ago. You'll know why."

"I already know," he said.

"You're growing up so fast," Alexandra said. "Do you remember stealing a jar of pills and playing with them, when you were a toddler?"

"No," Valya said, taking a delicate bite of the biscuit.

"That was the second time you came very close to dying," Alexandra said, staring at the fire. "Or maybe you didn't. I don't know for sure."

"Alexandra Igorevna," Valya said. "Children don't die, do they?"

"Call me Sasha," she said, shifting away from the fireplace and fixing her hair. It was tied back in a ponytail, like Portnov's. "We can be casual when we're not at the institute."

"I'm more used to calling you Alexandra Igorevna," Valya said, looking away. "Anyway . . . can children die or not?"

"I was born in a world in which children died," Alexandra said slowly. "And so did adults. And where aircrafts crashed."

Valya shut his eyes for a second. Even now, after many months of many discoveries, he shuddered at the memory of that red line on the scheduling board at the airport: *No survivors.*

"There was no threat to your parents," Alexandra said, reading his thoughts. "But only because I established universal laws where aircrafts don't crash. I made this decision, and I made it happen."

Valya took another bite and concentrated on the taste. There was something so familiar about it: orange peel, cinnamon. A ticking clock, a slightly open window, a kitchen curtain . . .

"Are you the creator of our world?"

"No," she said patiently. "Human speech is not designed to handle these concepts. A language in its infancy cannot explain the difference between a giraffe and case law. I am Password. I am what opens reality, like a key. But a key does not define the laws of the room it opens. Password does. To a degree."

Valya chewed his biscuit. It was so small, yet so full of smell and taste. A few grains of cottage cheese, vanilla, a hint of bitter orange peel.

"When I rid the world of fear, or so I thought," Alexandra continued, "I made a mistake. I shouldn't have destroyed concepts, erased Words from the memory of the Great Speech. Instead, I should have assigned them different values, but that's something I didn't understand until much, much later. You see, there is no such thing as 'the true world.' There is only the world we're ready to see and accept."

Her explanation reminded him of Portnov's tirades, but Portnov seemed to talk only to make students feel inadequate and lazy. Alexandra's words made Valya freeze inside, even though he understood very little, even less than in Oleg Borisovich's class.

"What do you mean, 'different values'?"

"Think of yourself before we met. What did the word 'fear' mean to you?"

"Something unpleasant," Valya said after a pause. "Like forgetting homework, getting yelled at."

"And after we met?"

Valya wiped sweat off his forehead. His hand shook.

"It's still hard for me to explain," she said, nodding in understanding. "But when you and I reach our goal, *fear* will return into this world as a concept, and *choice* will follow, as an idea. A directed effort in the name of love. The same thing that motivated you when you chose not to kill that hamster."

"'When you and I reach our goal?'"

Alexandra nodded.

"But I didn't love that hamster, not at all," Valya said. He felt shaken.

The hamster scurried inside its house, as if deeply offended.

"And why is fear necessary?" Valya asked. "I don't understand, what's the point of this stupid fear?"

"The sooner you understand, the better it'll be for both of us," Alexandra said, turning her face to the fire. "Then I would be able to speak to you on equal terms. Or nearly equal. And depending on your success or failure . . ."

She fell silent. Following her gaze, Valya looked into the flames.

Tongues of fire flickered before his eyes, forming abstract patterns from his textbook. Valya held his breath like a diver and forced a picture into existence: chaotic movement of gray and black dots, static interference, white noise. He blinked and realized he was blind. He blinked again, and his vision returned. Birch logs burned in the fireplace; there were no more streams, meanings, or multidimensional structures.

Valya exhaled and wiped his moist forehead again. He grabbed another biscuit from the plate and chewed it vigorously, not because he was hungry, but because the sense of taste brought him back to reality. Still chewing, he glanced at Alexandra and suddenly felt shy. Her face had a very strange expression. He'd never seen her look like this. Her face reflected tenderness. It showed pride. He wondered what was happening.

"You'll succeed," Alexandra said, her voice so soft the crackling of the fire almost drowned it out. "You're the best student I've ever seen, Valya."

Again, he knew she wasn't lying, and her admiration scared him a little. Involuntarily, he reached for the silver earring in his earlobe. "The best student," she said. They'd set him up quite cleverly by making Alyssa a hostage. He hadn't had a single failure in two and a half months; he'd learned to control himself almost automatically, and he applied this newly found self-control every time the world would begin to collapse into the system of abstractions.

Alyssa didn't know she was a hostage, and this tied Valya to her even more strongly. He was desperately horny all the time, and no amount of studying or exercises could dull his desire. As luck would have it, they couldn't find a place to be alone for a whole week after Valya got his earring. Having to find a place to hide only made them want each other more. When they finally found themselves alone, the piece of silver in Valya's ear became as hot as a chunk of coal. Valya's scream of surprise and pain had nothing to do with passion, and Alyssa got scared.

That night Valya found wire cutters in the closet and tried to cut the earring out. The earring wouldn't budge. In frustration, Valya was ready to cut his whole ear off, but at that moment, Alyssa knocked on the door and was so nice to Valya that he started crying.

They locked the door and secured it with a chair leg. A few minutes later they forgot about everything else. This time, Valya did not experience any transformations, and no ideas or abstractions bothered him. He saw Alyssa, he smelled and tasted Alyssa, he loved Alyssa. They fell asleep, comfortable and happy in each other's arms. Eventually, Valya woke up and looked at his watch; still grinning, he opened the door and peeked outside.

Across the hallway, Pashka sat on a borrowed chair, reading his Philosophy textbook.

"You're the best student I've ever seen," Alexandra repeated. This time she seemed embarrassed by her own grandiloquence. "I'll speak to the super. Hopefully, she'll find a room for you and Alyssa, just so you won't have to hide like mice, and that Grigoriev, P. won't have to sit in the kitchen or perch on windowsills."

"Thank you," Valya said sincerely. "These biscuits . . ."

He suddenly froze, analyzing the taste and the aroma, feeling each crumb on his tongue. Orange, cinnamon, cottage cheese, butter, flour . . . jam.

"It's Mom's birthday biscuit recipe," Valya said hoarsely. "When I was little . . ."

He saw a table set with a tablecloth, a clock in the shape of a cat moving its eyes from left to right, its tail marking seconds. Birthday cake, candles, a large platter of biscuits, and Mom, so very young, her hand resting lightly on his father's shoulder.

"You finally tasted it," Alexandra said softly.

"How do you know? How do you remember it, Sasha?"

"I remember a lot," she said, her eyes smiling. "I remember what happened, and what didn't. I think I'm about to remember what will happen soon."

The winter exam schedule was posted on the bulletin board. Alyssa waltzed around the lobby, singing.

"I got an automatic pass for Specialty! I got an automatic pass for Specialty, yay! And for the Introduction to Practical Studies, too!"

Her former roommates, a black-haired girl and a redhead, watched her with irritation and envy. The bell rang.

These days, Pashka sat in the first row next to Valya. Arthur was left alone in the last row by the window. At first, Pashka had to fight the urge to look back. Then he got used to it, in the same way a one-armed man gets used to no longer being able to clap his hands.

Sometimes Pashka thought it was a good thing that the provost bitch told Arthur the truth. At least now there were no more secrets or lies between them. And no dead hamster, either. There was an involuntary manslaughter and Arthur's face over the cage, but whatever, shit happened.

Obviously, Pashka never went to any of Alexandra's individual sessions, and no one said a word about it. He was rather surprised when she canceled Arthur's sessions as well but tried not to dwell on it. It was none of his business.

Arthur's current roommate was a third year named Igor. Pashka orchestrated a few "casual" conversations with Igor; the guy was obsessed with his studies and some basic life skills, like getting food, doing laundry, and replacing burned-out light-bulbs. "Matter is meaningless," Igor would say. "Our room on the second floor is warm and dry. Soon we'll have our next exams." He would sigh with such despair that Pashka eventually stopped talking to him.

In gym class, Arthur stood at the very end of the line into the locker room and would enter it when Pashka was on his way out. In the beginning, the entire class watched their "fight" or "disagreement," making bets on how soon the twins would make up or who would be the first one to ask for forgiveness. Some students thought the brothers fought over Eva. Miraculously, Eva finally learned to tell them apart.

She chose Arthur. She learned his habits and his routes; she entered the kitchen exactly when Arthur was making coffee and offered him an extra sandwich. Tonya and Stefa reported everything to Pashka, until he asked them to keep their gossip to themselves. His tone was polite yet firm, and now Tonya and Stefa avoided him.

Surprisingly, Valya never asked any questions. He was either that smart, or too preoccupied with his own relationship.

Portnov kept them very busy with homework. Mid-semester, everyone—not just the overachiever Shanin—were given books of mental exercises. All the chatter, all the gossip, and all the bets stopped immediately. Tears came more often, and some students were getting more aggressive with each other. When Irwing and Samvel came to blows in the kitchen, half the dishes had to be replaced. Only Valya and his Alyssa seemed to be above it all; they could do anything, and they did everything well. Pashka wasn't even mad about having to give up his room every now and then. They looked so happy together.

The weather was gloomy but dry, and Pashka spent hours taking solitary walks around Torpa. He'd go to the river and watch dry leaves float on the mirror surface of the water. He felt as if he'd been stuck in the fog all these months, from mid-October. These days he rarely reached for *Textual Module*. What could he possibly find in there? Either nonsense or lies, and the latter much worse than the former.

"Grigoriev, P., what did I just say?"

"That winter exams are coming," Pashka said without thinking. He was sure Portnov had said something similar, and fortune favored the bold.

"Please come up to the whiteboard," Portnov said, his tone rather unpleasant.

The auditorium went still. Portnov rarely called anyone up to the whiteboard, and when he did, it usually ended badly.

Pashka's heart skipped a bit, but he wasn't scared. With time, Portnov's threats turned into not much more than an annoying fly buzzing around. Pashka got up and walked toward the front of the class. He turned and faced them; the first person he saw was Arthur in the last row by the window.

Arthur stared at him with such horror that Pashka felt uneasy. He saw for the first time how much Arthur had changed. No wonder Eva could now tell them apart.

"Danilova, come up here, please," Portnov said.

Is he reading my thoughts? Pashka thought with displeasure. *Why did I think of her just now?*

Eva walked up the aisle like a model sauntering down the runway, and stopped by the door, staring above her classmates' heads. Her cropped black hair stood up on her head like feathers on a knight's helmet.

"These two are getting dangerously close to failing the upcoming exam," Portnov said. "I don't mean one or two takes, I mean *failing*, as in not passing, ever. Considering that recruitment was based on the new grammatical reform, that it was originally composed of particularly strong students, and that in the beginning of the semester nothing hinted at any sort of trouble—considering all these factors, this is a catastrophe."

Arthur got up and raised his hand.

"What's the matter, Grigoriev, A.?" Portnov asked, casting a heavy, inhibitory gaze above his glasses. Arthur stood still for a moment, then sat down without saying a word, hunched over so low that Pashka saw only the top of his head. Portnov remained silent, letting the "catastrophe" sink in. Pashka recalled how much Portnov had reprimanded him during the last few individual sessions. Considering that Portnov always reprimanded everyone, Pashka didn't pay any particular attention.

"Oleg Borisovich, I will pass," Eva said, her voice unusually high and fragile. "I promised!"

Pashka realized that Eva was about to cry in front of the

entire class, and that he couldn't let it happen. He wouldn't let it happen. He stepped toward Eva and took her hand, for the first time since they met.

"Don't take it personally. This is a teaching moment. Oleg Borisovich wants us to read his stupid *Modules* that are full of lies, and do exercises that are—"

"Shut up!" Arthur shouted. "Haven't you had enough? Shut your mouth!"

Eva pulled her hand away, staring at Pashka in distress; at least she no longer looked about to cry.

"You'll pass the exam," Pashka said again, a wave of courage coursing through him. He felt like an imaginary hamster breaking through the bars of its cage and closing its teeth on the throat of its observer. "Don't be afraid."

He turned to face his classmates.

"Our year is extremely talented, everyone says so! Alexandra Igorevna says so herself, although she lies more than *Modules*."

"Leave Alexandra Igorevna out of it," Valya said. "You don't know anything about her."

"What if we all stopped studying and got out of Torpa?" Pashka said. "Would our advisor catch everyone at the same time?"

"Idiot," Arthur groaned despondently.

"Hush," Portnov said. The silence returned; only Arthur breathed heavily, and the wind whistled softly in the slightly open window. "Grigoriev, P. and Danilova, take your seats, everyone has seen enough of you. And has heard enough of you."

Pashka let Eva go first. This time, she walked as if toward the chopping block.

"I am partly to blame," Portnov continued in the same tone of voice. "I didn't report you to your advisors when I should have done so. But it's too late now, the exam is scheduled for

January 2. The only student in Group A to get an automatic pass is . . ."

He paused, waiting for Pashka to sit down.

"Is Valentin Shanin," Portnov concluded. "End of class. You're free to go."

Alyssa caught up with Valya at the door to auditorium 1. She hugged him, openly, their relationship no longer a secret to anyone.

"I got an automatic pass for Specialty!"

"Me too," Valya said.

"Really?" she asked, jumping up and down like a little kid. "Yay! Can you help me with the winter concert? We are having one around New Year's Eve, and they are making me organize it. You'll help me, won't you?"

About ten paces away from them, Group A formed a tight circle by the equestrian statue. Something was happening in the center of the circle. Everyone was watching Arthur shaking his doppelgänger by the shoulders, silently screaming—almost hissing—into his face. Eva stood nearby, surrounded by her classmates. Her blue eyes seemed to be shielded by a layer of ice.

"What's going on?" Alyssa said, finally noticing her surroundings.

"Portnov said two people would fail the winter exam," Valya said. "Pashka and Eva."

"Oh no," Alyssa said, and her face fell. "But . . ."

Valya squeezed her hand, then let go and walked toward the twins.

"I'll fucking pass everything," Pashka said, shaking his brother's hands off his shoulders. "Get your paws off me. I will pass everything, and so will Eva. And even if we fail, whatever, no big deal."

"I'm going to kill you," Arthur said very clearly.

"Wouldn't be the first time," Pashka said, shrugging.

Valya had never seen a human being turn from dark red to gray in a matter of seconds. Arthur turned and walked toward the exit even though the bell was about to ring, and their next class was Philosophy. Pashka turned his head; Valya thought he was about to run after Arthur.

But Pashka stayed. He took Eva's hand and gazed into everyone's anxious, curious, frightened faces.

"Show's over. Forget what you've just seen."

That night Valya called Sasha. He didn't do it often; usually she called him. No matter how often she told him he could come over every day and no one would have to know, Valya did not abuse the privilege.

He did like her little place in the attic. He liked it very much. It was quiet and cozy, it felt homey, and most important, Sasha told him so much about their mom and all the years Valya didn't remember.

Sometimes he would ask:

"Which grammatical reality was it in?"

"The one that became my first," she'd say. "But I'm not vain enough to count texts starting with myself."

It was later that Valya learned about another reality, the one where Mom didn't have a husband named Valentin. In that reality, she had no son. She only had Sasha, who hadn't run away to Torpa. Valya listened to these stories as greedily as cave children listened to adults' conversations around the fire. The world in which Valya didn't exist did not scare him. It was just another narrative, just another text.

The day Portnov announced that Eva and Pashka would fail their winter exams, Valya dialed her number.

Something was different in her room, and Valya did not immediately understand what it was. Eventually, he figured it out: it was the pictures on the walls, all these strange drawings, from childish scribbles to remarkably accurate portraits. Some of them looked darker, as if another layer of shading was added to the pictures, and that made the room appear smaller.

"I know all about it," Sasha said as she shuffled papers on her desk. "Pashka stopped studying midway through the semester. Eva has been preoccupied with her emotions. But now everything will be fine: they will come to their senses, work hard, and pass the exams on the second try."

"On the second try?" Valya asked softly. "But . . ."

"Obviously, Oleg Borisovich made things sound worse than they are, just to motivate them," Sasha said, smiling faintly, as if sharing some excellent news. "They won't fail. They just need to apply themselves and to grow up."

"But Arthur says that if Pashka runs away or doesn't pass on the first try, their grandparents' house will burn down," Valya said, swallowing hard. "Is that true?"

Sasha nodded. It was a simple, common gesture, almost benign. Valya couldn't quite believe his own eyes.

"No," he said helplessly. "No. That means Arthur would be punished, too, even though it wouldn't be his fault."

Alexandra grew silent, as if what Valya had just said never occurred to her before.

"Arthur's feelings will serve as motivation for Eva," she finally said. "It will motivate her to work hard to avoid these situations in the future."

Valya glanced at the drawings lining the walls. He felt like a fish caught on a hook staring at the underside of the fisherman's boat. Dark, almost black pictures, some with nothing but three white dots in the center, like the eyes and mouth of an unknown creature.

"It could be worse," Alexandra said gently. "For both Pashka and Arthur. And for Eva. And as for Alyssa . . . Do you remember what we said about all this? It's necessary, Valya. There is no other way."

Valya didn't reply. The taste of Mom's biscuits was fading, not on his tongue, but somewhere deep in his throat, until finally it was gone forever.

Pashka heard voices before he even reached the gate.

He'd been visiting his grandparents every week. He never showed himself to them, let alone started a conversation. But now someone was talking to them. A voice very similar to Pashka's own was almost screaming, begging, pleading.

"Grandpa, there is nothing I can do to fix it! I need you to leave. In the winter, on the night of January second, you need to get out of Torpa, I am begging you!"

"But Arthur—am I to understand that you are threatening to light our house on fire?" a confused voice said in response.

When a troubled child says the house will burn down, it is easier to assume that the child may be an arsonist rather than imagine some inexplicable magical forces to be behind the fire. Pashka was amazed at how a simple, common, realistic point of view—could be so easily distorted. Reality reconstructed itself like a salt crystal or a snowflake, and it didn't matter that the result was ugly. If their grandfather could imagine something like this . . .

Arthur must have thought the same thing. At least he couldn't speak for a moment. Behind the bushes, Pashka froze and waited. He wasn't planning on speaking with his grandfather that day. He wasn't ready. He simply wanted to look at the house, the decorated tree, the snow-covered round window in the attic . . .

"I can't explain," Arthur said hoarsely.

"Should I call the police?" Grandpa said helplessly. "Tell them there is a potential threat of arson?"

"No!" Arthur shouted, and his voice was full of tears. "Grandpa, listen . . ."

Any moment now he'd say, *It's all because of him.* Or, *He doesn't care about you and Grandma, he doesn't care about anyone, he's not my brother anymore.* Or something else that would make Grandpa clutch his chest and slide down the steps.

"Hello," Pashka said, opening the gate.

Cleared of snow, the path glistened. Snow was weighing down the fir tree; someone had decorated its lower branches with gold tinsel. Pashka recalled the scent of the wooden pallet where decorations were kept. Grandpa didn't bother with the ornate glass icicles, balls, and stars, but the tinsel served as the sign that the house was still alive.

Arthur stood ankle-deep in the snow, next to the path, wearing his summer sneakers. Grandpa towered over him, holding his glasses in his hands and squinting, as if he found it difficult to look directly at Arthur. Both of them turned at the sound of Pashka's voice.

"Hello," Pashka said again. "Grandpa, what Arthur means

is that when winter comes, it's customary to check the wiring for safety reasons. Electricians are always called at that time. And everyone must have fire extinguishers; it's the safety rule for everyone in Torpa, there was an announcement recently."

"What the hell are you talking about?" Arthur asked him silently, not making a sound.

"The fire department is playing it safe," Pashka continued loudly. "Torpa has so many old homes. Arthur didn't mean to say your house is going to catch on fire. We just need to check everything, to make sure. To avoid accidents."

A snowflake could be reassembled. A salt crystal could be rearranged. Pashka sensed his grandfather's attempts to understand, to compare Pashka's words with what he'd just heard from Arthur, to destroy the absurdity. The absurdity had collapsed like a house of cards. After all, routine and normality were much more powerful.

Chills ran down his spine. Pashka felt that he could go further, but his window of opportunity was short, only a few seconds.

He came closer and took hold of Arthur's arm.

"Grandpa, we are going to call Mom and Dad soon. We had some trouble with addiction. We were too ashamed to admit it. But now everything is going to be okay. We're seeing a therapist."

Arthur flinched, trying to free his arm, but Pashka held on tight.

"We are going to get clean," he said, looking into his grand-father's dull, sickly eyes. "Our doctor is very good. We'll need more time, of course. But our prognosis is excellent. We'll be back with you soon."

Grandpa opened his eyes wider, his gaze becoming clearer. Pashka felt the air above the yard grow warmer.

"Do you need help?" Grandpa asked pleadingly. "Anything you need. Money, connections . . . Come inside, please. We—"

A door opened behind him. Dressed in a bathrobe, Grandma looked shorter than Pashka remembered. A white shawl was wrapped around her, like a layer of snow over a fir tree.

Pashka held his breath. Grandma looked at him the same way she did in his childhood when he brought her a bouquet of dandelions from the yard. She turned her gaze to Arthur and immediately tensed up.

"Arthur, honey, you're practically barefoot—in the snow?"

Arthur trembled, holding back tears. This time tears were inevitable. Pashka suddenly panicked, expecting to wake up over a book and realizing *Textual Module* had provided a false prediction yet again.

"I'll take care of him, Gram," he said loudly and confidently, forcing himself to either wake up again or confirm this was not a dream. "We are in therapy, it's a restricted rehabilitation center, we can't be absent for a long time. But we'll be back. Very soon we'll be back for good. And everything will be fine, you'll see. Just give us time!"

Grinning, stumbling, and practically dragging Arthur along, Pashka backed out of the yard and closed the gate behind him.

Trust, affection, all these threads that Sasha had woven between them like a spider—all was ruined. Sasha had made a mistake the likes of which deserved no forgiveness. She'd dived too deep into her dark projections.

Will the house burn down?

Yes. It's necessary. For everyone. There is no other way.

"Alyssa needs help with the winter concert," Sasha said, casually changing the subject. "This concert should be happy, with many jokes. Parodies, roasts, skits. Lots of music and dancing. Will you help her?"

"Is it necessary?" Valya asked, his voice full of grown-up sarcasm. "There is no other way?"

"Up to you," Sasha said, shrugging. "You don't have to help Alyssa. But you can do something else. If you are willing, of course."

He was staring at the wall plastered with her drawings. *I need to take them down,* Sasha said to herself. These drawings were not suited for his gaze. She'd let her guard down.

"If you are willing to help Pashka and Eva. We always helped each other during our first year. It's not against the rules."

A second passed while Valya processed her words. He turned his head and looked at her, making sure she wasn't making fun of him.

"It may be complicated," Sasha said. "There is no guarantee it will work out, but there is a chance it may, don't you think? What if you help Pashka and Eva, and they pass their exams from the first try? And to make up for this, I will allow you to try some exercises outside of class. I trust you, Valya. Deal?"

He gazed at her, not quite believing his ears. Trust, affection, all these threads Sasha had woven between them twitched, ready to come alive.

At that moment, the phone rang.

As they headed back, it started snowing.

"What the hell did you tell them?" Arthur shouted, or rather he tried to shout, but his voice was hoarse, and he was out of breath. "Why did you tell them we are addicts? What therapy? You do realize they believed you?"

"They've always believed it," Pashka said. "They live in their own reality, and we live in ours. We must lie if we want to make it easier for them."

Arthur's arm lay on his shoulder. To an outsider, it would look as if a relatively sober student was dragging a completely plastered friend back home.

"But we can't come back to them! We can't tell Mom and Dad the truth, and we can't do what you promised them!"

"At this point, we just need to survive January second," Pashka said heavily.

The courage that made him lie to his grandfather, the joy of seeing his grandmother, the realization that she had forgiven them after all—all this made Pashka invincible for a few blocks. Eventually, though, he felt so drained that a nearby bench was a welcome sight.

They collapsed on the bench without clearing off the snow.

"Don't be scared," Pashka said. "I'll come up with something. I'll find a way to pass this exam."

"Back in high school, I could've done it for you," Arthur said softly.

Pashka put his arms around his brother.

Something that had been broken had come together again. It hadn't healed, not exactly, but it did come so close that Pashka felt a huge surge of relief: there was no face leaning over the cage, there was no dead hamster. It was nothing but an anxious dream of a tired student in a dorm room.

"I'll talk to him," Arthur said. "You know who I'm talking about. I'll try to explain why you stopped studying. You had a reason. Maybe he would . . ."

Pashka appreciated his courage and his willingness to negotiate with the man in dark glasses, whose very name Arthur tried not to say out loud, but he didn't see how it would accomplish anything.

"Speaking with him is pointless," he said through gritted teeth. "It's all in the hands of this bitch—she rules everything. I told her, right to her face, what I think of her. I can try to kneel and beg, but I'm pretty sure she'll just smirk and tell me it's necessary for both of us."

"Then what are we going to do?" Arthur asked. He was starting to tremble. His light sneakers were covered in snow, and his eyelashes resembled icicles.

"First, we need to get you warm," Pashka said, pulling out his phone. "Let me try to get a car."

He was about to touch the screen when a white Nissan flew up the street. Nearly invisible in the snow if not for the dim headlights, it stopped in front of them.

"That was fast," Arthur murmured.

"This needs to be resolved before the winter break, Adele Victorovna," Sasha said. She stood on the balcony, looking at the snow-covered roofs and the *All Your Home Needs* sign across the street. "Otherwise, I may need to take some measures. We can discuss it at our final departmental meeting. Have a nice day."

She terminated the call but remained on the balcony a while longer. Under a thick layer of snow, Torpa gazed back at her in thousands of distant windows, trustingly, as if Sasha were that anchor, that boat, that island where fear was impossible, but freedom was within reach.

She congratulated herself on remembering her cigarettes.

···

Watching Konstantin Faritovich, dressed in black head to toe, climb out of a milky-white car, Pashka decided Portnov was a real asshole. Having promised not to report anything, he had clearly changed his mind and did just that. And he did it *today*, precisely when the good old prediction came true, when their grandparents forgave them.

Pashka got up and placed himself in front of Arthur, facing Konstantin Faritovich. He stood between them, having no idea what he was going to do next.

The man in dark glasses was in no rush to begin the conversation. Pashka realized he hadn't seen him since September. He'd forgotten what Konstantin Faritovich looked like. Too much time had been wasted rebelling and chilling out.

Snow swirled in the glow of the headlights.

"During my first year at Torpa, I failed my Specialty exam," Konstantin Faritovich said.

In his wildest imagination, Pashka would never conjure up Konstantin Faritovich as a first year. Dumbfounded, he stared at his own double reflection in the dark lenses: two pale skull-like ovals.

"I'm not going to share what happened next," Konstantin Faritovich said, and his tone clearly indicated that nothing good had happened. "But I had a classmate who helped me study and pass on the second try. If you want to have your own chance, this is it."

He opened the door of the white Nissan in front of Pashka.

As Valya watched, Alexandra ended her call and put away the phone. For a while, she remained standing on the balcony, finishing her cigarette. Usually, she smoked freely inside her apartment, and Valya's presence never seemed to bother her. She must have needed to be alone to think. Valya saw her back, her messy bun, her hunched shoulders, her bare neck. He wondered if she was cold; it was still snowing hard.

The tiled roofs darkened at dusk, dotted with distant weathervanes. From a certain vantage point, Torpa was a truly beautiful town.

Valya waited, wandering around the room, from the balcony door to the fireplace, over to the desk, to the wall, to the table. His pierced earlobe pulsated lightly: Alyssa was no longer a hostage. Alyssa was no longer a hostage . . .

Valya quickened his pace; he would have loved to jump into the hamster's wheel to get rid of his anxiety. He longed to be back in the dorm, but Alexandra was still smoking, and he didn't have the nerve to rush her.

As if hearing his thoughts, the hamster came out of its house and looked at Valya through the bars with its beady eyes.

"Greetings, colleague," Valya said. "How are you doing? Looks like you're quite well."

He stopped in front of the wall covered with pages ripped out of albums and notebooks. The drawings made him uneasy, especially the one in the upper left corner, the totally black one. Valya wondered how many pencils had been used to create it and how much patience was required to sit there and move the pencil over and over again, without a goal, without a system. He shuddered at the thought. Or perhaps there was a system and he just couldn't see it? Three white dots in the middle of a completely black sheet . . .

His eyes focused on these dots as if they had been covered in glue. The dots twitched and grew. They pulled him over, blinded him, and immediately turned dark. Valya blinked, trying to clear his vision, but at that moment an old city emerged—jumped or stepped out—of the darkness.

He saw the outlines of the streets, occasional paving stones underneath the rubble, cobblestoned paths and marble sidewalks. Shards of stately homes poked out like rotten teeth, and roof tiles scattered over piles of broken bricks. As far as Valya's gaze could reach, suburban buildings had been ground into crumbs; closer to the center, they kept some of their shape, but looked fragile enough to collapse at any point. Only in the very center of the city, a single tower, still intact, pointed its lopsided spire into the sky.

Valya writhed, but he no longer had a body. He tried to scream, but he no longer had vocal cords and there was no air. He recalled how to use a protective screen, how to flood his vision with interference, with white noise, how to cut off informational streams. To save himself. To get away.

A new blindness washed over him, and this time it was darker and deeper. Valya almost believed that he'd escaped, but the blackness was replaced with dark burgundy ripples, and once again, Valya saw a city in ruins, and watched a mountain peak fall on the horizon, and an arched bridge collapse under its own weight, its supports snapping like a dead spider's legs.

But it wasn't a bridge, and it wasn't a city.

Sasha burst into the room, nearly taking the balcony door off its hinges on her way. She jumped on him from behind, hung on his shoulders, pulling him like a child away from the precipice. Valya was taller than her, and heavier—a young male, no longer a teenager. When the visual contact with the "fragment" was broken, Sasha managed to hold him up, so he didn't collapse on top of the hamster's cage.

She sat him down on the floor and carefully looked *through* him. This boy, as transparent as a piece of glass for her before, now resembled a tornado funnel. Leaving him in this room, alone with all these completed and unfinished fragments, was beyond stupid. Sterkh would have killed her for this.

And yet, Sterkh had made the same mistake once. He didn't think Sasha could read this kind of information. But she could, and, as it turned out, so could Valya.

"Leave Alyssa alone," he said as soon as he regained the gift of speech. "It's not her fault."

"Yes, the fault is mine," Sasha said calmly. "These objects are not for you. It's way too early for you to see anything like that."

She removed the "fragment" off the wall, crumpled it, staining her hands with graphite, and placed it into the fireplace. The flames shot up, giving off an unpleasant sense of a large destructive fire rather than the expected warmth—like a city consumed by a conflagration, and not a piece of paper licked by small flames.

"Alyssa . . . " Valya said again.

"It's fine, I am not blaming you for anything, there is no penalty," she said, keeping her voice soft and monotonous, as if trying to hypnotize him. She watched his breathing grow steadier and his eyes regain their awareness.

"What did you see, Valya?" she asked, helping him off the floor and onto a chair.

"Ruins," he said, shuddering at the memory. "A city that looked like . . ."

"That looked like what?" Sasha asked, handing him a glass of water.

"That looked like an old city," he said, frowning and trying very hard to remember. Or perhaps he was trying to hide something from her?

"And what happened?" she asked patiently. "Why was this city in ruins?"

"I don't know," he said, looking at her pleadingly. "I . . . it's hard for me to think about it. It's too scary."

Sasha began speaking in a measured, teacherly voice.

"You must approach learning materials slowly and gradually, step by step. Every developmental phase has its tools, ways, its own possibilities. You must not try exercises you are not ready for."

Valya clung to her mentoring voice like a drowning man to a rope. Sasha had long been aware of how much Torpa students longed for a boring, tedious, exhausting lifestyle, a semblance of normalcy, something that saved them from madness. She had once wished for the same thing, and so she did her best to deliver that to him now.

He listened as he gradually calmed down. Sasha hid a sigh of relief: the boy had managed to read only the top layer of information. The thinnest layer of meanings. Visualization. It was a lucky break.

"We can discuss it after the winter break," she said. "Do you remember that you need to help Pashka and Eva?"

"Yes," he said, and his eyes lit up. "Thank you, Sasha. I thought you were going to stop me again."

"Valya, you're not my servant," Sasha said earnestly. "You and I have the same goal, we are allies. I don't reverse my decisions lightly."

He grinned; impulsively, Sasha reached out and hugged him, inhaling his familiar scent. Valya did not tense in her arms, like he did before. Instead, he relaxed and even clumsily hugged her back.

Only, on his way out, he paused at the threshold, turned, and glanced at the fireplace where the shaded paper had burned earlier.

"What was it?" he asked. "For real?"

"It's too early for you to know," Sasha said gently. "Be patient."

CHAPTER TWO

He ran all the way to the dorm. He mumbled and sang, and steam came out of his mouth.

"Alyssa . . . Alyssa . . ."

In the lobby he was intercepted by Arthur, whose cheeks were as red as if he'd just come back from a ski trip.

"Where the hell have you been? We're wasting time!"

"You already know?" Valya asked, surprised by this turn of events.

"We know!" Arthur said sharply. "We've been told, if you can imagine."

"We have plenty of time," Valya said with dignity. "Tell Pashka and Eva that we start tomorrow. What's our fourth block, English? We can skip it. We meet after the third block."

"Tomorrow?" Arthur asked. He seemed shocked, as if Valya had offered a delay of a hundred years. "Why not today?"

"Today they should read their *Module*," Valya said with authority. "There is a method to it. You know this—it's why you're not in the same predicament. They should read all the paragraphs they've skipped. I'll test them on the ones marked in red."

"You are a fast learner," Arthur said, taking a step back. "Aiming to be Portnov's assistant?"

Valya narrowed his eyes.

"If you want your brother and Eva to pass the exam, find both of them, go into the kitchen or wherever you want, and make them read *Module,*" he said. "But make sure you don't come back to our room."

"You're an asshole," Arthur murmured.

"An asshole whose help you desperately need."

Valya walked away. He had no time for bickering.

He knocked on the girls' door. Stefa opened, but not all the way—she simply allowed just enough space to poke her nose out.

"Hey, Alyssa is asleep."

"Now? Why?" Valya said, taken aback. "Is she sick?"

"No, just tired. She had a tough day."

"Doesn't she want to talk to me?"

"Don't be an idiot," Tonya said from the depths of the room. "She's on her period. She's not feeling well."

"Does she need anything?" Valya said, taking a step back. "Can I bring her some tea? Or something from the pharmacy?"

Suddenly he remembered that Alyssa's last period was two weeks ago, so she was either really sick or was lying, and the latter was more likely.

"Tell her I'm in my room," he said loudly, making sure his voice was heard by everyone inside. "I'm alone. And if she wants to swing by to talk about the winter concert, for example, I'll be there, waiting."

It had been a while since Valya spent the night on his own in an empty room. He hadn't seen the twins. The hamster slept in Alexandra's apartment, inside the walls lined with drawings shaded in graphite. And now, dozing off, Valya finally understood: all the drawings depicted the same thing.

Doodles, swirls, patterns, dots. A photographically precise self-portrait. Every single drawing represented Alexandra along with something else. That something was so enormous that Valya couldn't sleep; he was too terrified to close his eyes.

He wondered if Alyssa was going to come after all. Perhaps she was tired and would come after she'd rested. Valya waited in the dark, listening to the steps outside his door. None of them were Alyssa's.

That morning he had let Alyssa know he couldn't help her with the winter concert. Was this why she was upset? He knew Alyssa inside out, sometimes wishing he didn't know her that well. She had no directorial ambitions. She had no desire to subjugate anyone at all costs. Why didn't she come when he needed her so much?

The plan was set in motion. Shanin the overachiever was assigned to tutor two of his classmates. He was expected to teach them whatever the faculty had failed to deliver. Was Alyssa jealous of Eva? But it was common knowledge that Eva wanted Arthur, and Arthur was ignoring her.

Was Alyssa jealous of Sasha? That was crazy. Except . . . was it? Everyone was aware of Valya's status as a teacher's pet. No one knew that Alexandra Igorevna was Valya's sister. Except maybe the faculty, but they kept mum.

Three in the morning. Four. Valya realized Alyssa wasn't coming.

Turning on his side, he willed himself to sleep. Beneath his eyelids, he saw the black city in ruins.

●●●

At four in the morning, Pashka sat in the empty kitchen, wrapped in a blanket. The windows had been insulated, but not well, and the draft made it as cold as the Arctic. It had been snowing all night.

Pashka was reading *Textual Module,* volume 2. The nonsensical text made his eyes water. Every few minutes, Pashka would look away. He'd close the book, marking the page, and run the tips of his fingers along its spine.

The book was right; it was Pashka who acted like an idiot. The book always told the truth, and it was he who couldn't read it properly. Grandma on the steps, her gentle "Arthur, honey," and the fact that she could once again tell them apart—that meant she'd forgiven them. The book had kept repeating it for months. It was Pashka who'd lost faith and stopped reading.

He'd felt a tremendous amount of guilt before the book, before Arthur and their grandparents. For the first time, he wondered if that woman, Alexandra Igorevna, wanted to convey something important, just like the book had. Perhaps she did not wish him ill, perhaps she wasn't motivated by sadism when she'd placed him in the hamster's cage. Perhaps what was obvious to her had simply eluded Pashka.

Outside, it was snowing, and water rustled softly in the pipes. Under the influence of *Module,* Pashka perceived this rustling as a waterfall, then as rumbling combines in the field. He squinted in the bright light, even though the kitchen was dark, and read paragraph after paragraph. Somewhere on the floor, the doors were starting to slam, and sleepy students shuffled into the kitchen with empty teapots.

> But out of the ashes arose now seven other figures,
> and the first said: "Once I was called Pride. But now

my name is Nobility." And the rest spake after the same fashion . . ."*

The sentence stopped just as it began. Disappointed, Pashka realized it wasn't a fragment of the future, but only a snippet of someone else's meaning that had nothing to do with Pashka.

Eggs sizzled on the stove, supervised by sleepy, wan-faced Stefa. Valya entered the kitchen. He was wearing glasses, not contacts, and Pashka knew something had shifted yet again.

"How's Alyssa feeling?" Valya asked, ignoring the fact that Stefa pretended not to see him.

"She's better," Stefa said, looking away. "She's coming to the first block."

"Then I'll see her there," Valya said, heading out.

Valya ran up to the fourth floor, but once again, he was too late. Alyssa had escaped and was already in the auditorium, surrounded by her classmates. Valya didn't dare come in, especially since only two minutes remained until the bell. At the end of the corridor, Adele Victorovna appeared, trailed by her beautiful scent.

"What are you doing here, Shanin?"

"I was just leaving," Valya said grimly. He headed toward the gym but ran out of time to change, and so he showed up for the class wearing a T-shirt, jeans, and socks. Coach said nothing, but his face reflected his strong feelings on the subject.

---

* The Legend of the Glorious Adventures of Tyl Ulenspiegel
in the land of Flanders and Elsewhere
Author: Charles de Coster
Translator: Geoffrey Arundel Whitworth

...

They gathered in dorm room 6 after the third block. Arthur put up a short fight but eventually shuffled off to English class to avoid provoking the professor.

Valya surprised himself by understanding how Eva and Pashka managed mental exercises. Not by sounds, not by scent, not by a string of words, not by the ticking of a metronome—Valya sensed other people's mental processes like a blind person senses the texture of a fabric, like a deaf person feels vibrations with their entire body.

This discovery delighted him, and he struggled to keep silent. He had been terrified of failing, of not being able to help. And now this task seemed so simple that he barely contained his giddiness.

Both Eva and Pashka zoomed through the first part of the textbook, nimbly merging and separating the spheres, and then turning them inside out. Valya wondered what the issue was: Did Portnov pick on them out of spite, or was Valya himself that good of a teacher?

Alyssa is going to hear all about this, Valya thought. They'd clear the air; they just needed a chance to talk. Maybe Valya had inadvertently offended her. "Unclear things must be discussed," Mom used to say, even if she didn't always follow her own advice.

Thinking of Mom made him sad. They hadn't seen each other in four months; they hadn't even spoken on the phone. It wasn't normal. He wondered if Mom felt this layer of falseness, this crack forming between them. If she did, how did she justify it?

"Let's go further," he said, pushing aside his own, murky anxiety. "Eva, you go first."

She began a series of exercises, stumbling on the fourth one. Started again and stumbled on the second.

"You've done all of these things separately just fine," Valya said, trying to hide his aggravation. "They stretch on their own, flow into each other, like . . . like Escher's drawings. You've seen those, right?"

He found a few examples of M. C. Escher's art on his phone and made Eva study the tessellations and impossible geometry before returning to the exercises. Eva stumbled immediately, failing the very first exercise. She must have gotten tired.

"You're tired," Valya announced, faking control over the situation. "Take a break. Pashka, it's your turn."

A few seconds later he realized that Pashka had no idea how to link the exercises into a chain. Pashka reminded him of a child asked to draw a bird and painstakingly tracing first a feather, then a beak, a talon, a piece of fried chicken . . . and none of them remotely connected. Valya felt numb with fear.

"Uh-huh," Valya said, trying to seem unfazed. "What did Portnov tell you during your individual session?"

"I don't remember," Pashka said, shrugging. "He mostly yelled at me."

"No worries," Valya said after a pause. "I'll explain everything."

For the first time since he'd got his ear pierced and was forbidden to self-study, since Alyssa became a hostage—for the first time since then—Valya allowed himself to enter an exercise on his own, without any faculty present. It was so simple: abstract concepts grew, replaced each other, and flowed smoothly. All Pashka needed to do was to understand the principle and continue. It had been so easy with Alyssa, even if Valya didn't know what he was doing back then.

The thought of Alyssa made Valya stumble. Pashka watched him grimly.

"Explain away," Pashka said.

He didn't get it. The altered reality Valya entered with such ease remained closed for Pashka.

"Read the problem out loud," Valya said, trying to win some time.

Muscles on Pashka's cheeks twitched, but he didn't argue.

"'Complete exercises one through nine in sequence, avoiding pauses and internal interruptions.'"

"Do it this way," Valya said confidently. "First, and then immediately second. Get it?"

Pashka took a deep breath as if about to dive; he entered the first exercise, the simplest one. Unable to see the process, Valya nevertheless sensed Pashka's path through the mental metamorphosis. The first exercise had ended, and now he needed to . . .

Pashka lost his place and stopped. Wincing, he looked up at Valya.

"Now what?"

By the desk, Eva wrapped her arms around her shoulders, staring dimly at the page in front of her. The page was warped, as if it had gotten wet and then dried up. Just like in Alyssa's textbook, just like in all the textbooks of all the students here, so many pages soaked in tears.

Valya concentrated so hard that steam was practically coming out of his ears. The day Alyssa came out of the loop. Alyssa again; she was everywhere. The day Coach stopped time; the ball hung suspended in the air, and the rain froze outside the window . . .

"Hold on," Valya said, with even stronger conviction. "Let me give you a hint."

He stood in the middle of the room and tried to recall how many squats he had to do. Two hundred? Two thousand?

He began to bend his knees, then straighten them again, like a wind-up toy. That's how it worked with Coach and Alyssa. That's how it was going to work now. Through a physical effort, he would grant Pashka and Eva access to his own informational space. He must have looked ridiculous at this moment, but not a hint of mirth reflected on their faces.

Valya started a long chain of exercises. He modified four- and five-dimensional figures, took their projections, linked them with imaginary objects, and deconstructed them again. He didn't speak. The only sounds in the room were his gasping, Pashka's heavy breathing, and Eva's shallow sighs. Reality shattered, splintered, allowing meanings to peek from beyond harsh matter. It was getting darker.

New outlines appeared from the darkness.

Valya saw the ruins of the black city as a projection of absolute, pitiless, utterly inhuman evil. His leg twisted under him, and he collapsed on the floor.

Pashka sprawled across the mattress, his arms above his head. The radiators had been cooling off for a while, making a soft crackling noise. He listened to the howling wind and hoped the heat wouldn't be turned off.

Arthur sat on what used to be his bed next to a stack of fresh sheets. His stuff, a large suitcase and a few bags, stood in the middle of the room. Arthur had returned to his former room.

"She's mocking us," Pashka said softly. "Me, you, that nerd Valya. She grants us hope and then takes it away. I wouldn't be surprised if she tries to sweet-talk me tomorrow. Before she dunks my face in shit again."

"But what's in it for her?"

"I wish I knew," Pashka said. Then, after a short pause, he asked:

"Any idea what's happening with Alyssa? Why is she treating Valya this way?"

"Alyssa went crazy," Arthur said. "She lost her marbles after that time loop. I would, too, if I were in her shoes."

A gust of wind slammed into the window as if trying to come in for a visit, rattling the flimsy glass panes.

"I would love to burn down the entire institute," Pashka said.

Arthur quickly glanced at the door. Then, as if ashamed of his cowardice, he looked down and said: "Me too."

"What if we burn it down before they get to Grandma and Grandpa?"

"I am so envious of you," Arthur said.

"Why?"

"You're free," Arthur said. "For some reason, after all this, you're still free. And I'm not."

"If I am free, and that's a big 'if' . . ." Pashka said. "Come on, let's go get Eva."

"What for?"

"We're going to pass this exam. And then we'll roast a celebratory pig over the coals of this institute."

Valya wandered around Torpa. It got dark early, and the streets were empty, with only a few late headlights flashing in the distance.

The wind was brutal; Valya tightened all the cords on his jacket and pulled the hood low over his forehead. He was glad he'd put on glasses rather than contacts that day: at least glasses protected his eyes. He couldn't really see much through them, but then again, what was there to look at?

He wondered what kind of weather his parents were having in Bangalore.

Valya stopped across from a shop window. Quite a few downtown stores were still open—for whom, it was unclear. World news was broadcast on a giant monitor: space flight, an international water polo competition, an ice sculpture festival. Hunched over with his back to the wind, Valya watched the soundless images. There was something wrong with them, but he couldn't quite put his finger on it.

What was the weather like in India? Did India still exist? Was that water polo competition really taking place in Argentina? Were artists actually cutting giant sculptures out of blocks of ice in Norway? How could he tell whether these images weren't simply two-dimensional pictures on the fake screen?

Hold on a second, Valya said to himself. *I have been exchanging messages with Mom all this time she's been in India. I know my texts are fake, generated by Alexandra. But who said Mom's texts have been genuine?*

He took a few steps toward Sacco and Vanzetti. He was pretty sure Alexandra would be home at this hour. She'd told him he was welcome any time, even without an invitation, and right now he needed to ask her a few questions.

A terrifying thought stopped him in his tracks: *What if Sasha had been lying to him? About everything?*

Sasha had told him about his parents' first meeting and about Mom as a young woman. It had taken him so long to start trusting her, but now breaking that trust would mean destroying the world. Did he want to know whether she'd been lying? Wouldn't it be better not to ask?

He went back to the window of a store called Second Hands. Below it, the sign specified: *Vintage toys, clothes, tableware, accessories. Radio parts. Vinyl.*

A small portable transistor radio was placed in the window. Valya's dad used to have the exact same model.

As soon as he reached room 6, he heard a slap followed by a scream. Valya stopped, nearly colliding with the doorframe.

He heard Pashka's voice, devoid of aggression or surprise. Despite his shock, Valya decided to come in and assess the situation.

The door was unlocked. All the lights were on. Behind the desk, Eva sat in front of an open textbook, another book lying on the floor nearby; Pashka was rubbing a reddening handprint on his cheek.

"Valya, if you don't mind, would you give us some time alone?" Arthur said, as politely as a lord in a castle. "We are preparing for our exams and would appreciate some privacy."

"Just don't hit him anymore," Eva said meekly.

"As long as it works," Pashka said, still rubbing his cheek.

"If it worked, they would flog us every day since the beginning," Valya said grimly. "Like at a medieval school."

"Listen, Shanin," Arthur said. "Do you want to do some more of your squats here? Or will you grant us some privacy?"

Valya felt his face grow hot.

"Whatever," he said and walked out, clutching his transistor radio in his hands.

At this hour, the kitchen was crowded. Irwing and Samvel looked very busy pouring beer and crunching chips and cashews; a small group gathered around them. Group B was getting ready to celebrate someone's birthday; a few girls were collecting signatures on a birthday card. Stefa and Tonya studied some pictures on their phones.

"What do you have here? A transistor radio?" a second year asked Valya. "Whoa, cool. Does it work?"

"Yup."

"What does it get?"

"Shortwaves, sixteen and up. Medium. Pretty much everything. Want to listen?"

"Sure," the second year said vaguely. At that moment, though, someone called him over, waving a plastic cup, and he got distracted and walked away.

Valya remained standing in the middle of the floor, pressing the radio to his chest, puddles forming around his shoes. Stefa and Tonya were both in the kitchen, and that meant Alyssa was alone in her room.

A dim strip of light lay under the door. When Valya knocked, the light disappeared. Alyssa was not interested in talking to him.

Valya slid down, leaning against the wall, and turned his head in the direction of the keyhole.

"Listen, there is something that's really bothering me. Do you ever talk to your mom on the phone?"

Silence. It felt as if Alyssa had stopped moving and breathing, hoping Valya would think she wasn't there.

"I haven't spoken to my mom in a while. She doesn't even know I'm in Torpa, can you believe it? She thinks I'm enrolled at a totally different college. But that's not important. Do you remember the definition of 'solipsism'? It might come up on our Philosophy exam. Solipsism is when you believe that nothing but your mind exists. And if anything else does exist, then it's not what you think, because your senses affect your perception, and so nothing exists outside your mind. Do you remember how they kept telling us that the world is not what we imagined?"

No sound came from the room, but Valya thought that if he pressed his ear to the door, he'd hear her heart pounding.

"I bought a transistor radio today," Valya said in a whisper. "And it doesn't catch anything, aside from a couple of stations in Torpa: music, news, weather. But outside Torpa, there is nothing at all. White noise. Could it be because of the snowstorm?"

He heard some movement inside the room, a rustling, an intake of breath. He thought he heard the sound of bare feet stepping onto the floor. Valya stopped breathing, but at that moment, Stefa and Tonya showed up at the end of the hall.

"Stop following her," Tonya yelled, and in support, Stefa barked loud enough for the whole dorm to hear:

"Leave her alone!"

Valya got up and hesitated for a moment, watching the door, but all was quiet once again.

He walked away, tightening his hood and buttoning up his jacket. Perhaps, at night, when the wind died down, according to the weather report, his radio would start working better.

Overnight emergency lamps glowed dimly everywhere in the institute, and only auditorium 1 was fully illuminated. Sasha faced the whiteboard, holding a green marker. The marker was nearly out of commission, its plastic case cracked and twisted.

Model processes flowed and unfolded across the whiteboard. Sasha wove intricate patterns out of recurring structures: creation. Word. Name. Out of nowhere, time kept getting in the way, even though Sasha didn't want to, and couldn't, include it in her design. Time didn't belong in this diagram; with time, the task would become unsolvable.

Or perhaps, it was unsolvable from the beginning?

The door opened, but Sasha didn't turn her head. She picked up a sponge and began to methodically, thoroughly erase her designs as they twitched and crackled under her hand, unwilling to disappear and clutching on to existence.

"Even a simple diagram does not wish to be annihilated," Coach said behind her. "Everyone wants to live."

"I'm working on it," Sasha said grimly.

"Your brother . . ."

"Yes, I gave him a bit of freedom. It's good practice to alternate prohibition and permission. That's what Sterkh did for me."

"Your task is beyond his abilities. Neither Danilova nor Grigoriev, P. will pass their exam at the first try."

"I don't need them to pass it," Sasha said coldly. "I need my brother to trust me and to remain in my control."

She swiped the rest of the unusable diagram off the whiteboard.

CHAPTER THREE

Preparations for the New Year Eve's concert began only after Adele Victorovna threatened Alyssa to call off her automatic pass in Specialty and make her take the exam alongside everyone else. Thus motivated, Alyssa went around the institute asking everyone for help and participation.

She didn't ask Valya.

Third years ignored her entirely; they were facing their final exam, treating it like an execution. It seemed as if they'd stopped studying altogether, having lost any will to live. Second years attempted to weasel their way out but help suddenly arrived in the shape of Alyssa's own roommates. Tonya and Stefa turned out to be indispensable.

They presented a simple logic: Portnov had announced the losers in advance, naming Grigoriev, P. and Eva Danilova. The rest could relax and have a bit of fun on New Year's Eve. Samvel and Irwing, the usual jokers, decided to participate. And when an enormous tree was delivered to the assembly hall, the number of volunteers grew bigger than Alyssa could hope for.

In the evenings, music was playing at full volume and rehearsals were underway. Samvel and Irwing took over, writing and sorting new skits to ensure they were "funny enough." They planned a full program of limericks, parodies, dance numbers performed by men in tights, and all Alyssa could do was to try to veto the most inappropriate ideas: "The faculty will be there! What if they get mad?"

The room where some time ago Valya had made love to Alyssa was no longer his. Eva, Arthur, and Pashka spent every free moment there, studying for the exams. Valya offered his help on many occasions, but they refused, sometimes politely and sometimes not so much. Eventually, Valya left them to their own devices.

He could tell they were happy together, those three. Perhaps they worked well together. Perhaps they no longer feared failure. Eva's black hair stood up proudly on top of her head like the King's Musketeers ready for battle. These days, she could tell the twins apart under any circumstance, from the back, on the run. When they played basketball, Eva shouted: "Pashka, pass!" or "Arthur, here!" and never made a mistake even when the brothers wore identical T-shirts.

Valya took his radio set back to the store, but the salesperson laughed in his face, telling him he should've known what he was buying. Convinced that the radio was broken, Valya left it on the bench by the consignment store.

He opened one of the messages written by Alexandra to Mom and added a postscript: "Do you remember what color my jacket was that time I fell on the ice rink?" Mom responded immediately: "Red, with a squirrel appliqué on the pocket, it was your favorite. I was more scared than you, and the urgent care nurse reprimanded me. All children fall and their wounds heal quickly; there was no reason to panic."

Valya spent a long time rereading Mom's response. Could Alexandra know and remember such details? Or did Mom really write this, as she sat in a chaise longue waiting for Dad to finish his rehab session?

She didn't say, "I miss you; I love you." The sentiment was there, easily read between the lines. Wasn't it proof enough that the letter was genuine?

Valya wandered along the streets of Torpa. He knew it to the last alley. He deliberately exhausted himself so that he could collapse into bed by midnight and sleep without dreams, so he couldn't be disturbed by the black city in ruins.

Portnov removed the blinding ray of light and put away his ring. Pashka blinked. An individual session was in full swing in auditorium 38—the last session of the semester.

"If only you applied yourself earlier," Portnov murmured, and Pashka heard a note of regret in his voice.

"We have almost a whole week until the exam," Pashka said, rubbing his cheek. "I have time to study."

"Who's helping you?" Portnov asked, lighting a cigarette. "Your brother?"

"Yeah."

"Tell him physical violence is only effective in the beginning, and not always even then."

"He doesn't have to hit me anymore," Pashka said. "I got the concept of how to complete these exercises. I'll make up all my work. Oleg Borisovich, the stuff written in *Textual Modules*— is this the Great Speech?"

"No." Portnov glanced at Pashka with slight condescension, as if Pashka were a cute but dumb toddler. "You don't get to study the Great Speech until your third year. Assuming the institute still exists by then."

"Why?" Pashka asked with interest. "Is it possible that the students will burn it down by then?"

Portnov roared with laughter. Pashka stared. He'd never seen Portnov laugh before; he couldn't even imagine it.

Portnov removed his glasses and wiped away the tears welling in his eyes.

"My apologies, I am becoming inadequate."

He lit his cigarette that had gone out. Pashka suddenly felt shy.

"How much have you read in *Textual Module*?" Portnov asked sweetly.

"It's the same fragment," Pashka said. "It's gibberish."

"Tell me more."

"'But out of the ashes arose now seven other figures,'" Pashka recited, then hesitated, trying to recollect how many times he'd seen different versions of this text. "'. . . and the first said: "Once I was called Pride. But now my name is Nobility." And the rest spake after the same fashion, and Nele and Ulenspiegel saw how Economy came forth from Avarice; Vivacity from Anger; Healthy Appetite from Gluttony; Emulation from Envy; and from Idleness the Dreams of poets and wise men.' Something like that. 'And Luxury, on her goat, was now transformed into the likeness of a beautiful woman, and her name was Love.'"

Exhaling, Portnov asked:

"Which one of you is sleeping with Eva, you or him?"

"Neither," Pashka said, confused and disturbed by the question. "We figured we'd decide after January second."

"Good decision," Portnov said, inhaling. "See you at the exam."

Arthur took the English exam in Pashka's name, then put on a different sweater and took the same exam as himself. It was a smart move; the English professor didn't want to admit her mistake of grading Arthur's work as Pashka's and so she simply graded Arthur's next, pursing her lips but saying nothing.

Valya was the last one to pass English.

"Tell me about holiday traditions," the professor said. She spoke English with a very heavy accent.

"London is the capital of Great Britain," Valya began, collecting his thoughts. "Everyone loves Christmas trees."

It was December 29. Ahead was the winter concert, followed by the Specialty exam on January 2.

Alexandra stepped into his path in the hallway, as if meeting him by chance.

"How was your English exam?"

A dress rehearsal was underway in the assembly hall, shaking with the sounds of hard rock. It sounded like Samvel and Irwing had taken over the winter concert production.

"I can't help them," Valya said, looking into Alexandra's face. "I failed."

"You've already helped them," she said with conviction. "And not just with their studies. They are succeeding, they've regained their confidence, and they will pass. Why are you feeling so lost these days? Is it because of Alyssa?"

Valya took a moment to consider the level of trust he was willing to allow. He wasn't ready to tell her about the black city in his nightmares. Or of the broken transistor radio, or solipsism, or the real configuration of the world. He didn't want to look stupid.

"Don't be angry with her," Alexandra said solemnly. "Second year is harder than the first. She may have reasons you're not ready to understand. You must be patient."

Same old song, Valya thought bitterly. *Mom used to tell me to be patient all the time.*

"I tried calling them," he said, not bothering to specify.

"The connection is terrible," Alexandra said. Of course she knew what he meant. "Mom turns off her phone all the time. It's easier for them, don't you see? If you get through, Mom may think you're hiding something, judging by the sound of your voice. She'd lose sleep over it, but she wouldn't be able to come anyway. Valya, this is the time for you to grow up."

"Am I ever going to see them again?"

The words spilled out before he could stop them.

Alexandra pulled back. Her face changed from solemn to concerned.

"Come with me."

Valya tensed up as if before a dive into cold water; he cursed himself for losing control.

They went down to her basement office. Alexandra took out a pack of cigarettes and a lighter but did not light up. She strolled around the room, sparsely furnished with office furniture. Valya had a fleeting thought: her attic apartment and her office at the institute looked like they belonged to two different people.

"I forgot you're just a child," Alexandra said. "Completely grown up on the surface. But inside you're still a child. Sometimes you feel forgotten and neglected. Plus, the holidays, New Year's Eve. I always feel sad around the holidays."

She reached for her bag, took out a thermos, and poured the dark, steaming liquid into a mug.

"Have some tea. I brought biscuits, would you like one?"

At the very first sip, Valya felt his chest loosen. He felt warm. It was just tea, a little sugar, a pinch of cinnamon. And something else. The scent of Sasha's home? A faint aroma of birch logs?

"Of course you will see your parents again," she said, pouring him another cup. "They will see how much you've grown. They'll be so surprised and so happy."

"What about you?" he asked, feeling relaxed enough to smile. "Don't you want to see Mom?"

"I'd like to," she said pensively. "The question is, could I? We'll see. Everything is okay, Valya. We have a lot of work ahead of us. But we are not afraid of hard work, are we?"

The music in the assembly hall was turned up to full volume, loud enough to be heard in the basement and in the attic. In the cafeteria, tables had been set up with snacks and lemonade. Valya knew that quite an impressive amount of stronger stuff had been smuggled into the building and hidden all over the floors: in shower rooms, in closets, and even in the gym.

He wasn't going to swing by the institute that evening. But it so happened that Valya's boots, his favorite leather boots that he wore around Torpa in the rain and in the snow, decided to give up the ghost on December 30. Both soles had cracked as if on cue.

Unusually cheerful and chatty these days, Arthur found out and graciously lent (more like gifted) Valya his new, waterproof winter boots. The boots had been stored in his gym locker in the main building.

Lost in thought, Valya entered the institute from the back entrance just as the concert had begun: the walls shook and even the equestrian statue seemed to twitch. Walking across the empty dark lobby toward the stairs, Valya noticed a lonely figure by the window. Alyssa must have thought she was invisible behind the curtain. Or perhaps she didn't care—she was too busy crying.

"What's wrong?" Valya said, forgetting that he'd sworn never to approach Alyssa until she reached out first.

She shook her head, turning away from him and pressing her hands against her mouth to stifle her sobs.

"Is it because they ignored you and kept their stupid vulgar jokes? So what, it's almost New Year's Eve! Do you know anything about carnival traditions? It's when everyone suffers through a difficult year, but then they rebel, mock everything, insult their bosses, show their naked asses to everyone, and no one can get upset. It's fine, really, it is! Can you hear them laughing?"

They could, in fact, hear peals of laughter whenever the music was turned down.

She finally turned to face him. Valya had never seen people on the eve of their execution, but they must have had the same expression on their faces. He took a step back. Alyssa stared into his eyes, as a queen standing at the scaffold would gaze at the lords reading the verdict.

She was wearing a fuzzy white sweater with a high neck, zipped all the way to her chin. Alyssa pulled the zipper, and the sweater revealed a thin T-shirt underneath. Alyssa lifted the T-shirt. Valya glanced away instinctively, then looked back at Alyssa.

Skin was missing from her chest and stomach, replaced by a growth of algae and sea sponge, brown, green, yellow. The thinnest fibers moved as if they were alive. Valya felt nauseated.

"Do you see?" Alyssa whispered. "How do you like it? Is that what you wanted to see? Adele Victorovna . . ." Her voice broke. "Whatever. So now you've seen it, are you happy?"

She pulled her T-shirt down and turned back to the window.

"Have you seen enough? Get out. Can you love something like this? Can you sleep with something like this, huh?"

She struggled to zip up her sweater but kept missing the slider. Eventually, she gave up and screamed in a whisper:

"Get out! Why are you torturing me?"

Valya pulled her close and kissed her, barely touching her lips with a delicate, funny sound.

Stefa and Tonya were performing cancan on the stage, basking in the attention of their classmates.

"Please don't," Alyssa pleaded, not worried about being heard in the hallways. "You'll be sick! You already want to throw up, don't lie to me! I'm a monster, you can't touch me like this!"

Somewhere in the assembly hall, a giant tree was blinking in multicolored lights. Stone-faced faculty and administration sat in the front row. The audience snorted, giggled, and guffawed.

Samvel and Irwing were performing a skit, the first to laugh at their own jokes. The music thundered and roared. Valya and Alyssa were alone in room 8.

Valya *claimed* Alyssa; he became Alyssa, but this time it was different. Before, he'd nearly drowned in the sea of someone else's information. Now he floated in the stream of data, filtering out projections and meanings. He watched the big idea weave itself into matter, not always cleanly, not always precisely, breaking harmony, but it was fine, it would be easy to correct.

Somehow Valya knew: he longed for metamorphoses, he was ready and capable of changing, his mission was to alter everything. He fell into the deepest sleep—for about thirty seconds.

When he opened his eyes, Alyssa was crying softly in the corner, her forehead pressed against the large built-in mirror. Her naked reflection showed smooth skin and an elegant outline of a female body. Sparks flew off her tangled hair, but Alyssa paid no attention to such details.

"I'm human," she said wonderingly.

The winter concert went on, far too long, and some particularly impatient audience members had already snuck out in search of secret alcohol stashes. Alexandra Igorevna was still sitting in the first row, but pretty soon she'd get up, thank the actors, and leave the assembly hall.

"Valya, how did you do it?" Alyssa asked, sniffling. "Adele tried to fix me, but she failed. She said I'd have to deal with it for a while, that it was a spontaneous metamorphosis, and it could be permanent. But you made me human again . . . how?"

"You're growing as a concept," Valya said, avoiding her eyes, and by proxy, her question. He didn't feel like explaining to Alyssa that she'd never be human again. "You . . ."

Staring at Alyssa's reflection made him lose his thought. He shook his head and continued.

"You're very beautiful. I love . . ."

He swallowed the last word, hoping she'd know anyway. Alyssa laughed through her tears and immediately asked:

"Where are you going? My roommates are not coming back any time soon."

"I have to help my roommates and Eva," Valya said, pulling on his jeans and buttoning up his shirt. "I need to check on them—I promised to help."

"Are you seeing someone else?" she asked nervously. She'd forgotten that an hour ago she didn't know how to be jealous—she didn't even know how to exist.

"Only you," Valya said, putting on his shoes with their cracked soles. "Tomorrow's New Year's Eve. You and I will celebrate together."

He ran along Sacco and Vanzetti; with every step, he risked leaving the soles of his shoes behind in the deep snow. He regretted leaving Arthur's boots behind. The winter concert was almost over, and the fun part of the evening was about to start: dancing, food, and not-so-secret drinking. Alexandra Igorevna would not stick around for any of this. Neither faculty nor administration would be attending.

Valya saw the familiar entrance between two stone lions. The lion's faces were worn out from frequent touching. The right one looked sad, the left looked merry, and both had piles of snow lying on their heads like crowns.

Valya lowered himself onto the stone step. Just a few minutes ago he lay in bed, his arms around Alyssa, and he was warm, even hot. And now he felt the cold stone underneath him, and ice in his shoes, and wind under his unzipped jacket.

He recalled trying to catch radio signals amid vicious gusts of wind and failing to get even a hint of one. All he could get then was Torpa news, weather, discounts at local stores, and a local pop music channel.

He wrapped his jacket tighter around his middle. Any moment, Alexandra would show up and he'd ask her about everything. He was no longer worried about looking foolish. He would no longer accept half answers.

He briefly considered going back to the institute and catching her there but decided against it. He was being a sentimental idiot; to him, Sasha always seemed nicer, kinder, at home. In her apartment, she was his sister. At the institute, she was his provost. But what if she didn't go home right away, what if she went to see Portnov, for example, or back to her own office, to think, to have another cigarette, to cover a notebook page with a thick layer of graphite?

Valya wondered if he could wait for her inside. He knew that behind the door was a spiral staircase, and steam radiators lining the walls. Alexandra would be surprised, but . . .

He *claimed* the lock on the door. The feeling was unpleasant, as if he'd suddenly grown an extra arm joint, the limb cold, hard, semi-paralyzed. *It's nothing but matter,* Valya said to himself, *simple matter, the simplest form.* But it was also a projection of a great Word that blocked the entrance—and could unlock it on demand.

The lock clicked. Valya stood in front of the open door, rubbing his right hand with his left. His palm pulsed with phantom pain as if the lock were still an extension of Valya's body.

He entered. The lights switched on automatically. The thick railings curved like the soundboard of a musical instrument. The stairs made of dark wood led up in a spiral.

He sighed with relief and shut the front door behind him. Inside, the air was warm and smelled of pine needles. Had Alexandra decorated a tree? He struggled to imagine such a scene. He perched on a lower step, feeling the warmth return to his feet and the memory of the open lock leave his right hand.

He'd opened one lock, why not open another? Why couldn't he wait for Alexandra in her apartment, in front of the fireplace? If he were to believe his sense of smell, she had a tree in there. She'd invited him in so many times, she wouldn't be mad.

Valya rose and walked up the spiral staircase, higher and higher, passing a small round window. The higher he went, the more unsettled he felt, and the more aware he became of breaking into something forbidden. As if he had secretly snuck into the tower in the middle of the devastated black city.

He almost ran back down the stairs, but the narrow door to her apartment was right in front of him, and the light above glowed so invitingly.

...

Surprisingly, the first thing he saw was not a decorated tree. Rather, his eyes were drawn to the now-bare walls; all the drawings had disappeared. He saw white plaster, a few protruding decorative bricks, and an occasional fragment of double-sided tape. The apartment seemed bigger and brighter, even though the only source of light was a handful of ceiling bulbs. Rather too late, Valya thought that Alexandra would see the glow from the street. Perhaps it was for the best. It's not like he was hiding.

He stared at the wall, unable to look away. He felt as if all the meanings and concepts that used to be displayed here hadn't disappeared entirely, leaving behind a multitude of footprints, shadows, anxiety, and doubts.

There was indeed a tree: a small potted one, with three bright-red glass baubles suspended on paper clips. These red splashes on a green background looked ominous to Valya, and he wanted to leave. It wasn't too late to wait on the stairs. It wasn't too late to return to the dorm. The questions he had for Alexandra could wait.

Or could they?

Without thinking, listening only to his growing anxiety, he approached the vintage piece that served as a standing writing desk. There was also a tall chair. Small drawers with brass handles took up all the space on the left side of the desk, from the tabletop to the floor. The top drawer was slightly ajar.

Not sure what drew him, Valya pulled the handle; from that moment on, he no longer controlled himself. As if a giant magnet had been activated, pulling over a chunk of steel. Valya jerked the drawer open, it fell out, and a multitude of handwritten pages scattered around the clean wooden floorboards.

They moved. They forced their way from a one-dimensional plane into a three-dimensional space, and further into four dimensions. They hummed like a swarm of bees or a power line. A black sheet with three white dots lay above the rest, protecting this anthill of meanings.

Eva was the first one to give up. She terminated the exercise she was on and pressed her hands to her face.

"That's it. I can't do it. I can't see anything."

Pashka felt about the same, but said nothing, fearing another slap from Arthur. Eva had nothing to worry about; Arthur would simply sweet-talk her into continuing. He'd place his hand on her shoulder, whisper into her ear, and Eva would relax a little and go back to the goddamn mental spheres and vectors.

But instead, Arthur said:

"Why don't we go see what everyone else is up to? Maybe dance a little? It might be good for us. Might give us a second wind."

Eva beamed, making Pashka regret it wasn't his idea. Truth be told, if Pashka came up with something like that, Arthur would get angry and say it was a waste of time.

Eva ran to her room to get dressed. Pashka stacked all the books at the edge of the table. He was never a fan of dancing or parties, but tonight he wanted to dance so much his feet twitched.

Without consulting each other, they put on the same clothes: black jeans and sports jackets over T-shirts depicting cartoon characters. They glanced at each other, silently admitting that even those who knew the Grigoriev brothers well would not be able to tell them apart . . . and that was how they wanted it.

Eva walked in, dressed in jeans and a ridiculously oversized sweater. She had put on mascara and lipstick, and her cropped hair shone with hair spray.

"Pashka, I took your book," she said, addressing the right twin. "We can swap tomorrow."

"Forget the books for now," Pashka said firmly. He wondered what it would feel like to put his hands underneath that enormous, roughly woven yet delicate sweater. It looked like it was made for cuddling and making out at a party.

Arthur was thinking the same thing. Pashka made himself relax and concentrate on surviving January 2. Everything could wait until after they survived January 2.

They decided not to bring their jackets and ran swiftly across the courtyard. In clouds of steam, they burst into the institute. The walls had been adorned with garlands, paper snowflakes hung off the ceiling, and tinsel snaked around the railings. Loud music was coming from the ground floor, where the party was being held in the cafeteria and the basement lobby.

A man in a dark coat—a stranger, not a student—stood by the scheduling board at the entrance to the administration offices. Pashka glanced without curiosity, but Arthur stumbled, as if someone had tripped him, and nearly fell.

The stranger turned his head. It was Konstantin Faritovich, almost unrecognizable without his dark glasses. Chills running down his spine, Pashka thought it was the worst possible encounter to have before a holiday dance party.

Eva grabbed Pashka's elbow. Pashka automatically noted that it was his elbow she wanted, even though she'd probably choose Arthur as her dance partner.

Almost immediately, Eva let go of his sleeve and hid inside her enormous sweater, like a snail. Pashka felt a jolt of courage, even more daring now that Arthur and Eva were watching him.

He crossed the lobby, the garlands rustling above his head and colorful lights on the concierge booth blinking in time with his steps. Pashka stopped a few paces from Konstantin Faritovich and looked into the man's perfectly ordinary brown eyes.

"Happy New Year," he said.

"Same to you," Konstantin Faritovich said. Without any further comment, he looked back at the schedule, as if he were a student who desperately needed to pass an exam at the first try.

The corners of his mouth were pulled down, and he seemed to be gazing inside himself. If Pashka didn't know who was standing in front of him, he'd believe that Konstantin Faritovich was human, and that he was grieving. Suddenly, somehow, Pashka knew that Konstantin Faritovich was standing not in front of a scheduling board but in front of a mass grave. He wasn't reading the dates of the exams; he was reading a list of names.

Pashka took a step back, but not because he was afraid. He felt the presence of something else here, in the lobby, something Konstantin Faritovich knew and saw, but Pashka could only sense. But even that vague sense of something made his blood run cold.

"On that day, I remember everyone who didn't make it to graduation and failed to become a part of the Great Speech," Konstantin Faritovich said without preamble. "Many of them were my friends, my loved ones. Speech is just and harmonious, but that's not the point. Without Speech, there is nothing."

Below them, rock and roll replaced pop songs.

"What happened to them?" Pashka asked without thinking.

Konstantin Faritovich shook his head.

"Whatever it was, I will not let it happen to you. Just don't expect me to be lenient."

The dance floor was set up in the lobby across from the cafeteria. It was so dark that people had trouble telling apart not only

Pashka and Arthur, but everyone else. Eventually, the dancers got tired of moving, and someone asked the DJ for a slow song.

Eva went to dance with Arthur. Pashka found a spot by the wall and stood there, sipping his fruit drink spiked with vodka, thinking of what he'd just heard.

Just don't expect me to be lenient. No one ever expected anything like this from Kozhennikov. And yet, some time ago, Konstantin Faritovich was human, he was a student, and he was a first year. He said he failed his exam on the first try. And now he was an instrument of Speech that everyone talked about, but no one had ever seen. Why would Speech need sacrifices, especially ones like this?

What if Alexandra Igorevna was the Great Speech? What if it was a euphemism or a shady nickname?

He looked over and saw Eva and Arthur gently swaying in each other's arms. Pashka desperately wanted to pull them apart, tear Arthur's hands off her waist, and remind him of their agreement: no choices, no demands, no grievances, no kisses—nothing at all until January 2.

Or was it a drop of vodka in his sugary drink that made him feel like this? He wasn't sure he was ready for someone to stand between him and Arthur. He only had one brother.

But there was only one Eva, and that was a problem. Pashka wished January 2 would never come. He tossed his unfinished cup into a trash bin and made his way to the exit.

"Pashka?"

He was so lost in thought that someone's hand on his shoulder made him flinch. It was so dark in there.

"Have you seen Valya? I've been looking for him."

Why was Alyssa looking for Valya? Hadn't she broken up with him without an explanation?

"He said he was going to help you guys," Alyssa said anxiously.

"But you're here, I saw Arthur and Eva on the dance floor. Is Valya here?"

"I don't know," Pashka mumbled. Blinking lights brought Alyssa's uneasy face into view, then plunged it into darkness again.

"If you see him, will you tell him I'm looking for him?"

"Yeah."

The slow song ended, and the music stopped. The lights of the dance floor went on, along with all the lights in the basement. For a second, Pashka closed his eyes. He felt as if someone above had heard his secret wish: Arthur and Eva broke their embrace and stood apart, squinting, trying to figure out what was going on.

The first exclamations came, surprised and angry. A piercing screech of a mic drowned out the dissatisfied voices and made the most sensitive students cover their ears. Pashka looked at the DJ's podium and saw Valya Shanin standing there. His eyes were entirely black, and saliva collected in the corners of his mouth.

"Lis evr dy," he said into the microphone. "They are ly . . . to us. I saw. The whole wrld . . . nothing but tr . . ."

No one laughed. His broken mockery of speech sounded terrifying rather than funny. Everyone backed away from the podium, and some students started moving toward the exit.

"Too much studying," someone said in the ensuing silence.

"Valya, what's wrong?" Alyssa asked. She was the only one brave enough to approach.

He shook his head as if refusing to accept reality.

"Speech! No real . . . ty. Torpa!"

"He's had too much to drink," Samvel said calmly. "I had this happen to me at Vovka's birthday party. Let's not tell the faculty, we can just walk him back to the dorm."

Known for his kind and gentle manners, Valya Shanin threw the heavy microphone into Samvel's face.

Speech had betrayed him. Not the Great True Speech; the Great True Speech did not care about Valya. It was too busy deteriorating in agony. Valya's own human speech had deserted him, and he could only sputter and flap his arms.

He wanted to tell them what he had just seen, what he had felt, and what he had experienced. The black city in ruins and the ruins of Speech. There was no India, no Singapore, no Milky Way. There was nothing beyond the limits of this cursed city: no reality, no ideas, no matter. No one in the room had family members anymore, except for the Grigoriev twins, whose grandparents lived in Torpa. But even they didn't have much time left. The chaos was encroaching, the Speech was melting away. The stars were about to go out, and there would be no light, no darkness, no time.

They had been celebrating New Year's Eve, preparing for their exams, and dancing to slow songs. No one heard him. No one understood. Valya saw them from the inside: the foundations of new Words that would never *reverberate*. Alexandra knew it all along, she was *making it happen*; it was her mission to be the destroyer of grammar, the assassin of reality.

He threw the microphone. He wanted to transfer the information directly by breaking into the electric impulses of their tiny brains. He *claimed* everyone who was in the room at that moment as if gathering a handful of peas.

The lights went out again. Alyssa screamed, and the sound pierced Valya's eyes and seared the entire surface of his body. Losing connections, scattering other people's minds like pebbles, Valya failed to exist in his material form and flowed into the brick vault above. He became the building's communications system: pipes, couplings, tunnels, collectors—a complex knot of iron mandibles and tentacles. He shuddered with revulsion and moved on to become the tiles on the roof. He perceived the linden trees on Sacco and Vanzetti as the continuation of his own body. He sensed the cobblestones as skin covered with scales. He began to grow, spread, absorbing street by street, block by block, wishing to lock everything under a dome and keep it from disintegrating—or perhaps vice versa, assist the chaos, crush everything with his will, everything regimented and normal that remained in the world. What good was Torpa if there was nothing else left?

He cried in despair and almost immediately saw a white opening unzip in the black sky. A beam of bright light came from the other side of the sky, blinding him, pulling him upward. A black shadow fell from the opening, coming directly at Valya, and burying him under its weight.

The hired DJ ran off, leaving his equipment behind. A handful of students, the server, and the cook shuffled around the lobby: all those who had not witnessed the event because they had been peacefully sipping champagne from the secret bathroom stash, or enjoying the snacks in the cafeteria, or making out behind the hallway curtains or under the coatroom counters.

All the others had fled. *Tomorrow everyone will pretend they saw nothing and heard nothing,* Pashka thought. Shanin had simply suffered a nervous breakdown from drinking too much, scaring the wits out of his classmates, especially Alyssa, who'd been sobbing for the past half an hour. Eva led her to the bathroom, but Alyssa wept loudly enough to be heard over the running water.

"Where is he?" she wailed. "Where did he go? What if the cops come for him? What if he's punished?"

The celebration was over, but it didn't stop the most practical second years from collecting the secret stashes of vodka and taking the leftover sandwiches and pastries back to their rooms.

"They are going to go into full prohibition mode," one of the second years said with regret. "Room searches, all that stuff. It'd happened before, Igor told us."

"We just need to find better hiding spots," his friend said sagely. "I'd love to see Adele search our rooms."

They guffawed as if nothing had happened, as if things were already back to normal. Pashka wondered if he was the only one who knew that Valya never drank. Whatever happened to him must have been something so big and terrifying that he might not live long enough to graduate. Would Konstantin Faritovich stand by the scheduling board and remember Valya in his own private remembrance?

Finally, the girls emerged from the bathroom. Alyssa's face was covered with red splotches, and she kept biting her lips, but her eyes were dry. Eva looked so upset that both Arthur and Pashka reached out to hug her . . .

And stepped back, avoiding each other's eyes.

"I'm going to be put into a temporal loop," Alyssa said dully. "Forever."

"Why?" Arthur and Pashka shouted in unison.

"Because that's what they promised Valya," she continued without a hint of emotion. "For any failure of his, I would be punished. He thought I didn't know. But I did—all this time I knew everything."

CHAPTER FOUR

'm very sorry we have to hold this disciplinary meeting on New Year's Eve."

Sasha stood on a wooden stage; the back of the stage was plunged in darkness. The remains of the set from last night's winter concert were piled up behind the curtains. Confetti and crumpled streamers lay underfoot. Along the walls, thin threads of tinsel swayed in the draft.

Nearly all the first and second years were present in the assembly hall. Sasha let third years off the hook: their final exam was coming up in two weeks, and it was too late to discuss disciplinary issues with them anyway. Portnov stood in the right aisle, his arms crossed over his chest. Coach sat in the last row. Adele on a folding chair in the left aisle. A faint aroma of flowers wafted over the students, reminding them of summertime and freedom.

Silent, Sasha watched them. They probably thought that was her way of punishing them, making them nervous by holding a long pause. But they were wrong; she simply wanted a closer look.

Second years took up the back rows, huddling together. Sasha saw them before their summer internships—pitiful, mutilated creatures without a will. But now everything was different. She'd used inhumane, cannibalistic methods, but she had managed to reconstruct them, and now they were at least partly Words, still as soft as babies' skulls. And now the complex transformational processes had launched. The grammatical reform was in progress.

And first years—all personally selected by Sasha and recruited by Kostya. Those who had to revive the Speech and serve it. If only these first years had a couple more years of school at their disposal . . . But Coach was right yet again: *Time is against you.*

She raised her chin. The subjunctive mood, *if*, was against her nature. She'd experienced a moment of weakness. Time was a grammatical concept. Meaning was the projection of will onto the area of its application.

"Go ahead, Oleg Borisovich," she said, nodding to Portnov. She walked off the stage and took a seat in the first row, just like last night, when the amateur actors, driven mad by their workload, spouted naïve and vulgar nonsense from this stage. *I remember our winter concerts as truly funny, and our music selection was mostly classical,* Sasha thought.

Portnov adjusted his glasses and spoke in his usual even, icy, numbing voice. He talked about executions that would follow a sip of beer or a drop of vodka. He spoke of the upcoming raids and group responsibilities of roommates, floormates, and classmates. At first no one believed him, but eventually they were struck with horror, then depression. Sasha caught Portnov's eyes, letting him know it was enough.

Portnov reminded everyone that the first years' Analytical Specialty exam was coming up on January 2, second years' on January 5. He told them they had two tries; each retake had to be approved by their advisors. On January 11, second years had their Introduction to Practical Studies exam, and again they had two tries. On January 13, third years had their final exam, no retakes, but third years were well aware. None of the third years were present anyway.

After his speech, Portnov asked Sasha if she had anything to add. Without getting up, she said he'd covered it all and everyone was free to go. She wished everyone Happy New Year.

They began to disperse, some immediately, trying to escape as quickly as possible. Some hesitated, as if expecting to hear more. Adele left without saying good-bye to anyone. Coach gazed at Sasha for a few moments, then followed Adele out. A few people remained in the empty assembly hall: Alyssa in the center. The Grigoriev brothers on both sides of her. Eva Danilova behind her, like a bodyguard, traces of makeup still visible on her face.

Sasha glanced at Portnov. Portnov nodded and left, opening a new pack of cigarettes on the way.

Sasha leaned over the edge of the stage and crossed her arms.

Eva looked nervous. She seemed to regret staying behind with Alyssa and the twins. Grigoriev, P. remained silent, his face grim and stoic. Grigoriev, A. kept biting the insides of his cheeks. Alyssa stared straight ahead, past Sasha, her eyes unfocused.

"Questions?" Sasha said, shattering the silence.

"We'd like to know what happened to Valya Shanin," Arthur said. "Alexandra Igorevna, please tell us."

"He's fine," Sasha said. "However, there will be consequences."

Still staring ahead, Alyssa bit her lip.

"We all know he wasn't drinking," Grigoriev, P. said through gritted teeth.

"'We all know' is something you can say to your pals," Sasha said, smiling coldly. "Please address me as Alexandra Igorevna if you want to continue this conversation."

"He wasn't drinking," Pashka said, and his pupils became

as tiny as pins. "Alexandra Igorevna, we're not asking if he's okay. We're asking where he is right now!"

"For someone facing an exam the day after tomorrow, you're surprisingly self-assured," Sasha said.

"Alexandra Igorevna, Valya is our classmate," Arthur said, very politely and very firmly. "He was our roommate for the whole semester. Why can't we know what happened to him?"

"Here at the institute, students do not get all the information at once," Sasha said.

Without further explanation, she left the hall. Their stares stuck out of her back like daggers.

Down in the administrative wing, Sasha turned the key in the lock four times. Her hand trembled. This office had almost never been locked before.

Behind the desk, Valya sat in the same position she'd left him in: blindfolded, a pencil in his hand, hunched over a piece of paper, or what was left of it. The pencil had long ago become dull and nearly unusable, but Valya kept moving the stub over the page again and again, connecting the imaginary dots.

Sasha locked the door and switched on the fan, then collected and crumpled all the papers. She poured some water into a glass, pulled the pencil out of Valya's hand, and brought the glass to his lips.

He emptied the glass in one long swallow and froze like a machine whose task was suddenly terminated.

Sasha reached for his blindfold but stopped mid-movement, afraid of seeing a black film instead of his eyes.

Gritting her teeth, she pushed away her fear and took the blindfold off his face. Valya shut his eyes, disturbed by the bright light.

"Look at me," Sasha said.

He pressed his hands to his face.

From the moment the shadow fell from the sky and draped itself over him, something in Valya broke away, like some internal feature of an informational system. Since this something was *Time* as a philosophical category, Valya no longer understood the change of events, the sequence or duration of processes and objects in their existence, or the concept of movement and development.

Having gone through a series of painful metamorphoses, he saw himself from a distance: within a semiotic system where three-quarters of the signs and symbols were a mystery to him. Eventually, silence flooded his ears, and he saw the silence, smelled it, tasted its sharp bitterness on his tongue. The first sound he heard was the sound of the key turning in the lock. The key: Valya remembered himself, remembered his name, and knew what had happened.

To his surprise, the time had come back. Sound had temporary characteristics. Where there was no Time, there was only silence.

"I had figured it out a long time ago, I just didn't want to believe it. I bought a transistor radio, and it didn't work. But it wasn't broken. I looked inside—there were only ruins. The Speech is deteriorating. The world is falling apart. It's almost gone. And you, Alexandra Igorevna, you've been sending me messages from Mom all this time. And Mom doesn't exist anymore, no one does! There is nothing out there, only Torpa!"

He remembers Mom, Sasha thought, almost jubilant. He

hadn't dissolved in the irrational pocket like a teaspoon of salt in hot water. He hadn't turned inside out, hadn't fallen into *Untime,* he'd even regained his speech. She was delighted she was able to bring him back. Sterkh would have been proud.

"Are you . . . happy?" he asked, looking at her in dismay.

"I'm happy I could save you," she said sincerely. "Your fate could have been awful, Valya. You must have felt it."

"Why bother saving me if everything is falling apart, if it's all nearly gone? Or are you planning to stay in Torpa, hurting people, torturing them, terrorizing them?"

"All I'm doing," she said, exhaling a puff of smoke, "I do to fully restore reality in all its aspects. The Speech. Matter. Information. Systems of ideas and projections. I was hoping you'd understand what I'm doing, Valya, honey."

"Don't call me that," he said, his voice suddenly low, a real bass.

"I'm calling you by your name," Sasha said, taking another drag of her cigarette. "Your name holds you down like a pin that fixes the butterfly in place. You won't break away ever again. I granted you freedom, but you failed to use it properly."

"No, I didn't!"

"What you managed to realize is not freedom. You didn't even make a choice. You simply followed your nature, your curiosity, your whim. You could have simply asked me."

"You would have lied!"

"Yes, if I considered it necessary. I warned you from the very beginning: You wouldn't understand everything at once. You have to study; you have to grow."

"Blah, blah, blah," he said with a sigh.

"And now you're just being rude. You've lost your self-control. What would I do with a verb in the imperative mood when that verb can't control his own actions?"

"I've always been nothing but an instrument for you," he said, as if admitting for the first time that Santa Claus did not exist.

"You're an instrument of *Speech*. Just like me. Like all of us."

The cigarette smoke folded into a flat spiral; a tiny spark twirled inside the projection, at the beginning of time. Aggravated, Sasha waved her hand, and the tiny galaxy disappeared.

"Speech no longer exists," Valya said, still staring at the spot where the galaxy had formed.

"Of course it does. As long as I exist, so does the Great Speech. But it is in danger, as you have just seen."

"I saw you as well," he said, his voice so very grown up, almost old now. "You're *destroying* this world. You are the reason behind all of this."

"I am an assassin of reality," she said, nodding. "But if you had been listening to what I'd told you back in my apartment, you'd know that I am trying to fix my mistake. That's why I am teaching you everything. And that's why I need you. Needed you. Now I am not so sure."

"I turned out to be a broken instrument, didn't I?"

He bared his teeth in a scowl, reminding Sasha of a hamster hiding in the corner of its cage.

"Valya, do you want Alyssa locked in a temporal loop forever?" Sasha asked. She sighed heavily. "Your actions seem to indicate that's what you're trying to accomplish."

"If you do anything to Alyssa," he said with such hatred that she thought her hair was about to catch on fire, "anything at all, I will stay in the same loop. With her. Forever. You can't stop me."

"Yes, I can," Sasha said with regret. "You don't seem to understand that in our world, I make all the decisions."

He stood up, suddenly almost a head taller than the night before.

"So you decided to extinguish the stars and fold space into a single point? Or did you decide to stop the process? Are you missing the contradictions here?"

"There are decisions, and there are consequences of wrong decisions," Sasha said slowly. "At some point, I've made a mistake. And so have you. You broke into my home and opened my desk. You've committed an act of breaking and entering, Valya."

"Haven't you broken the world?"

"And I'm working to fix it. And you will have to fix your own malfeasance."

She fell silent, watching him struggle with his anger and fear. She watched his fury dissolve along with his determination.

"You've jeopardized my plans," she continued. "You've betrayed my trust."

Someone knocked lightly on the door.

"It's open," Sasha said loudly.

Kostya's short black coat was dusted with snow. Valya took a step backward, but almost immediately his hands clenched into fists and he looked up.

"I'm not afraid!"

"Are you sure?" Sasha asked gently.

The silence fell. The ceiling fan breathed softly, clearing away the cigarette smoke—the remains of the destroyed galaxies.

By 10 P.M. the dorm felt unusually quiet. Everyone was still recovering from last night's festivities. A few students gathered in the kitchen, but many stayed in their rooms, celebrating the new year with apple juice, canned meats, sandwiches, and thick slices of onion.

Television sets had been switched on and put on mute. After a brief consultation, Pashka, Arthur, and Eva invited Alyssa to join them. At first she declined, but shortly after ten, she knocked on their door.

Torpa's fireworks kicked off at a distance, in the center of the town. Samvel and Irwing released a dozen firecrackers out on Sacco and Vanzetti, but that was the extent of the celebration. The dorm windows glowed faintly in the night, the café across the street was closed, and the institute itself was dark and quiet.

Grandma and Grandpa must be waiting for us, Pashka thought, slicing a stick of bologna. *They have decorated a small tree in the living room, set up the table, and are listening for our footsteps, waiting for us. They believe we are coming soon. And Mom and Dad—Dad has just returned from a trip—have set up their table and are waiting for our call, checking and rechecking their phones. Two holiday cards from us simply weren't enough.*

Right after January second, Pashka said to himself. *We have three measly exercises left. Well, not exactly measly, but only three, not thirty! When I pass the exam, and when Eva passes it, and she surely will, she only has two exercises left to do . . .*

His imagination refused to go any further. It felt as if there was a wall in the time between January 2 and the rest of Pashka's future.

"Let's call our parents," Arthur said. "Just to hear their voices."

Pashka shook his head.

"Equilibrium. Balance. I'm afraid of upsetting it. What if they decide to come here? What if they start asking questions?"

Arthur shuddered as if from a chill. Assembling sandwiches, Eva said:

"I tried calling my family, but the connection kept dropping. I heard there was an accident on one of Torpa's towers. At least my text went through, thank goodness for that."

Sitting on Valya's bed, Alyssa remained silent. Pashka wiped his hands on a kitchen towel and sat down next to her.

"It's New Year's Eve. You know the old saying: *The way you greet it is the way you spend it.* Just relax, nothing has happened yet, the exam is ahead of us, and Valya gets an automatic pass."

Alyssa lifted her face with a dreamy, faraway look. Pashka felt a pang of anxiety.

"Alyssa, what is today's date?"

"Thirty-first," she said in a whisper.

"And what's tomorrow's date?"

Alyssa began to cry. Tears streamed down her cheeks, but her face remained motionless, and not a sound came from her lips, not a breath, not a sniffle.

"Alyssa, tomorrow is January first!" Pashka said, horrified. "Did you hear me? January first!"

Eva rushed over, grabbed Alyssa by the shoulders, and shook her, shouting:

"Tomorrow's January first! January first! Say it! And yesterday was December thirtieth!"

For some reason, Arthur looked at his watch, and Pashka followed suit. It was five minutes to eleven. What was going to happen to Alyssa at midnight? The carriage would turn into a pumpkin, and Alyssa would wake up today, on the morning of December 31, was that it?

The door opened. Pashka saw an unfamiliar silhouette and tensed up: Why would a stranger enter without knocking? But when the stranger stepped inside and the light fell on his face, Pashka recognized Valya. He did look different—as if he'd grown a few centimeters overnight.

Pashka jumped up. Valya looked around the room, saw Alyssa, and threw himself at her, nearly colliding with the table set with dishes. He sat down—or rather collapsed—by her side and put his arms around her.

"Don't cry. Everything is okay."

"She's in the loop," Arthur said grimly. "She's in a temporal loop of December thirty-first."

"No," Valya said, shaking his head vehemently. "She's not in a loop, and she won't ever be in a loop; why would she be in a loop? Never again, that's it."

"She knows she's being punished for your failures," Pashka said. "And you have failed."

"How do you know?" Valya asked, gazing into Alyssa's puffy eyes. She jerked her head away, unwilling or unable to provide the answer.

"Nothing will happen to you," Valya said, running his hand over her hair. "I gave up, I gave in. You can think of it as me killing my hamster."

Everyone inhaled. Alyssa stared at Valya with a brand-new expression of horror.

"Virtually," Valya said, forcing a smile. "Informationally. In projection. Anyway, I am not going to tell you anything. I can't explain it or help you guys, no matter what happens. But for Alyssa, tomorrow will be January 1. Let's celebrate New Year's Eve, shall we?"

Sasha sat behind the desk, moving her pencil over a piece of paper. A multidimensional image grew under her hand, shifting and folding into shapes.

"I brought carrots," Kostya said to her back. "For the hamster."

"Thanks," Sasha said, glancing at the cage. "Would you mind feeding it?"

The hamster ignored the carrots and hid in its tiny house. Sasha continued to draw. Kostya pushed away the plate of carrots and added a birch log to the fire.

"You saved your brother."

"I broke him," Sasha said, moving her pencil over the creamy textured paper. "I broke a verb in the imperative mood."

"If you didn't, you couldn't have held him back, and he would have destroyed himself."

"Well, now I've held him back," she said, building a shadow, a penumbra, a highlight, a gleam, a reflex on the paper in front of her.

"Does your plan remain in effect?" Kostya asked softly, gingerly, as if pulling a brick from the base of a tall tower.

"I don't know," Sasha said. "Look at this."

She pushed her drawing toward him. A human face—or perhaps not. Possibly a burning anthill. Or a flock of birds flying into a jet engine.

"It's not you," Kostya said quickly. "It's your exhaustion. Your anxiety. You need to rest."

"It is me," Sasha said, taking the drawing back. "I've changed as a concept. Every decision has changed me from the inside. Do you know what makes me different from Farit?"

"Everything," Kostya said.

Sasha shook her head.

"Farit never asked for the impossible, Kostya. And I do. And looking at this," she touched the drawing, "I keep asking myself: Am I demanding the impossible from the True Speech?"

PART V

CHAPTER ONE

P ashka gazed at the sunbeam on the ceiling and smiled, knowing he was still asleep.

The room smelled of pine needles and tangerines. The living room clock was ticking softly. Someone was snoring gently. Pashka turned his head and saw Arthur sleeping on a foldout bed. Arthur lay on his back, arms thrown to the sides; he looked about ten years old. It felt like the winter vacation had finally begun, and Grandpa had already prepped their skis with wax and resin.

Pashka sat up. This wasn't a dream. And yet it was impossible.

Under his stare, Arthur woke up and shifted, and the foldout bed nearly collapsed under his weight. They stared at each other for a moment; Arthur looked up at the ceiling, at the stripe of the morning sun.

The night before, they'd arrived at five minutes to midnight, fighting their way through the blizzard. They rang the doorbell, and their grandparents opened the door.

They collapsed at the festive table set not for a small family of two but for a large party. They clinked their champagne glasses, disregarding the fact that it was already a quarter past midnight. The twins had brought an armful of branches from the nearby pine tree as a gift, and Grandma lovingly arranged them in her prettiest vase.

They laughed together, sharing funny stories from their childhood, and the house enveloped them with sounds, smells, and warmth. Eventually, the living room grew so hot that Grandma had to bring a pile of old T-shirts and shorts from the closet. Arthur and Pashka changed into summer clothes, and it made them think the last six months in Torpa had been a dream. They thought they had dreamed up the institute and it existed only in their nightmares.

Grandpa insisted on calling the twins' parents, but the connection kept dropping. At the end, they simply sent a celebratory text. An hour later, Pashka and Arthur went to bed, Pashka on the sofa, Arthur on the folding cot, just like when they were kids, just like always. Just like in ordinary life.

And now it was morning.

The door opened a smidge. Grandma peeked in, saw that the brothers were awake, and opened the door wider.

"Breakfast is ready!"

"Just one more minute, Gram," Arthur whined, pretending to be a five-year-old being woken up before a fishing trip.

Grandma laughed. Pashka laughed with her.

They finished all the leftover salads and polished them off with bread smeared with jam. The house, slightly cool by morning, was warm again: Grandpa was generous with firewood.

"Eva is still sleeping," Grandma said when there was a lull in the conversation. "She must be hungry. Should we wake her up?"

Arthur and Pashka glanced at the tightly closed guest room

door. Last night Eva had put up a fight, refusing to go all the way across Torpa and saying, "But this is your family, not mine."

Later she laughed at the stories and helped with the dishes.

"When she gets hungry, she'll get up," Arthur said. "We are free all day, there is no reason to hurry."

Grandma nodded agreeably.

"We have plenty of food left, I'll send some back with you. She's such a nice girl. Those eyes . . . My great grandmother had eyes like hers. So blue. And very kind."

"Yeah, she's sweet," Pashka said. He didn't think Grandma's simple words would make him this happy. "Sometimes she acts like a hedgehog when she thinks she might get hurt. It's a defense mechanism."

"She's a good girl," Grandma said, smiling. Then, unexpectedly, she said, "Arthur, Pashka, my darlings. You're not addicts. Not a bit. I can tell. Grandpa and I can tell."

Pashka froze with his mouth open, as if he were a toddler caught in a lie. It was his own fault; he had allowed himself to relax, to sink into his careless childhood. He had thought the reality woven for his grandparents—not particularly joyful, but with a promise of a happy ending—was still holding up, like a reliable cover identity for a spy.

"I have worked in pedagogy for so long," Grandma was saying with a sigh. "I have quite a bit of experience with teenage addiction. You guys know nothing about drugs. And that's perfectly fine."

Sap glistened on the pine branches in a crystal vase, and the pine cones looked like decorations.

"We don't know why you made this choice," Grandma said. "But we made a choice, too, long ago:

"We'll never desert you."

Both boys wrapped their grandmother in a hug, and for the first time in months, they thought they might be whole.

On the morning of January 2, Sasha looked out the window. The streetlights were still on, the snow had stopped falling, and the bright sky peeked through gaps in the clouds. A man stood in the middle of the street, across from the institute's entrance with its stone lions. It would be impossible to see him if it weren't for his shadow. Snow lay on his head like a hat and piled up on his shoulders. There was no trace of footprints on the white field around him, not a sign of a human, a bird, or even a car. He'd been standing there since the beginning of the blizzard; an orange streetlight behind him made his shadow look dark blue.

Sasha put a jacket over her pajamas and stuck her bare feet into boots. Nearly falling as she ran down the stairs, she threw the door open. The stone lions were wearing tall white caps.

Valya was fully conscious. He didn't plunge into mental exercises, did not try to shake off his human body like a straitjacket, did not become a part of the sewer pipes, did not claim shapeless fragments of space. He simply stood in the middle of a snow-covered street.

For some reason, Sasha thought of her former roommate Lisa firing at Farit, of the bullets going into Farit's chest, into his neck, into the right lens of his dark glasses. She recalled the gun dropping on the polished floor with a hollow sound, and Lisa stretching her lips in a contemptuous yet beseeching smile. Lisa aimed at a shadow, hoping to kill the one who threw it. Or perhaps she had no hope, but rather only a dream.

"I want to pick up my hamster," Valya said.

"It'll freeze before you get it home," Sasha said, only now realizing how cold it was outside.

"I'll hold it under my shirt, it'll be warm there."

"That's fine," Sasha said. "I'll give your hamster back to you. Come upstairs."

She was afraid Valya would say no, but he took a step, then another. Snowflakes flew off his uncovered head and his jacket. Clumps of snow turned the smooth fabric of the street into a semblance of a lunar surface. Valya stopped, as if only just realizing where and how he'd spent the last few hours.

She changed her clothes, donning a pair of slacks and a sweater. Valya was feeding Kostya's carrots to his hamster. Valya didn't know where the carrots came from, and the hamster didn't care.

"I didn't tell them anything," Valya said, addressing the hamster.

"I know," Sasha said from behind the screen that separated her "bedroom" from her "office." "How are they doing? Are they ready for the exam?"

"They are ready," he said grimly. "I just wish I knew who needs this exam and why."

"The Speech needs it," Sasha said, standing at the balcony door with her arms crossed. "The Great True Speech needs new Words to operate."

"Pashka and Arthur don't know anything, they are visiting their grandparents," Valya said quickly. "With Eva. They are happy, do you understand? They plan on living. Alyssa hopes to go on living. She asked if I wanted to marry her someday. She wants to graduate and live like a human being! And I didn't tell her anything, not even her," he said, then paused. "It's probably for the best. They can live and not know that their world no longer exists, and that they are doomed."

"Perhaps you're right," Sasha said, nodding.

He looked into her eyes.

"What's going to happen with everyone? All the people who live in Torpa? Salespeople, cops, bus drivers?"

"What happens to unspoken Words? Or the rules to a long-forgotten game? Where does the light go when you switch the lamp off?"

"You speak of it so calmly," he said with difficulty, as if speaking through agonizing pain. "I thought that living with Alyssa repeating the same day over and over was not such a bad idea."

"If the True Speech is destroyed, there will be no time as a grammatical concept," she said. "And that means no one would be able to escape by staying in a loop."

Valya opened the cage and picked up the hamster, pressing the tiny animal against his chest, as if trying to protect it.

"And you? What will happen to you? Will you disappear as well?"

"No, I'll remain," Sasha said. "Only me, in the vacuum, beyond mass and space, beyond matter, beyond ideas, beyond time."

He opened his mouth, wanting to say something—and closed it. He began to tremble—noticeably, unable to hide it. The hamster fidgeted, and Valya let it back into its cage.

"Did you bring me your fear, Valya?" Sasha asked gently.

"I came here for my hamster," he said, looking away.

"We talked so much in this room," Sasha said. "Or rather, I talked, and you pretended to listen."

"I listened."

"Do you like my apartment?"

He nodded, pressing his lips together.

"This room, oh, this room," Sasha said, smiling. Her smile caught him off-guard. "This room is the only place where I feel like the old me. I loved someone here once, and I saved someone's life in here once. My mom waited here once while I was in class. I made biscuits for you here. This is my anchor, my home. It's where I decorate my tree for New Year's Eve."

"This place is going to be the last one to disappear when reality collapses, isn't it?" he asked, wanting to hurt her.

"Reality is not going to collapse if I don't let it."

That's what he'd come to her for. For hope. Trusting Sasha once again was torture for him, but, struggling as he was, he needed to hear this.

"But you destroy everything," he said, looking into Sasha's eyes. "I saw it."

"I destroy *and* I create; there is no contradiction here, only dialectics. If only you paid attention to what I'd told you."

"I remember." He spoke hastily, as if afraid that she wouldn't let him finish. "Big ideas cannot be canceled; they must be given new names. Fear cannot be canceled, it has to be brought into life, like in Torpa. The whole world should be like Torpa; is that what you're trying to accomplish? Is that really your goal?"

"Do you remember what I told you about choice?" Sasha asked, deliberately slow and calm, in contrast with his frantic rhythm. "'Directed effort in the name of love.' Do you remember?"

"But you have no love within you," Valya said. "There are just huge containers labeled *love,* but they are empty inside. They are just decorations."

"You've already said something like that to me," Sasha said, her heart sinking.

"Back then I just blurted it out in anger. But now I've *seen* it. I saw it when I looked at your pictures and turned into a monster."

"Well then," Sasha said, picking up a pack of cigarettes. "You've seen a lot during your time at the institute. But you still understand nothing. Nothing at all."

Pashka spent the night before the exam in the kitchen, struggling with one last exercise. He had to mentally build a chain of abstract notions, not from simple to complex, but from complex to elementary. Pashka couldn't do it. He tripped, he stumbled over and over again. He never managed to complete the chain, not even once.

Eva was asleep in her room on the second floor. The night before she swore on her life that she was ready for the exam.

Alyssa was also asleep, in her bed in room 8. She didn't have any exams coming up, only consultations. Tonya and Stefa slept with their textbooks under their pillows: they believed it would give them a boost when they faced Portnov the next day.

Valya was gone the entire night. He'd done this before. The rubber boots Arthur had lent him were about to fall apart, like his previous pair of shoes.

Arthur was asleep, likely dreaming of summer, fishing gear, and his grandfather's old boat.

It was five o'clock, the morning approaching quickly. The last exercise refused to obey. Pashka thought of Grandma and Grandpa, of the way their house smelled; he thought of the grandfather clock with its enormous pendulum, of the wooden staircase, the attic where one could find a typewriter, a hundred-year-old chess set, and other marvelous things. But the more Pashka thought about it, the more terrified he felt.

He saw flames bursting out of the round attic window, and this terrible fantasy refused to be contained.

CHAPTER TWO

Hello, first years, Group A. Welcome to your first Specialty exam. We have esteemed guests here today: my colleagues Alexandra Igorevna, our provost, and Adele Victorovna, the faculty member you will be working with next year. We also have Dmitry Dmitrievich here, although there's no need for an introduction since you all know him already."

A few students had to find new seats since the last row by the window was taken up by the esteemed guests, as Portnov called them, his voice dripping with sarcasm. Arthur and Pashka were no longer sitting together. Eva sat in the first row, next to Valya.

"This is what is going to happen," Portnov said, waving in the direction of the pieces of paper arranged on a long table. "I am going to call you one by one, not in alphabetical order, but in the order I decide on. You will choose an assignment, answer it, get your grade, and get the hell out of the auditorium so we can go on with our lives. Concentrate, remember what you've been taught, and don't embarrass me in front of my colleagues.

"Shanin!"

Valya jumped in his seat. His first thought was, *Portnov is about to fail me in front of everyone, and I am going to do something terrible. I might kill Portnov, or I might admit that I'm her brother.*

"Valentin Shanin passes automatically," Portnov said, opening a student attendance journal. "Based on his academic achievements during this semester. Shanin, give me your report card."

Valya tripped on his backpack and nearly fell in the aisle.

"Don't forget your belongings," Portnov said with distaste, writing "A" in Valya's card. "I hope you remember that pass/fail results are always differentiated. Get out of here, Shanin. Go get ready for your Philosophy exam. Makarova!"

Valya proceeded toward the exit on stiff legs. By the door, he turned and looked at Arthur, but it was Pashka who looked back at him, smiling. The smile was forced.

Pashka watched him leave. He longed to follow Valya out. He felt like a condemned man watching his friend draw a long straw and walk away unharmed.

He never mastered the last exercise, not during the night, not in the morning. Portnov used to say in almost every class: "Study. That one missed day, or hour, or minute might be the one that matters. Don't waste any time."

He thought of all the time he had wasted.

Grandma and Grandpa must have already had breakfast; they were early risers. Grandpa was probably on his way to the chess club. What day was his club meeting in the library? Grandma was probably busy with her embroidery. She'd never done any arts or crafts before, but recently she'd developed an interest and bought a huge magnifying glass. And now she was probably moving the needle in and out, watching a show on TV, while snow fell outside the window. If Pashka turned around, he'd see the snow outside; but he'd also see Alexandra Igorevna.

He never said anything to Arthur. All he said was that he was ready. Arthur had sighed with relief and clapped Pashka on the shoulder so hard it still hurt.

Visibly nervous, Tonya Makarova took a while to choose her question. Finally, she made the decision, and it appeared to be the right one. She read the assignment out loud: "'Complete the sequence of mental exercises from Chapter Four, numbers five through fifteen.'" Pashka could have done that one easily.

He perked up a little. Perhaps he'd get lucky and pass without the last exercise? Portnov couldn't possibly test everything; there were twelve students in Group A, in addition to the straight-A student Shanin. How long would this exam possibly last?

Tonya froze, her gaze fixed, her eyes bulging—a terrifying sight if one didn't know what she was doing. Portnov watched her dispassionately. Pashka wondered how many students Portnov had seen. Ten thousand? A million? How many of them had failed?

"Enough," Portnov said, putting his ring on top of the journal. "Your report card, please. You get a B."

For a moment, Tonya didn't move. She smiled, blinked—and suddenly began to cry, large round tears streaming down her face.

"Go, go," Portnov said, signing her report card. "Zhuravlyova!"

Pashka and Arthur exchanged glances. They were used to their place on top of the list. Arthur liked order; Pashka liked systematic approach. And now everything felt topsy-turvy, and Arthur still didn't know Pashka hadn't finished the last exercise.

What if Grandma were home alone when the house caught on fire?

It won't catch on fire, Pashka said to himself. He intertwined his fingers so tightly they hurt. *I will pass. I will pass. Why isn't he calling on us? At least on Arthur. He looks so nervous . . .*

The auditorium was emptying out. Behind him, Pashka felt the presence of the *esteemed guests*. He wondered what Coach was doing there. Obviously bored, Coach was fidgeting, making his chair squeak. Adele wore her winter perfume, cold and crisp. And this bitch, Alexandra Igorevna—now she knew what he thought of her, he certainly didn't hold back—she'd be a witness to his humiliation.

Squinting, Sasha watched the process. This was a new experi-ence for her. When she herself was a student here, she would simply get her report card marked with an A and leave. She wasn't sure what was worse—sit in the auditorium waiting to be called, or sit outside and wait for your classmates, unsure of who'd pass and who'd fail.

This was a good class, solid and smart. Sasha had done well, and Kostya was good at his job, and the kids themselves had worked hard; it had turned out to be an excellent semester. So far, they'd earned three A's and three B's, all well deserved, all the students with enormous potential. According to Portnov, Group B was just as good.

She wondered whether the Grigoriev brothers always asked for the same haircuts. She gazed at the backs of their identical heads, knowing neither one would turn around.

Why, oh why, were there two of them? If Yaroslav had one son, Sasha would be able to find his projection, the lost fragment, the magic Word. But these two flowed back and forth, complementing and negating each other. She noticed the tension in Pashka. Did he know how unprepared he was?

"Danilova," Portnov said.

A girl stood up; she was dressed in overalls that resembled a pilot's uniform, her cropped hair standing up on the top of her head like the needles of a hedgehog.

Pashka bit on his index finger. Across the aisle, Arthur repeated his gesture.

She can be yours, Pashka pleaded silently. *Let her choose you forever and ever. Just let her complete these goddamn exercises, let her pass the exam.*

Eva stopped by the whiteboard, facing the auditorium. Just a short while ago, she'd stood in the same spot, as if on the scaffold, Pashka by her side, and Portnov had informed the entire group that these two were doomed to fail.

"Go ahead, choose," Portnov said, shuffling the pieces of paper on the table.

Eva looked at Arthur, then at Pashka, then again at Arthur.

"I didn't say choose one of them," Portnov said, smirking. "Choose your assignment, please."

Pashka and Arthur inhaled and got up, ready to fight. Sudden tears made Eva's eyes look enormous.

"Stop," a woman's voice said behind them. "This is not the time. Please maintain discipline during the exam."

Arthur and Pashka returned to their seats, avoiding each other's eyes. *Just let her pass,* Pashka thought and felt—almost heard—Arthur thinking the same thing.

Choking on her tears, Eva picked the closest piece of paper and read the assignment. The room was so quiet that the rustling of snow outside seemed as loud as a hurricane.

Eva turned to face Portnov, her back to the audience. An electric spark flew out of the black hair on top of her head.

Minutes passed. Portnov gazed into Eva's face above his glasses, twirling his ring around his finger. Pashka couldn't see what was happening, and neither could Arthur. All they saw were the sparks in her hair growing stronger and crackling louder. A scent of ozone filled the room.

"Enough," Portnov said. "Your report card, please."

Eva did not move.

"You get an A," Portnov said, marking the journal. "How predictable humans are. No matter how hard we're trying, they remain . . . human. Your report card is in your right hand, Danilova."

Eva loosened her grip, letting her report card slide toward the floor. Portnov caught it, opened it on the correct page, and signed it.

"Get out of here; go get ready for Philosophy."

On her way out, Eva walked into the doorframe. She took a step back and tried again, holding her head high. Pashka and Arthur watched her exit. Pashka asked himself what had happened to the anticipated joy. His reaction was delayed, probably because he hadn't had enough time to process what had just happened.

Eva got an A.

"Mikoyan," Portnov said. Pashka came to his senses: only he, Arthur, Samvel, and Irwing remained in the auditorium. Was Portnov leaving the Grigoriev brothers for dessert?

After hours of waiting, Samvel was visibly nervous and asked for more time. Portnov gave him a look above his glasses, and Samvel almost started crying. Pashka had a bad feeling, but Samvel managed to pass.

"You get a C," Portnov said, signing his report card. "Taking into account your work on the winter concert, which turned out as successful as your preparation for this exam. I expect an uptick in your efforts in the beginning of the next semester. Otherwise, I'll be forced to report you to your advisor without waiting for the spring exam. You have been warned."

Samvel staggered out of the auditorium. Portnov reviewed his attendance journal, choosing the next victim. Pashka shrunk in his seat. He couldn't wait any longer. But he didn't think he could handle hearing his name, either.

"Klimchenko," Portnov said, and Irwing nearly toppled his chair on his way over to the whiteboard.

Valya waited, sitting at the base of the equestrian statue. He'd never imagined how painful an automatic pass would feel.

One after another, his classmates came out of the auditorium, jumping into each other's arms. Tonya and Stefa sniffled, then burst out laughing, then sniffled again.

Drenched in tears, Eva came out sideways, clutching her report card. Everyone stood still. Tonya ran over and looked at the grade.

"She got an A!"

Everyone hugged Eva, even those who didn't like her much, and even the girls from Group B, who'd ignored her so ostentatiously before.

Valya felt very strange, as if he still stood frozen in front of the building with an attic apartment and stone lions at the entrance. As if it was snowing here, inside, the snow, heavy as marble, falling onto his classmates' shoulders and covering the floor. Valya watched his happy classmates, who knew nothing and were simply celebrating passing their exams. The world hadn't changed for them; to them, everything was well outside Torpa and billions of people went on living their lives.

"Did you bring me your fear?" Alexandra Igorevna had

asked. Yes, he went to her door because living among unsuspecting people and knowing what he knew terrified him. But mostly, he went to get an answer. He wanted her to tell him that reality would survive.

Sitting at the base of the statue, Valya recalled all their conversations in her attic apartment, all the minute details about the world where children died and aircrafts crashed. He thought of the world without fear, despair, and childhood mortality; the world that had no chance of survival, the world that was being destroyed. He thought of Chaos approaching their threshold.

Alyssa came over, sat down, and pressed her warm side to Valya's.

"Are you worried about your friends?"

"Eva passed," Valya said absently.

"Yay!" Alyssa hugged him and kissed his ear. "You did it! You helped her!"

"Not in the least," Valya said. He was not in the mood for her affection, but to push her away would have been rude. "I couldn't do it. It was all Arthur and Pashka. Somehow they managed."

"Have they passed?" Alyssa asked anxiously.

The door of the auditorium opened. Valya stood up. Irwing emerged, red as if straight from a sauna.

"Whoa, I got a B. Holy crap!"

Valya sat back down on the edge of the pedestal. Portnov had left the Grigoriev brothers for the final part of the process.

He'd left them for dessert.

The auditorium was almost empty. Only Arthur and Pashka were still there, sitting across the aisle from each other and staring straight ahead at the board above Portnov's head. Portnov was slowly and deliberately reviewing his journal even though he only had two names to choose from.

"Well, Grigoriev, P. Please, come up."

From the way Pashka got up, Sasha knew: He wasn't ready. He hadn't finished. He was happy during those two weeks they'd spent in the same room with Eva and felt no remorse over it. He'd drowned half of his studies in his happiness. He was arrogant. His frivolity offset Arthur's iron willpower and diligence.

Sasha met Portnov's eyes. Portnov lifted his narrow glasses higher, shielding himself with the flickering reflections of the snow outside the window. Portnov was a function; there was no reason to plead with him. If a student wasn't ready, the student would surely fail.

"Choose your assignment, Grigoriev," Portnov said.

Adele and Coach looked at Sasha. Their gazes carried different connotations, but Sasha would have preferred to be invisible.

Pashka reached for the nearest piece of paper. Unsurprised, he saw the assignment he did not complete the night before. He'd run out of time.

"Complete the sequence of exercises from Chapter Thirty, backward from ninety-two to seven."

Pashka glanced at Arthur. His brother intertwined his fingers, tense but not panicking. It was a complicated assignment, but Arthur himself had completed it several times.

Pashka looked past Arthur. Alexandra Igorevna sat against the light, snow falling behind her. Her face remained in the shadows.

"You may begin," Portnov said.

Pashka inhaled, exhaled, and mentally re-created an object that encompassed qualities of both a cone and a sphere. He followed a chain of exercises, just like he did the night before, knowing where the sphere would rupture but fervently hoping he'd manage to repair the gap this time.

He failed. His concentration was lost, the imaginary figures melted, and the exercise chain sagged and ceased to exist. The first thing Pashka saw when he returned from abstractions to reality was Arthur's face. It bore the same expression as on the day Konstantin Faritovich ordered him to slap Grandma.

Coach shifted on his squeaky chair. Adele said something softly. Portnov glanced at the clock.

"Well. You have a couple more minutes. Want to have another go?"

"Sure," Pashka said hoarsely, even though he should have stayed silent.

Gritting his teeth, swimming in his own sweat, he imagined an unknown, foreign space and within it, the goddamn object that encompassed all qualities of a cone and a sphere. He followed the chain of exercises, knowing that . . .

The picture in front of his eyes—an imaginary, abstract picture—had a very subtle shift. It was as if the path were now outlined by a faint dotted line. As if someone had built the exercises for Pashka, highlighting his next move. As if someone had offered him a hand on a steep slippery slope. Pashka passed the spot where he failed the first time, then the next one, where he failed last night, and entered the phase of the exercises he'd never reached before.

Someone supported him, guided him forcefully, the life-line weakening, strengthening, and occasionally disappearing completely. But the chain of exercises was built from the most complex to the simplest one, and the farther he got, the easier it became for Pashka to manage on his own. Finally, he reached the simplest, most elementary task: "Convert the resulting object into a single point."

If I fail now, I will die, Pashka thought. He opened his eyes and realized they'd been open all along. Before his gaze, a single point was melting into the darkness. A single point, the last one.

"Your report card, please," Portnov's voice said in the dark. "Earth to Grigoriev? Regarding next semester: if you don't hit the ground running on the very first day . . ."

There was something unusual in his voice. Something aside from the habitual grumpiness and cold distaste toward student indolence. Pashka blinked. The auditorium emerged from the fog. The esteemed guests sat unmoving, like cardboard cutouts. Arthur visibly trembled, his head lowered, his fingers buried in his hair.

"You get a C," Portnov said. "Because you lost your place in the beginning, otherwise you'd get a B-plus for technical skills. You're done, get out of here."

"Did I pass?" Pashka asked hoarsely.

"You sure did," Portnov said grimly. "But you're sloppy. You have no work ethic. Go, prepare for Philosophy."

"Arthur," Pashka said.

His brother raised his head and looked at Pashka. Arthur's face was wet, with tears or sweat, and his eyes looked red and inflamed. Was it really because of Pashka?

Pashka smiled encouragingly. Once again, he felt no joy, even though what had just transpired was akin to a true miracle. A few more minutes, and this nightmare called Specialty exam would be behind them.

Pashka left, with one final glance in Alexandra Igorevna's direction.

...

The door closed behind Grigoriev, P. When he turned his head and gave her one last look, Sasha stopped breathing. At that moment, Pashka looked exactly like Yaroslav. A courageous man in the world full of fear. An ideal projection of someone capable of landing an aircraft in the storm.

Sasha lit a cigarette. It was absolutely unacceptable, beyond unacceptable, but she couldn't help herself. Portnov hunched over the attendance journal. Coach sighed dramatically. Adele moved her shoulders as if she had a backache.

"Under the circumstances, do you consider this a pass?"

"Objectively, he did pass," Portnov said dryly.

"But it's cheating!"

Sasha glanced at Adele; Adele fell silent and shifted in her seat, waving the smoke away from her face with visible displeasure.

"Grigoriev, A.," Portnov said, studying the journal. "Who taught you to enter into contact with the grammatical structure of another object? This is a syntactic connection, which is a part of the fourth-year curriculum. Who taught you?"

Arthur got up from his seat. Sasha saw his back but not his face. Unable to resist, she stepped toward the whiteboard and switched on the lights; the winter day outside was too close to twilight. She looked at Arthur's face in the fluorescent light. She looked *through* him and took another drag of her cigarette with aggression worthy of an old seaman.

Demonstratively, Adele opened a window.

"No one taught me," Arthur said softly. Sweat was drying on his face, leaving salty stripes and tightening his skin. "I didn't even know it was possible. I simply wanted to help him but didn't know how. I just wanted to help him."

Portnov removed his glasses and vigorously rubbed his eyes, then looked up at Sasha.

"What is this?"

"He's a particle," Sasha said. "A universal particle. Capable of changing modes."

Portnov swore under his breath.

"Negation, affirmation, motivation, instruction," Adele murmured, aimlessly flexing her fingers with their shiny lilac nails. "Strengthening or softening the demand. Wait a minute. What year is he?"

"He'll learn," Sasha said. "Right now he's still human, but ahead of him, he has—"

"He has nothing ahead of him," Coach said sharply. "None of us do."

The fluorescent lamps crackled, burning brighter. Arthur stood in the center of the auditorium, first red in the face, then growing pale. He looked from one faculty member to another, trying to figure out what they were talking about, and what it meant for him.

"Oleg Borisovich, Group B is already here, waiting," Sasha said. "Let's wrap this up."

"Grigoriev, A., choose your assignment," Portnov said, returning his glasses to the bridge of his nose. "Stop wasting our time."

Arthur flinched. Sasha recognized Portnov's cheap trick, the same one he applied to Eva: an unfairly insulted student performs better than expected.

"'Imagine a sphere,'" Arthur read out loud. "'Sequentially transform it so that its diameter is twice its original size, but the area of its surface remains the same.'"

He stood still, facing the desk, with his back to the whiteboard.

...

Ten minutes had passed since Pashka left the auditorium, then twenty minutes. Arthur remained inside.

First years, Group A, faced the door, unaware of holding each other's hands. Eva squeezed Pashka's palm. *He's coming out,* Pashka said to himself. *Any moment now.*

Group B sat on the floor leaning against the wall, textbooks in their laps. Their exam was scheduled to start a few minutes ago, but no one was reviewing the exercises. Everyone was waiting; more and more often someone would break into laughter, a sign of acute anxiety.

No one noticed the front door open, except for Valya, who stood a few paces away. Konstantin Faritovich was dressed lightly, like someone whose winter mode of transportation was a private car. A few snowflakes melted on top of his head. A handful of snow fell onto the rug by the entrance. Konstantin Faritovich caught Valya's gaze and waved in a simultaneous greeting and warning: *Don't attract attention.*

Valya moved forward as if trying to stop him, to block his path. Konstantin Faritovich bowed his head; it was a friendly gesture, but one that made Valya freeze mid-move. The man in dark glasses proceeded toward the administration wing, unnoticed by the first years: everyone's eyes were on auditorium 1.

Arthur was still inside. Valya couldn't come up with any plausible explanation.

Coach was impudent enough to remove a nearly empty cigarette pack from Sasha's hand. It wasn't just one window open now, all the windows were opened wide; gusts of wind threw handfuls of snow inside, and a large puddle grew under the radiator.

"Samokhina, enough with the smoking," Coach said, turning his perfectly human face with utterly inhuman eyes in her direction. "It's not going to help you."

Sasha stuck her cigarette into a pile of snow collected in the window frame, then pocketed the butt, staining her blazer.

"This was a pedagogical failure on your part," Adele forcefully said to Portnov. "You had to predict that the boy is capable of establishing syntactic connections! And now, after he served as a donor for his brother, he's been squashed dry!"

"Squeezed dry," Portnov corrected her out of habit.

"He's good for nothing! How could you not know something like this about your own student!"

Adele was taking many old grievances out on her colleague. She was mostly angry with Sasha, but Sasha was way out of Adele's reach, and so she pounced on Portnov.

"Let's wrap this up," Portnov said over Adele's voice. He patted the table looking for a pen. "Grigoriev, A., your retake is scheduled for January thirteenth."

Arthur stood still, his back to the board, his face to the audience; he'd clearly missed the point of what he just heard.

"You are to complete no exercises until January thirteenth," Portnov continued in a monotone. "Do not open your books. You must recover fully."

"No," Arthur whispered.

"By January thirteenth, you'll have rested, pulled yourself together, processed this new experience, and you will pass the exam."

CHAPTER THREE

The first person to step out of the auditorium was Portnov; he announced that the Specialty exam for Group B had been pushed back by fifteen minutes. First years were surprised, but not shocked. They hadn't been at Torpa long enough to know that Portnov would never, under any circumstances, postpone an exam.

Sasha followed Portnov out of the auditorium. Arthur was still inside. Sasha couldn't handle being in the same room with him; she suspected Arthur would not welcome her sympathy.

Pashka Grigoriev stood so close to the door that she nearly collided with him. She managed to look away. She followed Portnov to the administration wing, leaving behind a trail of general confusion, sympathy, shock, but also curiosity and a touch of gloating. A typical cocktail of emotions for first years.

Inside her office, Kostya was waiting for her, pacing from wall to wall, still wearing his coat. He said a terse hello to Portnov and turned to Sasha as if ready to deflect a harsh accusation.

"I am an instrument of Speech! You called me yourself!"

"It's fine," Sasha said. "Relax."

"Formally, we could consider the mitigating circumstances," Portnov said carefully. "I should indeed have known—

predicted—that Arthur was capable of syntactic connections. He should have taken his exam privately."

"Without his help, Pashka would have failed," Sasha said wearily. "Either way, one of the Grigoriev brothers would need a retake."

"You yourself," Kostya began, but Sasha interrupted him.

"Don't even go there, I know better than you who you are and what you must do! You are a pronoun; you must react as Farit would have done."

Kostya shuddered.

"If I can't convince you, I'm going to go," Portnov said softly. "I still have Group B."

"Thank you, Oleg Borisovich," Sasha said. "This is a very strong class, and it's very well prepared. I hope Group B avoids retakes."

Portnov nodded and left. Sasha waited for the door to close and sat down heavily behind her desk.

"Do I not have any love left inside me? Not a drop?"

Kostya stuffed his hands into his coat pockets and paced around her office, then stopped.

"Listen to me. I remember everything. But do you? Do you remember the first time you *expressed* love on a piece of paper and then burned it in the fireplace? It was our love, by the way, yours and mine."

"I'm very sorry," Sasha said. "Had I been smarter back then—"

"Had *I* been smarter!"

"We were teenagers, we couldn't have known." Sasha laughed bitterly. "So much love. So little understanding. And now it's the opposite."

"But you—you do love your pilot, don't you?"

"He doesn't exist," Sasha said softly. "I love someone who

doesn't exist. He's made up, this love of mine. He's the light that takes so long to make its way from a star that, on its way, it scatters into nothing and violates the law of conservation of energy."

"But you loved him, Samokhina! You trusted him! You wanted to bring him back! What happened?"

"I happened," Sasha said. "I changed. I've taken too long to gather my own fragments. I tortured people, forcing them to jump over their heads and become true Words. I lied to them. I made them kill hamsters. Go, Kostya. Do something useful. I hope it teaches them a lesson in discipline."

Crying, Eva wrapped her arms around Arthur. At some point Pashka considered leaving them alone together, vacating the room and letting Eva make her choice. But Arthur was adamant: *Tonight we must be with Grandma and Grandpa.*

"I'm coming with you," Valya said. To Pashka's surprised glance, he responded: "With the three of us there, let them try and burn this house down."

On the way, they stopped at a housewares store and purchased as many handheld fire extinguishers as they could carry. Sidewalks had been cleared, but not diligently, and they kept sinking knee-deep in the snow.

"They said I was a particle," Arthur said hoarsely. "And that I am too powerful for a first year. And that I also can't do enough. They talked right in front of me as if I were a log. And that's exactly what I was. I didn't understand anything."

"Save your breath," Valya said. "There is no point in listening to them, they always lie."

"You've stood up for Alexandra before," Pashka said, shifting a large red extinguisher on his shoulder.

"That's because she's my sister," Valya said, staring at the ground.

Pahka nearly dropped the fire extinguisher on his foot.

"*What?*"

"It doesn't mean anything. I've never . . . I only met her when I came to Torpa."

They walked in silence for a few minutes, snow crunching softly under their feet.

"You can't make any deals with her, can you?" Arthur asked.

"Nope. She's all about velvet gloves," Valya said, smiling wistfully. "But right now it doesn't matter because . . . How far is the house?"

"Two blocks," Pashka said, breathing heavily. "But uphill. Not a steep hill, though."

It looked as if Valya was about to say something important. He took a deep breath and opened his mouth, but then he changed his mind.

Standing at the door, Grandma clasped her hands.

"What in the world is that?"

"It's regulations," Pashka said. He was almost out of breath. "Torpa's administration wants everyone to observe fire safety."

"But these things are so ugly," Grandma said, studying the fire extinguishers with distrust. "Can we put them in the closet?"

"No, Grandma. The regulations demand that they are placed in every room," Arthur said softly. "We can decorate them or drape them with something."

"Arthur, honey," Grandma said, gazing into his eyes. "What's wrong?"

Arthur flinched. Pashka worried that Arthur would give

himself away, but his brother's laugh sounded cheerful and carefree. Pashka marveled at Arthur's willpower. At the next moment, Arthur wrapped his arms around Grandma, and she laughed, too, and Pashka dragged the fire extinguishers up the stairs.

January 2 was drawing to a close. The sun was setting early.

They had tea with apple cake. Whispering, they assigned responsibilities: who was going to do what when the house caught on fire. They tried to identify the most critical zones: wiring in the living room? The attic? Grandma wanted to light the tall holiday candles, but Pashka gently talked her out of it.

The attic was cramped with all sorts of flammable rubbish. Old magazines, children's furniture, Lora and Antoshka's toys, and even the toys that belonged to Arthur and Pashka. Teddy bears with sweet dirty faces: some time ago they had been lovingly fed with breakfast oatmeal. A small bike and a red beach ball: Pashka flinched when he saw it. The ball hadn't deflated in six months; it looked ready for a game in the water.

"It looks like our world," Valya whispered. "A projection of reality."

"That's bullshit," Pashka said sharply. "If it's a projection, it only projects our own sentimentality."

And our fear, he added silently.

"We shouldn't stay here in the attic," Arthur said. He kept sniffing the air, like a smoke detector in search of carbon monoxide. "Let's spread out as we discussed."

But they didn't want to spread out. They kept clinging to each other. Valya looked particularly dejected. Did he regret coming with the brothers? Did he miss Alyssa? Was he afraid of retaliation from his insane sister?

"Listen, guys," Arthur said, as if responding to Pashka's internal monologue. "So if we manage to put out the fire, what will *he* do next? Will *he* forgive us? Or . . . ?"

"Let's start by putting out the fire," Pashka said.

He picked up the red beach ball and squeezed it like the head of a bitter enemy.

"We'll never obey them again. We're going to get out of Torpa."

"There is nowhere to go," Valya said softly.

The clouds parted. The stone lions looked up at the sky, at the place where Orion would rise in February; at this moment, Orion was still low, behind the horizon, obscured by the tiled roofs. Sasha stood on her balcony, gazing at the jagged edges of the tiles, at the copper weathervanes. The wind blew the remaining smoke out of her lungs.

The last pack of cigarettes was smoldering in the fireplace inside.

Taking one more deep breath, Sasha parted from her body and rose above Torpa, rose above the world. The old city with a tower had been destroyed, and so had the distant bridges and mountains. The tower itself was leaning precariously, about to topple over. Sasha could see reality as Valya, a human child, saw it: in ruins. She could see it as a network of colorful Platonic eide. Or as pure information that a human brain could never perceive nor describe.

That night she made a decision. She felt light. She was in a great deal of pain.

"But we have their messages." Arthur shook his phone demonstratively. "Just a few, but here they are. 'Happy birthday!' 'Are you ready to apologize?' 'We spoke to Grandpa, happy about your news, but perhaps you can get in touch yourselves?' The last message was the day before yesterday, they wished us a happy New Year."

"If Alexandra wants to, she'll make it possible for you to talk to your parents, even on video," Valya said. "They will say exactly what you'd expect, what you want them to say or are afraid to hear. But everything outside of Torpa is . . . how can I explain it? There was this short story about a guy who kept getting letters from a woman who'd been dead for a hundred years. That's what it's like."

"What about our grandparents?" Pashka said. His voice broke slightly, and Valya knew that Pashka believed him and had stopped torturing himself with "what ifs."

"They are real," Valya said. "I'm happy I had a chance to meet them."

"What will happen to them?"

"It might be that things will remain the same in Torpa," Valya said. He didn't feel like sharing what Alexandra had said on this topic. "It's possible. Torpa is—"

"Torpa is this bitch's lair," Arthur said quietly. "And everyone at the institute is her servant."

"*The world is not how you imagine it,*" Valya said, as if spitting out something bitter. "They said it so many times. They are turning us into someone like them."

"Fat chance," Pashka said grimly.

Arthur sniffed the air again. Valya listened to the ticking of the clock behind the wall, a warm, cozy sound. They'd gathered in a small room where the twins usually slept. It was long past midnight; in the summer, at this hour the sun would already be coming up.

"When I believed that my parents no longer loved me, I

got one step closer to what she wanted me to be," Valya said. "An instrument of True Speech. I wish I knew what it was."

"When I killed that hamster . . ." Arthur began, but Pashka placed a hand on his shoulder.

"Never mind, it's all in the past."

They fell silent. The clock kept ticking. Silence reigned over Torpa; small towns go to sleep early.

"What if it doesn't happen today?" Arthur said, finally verbalizing his biggest fear. "My retake is not until the thirteenth. What if *he* waits until we turn away, get tired, leave . . ."

"We won't leave," Pashka said firmly. "We're going to protect our grandparents. We will stay here until the end of the world if we—"

A distant siren cut through the silence, like a howl echoing inside a cave. It roared again, then again.

All three of them jumped up and made their way into the living room, trying to be stealthy but tripping over chairs. The living room did not smell of smoke. Nothing indicated faulty wiring. Two enormous fire extinguishers stood sentinel on both sides of the decorated tree like armored elves.

The siren howled somewhere very close. Headlights flashed around the corner: a fire truck was rushing from the small suburban fire department to the other side of Torpa, through the center of the town.

"It's not our house, is it?" Arthur said hesitantly. "Are we being tricked? Are they trying to smoke us out?"

"I know where the fire is," Valya said softly. "But it can't be . . ."

A thick layer of soot blanketed the stone lions. Black snowflakes fell from the sky, and Sasha was forced to step away. The fire trucks had already blocked Sacco and Vanzetti. Sasha raised her head, watching the flames burst out of the balcony door, singeing the grapevines.

"Too bad about the grapes," Kostya said. Sasha didn't see him approach, but now he stood just behind her, as if trying not to get into her face.

She sighed and took his arm.

"It is a pity, yes."

The house burned like a candle. Aside from Sasha, no one had lived there for years. Maria Fedorovna, the landlady from the previous grammatical reality, had moved in with her granddaughter a while ago. Or perhaps she had never been born.

Snow melted off the roofs across the street. Neighbors ran around in a panic. The owners of the *All Your Home Needs* store were shuttering their windows. But Sasha knew the fire wouldn't reach that far. Within seconds, Sacco and Vanzetti Street turned from a snowfield into a dark, smoky mess. Like a bride who'd been tarred and feathered. Black streams ran among boulders as if signifying the arrival of the final spring.

Firemen brandishing thin water hoses looked like a bunch of children trying to put out a fire with their own feeble rivulets. The image amused Sasha and she laughed out loud. The neighbors stared at her fearfully, wondering if the poor woman had lost her marbles from grief.

The lower the flames, the brighter it was outside. When the tiled roof collapsed, the sparks flew into the gray sky with a hint of the morning blue light. The firemen lowered their hoses, admitting the futility of their efforts. Water soaked the burned building, heavy drops falling as in a forest in early spring.

"Everyone, please disperse," a local official in a coat thrown over his suit jacket and tie commanded, wiping soot off his snub nose. *He must be someone important,* Sasha thought.

Running over here at such an early hour, on January 3—they must have dragged him out of bed. This will surely end up in the local paper.

Onlookers recorded the charred ruins on their phones. Still holding Kostya's arm, Sasha took a deep breath—and saw the boys, all three of them.

They ran across the small town. Their jackets were unbuttoned, their faces flushed, eyes watering from the wind. They couldn't resist. They came all this way only to see the ruins of her apartment, to see Sasha and Kostya, to take a step back in horror . . .

Valya was the first one to come to his senses. He assessed the fleet of fire trucks, clenched his fists, and stepped toward Sasha as if he was about to hit her.

"Is their house going to burn down? Because the entire fire department is here?"

The twins stood behind him, Pashka red in the face, Arthur growing paler by the minute.

"Do you really think a fire like that can be put out with a hose?" Sasha asked softly. "Or with a fire extinguisher?"

Kostya stood by her side, not saying a word. At this moment, Valya knew no fear; in him, Sasha saw her own reflection, like a strange light underneath a body of water.

"Their house is not going to burn down," Sasha said, smiling. "Because mine just did."

"This room," Alexandra Igorevna had said a while ago. "This room is the only place where I feel like the old me. I loved someone here once, and I saved someone while living here. My mom waited here once while I was in class. I made biscuits for you here. This is my anchor, my home. That's where I decorate my tree for New Year's Eve."

"Have you sacrificed your own home instead of . . . ?" Valya asked without thinking. Arthur and Pashka stepped closer, trying to understand.

"It's just an old building," Alexandra said lightly.

"It was a projection," Valya said faintly. "Of something very big. It was . . ."

The sun came up, reflecting in the weathervane across the street, its copper silhouette untouched by soot. The beam of light fell onto Alexandra Igorevna's face and made her squint. Suddenly, just for a second, Valya saw her—all the way *through*.

He staggered and became blind.

"Stop it!" Alexandra barked. "You're not ready! When are you going to learn not to jump ahead?"

"Forgive me," Valya said, forcing himself to regain his human vision. Then, quietly, "Regarding love . . ."

"Regarding love?" Alexandra Igorevna said, glancing at the smoldering ruins dripping with water.

"Sasha, if you need something—anything in my possession— please take it, it's yours," Valya said.

The sun was fully up. The firemen cordoned the scene with yellow tape to keep the gawkers away. The tape connected the two stone lions like a double leash or a tie. Sasha felt Kostya's warm breath on her left ear, her cheekbone, and her temple.

The three boys stood in front of her, and Sasha struggled not to let herself stop the time. Just for a moment, a half measure. Just to take a better look.

A better look at Valya, like into a mirror. When did he

manage to grow up? And these two—reflections of Yaroslav, all the while mirroring each other. A system of projections, dynamic and very beautiful. It was a shame no one but Sasha would truly appreciate it.

"Thanks, Valya," Sasha said. "I'm very grateful for your offer. But . . ."

Across the street, the sign creaked, drowning her voice. The first letter in *All Your Home Needs* fell, followed by the crossbeam of *N*. After a short pause, the last letter dropped onto the dirty cobblestones.

The onlookers reached for their phones. "It's from the heat," someone yelled. "Good thing the window didn't pop. Move away!"

Firemen began to replace the yellow tape. The letter *H* swayed precariously.

"What is this?" Arthur asked, the first words he'd uttered since seeing Alexandra's home on fire.

"Verification," Sasha said, forcing a smile. "'An empirical confirmation of the theoretical provisions of science by "returning" to the visual level of cognition when the ideal nature of abstractions is ignored and the abstractions in question are identified with observable objects.'"

No one knew what to say. Kostya squeezed Sasha's elbow harder.

"It's an illustration of certain processes," Sasha explained. "A primitive, visual one. Like a children's cartoon."

"The Speech is deteriorating," Valya said in a faint whisper. "But . . . Sasha, you promised not to let this happen! And . . ."

He faltered, struck by a terrible thought.

"Is this because of me? I ruined everything . . . I spoiled things. I failed!"

"It was me who failed," Sasha said with a sigh. "I needed

three fully formed Words. And instead, I have three little boys who have learned a lot but who are still human."

She took one last look at the ashes of her home.

"Let's go, Kostya."

"Wait!"

Grigoriev, P. stepped in her way. His eyes shone; Sasha knew this look, harsh and sharp. It made her feel hot.

"Where do you see 'three little boys'?" he asked, his teeth bared in rage. "Are you lying to us again? Are you manipulating us? Is this because you don't want to change anything, because you are an assassin of reality?"

Sasha looked up at the sky and saw stars no one on Sacco and Vanzetti could see anymore. The air smelled of smoke, a revolting, disturbing odor.

"Either you fix everything, or you are truly a murderer," Arthur said.

Sasha did stop the time then, and the letter *H* hung suspended dramatically in the middle of its fall, and the black streams froze among the cobblestones, and so did a cloud of smoke above the street. If the world was cannibalistic by nature simply because its foundation presumed no alternatives, then for such a world to be annihilated was a necessity and a blessing.

And yet, here was Yaroslav, very much alive, very young, angry and confused, glaring at her through the eyes of his twin projections. And Valya stared at her, too, with their mother's eyes. It had been a while since Sasha had thought of Mom.

Scattered shards gravitated toward each other, and the last fragment, the one Sasha thought had been lost forever, clicked into place. Sasha saw the world the way it was supposed to be and the price she would have to pay for it.

"At this point in time, you will have to believe me," Sasha said, restarting the time. The letter *H* crashed onto the pavement.

"Or rather, you must believe *in me*. Can you manage this, after all I've done to you?"

Onlookers and passersby bustled around them, water squelched, and soot crunched under their feet.

"The assembly hall key, please," Sasha said to the guard on duty.

She had her own locked in a safe, but she didn't have time to go to the administration wing.

The guard hesitated but obeyed. Sasha took the heavy key on a large wooden key chain and walked across the lobby, pausing in front of the scheduling board. A multitude of names appeared, then melted into nothing—like a memory plaque.

Followed by Valya, Pashka, and Arthur, Sasha passed the bronze stallion, moved the dusty curtain covering the entrance into the assembly hall, and unlocked the door.

Coach sat in the last row, his muscular arms crossed over his chest. Surprised, the three boys stopped in their tracks.

"No exams or tests have been scheduled for today," Coach said.

"We are having a consultation."

"Is Oleg Borisovich aware?"

"For your information, Dmitry Dmitrievich, I decide whom to involve in my plans."

"May I be of assistance?" Coach said, touching the whistle hanging around his neck.

"No," Sasha said with regret.

"The twins are showing signs of interference. Self-oscillations are not out of the question."

"I know," Sasha said, raising her voice slightly.

"Whatever happens now, there is one thing that makes

me happy," Coach said after a pause. "I am glad you've once *reverberated*."

He closed the door behind him.

"What self-oscillations was he talking about?" Arthur asked anxiously. "And also, is 'interference' a grammatical term?"

Sasha looked around the assembly hall. Nothing in there had changed in millennia. The hall was the true center of Torpa. Rows of creaky chairs, heavy velvet curtains, a tiny window of the sound booth. Above the stage, a thousand-year-old banner announced: *Gaudeamus Igitur, Juvenes dum sumus.*

"This is not a place, and this is not time. It cannot be described, nor can it be understood through human experience. But I will create a visualization for you, albeit a crude one. You will see only what a human being can imagine. The true processes and events will be concealed from you."

"Like with the sign over the store," Valya said hoarsely.

"Please don't talk," Sasha said, not unkindly. "From this moment on, everyone must remain silent, unless I address you directly."

Valya pressed his hands to his mouth.

"If you cease to exist there, you will not die," Sasha said. "You simply will not have been conceived. It will be impossible to remember you, and it will be impossible to imagine you. This is how it will be forever."

They didn't look scared. Moreso, their eyes lit up. All three of them *believed* in her intention.

"Pashka, you're an adverb," Sasha said. "An adverb of direction, signifying a dynamic relocation toward an object or away from it. Arthur, you were asking me about interference:

355

when Pashka indicates a direction you will subjectively judge to be correct, please support him through your syntactic connection. If he makes a mistake, suppress his move, extinguish his will."

"How will I know if it's correct?"

"You're a particle, an auxiliary part of speech," Sasha said. "You determine the probability of an event or a process. If you cannot support the right solution, we will fail. All of us will fail. Yes, you're a Word that has never *reverberated*. Yes, we're taking a risk. Do you think I'm an idiot, not taking you to the beginning of time on the first day of school?"

It became very quiet. Sasha felt a chill: it was such a human emotion, a bad temper tantrum. Sterkh would never believe his best pupil was capable of something like this.

Valya raised his hand like an obedient pupil.

"Sasha, is everything all right?" he asked softly.

Grateful, Sasha nodded.

"Valya, you are a verb in the imperative mood."

"I'm a part of you," Valya said quickly.

"No. You are a part of yourself. But at some point, I will miss . . . I will want for my missing fragment. That's when I will need you to act. I will need you to express a command."

"What kind of command?" he said, and now he was terrified.

"You'll figure it out," Sasha said. "Now, all of you: Take a deep breath and hold it."

Sasha raised her hands; the ashes from all her drawings, all the self-portraits, doodles, sketches, tactical plans—all the ashes remaining in the fireplace of her attic apartment along with the ashes of the house itself flew off her hands, filled the assembly hall, and folded into a model of a dying universe.

He couldn't breathe; he felt as if he were sliced across the chest with an edge of a tin can. Pashka opened his mouth wide, choking. He felt a stream of air on his face.

He saw a very low white plastic ceiling and an air-conditioning grille directly above. Without thinking, he reached up and directed the air stream off to the side.

An empty chair to the left of him, another empty chair to the right. A black window reflected the lights inside the aircraft.

"Dear passengers, our aircraft is moving along the set route," a familiar voice said through the speakers. "Bathrooms are open. Please keep your seatbelt fastened when in your seat."

"Dad," Arthur said somewhere very close. There was a click of a seatbelt being unfastened. Pashka turned his head and saw Arthur crawling along the aisle on all fours, breathing heavily.

"Wait!" Valya shouted, trying to unfasten his own seatbelt. "It's not a real plane!"

"Our dad is there!" Grabbing onto the back of empty seats, Arthur made his way toward the cockpit. "Dad, forgive me, I will explain everything."

"Dear passengers, our flight is right on schedule."

There were no passengers on board this plane, and no flight attendants. Pashka caught up to Arthur right by the cockpit and grabbed his shoulders.

"It's an illusion. A visualization. Dad's not here. We have to—"

Arthur pulled the cockpit door open.

Beyond the windshield, a flat vortex resembled an enormous staring eye. The aircraft was heading straight at the pupil, directly at its black center. The instrument panel glowed in the dark. The cockpit was empty.

Pashka and Arthur stopped at the threshold, hypnotized by the colorful clusters of stars, nebulae, masses of energy, and matter ready to pass beyond the event horizon. What they were witnessing wasn't just visible, it was audible; music passed through their skin and left a bitter taste on their tongues.

"Take your seats," Alexandra said, appearing behind them. She wore a white suit, the same one she wore on September 1. "Pashka, take the captain seat. Buckle up."

"But I don't know how . . ."

"There is no plane, no steering, there is only you, the adverb of direction. Arthur, take the first officer's seat. Fasten your seatbelt."

Seatbelts clicked, a mundane sound breaking through the inhuman music of the beginning of time. Sasha looked at the Grigoriev brothers and felt almost calm. Yaroslav was close now, so very close: the one who flew a plane through the storm. The fulcrum.

"Valya, go back to the cabin, to the emergency exit on the right," Sasha said softly. "Take a seat and fasten your seatbelt."

"What about you?"

"I'm a stream of particles, a conceptual activator. I'm a sum of galaxies, Valya. I can stand up during turbulence."

The Grigoriev brothers froze in their assigned chairs, gazing at the view in front of them: the embodied *Nothing* devouring matter, energy, and time.

"Pashka, look for the course," Sasha said from her spot at the cockpit door. "Arthur, assess the probability of success."

Pashka clutched the steering wheel. The aircraft shook like a bus going over speed bumps, once, then again, then again.

"Unlikely," Arthur whispered.

Arthur sat upright, not looking at his brother, but remaining in direct communication with him. This was the connection that their teachers and psychologists had tried so hard to break. Only Sasha succeeded at destroying it, then allowing for this connection to rebuild not at a biological level, but at a grammatical one. Arthur was a particle, a blind navigator; his mission was to lead Sasha following his intuition, employing Yaroslav's reflection he carried within. Pashka's job was to direct him through his will.

The course changed again.

"Doubtful," Arthur said, barely moving his lips. He was trying to define the true Meaning using human language; it was a futile attempt, like painting a windy sunset with a soot-covered finger. "Dubious."

Sasha tensed up. Was he acting as a navigator—or as a confused first year? A pilot—or a boy lost in the dark? Doubt turned into self-oscillation; the twins were human beings, teenagers, dependent on each other since sharing the same amniotic sac.

"Not at all," Arthur said. He was losing his voice; all that came out was faint wheezing. "Absolutely not. No way."

The aircraft leaned to one side, about to go into a tailspin. The interior lining of the cabin shimmered like fish scales, breaking into signs and symbols. Sasha was losing her grip on the synthesized model.

"Dear passengers," the voice spoke again, and this time it sounded different, low, and very authoritative. "We are entering an area of turbulence, but I'm here. I exist. I'm here."

"Exactly!" Arthur shouted, his voice barely rising above a whisper. "Right now! Exactly! We're here, Dad!"

Sasha didn't know whom or what Arthur saw at that moment, but Pashka saw it, too, and he screamed, indistinctly and joyously.

Pieces of the puzzle had come together. The event whose probability was so low it couldn't even be expressed in numbers had taken place. Sasha had reached the starting point: without mass, without gravity, volume, or temperature. She made it to the point of the first cry of an infant with no hint of Speech. Staggering, clinging to the backs of the rows, Sasha walked toward the emergency exit, where, huddled in a seat, Valya was waiting for her.

"Will it be much longer?" he asked, licking his cracked lips.

"Now," she said, unlocking the emergency door, one latch after another.

"You'll depressurize the cabin," Valya said faintly.

"Yup," Sasha said. "The absolute true Fear is outside, and I'm about to let it in."

"Don't!"

"It's okay. I will become a part of the Fear, and it will become a part of me. I will not be able to overcome it because it is unsurmountable by design."

The last lock gave way.

"I'll hand the Fear back to the Speech," Sasha said softly. "Along with other things. Like a directed effort in the name of love. Or believing that all fairy tales have happy endings."

"What about me?"

She smiled.

"Without you, I will fail."

The emergency door opened.

Valya saw the pupil of the universe's eye framed by the bright and happy green iris of collapsing galaxies. Valya saw Alexandra's face, the face of a little girl, terrified, paralyzed by fear, frozen in panic.

He was only a first year, far from being able to *reverberate,* and so he simply took her hand.

"*Trust me,*" he said.

Pulling her along, he took a step forward, as if jumping with a parachute and knowing full well that the parachute never existed.

EPILOGUE

Y aroslav Antonovich, it is with deep regret that we must inform you: your sons are expelled from the Institute of Special Technologies. The reason is professional incompetence. They will receive their last stipend in January."

He was sitting in her office, dressed in a black sweater over a black shirt. He never once looked up, staring down at the desk during their entire, brief conversation.

"I'm glad you came here," Sasha said. "I always prefer speaking with parents in person."

He nodded, still avoiding her eyes.

"Well then," Sasha said, getting up. "I'll walk you out."

Together, in silence, they passed through the lobby and walked out onto Sacco and Vanzetti.

The linden trees stood naked, their ice-covered branches glimmering like glass and thawing slowly under the bright sun. Heavy drops fell onto the pavement, as shiny as the scales of a healthy young fish.

A minibus was parked by the side of the road. Pashka and Arthur were loading up their suitcases; Anton Pavlovich was trying to help, but the boys' grandmother wouldn't allow him to pick up anything heavy.

Eva was waiting nearby. Like most teenagers, she didn't bother with a hat, and her black hair stood on end like hedgehog's needles.

"Sasha, I . . ." Yaroslav said quietly.

Sasha turned. A mere meter separated them, and the entire street could see the two of them standing a mere meter apart.

"Would you prefer to forget everything?" she asked, smiling and holding back tears. "Your memory contains enormous clusters of information unsuitable for a human being. It may be unpleasant. It may even be dangerous."

"Don't you dare," he said, nearly choking on air. "I'd never forgive you."

"You have so much to not forgive me for."

"No," he said, shaking his head. "I want to remember all my lives. All the versions of my fate. Don't worry, I can handle it. I will write a book, then another. And you will be in all of them."

Once again, he was himself, the real Yaroslav Sasha remembered and loved so deeply. Listening to him, she grinned like a high school girl, and there was nothing she could do to stop her lips from smiling.

"Promise me I'll always remember you," he said in a soft whisper. "I know what you're capable of, so promise me."

"Won't it make it worse for you? Won't it make you feel anxious and sad? Will it stand between you and the mother of the boys?"

He shook his head.

"Then you have my promise," Sasha said. "You will never forget me."

Arthur and Pashka finished loading up the minibus and dusted off their hands in the same gesture. Neither one showed even a shadow of a Word, not a bit of the information directly connected to the Speech. Arthur and Pashka were simply two healthy strapping young men; one was clad in a formal dress suit despite the long travel ahead of them. The other—in ripped jeans and a light jacket, despite the winter weather. They were the same, but it would be impossible not to see the difference.

Exchanging glances, the Grigoriev brothers approached Eva. The driver waited, strolling back and forth and squinting at the sun. Arthur and Pashka put their arms around Eva. She hung on their shoulders, sobbing.

"This is for the best," Sasha said. "She could never love them both; it would be a betrayal of all of them. And should she choose one of them, all three would be unhappy."

"Is she staying?" Yaroslav asked.

"Yes," Sasha said, nodding. "She's a very good student with a lot of potential. She'll pass her third-year exam, she'll *reverberate* and learn how beautiful and harmonious the Great Speech is. And you—you should prepare for a future with grandchildren."

The driver honked impatiently. Arthur and Pashka seemed to be promising Eva to text, call, and come for a visit in the summer.

"Sasha, will I ever see you again?" Yaroslav asked.

"I'll always be with you," Sasha said. "Every time you enter the cockpit, I will be sitting in the cabin behind you. Your aircraft will never crash. Not because there is no fear and there is no death, but because I will always be in the seat behind you."

The beds looked bare without mattresses. Plastic bags, shreds of paper, and fragments of packing tape were scattered around the room. The hamster was munching on an apple. Valya sat behind his desk, looking through his book of exercises.

Sasha knocked before entering. Valya looked back, got up, and hugged her.

"Don't be sad," Sasha said. "Everything has a price. You saved reality while I was murdering it."

"I will never again . . . won't see . . . I won't be able to . . . all these spheres, all these dimensions . . . The Speech . . . I won't hear . . . won't understand . . ."

"You will meet Mom and your dad at the airport. Tomorrow, very soon. Your cab is coming in ten minutes. You need to pack the hamster and its cage in a duffel bag so that the hamster has enough air and is warm but not hot. And take off your earring—no reason to annoy Mom."

"No," he said, touching his silver earring with the tip of his finger. "Listen, I couldn't say good-bye to Alyssa. She didn't believe me, she got upset and ran away. Sasha, can you release her? Can we leave together?"

"I can't," Sasha said. "Students must pass their exam, and the Great Speech must have its new Words. Each graduate is worth their weight in gold. Just think—Alyssa will never find herself in a temporal loop again. And she will once again learn to love the rain."

"Then let me stay here, at the institute," Valya said quietly.

"No. You're no longer a verb, you're just a normal young man. With a normal life. With a family, a future. You used to want this."

Valya shook his head.

"I didn't know. I couldn't have known."

"Tell Mom I love her."

"Sasha!" he said, choking on air. "Come with me! Let's go

get them from the airport! Can you imagine how happy they would be? Mom's been waiting all these years."

"No. Just believe me. Trust me."

Portnov and Adele stood by the open door of auditorium 1, by the base of the marble staircase.

"Third years are doing reasonably well," Portnov said. "They have a good chance of passing the final exam. All of them. Do you agree, Adele Victorovna?"

"Most assuredly, a total success of the grammatical reform," Adele said, her expression resembling that of someone trying an oyster for the first time.

"Great," Sasha said. "Then I have nothing to worry about."

"You were my best student, Samokhina," Portnov said, looking over his glasses at the space above the tall arched ceiling.

"I wish I could say the same thing," Adele said in a sugary singsong voice.

"Good luck," Sasha said. She went up the stairs to the third floor, feeling their eyes on the back of her head.

In the gym, a basketball was bouncing off the floor. In the rear of the room, Coach strolled back and forth, watching the game. Sasha stopped at the entrance, but he didn't even look in her direction. First and second years, done with their Applied Specialty exams, haphazardly ran around with no strategy, like a bunch of toddlers with the sole purpose of getting their hands on the ball.

"Pity them, Kostya," Sasha said.

Kostya immediately materialized behind her left shoulder.

"What did you say?"

"Just pity them occasionally. They will think of it as a miracle, and it will make them study harder."

"That's debatable," Kostya said after a pause. "But I will consider it."

Sasha walked along the creaky fourth-floor corridor, glanced through the round stained-glass window at Sacco and Vanzetti Street, and entered the deserted auditorium 14.

She opened the window shutters and inhaled the frosty air. She looked at the roof across the street. There, amid the chimneys, amid the copper weathervanes, she saw the person she'd been longing to see for a very long time. He was patiently waiting for her, his enormous wings folded behind his back.

"I'm ready, Nikolay Valerievich," Sasha said. "I'm ready to fly."

The End

ACKNOWLEDGMENTS

I would like to thank Sergey Dyachenko, my husband, friend, and coauthor. I promised him to complete the Vita Nostra trilogy, and now I have fulfilled my promise. I believe his voice can be heard in this book.

I would like to thank our daughter Anastasia, who is always there, forever in my memory.

I would like to thank my parents and my sister Natalia, my beloved New Zealanders, who have supported me through thick and thin. I am proud of my friendship with David Allen, a man with a huge heart, who became a member of my family.

I would like to thank Julia Meitov Hersey, without whom this book would not exist. She is not just a friend and translator, she is a path and a guide, and I wish for myself that our cooperation would last another hundred years.

This book wouldn't have happened without our agent, Josh Getzler, to whom I wish health, strength, and energy. I also want to thank Jillian Schelzi, Jon Cobb, Soumeya Roberts, Ellen Goff, Alex Reubert, and everyone else at HG Literary. I am very grateful to you all.

Special thanks to David Pomerico, our wonderful editor, who always puts a part of his soul into books, and to his colleague Isabella Ogbolumani. I thank the Harper Voyager team: Art

Director Owen Corrigan; production team: Robin Barletta, Hope Ellis, and Jessica Rozler; marketing and publicity team: Lara Baez. I wish everyone on the Harper Voyager team much success and prosperity.

—*Marina Shyrshova-Dyachenko*

Much gratitude to Marina and Sergey for letting me be part of this remarkable adventure. A special thank-you to Marina for teaching me resilience and dignity. Much love to Josh Getzler for his support and guidance (and especially for the precious gift of his friendship), and to David Pomerico for his talent and infinite patience. Many thanks to Harper Voyager and HG Literary teams for all their hard work and their appreciation for good stories.

I first fell in love with *Vita Nostra* about fifteen years ago, and my family has been on this journey with me all this time. They have listened to me talk about the novel and its sequels, read early drafts, and held brainstorming sessions on translating the titles. The trilogy translation may be completed, but I know my family is standing by, ready to discuss my next project. Malcolm, Sasha, Veronica, Mom, and Sue Peach—my sister by choice—I'm forever in debt to you all.

—*Julia Meitov Hersey*

ABOUT THE AUTHORS

Marina and Sergey Dyachenko, a former actress and a former psychiatrist, are coauthors of over thirty novels and numerous short stories and screenplays. They were born in Ukraine and moved to California in 2013. Their books and screenplays have been translated into several foreign languages and awarded multiple literary and film prizes. Marina and Sergey are recipients of the Award for Best Authors (Eurocon 2005), Prix Planète SF des blogueurs (2020), Grand Prix de l'Imaginaire (2020), and of the Science Fiction and Fantasy Rosetta Awards (2021).

Sergey Dyachenko passed away in 2022, but his memory lives on in his books.

ABOUT THE TRANSLATOR

Julia Meitov Hersey originally began her translation of Vita Nostra because she wanted her family to share her love for this striking example of urban psychological science fiction and fantasy genre, with its literary allusions and ominous atmosphere. Born in Moscow, Julia moved to the U.S. at the age of nineteen and has been straddling the two cultures ever since. Julia is the winner of the 2021 Science Fiction and Fantasy Rosetta Award for best translated work (long form). Currently, she is working on translating other Dyachenko novels into English.

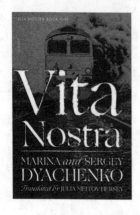
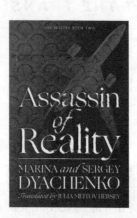
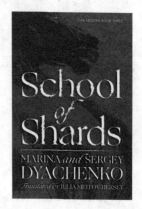